LINDA HOWARD

EXPOSURE

ISBN-13: 978-0-373-77700-6

EXPOSURE

Copyright © 2013 by Harlequin Books S.A.

The publisher acknowledges the copyright holder of the individual works as follows:

THE CUTTING EDGE
Copyright © 1985 by Linda Howington

WHITE LIES
Copyright © 1988 by Linda Howington

This edition published by arrangement with Harlequin Books S.A.

For questions and comments about the quality of this book, please contact us at CustomerService@Harlequin.com.

® and TM are trademarks of Harlequin Enterprises Limited or its corporate affiliates. Trademarks indicated with ® are registered in the United States Patent and Trademark Office, the Canadian Trade Marks Office and in other countries.

www.Harlequin.com

Printed in U.S.A.

CONTENTS

THE CUTTING EDGE

CHAPTER ONE

"THAT," SAID BRETT RUTLAND in a quietly appreciative voice, "should be illegal."

Evan Brady had been watching the young woman who had just walked past them, too, and he could only agree. He'd already been in the Los Angeles office for a week, and he'd seen her several times. "You'll have to get in line, along with the rest of us," he advised Brett dryly. "Her social life would make a Philadelphia debutante green with envy."

A cool, hard smile touched Brett's lips. "Sorry; I think I'll cut in and go to the head of the line."

Evan was a little startled, for he'd never known Brett to become involved with anyone in the company before, and he'd really only been teasing. Still, when a man looked at Teresa Conway, other considerations tended to fly right out of his mind. Then he shrugged. "She doesn't look like the general idea of a bookkeeper, does she?"

Brett's dark blue eyes cut sharply to him. "Bookkeeper?"

"And damned good at what she does, too. She has to automatically be considered a suspect."

Brett nodded, turning his gaze once again to the slim back of the woman and watching until she entered the elevator and he was no longer able to see her.

He and Evan were in Los Angeles to quietly investigate the mysterious discrepancy that an internal audit had turned up in the Los Angeles office of Carter Engineering, which was under the corporate umbrella of the Carter-Marshall Group. When Joshua Carter had heard of the possible embezzlement in his base company, he'd been livid, and Joshua Carter in a rage was something to behold, even though he was now pushing seventy. He'd called in his prize troubleshooter to investigate and handle the problem, and he'd instructed Brett to prosecute to the full extent of the law. Nobody stole from Joshua Carter and got away with only dismissal and a slap on the wrist! Bad publicity could go hang, for all he cared.

Brett shared with Joshua Carter the same cold distrust for a thief; he'd worked too hard to achieve his success to feel anything but contempt for anyone who tried to do it the easy way, by stealing the fruit of someone else's labors. It might take a while, but he and Evan would find the thief, and their handling of the situation would make everyone else in Carter Engineering think twice before they took so much as a pencil home.

Computer theft, by someone who really knew computers, could be a real bitch to track down, but Brett had full confidence in Evan's skills. There were few other people in the United States who could match Evan's expertise with a computer. With Evan working on the technical end, and Brett investigating the people, they'd have this wrapped up before the thief even knew they were coming. The cover story that had been given out was that they were in Los Angeles to investigate the feasibility of a new computer system that was being considered. Evan could make that look legitimate for an indefinite length of time.

Brett rubbed his jaw consideringly. "Do you know her name?" he asked Evan in an almost absent manner.

"Every man in this building knows her name," Evan replied, grinning. "Teresa Conway, but everyone calls her Tessa. She isn't married; I…uh, pulled her personnel file."

"Interesting reading?"

"Depends on what you're looking for. No obvious skeletons in her closet, though."

"I think I'll combine business with a little pleasure, and take Miss Conway out to dinner," Brett drawled. "I'll pump her for information on the rest of the department; she may know of someone with financial problems, or have noticed any sudden riches."

"I hate for you to have to work so hard." Evan lifted his eyebrows sardonically. "I'll pull night duty for you and take the lady out, so you can get a good night's rest."

In admirably succinct language, Brett told him what he could do with his suggestion, and Evan grinned. He was thin and dark and intense, and he'd never suffered from a lack of female companionship. Probably he would have asked Tessa Conway out himself before the assignment was finished, but he'd been too busy and now Brett was stepping in, which meant that no one else would have a chance with her until Brett decided to walk away. Women didn't deny Brett Rutland; nature had given him a burning sexuality, a rawly demanding virility that drew women like moths to a candle, but his physical appetites were tempered by the icy control of his brain. Evan had never met a man more in control of himself than Brett Rutland.

Joshua Carter couldn't have picked a better choice than Brett to send in; he was cool, alert, and he didn't become emotionally involved. Evan had heard it said that Brett Rutland didn't give a damn about anyone, and on occasion he'd thought that the rumor just might be right. The clarity of Brett's thought processes was never clouded by sentiment or emotion. He had a guarded personality; he kept his thoughts well hidden, though most people never realized that, because he was so adept in handling them and bending them to his will.

"When we get back from lunch, I want to read her file," Brett said now. His navy blue eyes were intent, and Evan felt a moment's pity for Tessa Conway; she didn't have a chance.

As Tessa reentered the building after lunch, she smiled at the security guard at the front door, earning an ear-to-ear grin from him and an exasperated snort from Martha "Billie" Billingsley, who worked in the payroll department of Carter Engineering and who was also Tessa's closest friend.

"You'd flirt with a dead man," Billie growled.

"I wouldn't," Tessa defended herself good-naturedly. "Besides, there's a difference between flirting and just being friendly."

"Not where you're concerned, there isn't. You have every man in this building falling all over himself whenever you're anywhere near."

Tessa laughed, not taking Billie's charge at all seriously. She was a cheerful flirt, laughing and teasing, but doing it so lightheartedly that it was almost impossible not to laugh with her. Most people liked Tessa—even women—because she wasn't a poacher, despite the sunny charm that drew men to her like iron filings to a magnet. She was always the first person invited to a party because she was so lively. She had a sharp but kind wit, the sort that had people hanging on her lazy words, waiting with almost painful anticipation for her to get to the punch line, then exploding with mirth when she finally got it all said. Tessa's drawl would have driven everyone crazy months ago if the lazy music of it hadn't been so distracting. She was originally from Mobile, on Alabama's Gulf Coast, and Billie had long ago concluded that it would take an earthquake to make Tessa hurry. It was really odd how she managed to accomplish so much on her job, because she approached it with such calm laziness, never appearing ruffled or frantic no matter what crisis was crashing down on the office. Tessa just sort of strolled around, and things somehow got done. It was a complete mystery.

They entered the elevator, where they were joined by the company's computer genius, Sammy Wallace. Sammy was tall and thin and blond, with vague, sweet blue eyes behind horn-rimmed glasses that made him look like even more of a genius. Put him at the keyboard of a computer and he could practically make it sing opera, but he was almost painfully shy. Tessa felt protective of him, even though he was actually a few years older than she, and she greeted him warmly. He still blushed whenever she spoke to him, but he'd learned that the kindness in her eyes wasn't a lie, and he returned her smile. He might usually have his mind on computers, but he'd noticed how men looked at Tessa, and he felt a little proud that she always spoke to him.

"Do you have a free night for another chess lesson?" she asked, and he blushed a little more at the way she suggested that his social life was so busy that his free nights were few and far between. He liked that, and he gave her his sweet smile.

"How about tomorrow night?"

"Wonderful!" She rewarded him with a dazzling smile, her deep green eyes sparkling. "About seven?"

"Sure. Do you want to play poker again, too?"

"Now, you know I never turn down a poker game." She winked at him, and Sammy winked back, surprising even himself. He was teaching Tessa chess, and in return she was teaching him poker. He was so good with numbers that he was picking up the basics of poker far more easily than she was handling chess. Tessa played chess with verve and dash, going on instinct rather than strategy, and the board was often chaotic before her adversary figured out what was going on and began methodically boxing in her king. On the other hand, she was very good at poker; she liked the sheer exhilaration of blending skill and luck.

The elevator stopped at the next floor, and several men entered; Tessa moved toward the rear, holding the rail as the doors closed and they all moved upward again. It was lucky that she did hold on to the rail; when the elevator reached the next floor, it lurched violently before shuddering to a stop. Ted Baker, the man standing in front of her, lost his balance and flailed wildly in an effort to keep from falling. He succeeded, but his elbow crashed against Tessa's cheekbone, and she stag-

gered from the force of the blow. Instantly, the man beside her had his arm around her waist, holding her up,
and he swore softly.

The man who had hit her turned around, apologiz-
ing profusely. "It wasn't your fault," Tessa tried to reassure him.

"Baker, have a repairman called to check out the
elevator," the man holding Tessa ordered, and Baker
quickly murmured an acknowledgment.

Tessa had already recovered from the brief dizziness
caused by the blow, and she tried to move away from
the man, but he held her firmly within the hard circle
of his arm. Billie squeezed over to them, her eyes anxious. "Tessa? Are you all right?"

"Yes, I'm fine." But she probed her cheekbone gingerly with her fingers, not certain if she was being
truthful or brave. Her face felt a little numb.

"I'll take her up and put ice on it," the authoritative
voice above her head said, and she doubted if anyone
ever disobeyed that note of command. Certainly no one
in the elevator made any other suggestion. Billie got off
at their floor, looking back worriedly at Tessa, but she
didn't try to accompany them. Little by little the elevator emptied as it rose higher and higher in the building, and Tessa pursed her lips thoughtfully at what that
meant. She wanted to tilt her head back and get a good
look at her rescuer, but he was standing slightly behind
her, and she really didn't feel safe in moving her head
that much. Sensation was returning to her face, and her
cheekbone was throbbing painfully.

They exited on the executive floor, where Tessa had
been only a few times in the past, since there was sel-

dom any need for someone from bookkeeping to venture that far afield. He opened a door that had no name on it, but a secretary sprang to attention at her desk.

"Helen, do I have any ice in my office? There's been a slight accident."

"Yes, sir, I'm certain you do." Helen jumped to open the door for him, then walked straight to the small built-in bar in the corner of the large office to check the supply of ice. "Yes, there's ice. Do you need anything else?"

"I'll get a towel from my washroom," he said easily. "That'll be all, thanks."

The secretary left, closing the door behind her, and Tessa was alone in the big office with a man she'd never seen before. "Sit here," he instructed, easing her into the huge leather chair behind the desk that stretched out like a football field. He turned away to fetch a towel from his private washroom, and Tessa promptly got to her feet, propelled by both curiosity and an instinctive wariness of a man so used to giving commands and having them obeyed. She walked to the wide windows and looked out at the almost endless vista of Los Angeles. She heard him when he came back into the office, but she didn't look around.

"I told you to sit down," he said abruptly to her back.

"Yes, you did," Tessa agreed in a mild voice.

After a moment, he walked over to the bar, and she heard the clink of ice cubes as he got them out. "I'd feel better if you sat down; that was quite a crack you took."

"I promise I won't faint." She could hear him approaching…no, the thick carpet muffled his footsteps. She *sensed* his movements, as if her skin had become acutely sensitive to him; she actually felt the warmth of his body as he came closer. Turning, she faced him for the first time.

While he'd been holding her so closely against his side, she'd noticed several things about him. The first was that he was very tall, probably six-four, and very strong. She was of medium height, but her build was delicate and graceful, and she'd had the feeling that he could have lifted her with one hand. The heat and power of his hard-muscled body had been almost overpowering. She'd also noticed his clean male scent, and felt the lean strength of his hands.

Now he stood before her, looking at her with narrowed, intent eyes, and Tessa looked back.

A curiously light-headed feeling began to creep over her, and she wondered for a moment if she might have a slight concussion; then she realized that she was holding her breath. She let it out in a soft sigh, still staring up at the hard, distinctly unhandsome, but remarkably sensual and arresting face. He had the most beautiful eyes she'd ever seen on anyone: navy blue eyes, fringed by thick dark lashes, a blue as pure and deep as she could ever imagine. His hair was tawny brown, with strands of gold running through it, and verging on shagginess. He looked hard and sensual and perhaps a little cruel, and Tessa couldn't look away from him.

His chin was a little too prominent, his jaw a little too long, his cheekbones a little too high and raw and hard; his nose could almost be called beaky. His features were so roughly hewn that he might even have been called homely if it hadn't been for the dark blue beauty of his eyes and the sensually chiseled perfection of his mouth. That mouth was positively wicked, and she stopped breathing again when she looked at it. His mouth was just the right size, neither too wide nor too small, and his lips were mobile and clear cut, with a small curl to them that could be either cynicism or amusement. It was the mouth of a man of wide and varied experience, a man who knew how to kiss, how to savor the taste of a woman's skin. Tessa found herself suddenly shaken by the compulsion to rise on her tiptoes and find out for herself just how well he could kiss.

Very gently, he put one finger under her chin and tilted her face to the light so he could examine her cheek. "You'll have a bruise," he told her, "but I don't think your eye will turn black."

"I hope not!"

Cautiously he placed the makeshift ice pack against her cheek, and Tessa reached up to hold it in place. Her hand touched his, and she noticed that his fingers were slightly rough, not the hands of a man who never did anything more strenuous than sign his name. He didn't drop his hand, but kept it under hers, and he looked down at her with such calm, self-confident awareness in his eyes that Tessa automatically wanted to put a safer distance between them. She was used to charming men so easily that it wasn't even a conscious effort, but it was a lighthearted charm, and she always danced away before emotions could become intense. She couldn't have said how she knew it, but every bone in her body, every fiber of her flesh, every instinct of her very female personality, recognized him as being more than she could handle. He wasn't a man of easy charm; he overwhelmed women with the intensity of his maleness. He wouldn't let the butterfly flit away after

dancing tantalizingly before him; he would reach out
and capture her, and hold her for as long as her beauty
intrigued him. Tessa knew that she had to go, then, in
order to protect her own best interests. But she didn't
want to go, she thought wistfully. She wanted to stay
near him....

Beneath all the light and laughter, Tessa had a strong
streak of common sense, and it surfaced now. "Thank
you for the ice," she murmured as she stepped away
from him. "I'd better get back to my job before I'm fired
for being late. Thanks again—"

"Stay," he commanded softly, and it was definitely
a command, despite the evenness of his tone. "I'll call
your department head and cover for you."

"That won't be necessary. I'm really all right, so I
can go back to work."

"If you insist." His lids dropped lazily over his deep-
sea eyes. "I'd like to talk to you, though, so I'll take
you out to dinner tonight. Will seven-thirty suit you?"

"Whoa!" she said, startled. "I don't even know you!"

"That's easily remedied." He held out his hard,
sun-browned hand. "I'm Brett Rutland, from Carter-
Marshall."

Tessa's eyes widened fractionally. She'd heard the
name so many times during the past week, and so many
people seemed to be a bit cautious of him that she'd
begun actually to believe all the things she'd heard
about him. Just the rumor that he might descend on
Carter Engineering had made a lot of people nervous.
He must have arrived that morning. But he was still
holding out his hand, and slowly Tessa put her hand out
to clasp his. His fingers wrapped gently around hers,

as if he were very aware of the difference between his strength and hers.

"Tessa Conway," she said as a self-introduction. "I work in the bookkeeping department."

He didn't release her hand. "Well, Tessa Conway, now you know who I am and I know who you are. Dinner?"

She eyed him warily for a moment; then her natural sense of humor began to surface. Was this man the ogre everyone had been telling horror tales about? He was no one's tame pussycat, that was for certain, but he didn't look as if he ate raw meat for breakfast, either. Teasing lights began to dance in her green eyes. "I'm not certain I'd be safe with someone known as the *Ax-Man*," she pointed out cheekily.

He threw back his head and laughed, a good, deep sound, and a warmth began to grow inside her. "Ax-Man? That's better than what I'd thought! But you won't have anything to worry about, Tessa Conway. I won't chop you up into little pieces."

No, but he was a man who could put a woman's emotions through the meat grinder. Just standing there in the office with him, Tessa could feel her heart beating a little faster, and the way her blood was humming through her veins made her feel warm all over. Temptation was weakening her because she really wanted to go with him, but she knew that the smartest thing to do would be to run, not walk, to the nearest cover.

"If we went out together, the grapevine would short-out from the overload of gossip. I really don't—"

"I don't give a damn about gossip, and neither do you." His fingers tightened over hers. "Seven-thirty?"

She looked up at him again, and that was a tactical error. With a low, musical laugh, she cast caution to the winds. "Make it six-thirty. I'm the original sleepy-head; if I don't get my eight hours, I'm incapable of functioning. During the week, I don't even stay out as late as Cinderella did, and we all know she was a party-pooper."

Brett veiled his eyes with his lashes, not letting her see the predatory gleam in them. He'd be glad to make certain she was home in bed at an early hour; letting her sleep was something else entirely. "I'll be there. Write down your address for me." He planned to read her file, and he could get her address from there, but she didn't need to know that.

Tessa held the cold compress in place with her left hand while she scribbled her address on a scrap of paper, along with her telephone number. Then she looked at him again, and shook her head a little. "I must be out of my mind," she murmured to herself, and walked quickly out of the office before he could somehow entice her to stay even longer.

Brett sat down at his desk and toyed idly with the scrap of paper that contained her address. That was just how he wanted her: out of her mind, totally sense-less with the pleasure he intended to give her. He'd had a number of affairs, enough that the prospect of an-other woman in his bed should produce only a feeling of mild anticipation, but the way he felt could never be described as mild. Whatever it was about Tessa Conway, he wanted her. He couldn't really remember a woman he'd wanted whom he hadn't eventually gotten, and usually within a fairly short length of time. There was no reason for things to be any different with Tessa. He thought of the way she walked, her slender hips moving in a way that made sweat pop out on his forehead. It might take a while for him to tire of her.

"I'm an idiot," Tessa told herself over and over as she returned to her office, still holding the ice-filled towel to her bruised cheekbone. She'd actually agreed to go out with a man who occupied a rather high rung of the corporate ladder in her company, and that in itself could give birth to a bumper crop of gossip. Not only that, the man had a horrible reputation; whenever he appeared, people lost their jobs. "Ax-Man" was a singularly appropriate nickname. But all of that aside, he was also the sexiest man she'd ever seen, or imagined. It wasn't his looks particularly, though his eyes were almost stunning in their beauty. It was the way he looked at a woman, as if she were his for the taking, and as if he knew all sorts of delicious ways to do the taking, and would linger over every moment of it. The eyes of a rake…except that there was something cool and controlled in his gaze, too, as if he held a part of himself aloof, totally untouched by the heat of his own passion.

What was a woman supposed to do with a man who would want more of herself than she felt safe in giving? Her heart had never been broken, but it had been battered badly enough that she didn't want to risk her emotions again, especially with a man like Brett Rutland. He'd ignore the barriers of laughter and lighthearted teasing, knocking them aside to get to the woman behind them. Tessa loved flirting and partying; it was a lot of fun, and frequently made people feel better about themselves. But the thought of getting serious with anyone was a little scary, and she was very much afraid that keeping things cool with Brett Rutland was only a remote possibility.

After two broken engagements, Tessa no longer had so many stars in her eyes. She was optimistic and level-headed enough not to condemn all men because of two failed relationships, but she was also more cautious now in the way she handled romantic entanglements. She knew danger when she saw it, and that man flashed danger signals like a neon sign. So why was she tossing aside all caution now, agreeing to go out with him when she knew better?

"Because I'm an idiot," she muttered to herself as she sat down at her desk.

Perry Smitherman, head of the bookkeeping department, came out of his office and approached her small cubicle. His high forehead was knit in a perpetual frown. "Billie Billingsley called to say you'd had a small accident. Is everything all right?"

"Yes, I'm fine," Tessa removed the cold compress and explored her swollen cheekbone with a light, cautious touch. "How does it look?"

His frown pulled even tighter as he bent down and examined the bruise as thoroughly as he would check the books. "Painful," he finally pronounced. "Do you need to go home?"

Tessa concealed her startled laughter. "No, I'm able to work," she assured him demurely. Perry was a fuss-budget, but he was kindhearted enough, and she liked him, for all his fussy ways.

"Did you go to the infirmary?"

"No. Mr. Rutland took me up to his office and put this compress on it—"

"Brett Rutland?" Perry asked sharply.

"Yes, he was in the elevator—"

His high, white forehead began to glisten with sweat. "Did he ask you anything about the department? Did he say anything about going over the books?"

Anxiety was evident in his face and his raised voice. Soothingly, Tessa said, "Not a word. He simply got the ice from his bar and wrapped it in the towel."

"Are you certain? He never does anything without a reason. He can be subtle, when it suits him. I'm sure he's going to go over everything; but he'll ask around first, and try to find out if we're slack or careless in any way."

"You don't have anything to worry about; the department is in good shape, and you're a very competent manager."

"You never know," he said, wringing his hands. "You never know."

He was determined to think the worst, and with a sigh Tessa gave up the effort of cheering him; he was probably happier looking for a dark lining in a silver cloud anyway. Some people simply had a melancholy outlook, and Perry was one of them.

Billie popped in during the mid-afternoon break to check on Tessa. The other woman was full of curiosity about Brett Rutland, her big brown eyes even rounder than usual as she stared at Tessa and shot questions at her faster than they could be answered. "What did he say? How long did he keep you? Were you scared? My gosh, of all the people who could have been in that elevator! Did he say why he's here?"

Tessa picked out one question and ignored the others. "Why should I have been scared? I didn't know who he was."

Billie gaped. "You didn't know Brett Rutland?"

"I knew the name, but I'd never seen him, so how could I have known him?"

Looking impatient with such logic, Billie still tried to pry more information out of Tessa, who could be infuriatingly hard to pin down when she wanted to be. "What did you say? What did he say?"

"Among other things, he told me to sit down while he got a towel," Tessa murmured. She wasn't going to tell Billie that he'd asked her out to dinner; just the thought of going out with him affected her nerves, jarring her out of her usual lazy contentment and making her feel jittery, and both afraid and excited at the same time. She was still tingling from the sizzling electricity of his masculinity.

Aunt Silver would adore him.

Just the thought of her aunt made Tessa smile, because Silver was the warmest, liveliest, most lovable woman in existence, and if there was anything Silver appreciated, it was an exciting man. "Sugar," Silver had told her more than once, "if I ever stop man watching, you'll know to bury me, because that's a sure sign that I'm dead." Since Silver was prospering with her small, exclusive doll shop in Gatlinburg, Tessa was certain that her aunt was still happily man watching, too.

"You're smiling," Billie accused. "*Teresa Conway!* Don't you dare try flirting with that man! I know that look in your eyes; have you been batting your eyelashes at him?"

"With my face looking as if I'd just gone ten rounds with a heavyweight boxer?" Tessa asked in a mild voice.

"Would you let a little thing like that stop you?"

"I promise, I haven't been flirting with Mr. Rutland." Her eyes twinkled; evidently Mr. Rutland didn't wait for a woman to flirt with him before he made his move.

"I hope not! He's been known to tear strips of flesh off people who have looked at him wrong."

Several things about Brett Rutland alarmed Tessa, but not the fear that he'd tear strips of flesh off her. No, what he'd do to her flesh wouldn't be painful at all, and that inner certainty was probably the most alarming thing she felt about him. Whenever a woman looked at a man and knew, instinctively and without doubt, that he would be able to give her exquisite pleasure, her defenses against that man were dangerously weakened. Tessa didn't want her defenses to be weakened; she'd been hurt badly, not once but twice. Later, after time had completely healed all her emotional wounds, she wanted to try love again. But not now, she thought despairingly. I'm not ready now.

She managed to assure Billie that she hadn't done anything shocking that could cost her her job. Billie was an uneasy mixture of laid-back California casualness and a surprising streak of prudery that was frequently shocked by Tessa's flirtatiousness. Because she was also a loyal friend, Tessa looked out for Billie in subtle ways that no one had ever realized, though many thought that Billie had guided Tessa through the mazes and pitfalls of life in Southern California, where the normal flow of traffic was practically a death sen-

tence for a young woman used to using a much more leisurely pace in getting from one place to another. Since
Tessa had become Billie's friend, Billie's clothes had
become simpler, more classic in style, and more suited
to her short, rather rounded figure. Billie's hairstyle
now flattered her face, her makeup accentuated her
large brown eyes and camouflaged her rather sallow
complexion. Before, Billie's taste in jewelry had run
to heavy, clunky pieces in neon colors that had tended
to make her look like a midget in the circus. Now she
wore smaller pieces, well coordinated with her clothing. Billie's social life had picked up considerably in
the last year, but she never wondered why. Tessa knew
why, and the knowledge filled her with quiet satisfaction. She'd been lucky; she'd had Aunt Silver to guide
her in her confusing teenage days, to teach her how to
dress and use makeup; not many girls were so lucky.
Spreading around a little of Aunt Silver's knowledge
was the least she could do.

She'd have to remember to write to Aunt Silver about
Brett Rutland; her aunt would definitely enjoy hearing
about a man with navy blue eyes and a mouth that made
a woman go a little crazy.

BRETT LEANED BACK in his chair, his eyes narrowed as
he flipped through the scanty information in Tessa's
personnel file. There wasn't a lot in there: She'd never
been arrested, never been married and had no identifying scars or birthmarks. Her supervisor, Perry Smitherman, had given her a good evaluation, but Brett thought
cynically that any normal man would find it difficult

to say anything unfavorable about Tessa, even an old-maid type like Perry Smitherman.

He tossed the file onto his desk; its contents were useless. He'd find out more about her tonight.

CHAPTER TWO

TESSA LEANED CLOSER to the mirror and examined her discolored, swollen cheekbone, then frowned. Her normal makeup hadn't covered the bruise as well as she'd hoped; she carefully applied a concealer, and blended it until she was satisfied that the bruise was hardly noticeable.

She'd gotten caught in the snarled traffic, and as a result had only arrived home a mere half an hour before, but the situation was well in hand. She'd plugged in her hot rollers, then stripped and taken a fast shower and washed her hair. By the time she'd blown her hair dry, the rollers were hot, and she'd set a few of them in her hair for lift and control. Makeup had taken an additional ten minutes. Now she took the rollers from her hair and deftly brushed it into a casually sophisticated style that swirled about her shoulders. A glance at the clock told her that she had twelve minutes left, ample time to get dressed.

Tessa disliked hurrying, but she seldom had to hurry, because she had everything organized. Organization was insurance against haste. She knew where everything was, and had her routine well planned; if circumstances conspired against her and she was thrown off schedule, she would hurry, if work were involved, but she never hurried for personal reasons. Oddly, she was almost never late, as if the little gremlins who disrupted schedules realized that they wouldn't get any satisfaction from watching her dash around madly, so they seldom bothered with her. At least, that was the explanation she'd worked out in her mind, and it suited her as well as any other.

She sprayed herself lightly with her favorite perfume, then put on her underwear, her hosiery and her dress. The dress was cream-colored silk, with a slim skirt and a wrap bodice, and long sleeves to keep her arms warm in the April night. She slipped pearl studs into her ears, then fastened a single long strand of creamy pearls around her neck. Pale beige sling-backs lifted her a few inches higher, giving her a willowy, swaying grace. Just as she picked up her matching beige evening purse, the doorbell rang, and she nodded in satisfaction. "Right on time," she told herself in congratulation, and she meant herself, not him.

She opened the door to him, and as soon as she met his dark blue eyes she felt a sudden rushing warmth inside. Darn, but the man packed a wallop! All he had to do was smile and a woman was reeling on the ropes. But none of what she felt was in her lazy smile as she invited him inside. "Would you like a drink before we go?"

"No, thanks." He looked around her small, cozy apartment, full of comfortable furniture and warm lighting, with her many unrelated collections filling every nook and corner. "Nice. It looks homey."

With some people, "homey" would have been a polite way of saying "cluttered," but somehow Tessa felt that he meant it. Andrew would have turned up his nose at the comfortable but definitely unfashionable decor, but then Andrew was very much concerned with keeping up his image. She sighed; she'd promised herself several times that she'd never think of Andrew again, but somehow he sneaked back into her mind at odd times. Why should she think of him now, when she was going out with a man who put Andrew completely in the shade? Perhaps her subconscious was dredging up Andrew's memory in an effort to put her on her guard and protect her against a man who was so much more dangerous than Andrew had ever been.

His car was a rental, but a luxury model for all that. She'd heard it said that Brett Rutland was Mr. Carter's fair-haired boy, and perhaps he was. After helping her into the car, he walked around to the driver's side and folded his long length behind the wheel. When she considered his height, she realized that he had to have a large car; a man with legs that long would never be comfortable in a sports model.

"I made reservations for seven o'clock," he said, and she caught a glint of amusement in his normally controlled expression. "You should be home by ten-thirty; can you stay awake that long?"

"I might," she drawled, not giving him an inch.

A tiny smile tugged at the corners of his mouth.

"I'll try to make sure you stay awake," he said in a voice that almost purred with sensuality.

Oh, she'd just bet he would! Probably the only time any woman had gone to sleep on him was in his arms, after the loving was finished.

"What part of the South are you from?" he asked casually, as if he hadn't read her file.

"I was born in Mobile, Alabama. But when I was

thirteen my mother and I moved to Tennessee to live with her sister." Those were the bare facts; they didn't tell of her mother's long battle with ill health, the poverty they'd endured, the times when there simply hadn't been anything to eat because her mother hadn't been able to work. Finally her mother had given up and swallowed her stubborn pride and asked her sister to drive down from Tennessee to get them, and even then she'd asked for Tessa's sake, not her own. It was just that her mother's entire family had been against Tessa's father, and they'd been proved right, for he'd walked out on his family when Tessa was too young even to remember him. Tessa's mother had lived barely a year after the move, and after that there'd been only Tessa and Silver in the old farmhouse just outside of Sevierville.

"What made you move out here?"

"I wanted to see something of the country," Tessa replied easily. She wasn't about to tell him about Andrew. She'd hated the idea of leaving, but Aunt Silver had talked her into it. She wasn't running, Aunt Silver had said; she was turning her back on a bad situation and walking away from it. Well, Andrew thought she'd run, but eventually Tessa had come to realize that what Andrew thought didn't matter worth a hoot. If only Andrew hadn't been a hot, rising young executive at the company where Tessa had worked!

"Do you like it?"

"Well enough. What about you? You have a bit of a drawl yourself, but I can't place it."

He looked surprised, as if she wasn't supposed to ask any of the questions. "I'm from Wyoming. My father and I own a ranch there."

"A real ranch? Don't you miss it?" Her eyes had brightened with interest, and she'd turned in her seat to face him, a movement that made the draped bodice of her dress gape open just a bit, enough to allow his quick glance to caress the soft, beginning curve of her breast. He wanted to put his hand inside her dress and feel the satiny swell, to make her nipple pucker against his palm. The jolt of pure desire that hit him took him by surprise, and he had to force himself to concentrate on her question.

"Yes, I miss it." The admission surprised him, because he'd been ignoring the increasing need to walk away from the whole rat race and go back to what he'd grown up doing, ranching. Old Tom was proud of his son for making it big in the business world, and Brett had to admit that he'd enjoyed the challenge of it himself. But now…he was getting older, and so was old Tom, and when it came down to it there was nothing that gave him the satisfaction of a hard day's work in the saddle. He wondered what this soft, sleekly sophisticated creature beside him would say if he told her that more and more often he wanted to go home, to Wyoming and the growing Rutland spread.

"I'm going to go home, someday," she said softly. "This isn't going to be my permanent home. Home is an old farmhouse that needs a coat of paint, and a dilapidated barn behind it that even the old cow was afraid to go in." She laughed a little at her memories, but they were good, warm memories, because Aunt Silver had filled that old farmhouse with enough love to completely shelter her young, confused niece. Aunt Silver had left the old farm now, though she still owned it, and moved to a modern house in Gatlinburg, but Tessa meant to fix up the old farmhouse and live in it some-day. The best times of her life had been spent there.

Looking at her now, Brett found it hard to believe that her childhood had been a deprived one. She looked as expensive as a woman from a moneyed, blue-blooded background, educated in a private school in Virginia. Why would she want to go back, if she had it so much better here?

Tessa thoroughly approved of the restaurant he'd chosen; she'd never been there before, but the interior was dim and the diners were all discreetly isolated, while the music was low and pleasant. They were shown to a private little alcove, where a candelabrum with three tall white tapers was the only light. The table was small, and she found that when they were seated their knees bumped. Their eyes met across the table, and a slow, sleepy smile touched his lips and made his eye-lids droop heavily. He spread his legs until they were on either side of hers, then gently closed them so that his calves clasped hers. Her heartbeat bolted into a faster rhythm as she felt the warmth of his legs, the muscu-lar strength of his calves. He'd have legs like a line-backer, she thought suddenly, and her legs felt burned from his heat.

Over a glass of very good wine, he continued ques-tioning her, small, innocent questions that she answered willingly. She was too bemused by the possessive clasp of his legs to really pay any attention to the polite, get-ting-to-know-each-other questions that he gently posed to her every so often. Inevitably, they talked about work, since that was a common ground for them. He didn't

seem to be digging for any dirt, and he was so knowl-
edgeable about the firm anyway that she found herself telling him funny anecdotes about the people she
worked with, nothing that would get anyone in trouble,
but the humorous little things that happened to everyone. She didn't spare herself, either, and laughed as
hard at the spots she'd gotten herself into as she did
at any of the other stories. He countered with his own
tales of the things that had happened to him during the
years he'd been with Carter-Marshall, and Tessa completely relaxed.

Brett was too coolly controlled ever to be a social lion, but in a private situation with a woman he
wanted, he was unrivaled. He charmed without threatening, making her feel appreciated without coming on
too strong, skillfully wearing down any inner defenses.
He wanted Tessa very much. It wasn't that she was
the most beautiful woman he'd ever seen because she
wasn't; but she was almost certainly the sexiest woman
he'd ever met. It wasn't anything he could really put
his finger on; she was slender rather than voluptuous,
though very shapely indeed. But her soft green eyes
sparkled with teasing amusement, and her wide, generous mouth was made for passion. Her dark brown
hair looked like thick silk as it curled around her delicate shoulders. With those high, beautiful cheekbones,
she looked exotic and a little foreign. She teased and
flirted…oh, she had flirting down to a fine art. Every
time her long dark lashes languorously swept down to
veil the cheerfully wicked glint in her eyes, he felt his
body tighten with need. She played at being the vamp,
but she did it so boldly, laughing at herself and enjoy-

ing the role so much, that it was unbelievably effective. She invited everyone else to enjoy themselves as lightheartedly as she did, but she didn't seem to realize what a challenge she was. Brett thought of having her beneath him in bed, that full mouth no longer laughing but swollen from his kisses, and her sweet, satiny body accommodating his passions. He'd have to be gentle with her, at least at first, he thought as his eyes narrowed intently on her. She was delicately built, with slender, fragile bones.

Tessa looked up from the prime rib she was devouring with elegant greed, and found him watching her with sexual intent burning with obvious fire in his eyes. She went suddenly still, her mouth soft and a little tremulous. Without taking his eyes from her, he lifted his wineglass and drank the rich red liquid.

"Finish eating," he said gently.

"I can't." Despite the way he made her feel, so shaky inside, she smiled at him. "You're staring at me."

"I know. I was thinking how much I'd rather be having you than this roast beef."

His voice was so tender and low that it was a moment before she realized exactly what he'd said, and her eyes widened even more. She felt utterly hypnotized, sitting there and staring at him as helplessly as a rabbit must stare at a lion about to pounce. Giving herself an inner shake, Tessa gathered her senses. "Finish your roast anyway," she admonished him. "Aunt Silver always told me that the only thing worth betting on was a sure thing, so don't turn down your bird in the hand...or in this case, beef on the plate."

His hard mouth curved in amusement. "Do you really have an Aunt Silver, or do you just use the idea as a diversion?"

Feeling more on top of the situation again, Tessa gave him a look so innocent that it should have been patented. "Now, could I really make up an Aunt Silver?"

"If it suited you."

"You're probably right," she agreed comfortably, smiling at him. "But in this case, I don't have to rely on my imagination. Aunt Silver is my actual, living, breathing aunt."

"The one you and your mother went to live with?"

"Yes. Mother died not long after we moved to Tennessee, so Aunt Silver and I were closer than we'd normally have been. All we had was each other. She's fantastic; she's my aunt, my mother and my best friend all rolled into one."

"Does she still live in Tennessee?" That was another bit of information that he'd already gotten from her file, but Brett's cool attention to detail never faltered. He wanted her to give the details of her life herself, partly to account for the knowledge he already had, and also to give him the chance to see if she told it exactly as she'd put it in her file, or if she was reluctant to answer any personal questions. So far, she was an open, warmly responsive woman, and he wanted her more and more as the minutes passed.

"She owns a doll shop in Gatlinburg; she lives there now. The old farmhouse needs a lot of work done on it, and the only heat is the fireplace and old woodstove, so it was a lot easier on her just to move to Gatlinburg, as well as being safer during the winter. Now she doesn't have to drive on those icy roads." Tessa gave her slow smile. "I hope she'll close the shop for a couple of weeks of vacation this winter, during the slow season, and come out here to visit."

Brett's eyes sharpened with interest. "Slow season?"

"The Smoky Mountain park headquarters are in Gatlinburg. The summer months, and through October, are the busiest, though a lot of people go during the winter, too, for the snow."

He shook his head. Wyoming born and bred, he still couldn't understand why anyone would actually *want* snow. It seemed to him that every winter they'd always had more snow than anyone could want in a lifetime. He skied, and did it well, but he'd never been enthusiastic over the sport or the snow necessary for it. But more and more he found himself missing Wyoming, even those god-awful winters.

Tessa laughed at his expression. "Listen, when you live in the South, snow is rare. I'd never seen snow at all until we moved to Tennessee."

They finished their main courses, and the waiter promptly cleared the dishes away, while they lingered over the wine. Tessa had thought that she wouldn't be able to eat any dessert, but when the waiter brought the dessert cart, she stared at the scrumptious pastries until her mouth was watering. "I can't resist it," she sighed, choosing her dessert.

Brett declined a sweet, but they both ordered coffee, and he slowly drank his as he watched her attack the pastry. She certainly enjoyed her food, for someone so slim. She glanced up at him and caught his gaze, and smiled as she read his thoughts. No words were necessary; it was one of those strangely intimate interludes when two minds march together, and she felt closer to him at that moment than she ever had with anyone else.

His gaze lowered. "You have a crumb on your lip," he said softly, and Tessa ran her tongue slowly, searchingly, over her lips in quest of the errant crumb.

His navy eyes darkened to black. "You missed it. Lean over and I'll get it off for you."

Obligingly Tessa leaned over, smiling at him, so he could flick the crumb off with his finger. He paused for a moment, searing her with the dark heat of his gaze, then leaned over slowly, like a man moving at the command of a force stronger than he. As the distance between them lessened, Tessa's eyes widened until they were large green pools, soft and deep. Surely he wasn't going to kiss her, was he? Lightly his mouth touched her, found the crumb, and his tongue captured it. Tessa quivered under that light touch, filled with his taste, the heat and smell of his skin surrounding her. She felt almost paralyzed, totally unable to move away from him. She was as overwhelmed by him as if he'd put his arms around her and was holding her tightly to his lean, hard frame, though he'd touched her only with his mouth, and that so lightly and delicately that she'd scarcely been able to feel it.

He moved away, and the heat in his eyes had intensified, his gaze locked on her face. His expression hadn't changed, but Tessa's tingling nerve endings picked up the small, almost imperceptible signals of his growing arousal. His skin seemed to be pulled tighter over his fierce cheekbones; his lips were redder, a bit fuller. Tessa's body throbbed in rhythm with his thundering heartbeat, as if his body set the pace for hers. His heat lured her, pulling her closer.

"Are you ready to leave?" he asked, and his raspy voice was even rawer than usual.

Tessa had a mental image of herself cheerfully, blindly wading ever deeper into the dark sea of temptation. In over my head, she thought with faint despair, then threw caution to the wind and nodded. "Yes. I'd like to go home now, please."

He didn't even take her arm as they walked back out to his car, but tension vibrated between them. Tessa glanced up at his controlled face, wondering how a man with such steely self-control could at the same time project the raw, steamy sensuality that was overwhelming her own instinctive caution before he'd even made a real move toward her. That fleeting brush of lips in the restaurant hadn't qualified as a real kiss, but even that had sent rockets of pleasure zinging through her body.

She was a little stunned by the intensity of her feelings. Not even with Andrew had she *wanted* so badly, and she'd loved Andrew. Nor had she been physically attracted to Will, but Will had been an infatuation, not love. She was accustomed to attracting men; it was effortless on her part, and she simply accepted it as part of her personality. She kept it light, enjoying herself and enjoying the knowledge that the men in her life had *fun* when they were with her. Life was for laughter, for teasing and joking and dancing, for feeling good. It was for love, too, but she knew that love didn't come as easily as laughter.

Tessa was a creature made for the sunlight, warm and bright; the man beside her was controlled, even a little grim, though she'd been able to bring the light of laughter to his eyes several times. For all the warm golden streaks in his hair, for all the heat of his sexuality, he was a man who held himself aloof mentally, whose emotions were cool and even. But he made her heart jump at the sight of him, as no other man had ever done. He made her ache, as if she were suddenly incomplete, and yearning to be a part of a whole, with him.

What if I fall in love with him? she thought in sudden panic, and looked at him with apprehension plain in her eyes. He wasn't like other men; with him, she wouldn't be able to control the relationship as she'd always done before. He would take everything she had to give, all of the sunlight and sweet secrets, and she wasn't certain that he would give her anything in return. Oh, she knew that he was physically attracted to her, but he kept his emotions, his thoughts, carefully shielded. She was totally uncertain of herself in that regard, and she wasn't used to feeling as if she was walking in emotional quicksand.

Brett had seen the brief moment of fear that had glimmered in her eyes, and he wondered what had caused it. What was she afraid of? She certainly wasn't afraid of him as a man; she was too damned enticing and flirtatious. His brows pulled together in a momentary frown, before he smoothed them again. He'd solve all her riddles, eventually.

As he pulled the car to the curb at her apartment, he glanced at his wristwatch. "Ten o'clock, Cinderella. You're safe for the night."

She chuckled, then quickly sobered. Was she safe? She wasn't certain yet, and she wouldn't be until she'd seen him on his way. What if he wanted to stay? She'd already learned that her toughest problem with controlling him would be controlling herself. If he could make her melt with a barely-there kiss, what would she do if he turned his charm on full power?

His hand rested lightly on the small of her back as they went up the walk, but even that touch affected the rhythm of her heartbeat. "Let me have your key," he murmured. She got it from her purse and gave it to him. He unlocked the door, then stepped inside the apartment before she could think of a way to keep him from coming in. She stood just inside the door and watched as he turned on the lights and checked all the rooms. "All secure," he said, smiling a little.

"Is this security check standard?" she asked, curiosity momentarily taking her attention.

His eyes were like the deep Pacific, with golden lights dancing on top of the blue waves. "Yes," he said simply, and came over to her where she still stood by the door. Taking her arm, he drew her farther inside and pushed the door closed. He cupped her face in his hard, warm hands, turning it up and studying the generous mouth, the languid sweep of her thick dark lashes. It was a passionate face for all its delicacy, and he wanted the taste of her mouth on his.

She clasped her hands around the thickness of his wrists, and he felt the faint quiver of her body. Without a word, he bent his head and covered her lips with his mouth, feeling the sweet softness tremble and part, and he kissed her harder, tilting her head back even more so he could slant his mouth across hers and deepen the caress. Tessa helplessly opened her mouth to his tongue.

No man should taste this sweet and heady, but he did, and she cried a little inside because she was afraid he would hurt her if she gave him any opening into her emotions, but she was also afraid that she wouldn't be able to protect herself.

He lifted his mouth from hers a fraction of an inch, and his wine-sweet breath wafted over her lips as he demanded in a low, harsh voice, "Kiss me the way I'm kissing you. Give me your tongue. I want it now; I want you to kiss me the way I know you can." Almost fiercely, he put his mouth over hers again, and with a little sigh Tessa gave in to the delicious, erotic demand. She kissed him as if he were hers, as if she had every right to him, every right to demand everything from him. With her lips and tongue she claimed him, kissing him deeply, forgetting the need to protect herself. His frank, heated sensuality overcame the barriers of laughter that she used to keep people from becoming too intimate, and tapped into the deep, passionate core of her womanhood. Tessa was a woman with a deep reservoir of love and passion waiting to be given to the one man who would be the love of her life. She knew the worth of her love; she wasn't about to waste it on a casual, fly-by-night relationship no matter how attractive the man. Always before, she'd been able to keep the necessary mental control to ensure this, but now she felt her control slipping away, felt herself giving him the first taste of the searing magic of her passion.

His hands left her face; one arm went around her rib cage, locking her to him with a steely strength that made her shiver as she realized how very strong he was. His other hand went to the back of her head and seized a handful of hair, exerting just enough pressure to hold her head back without hurting her. He lifted his mouth from hers again, and his breathing was ragged, his eyes burning with need.

Tessa quivered against him, well aware of his need; pressed against him as she was, she could feel every taut line of his body. She knew that she should say something light, something to make him laugh, to break the mood, but she couldn't seem to think of anything very effective. "Was that what you wanted?" she finally managed, but her voice was so low and whispery with her own need that the words were more of an invitation than the light mockery she'd intended.

"That was part of it," he said in rasping admission, and began kissing her again. Her senses noticed the roughness of his voice, and she knew the more aroused he became, the lower and rougher his voice was, until he spoke in little more than a growl. She clung to his heavy shoulders, helplessly giving his mouth everything it sought, the freedom and depth and response of her own mouth. He was teaching her the power of physical desire, making her want him in a way she'd never wanted a man before, so deeply and powerfully that it was becoming desperation.

In Brett's experience, the unguarded response she was giving him meant that she was his for the taking. Though his loins were throbbing heavily, his mind was cool as he deliberately put his hand inside the wrap bodice of her dress, cupping the warm silk of her breast in his palm and discovering with delight that the curves of her breasts were lusher than he'd expected, given her almost fragile slenderness. His slightly rough thumb moved over the velvet nipple, gently turning it into a firm, impudent little nub.

Tessa jerked away from him.

Her instinctive action startled her as much as it did him. She blinked in bewilderment, then stared at him as she wasn't quite certain what had happened. Her eyes were enormous, her face a little pale. "I wasn't expecting that," she said a little helplessly.

Brett ground his teeth in mingled rage and frustration. His entire body ached; his hands twitched, wanting the sweetness of her flesh beneath his fingers again. "Damn you, I ought to——" he began gutturally, then stopped before he said too much, before his male frustration led him to say things he didn't mean. He meant to see her again, even if tonight wasn't ending the way he'd planned. He'd have her yet, and he also thought he might be able to get more information about her fellow employees from her.

Tessa pressed shaking fingers to her mouth. "I know. I'm sorry," she said weakly. "I never meant to let things…that is, you startled me when you touched… oh, damn it."

He looked at her sharply. She was visibly trembling, and something very like fear was in those wide eyes as she stared at him—fear like he'd seen before, during dinner, and he felt a sudden, keen curiosity. No, he had to reassure her, calm her down so she wouldn't refuse to see him again.

He took a deep breath to calm the ragged pace of his breathing, and to bring his voice back to normal. "It happened too fast, didn't it?" he asked quietly.

Tessa brought herself back under control, too. "I'm

not a tease, but I don't sleep around either. I don't believe in casual encounters. We just met today, after all. I didn't mean to let this happen."

"I understand." He managed a smile, a brief, grim smile. "Not that I think there would be anything casual about our encounter. We'd probably blow the needle off the Richter scale."

Tessa had thought herself long past the blushing stage, but the color that rose to her cheeks was from excitement, not embarrassment. He was looking at her in a way that almost scorched her, and the painful part of it was that she still wanted him, too, in just the way he was imagining. Her body had reacted instinctively, independent of her mind and common sense, and her flesh had recognized him immediately as a worthy partner.

"Tomorrow night. Dinner again."

She couldn't take her eyes from him. "I can't. Sammy Wallace is trying to teach me how to play chess."

Brett remembered overhearing her make the date in the elevator, and his almost photographic memory dredged up an image of Sammy Wallace: thin and blond and no match at all for this sweet little Southern Delilah.

"All right," he allowed grimly. "The night after, then. And don't tell me no."

"I wasn't going to." Never off stride for long, Tessa felt enough like herself to give him her slow-breaking smile that held him breathless as he watched the beginning curve of her lips and waited for the smile to reach full bloom. "I must have more courage than brains."

He didn't feel like smiling, but the twinkle in her eyes invited him to share in the laughter at herself. He didn't want to laugh; he wanted to take her to bed, and the coiled tension in his body told him that he'd have to take a cold shower before he could sleep. "I'll see you Thursday night. Six-thirty?"

"Yes, that's fine."

He'd turned to the door, but he paused and glanced back at her, his face grim. "This Sammy Wallace, is he special to you?"

"He's a very sweet and very shy man, and he's also a genius. He's teaching me chess." Why was she explaining herself to him? But from the way he was looking at her, he didn't think that was explanation enough.

"Don't make any more dates with him, or with anyone else except me."

The possessive order made her eyes widen. "Are you going Neanderthal on me?" she asked suspiciously.

"If I have to. You shouldn't have kissed me the way you did if you didn't want me to lay claim." Very calmly, he caught her chin in his hand and kissed her, slow and hard. "Remember that."

When he was gone, Tessa creamed off her makeup and brushed her hair, then pulled on her light nightgown and tumbled into bed. She was a hard sleeper; nothing interfered with her rest, and tonight was no exception. She went immediately to sleep, but her subconscious played the night for her again and again in dreams that didn't stop with the touch of his hand on her body.

EVAN'S EYES WERE tired and red-rimmed from the work he'd been doing at night as well as the bogus work necessary during the day, but his mind was still running at full speed. He was totally caught up in their covert search for the embezzler. "Did you get any useful information from Miss Conway last night?" he asked absently when Brett entered the office.

"I've made notes," Brett answered, taking a small notebook from his inside coat pocket. The details he'd noted were insignificant, except to himself and Evan. He'd had to be careful in his questioning, since Tessa wasn't a gossip, but he'd gotten a surprising amount of information from her humorous tales.

Evan read the notes, frowning as he added the information to the profiles he was compiling on each employee under suspicion, which was, at that point, virtually everyone.

"What do you have on Sammy Wallace?" Brett asked slowly, frowning at himself for asking the question. He didn't like the possessive jealousy he was feeling; he'd never felt it for any woman before, and he didn't want to feel it now.

Evan's head snapped up. "He's a computer genius," he said slowly. "He has a system at his apartment that the CIA could use. From what I've found so far, he has to be the prime suspect. What made you ask?"

Brett shrugged, his eyes intent. If Wallace was the prime suspect, he'd make damned sure Tessa didn't have anything else to do with him.

CHAPTER THREE

ALL DAY LONG, Tessa had looked forward to Sammy's undemanding company as an antidote against the tension that curled in her stomach at just the thought of Brett Rutland, and Brett had occupied her thoughts so much that day that she wondered if she'd made a mess of everything she'd done.

"Aunt Silver, you never warned me about men like him," she grumbled aloud, as if her aunt were in the room with her instead of almost an entire continent away. "I think I've met the man I could really love, but it's not safe to love him. He's a real heartbreaker. So what now?"

Take it as it comes.

That was exactly what Aunt Silver's answer would be. She was a wonderfully romantic woman, but soundly based in common sense. Silver had probably faced the same dilemma when she met the man who would eventually be her husband. From what she'd heard from both her mother and Silver, Tessa had surmised that her uncle had been as wild as a mink, with charm to burn and an itch for Silver that Silver had been determined he wasn't going to scratch. Their running battle had lasted for almost two years and kept three counties enthralled, wondering who would win. Silver had won, and their marriage had been as tempestuous and as loving as their courtship. It must run in the family for the women to fall in love with rakes and rascals, she thought.

"I won't fall in love with him!" Tessa said fiercely as she took the stairs up to Sammy's apartment, then admitted to herself that she was whistling in the dark.

When he answered the door, Sammy's face was flushed with excitement and his hair was mussed. "Tessa, just wait until you see the new computer we've put together! It's a real honey."

Tessa was thoroughly familiar with computers, but only from a user's standpoint. She knew absolutely nothing about microchips or interfacing, and wasn't interested in learning, but she smiled at the enthusiasm on Sammy's face. "Tell me about it," she invited.

"See for yourself. Hillary's here, too."

Tessa had never met Hillary before, but Sammy had often talked about her. Hillary lived on the floor above him, and she was as wild about computers as he was. Tessa supposed it was a case of kindred spirits. The young woman she saw seated at the display terminal and practically attacking the keyboard only reinforced that original supposition, for Hillary was as blond as Sammy. Her slim figure was encased in jeans and a jersey, and her long blond hair was pulled back in a simple ponytail. Glasses perched on her small nose as she peered at the monitor.

"Hillary, this is Tessa Conway. I've told you about her; she works with me. Tessa, Hillary Basham."

Hillary looked up, vague surprise in her brown eyes. "Oh, yes, I remember. How are you?"

"Fine, thank you," Tessa said gently.

Sammy launched into a spirited explanation of his

new computer, and Hillary was as carried away by it as he was. Tessa listened and nodded, trying to make sense of what they were telling her. They both seemed very excited, and because of that she asked questions, letting them enjoy the moment. Intuitively, she realized that Hillary was so much in love with Sammy that the girl was almost sick with it, but was too shy to let him know. Of course, with Sammy, a woman would have to put up a billboard and point it out to him to get him to notice it, and even then it might be a week before he realized he was the man involved. He was so deeply involved with his computer that everything else passed him by.

She didn't get her chess lesson that night; Sammy was so high from whatever great strides he'd made in the computer industry that there was no question of settling him down. He and Hillary played with the computer as if it were human, and they devoted over an hour to the naming of it before they finally settled on Nelda. Tessa groaned when she heard the name, and Sammy looked hurt, since it had been his idea. Hillary jumped in immediately in favor of Sammy's choice, and Nelda it was. Shaking her head, Tessa looked around at all of the equipment that Sammy had in his apartment. He must sink most of his salary into his hobby, she thought. In fact, she wondered how he even had money left to eat on.

Sammy wasn't a complete social wasteland; he eventually realized that he was hungry, and evidently recalled the manners his mother had tried for years to drill into him. Blushing, he jumped to his feet and offered to fix sandwiches and cold drinks, and refused

Hillary's quick offer to help. He rushed out of the room and left a pool of silence behind him.

Tessa looked at Hillary's downcast eyes and saw the way the girl had suddenly withdrawn. "Where do you work?" she asked, since it was evident that Hillary wasn't going to begin the conversation.

"At a bank." Hillary gave her a shy look, then quickly looked down again. "Sammy talks about you a lot. You're…you're as beautiful as he says."

Tessa wondered if she'd gone too far in her friendship with Sammy, trying to make him more comfortable in female company. "That's sweet of him, but I'm not beautiful at all," she said honestly, and that brought up the bent blond head. "It's just that he's shy with women, and I talk to him and make him laugh. He talks about you a lot, too."

"Yeah, but that's different. I'm a buddy, someone to talk computers with." For a brief moment, hostility was plain in her brown eyes.

"Then talk about something else when you're with him." The last thing she wanted was to get involved in some sort of triangle, especially when the man in question couldn't see the forest for the trees.

"That's easy for you, but not everyone's a…a flirt like you!" As soon as she flared up, hot color rushed into Hillary's rather pale face and made it rosy. She looked down again, as if appalled at her rudeness, and Tessa sighed.

"Hillary, I'm not a threat to you. Please believe me. Sammy's just a friend to me, nothing else."

"But what about the way he feels about you?"

"He's definitely not in love with me; I promise!"

Before she could say anything else to reassure the girl, Sammy came back into the room with a tray of drinks. He carefully set it down away from his equipment.

"I'll be right back with the sandwiches."

"I'll help!" Scrambling to her feet, Hillary hurried after him.

Feeling definitely *de trop,* Tessa called after them, "Just one sandwich for me; I have to be leaving soon."

When they came back into the room, Sammy frowned at her. "But we haven't played chess yet."

"It's later than I thought, and tomorrow is a working day," she reminded him.

He looked guilty. "I guess I got carried away over Nelda."

"I enjoyed hearing about Nelda," she reassured him.

"I know you've probably been bored, but really, I think we're going to be able to market Nelda. Hillary and I have put a lot of time and money into her; she's really something."

Was he talking about the computer or Hillary? Probably the computer. Deciding to give him a nudge in the right direction, Tessa said blandly, "It must be marvelous to have someone like Hillary, someone who understands your work and wants the same things you do."

Hillary flushed, but Sammy wasn't paying any attention. "Yeah, she's really great."

As quickly as she could without appearing rude, Tessa downed her sandwich and drank her cold drink, then gathered up her purse and light coat. "I really have to be going now."

Sammy walked her to the door. "I owe you a chess lesson," he said, smiling. "How about tomorrow night?"

For some reason, Tessa thought she'd probably had her last chess lesson. It was better not to cause trouble. "I already have plans for tomorrow night, and I know you better than that, anyway! You're still going to be playing with Nelda to see if she can do everything you think she can."

He rubbed the back of his neck, shrugging his shoulders to work out the kinks. "You're probably right. We still have a lot of work to do on her. Maybe next week?"

"Maybe," she said, giving him a smile. He'd be so involved with his work that he'd never notice; she had been the one who had pursued their friendship, easing him out of part of his shyness.

Later that evening, when she was ready for bed, she sat with pillows behind her back and a pad of writing paper on her knees. Her weekly letter to Aunt Silver was its usual mixture of news and comment, and at the end of it she mentioned Brett Rutland. As she sealed the envelope she smiled to herself. She'd deliberately been casual in her mention of him, knowing that Aunt Silver's antennae would begin quivering as soon as she read the name.

BILLIE HAD BROUGHT coffee and doughnuts for their mid-morning break, and they had just begun their second doughnut when Tessa's phone rang. She answered it absently.

"I just want to confirm tonight. Six-thirty."

She hadn't heard his voice on the phone before, but there was no mistaking his identity. She closed her eyes briefly at the pleasure that rippled through her at just the sound of his voice. "Yes. Six-thirty."

"Do you like to dance?"

"Did granny wear garters?"

His low, rough laugh filled her ear. "Wear your dancing shoes."

When she hung up the phone, Tessa was aware that her heart wasn't beating in its regular rhythm, and she felt a little breathless. Even over the phone, his impact almost knocked her down. She thought of his thick, tawny brown hair and navy eyes, and it became even more difficult to breathe.

"Don't you ever stay at home?" Billie said automatically. It was practically standard procedure for Tessa to have at least one offer to go out every day.

"Of course I do. You know Monday night is laundry night."

They laughed together, but Tessa's mind was already on the coming night. They would have dinner, go out dancing…and then what? Would he try to make love to her again? She was afraid that he would, and even more afraid that he wouldn't.

Billie regarded her friend thoughtfully. "You know, this is the first time I've seen you get cloudy-eyed over a man. Is this one special to you?"

"I'm afraid he will be." Well aware of the admission in those few words, Tessa wound her suddenly shaking fingers together.

"You don't want to fall in love? Sometimes I think I'd give anything I own to find the right guy, the real McCoy." Why should Tessa, of all people, be nervous about a man? Of all the people Billie knew, Tessa was the most comfortable with men, a woman who honestly enjoyed a man's company. It didn't make sense for her to be so wary.

Tessa didn't volunteer Brett's name, and Billie didn't ask, for which Tessa was grateful. She didn't know how Brett felt about their connection being known, but she knew she wouldn't like the gossip that would flow as surely as the tides followed the moon if it became known that she was seeing Brett Rutland. His position automatically made their relationship difficult. She was totally uninterested in climbing the corporate ladder, but that wouldn't keep people from saying that she was trying to get ahead on the strength of her performance in the bedroom rather than in the office.

Because of her uneasiness at both the way she was beginning to feel about him and the difficult situation she could find herself in at work, she was quiet that night. She could feel his cool gaze dissecting her, trying to probe her thoughts. Over coffee, he asked, "Has something upset you?" His voice was so even that it took her a moment to hear the steel in it.

She blew across the steaming surface of the coffee, then sipped it. "Not really. I'm a little at a loss. Would you rather not have people from the office know we've been out together?"

"I don't give a damn who knows."

"I know I'm being premature in worrying about it. After all, we've only been out twice, and that doesn't mean—"

"Yes, it does mean," he interrupted, reaching for her hand. He put his hand on the table, palm up, and looked at her slender fingers as they lay across his palm. The contrast in their hands was striking, in ways besides the obvious one of size. His hands were powerful, lean and hard, with long fingers and short clean nails, his fingertips rough, his skin bronzed. Her hands were slim and delicate, the bones so fragile that her fingers were almost translucent, her oval nails polished. Her hands bore no rings.

"Have you ever been married?" he asked abruptly, looking at her bare fingers.

"No."

"Engaged?"

She sipped her coffee for a moment before replying. "Twice."

His eyes narrowed. "What happened?"

"I found out that I didn't love either of them enough."

"You must have thought you did, at one time."

She sighed and looked away from him. She didn't particularly want to talk about her failed engagements, which to her were almost as bad as failed marriages, but she could sense his determination to get the details out of her.

"The first time, it was an infatuation that I took for love, that's all. I was in college, and Will was a medical student. He wanted us to get married right away; he'd already planned for me to quit college and put him through school. I gave him his ring back."

He was watching her very closely, reading every nuance of expression that crossed her face. "And the second time?" he asked, dismissing Will as unimportant because he sensed her reluctance to continue.

"Andrew," she said slowly, somehow feeling compelled to answer him. "He did something that hurt me, and I didn't love him enough to forgive him."

After several moments of silence, Brett realized that she wasn't going to enlarge on her explanation. His hand tightened on hers. "Tell me," he insisted. The dim light above his head turned his tawny hair into dark gold and cast shadows on his face that made it seem harder, more dangerous.

Her hand moved restlessly in his. "I don't believe in raking over old coals. I don't think about it anymore. I picked up the pieces and moved on."

"Tell me," he whispered, his eyes as dark as midnight.

"He was unfaithful." Simple words, old-fashioned words, but for her they were the epitaph for a romance. With her heart, Tessa gave fidelity, and she expected the same in return. Andrew had cheated her, promising her faith and giving her only deceit.

Brett's eyes brushed over her throat and shoulders and breasts, his gaze as hot as a touch. "He was a fool. Why would any man want to sleep around when he could have you in his bed every night?"

Tessa looked up at him, and color rose in her cheeks at the way he was looking at her. Still holding her hand, he rose to his feet. "Dance with me," he invited.

She went willingly into his arms, grateful for the hard strength that enfolded her, for the warmth of his body. The virile impact of his masculine appeal made her tremble, but being in his arms also made her feel safe, as if his strength held the rest of the world at bay. She put her arms around his shoulders, sighing a little in contentment.

"Did you enjoy your chess lesson?" he murmured, brushing her soft hair and temple with his lips.

She laughed against his throat. "We never got around to it. Sammy was so excited over his new computer that he couldn't think about anything else."

"What sort of new computer?"

"Nelda. He swears it's going to revolutionize the personal computer industry, and maybe it will. For his sake, I hope so. He has to have a small fortune sunk into all of that equipment he has in his apartment. I don't see how he can afford to eat."

Above her head, Brett's eyes narrowed as he filed that bit of information away in his memory. Automatically his arms tightened about her, pulling her closer so that her breasts flattened against his muscled chest. "Did you tell him there wouldn't be any more chess lessons?"

"No, there was no need. He's so involved with Nelda, he won't even notice."

"Why did you get involved with him in the first place? He isn't your type."

Tessa stiffened a little in his arms. "He's a nice man; why isn't that my type?" She seldom bothered herself enough to take offense at anything anyone said, but she couldn't ignore Brett. She was vulnerable to him in ways she didn't even want to think about. Just what did he think her "type" was?

"He'll never be the life of the party," Brett said coolly. "And for all his electronic genius, you could wind him around your little finger and he'd never realize it. If you had him as steady company, you'd be bored to tears within a week."

She stared up at him, trying to read his thoughts in his hooded enigmatic eyes. She was more than a party-girl, and she wanted him to see that, to see the woman beneath the gay and frothy facade. Did he think she was just out for a good time, that she was only attracted to people who were as comfortable socially as she was? "I'm never bored with Sammy," she said, her voice steady, concealing the faint hurt that was welling in her. "I like him very much, whether he's my type or not."

Slowly his arm tightened about her waist, pulling her so close to him that his hard body felt imprinted against her softer one. "He doesn't matter, since you won't be seeing him again. I want you; I'm going to have you. And I don't share."

Tessa caught a quick breath at the hard, determined note in his voice. She was accustomed to being pursued, but Brett was a man who not only chased, but caught his prey. Her frail butterfly wings would be useless against his power, yet she wouldn't feel threatened at all if she knew she could entrust herself to him. Did he want her for herself, or did he only want to conquer her because of the challenge she represented, to catch the fragile and elusive butterfly simply so he could say she'd belonged to him for a while?

Perhaps he saw some of her doubts reflected on her face, in her clear green eyes, because he slid his hand down to boldly cup her bottom, propelling her forward to press her hips against his in a gesture so provocative and possessive that she barely stifled the startled cry that came to her lips. "Get used to it," he drawled, and something frightening moved in his navy eyes.

Her face burning, Tessa looked around hastily to see if anyone had seen him, but no one was paying any attention to them, and she felt her color begin to fade. The evening, which had begun so quietly, was getting out of hand. "I want to go home now, please," she told him evenly.

"Are you certain? It's still early."

"Yes, I'm certain. I'd like to go now."

Perhaps she was being foolish in abandoning a public place for a private one, but Tessa felt that she could handle herself better without an audience. He wasn't the kind of man to force a woman; she had no fear that the evening would end in a wrestling match. Even given the provocation of the way she'd kissed him the first time they'd gone out together, he'd been more understanding than she would have expected any man to be, under the circumstances. The problem was that when he kissed her, she didn't want him to stop. Ever. And there was a sensual determination about him now that made her pulse rate increase. If he pressed the issue, would she give in? She was weak, because she wanted very much to give in; she wanted to be in his bed and give herself to him. The strong physical attraction she'd felt for him from the beginning was rapidly intensifying. She was beginning to love him, despite everything her common sense was telling her. She knew that he was a walking heartache, a man who had such a strong sensual appeal to women that he probably couldn't even remember the names of those who had shared their beds with him.

She was silent on the drive to her apartment, and so was he, though occasionally she could feel his intent gaze on her. If only she could read his thoughts! But he kept them well-hidden, and she had no idea what he wanted from her beyond the obvious: physical gratification. To really know him would be a lifetime occupation, she thought. He kept himself too well guarded; he was so cool, so controlled even in his passion. The woman who broke that control would find herself with a volcano on her hands, but Tessa shivered with excitement at the thought of being that woman.

Once again he preceded her into the apartment and checked all of the rooms before returning her key to her. She stood still, a little wary as he approached her, and a faint smile touched his chiseled mouth as he put his hand beneath her chin and tilted her face up to him. "You pretty little witch," he whispered, his warm breath caressing her face. "You tie a man in knots with your flirt-and-retreat games. You can keep on flirting, baby, but I'm going to put an end to those teasing retreats. Kiss me. I've been driving myself crazy for two days, thinking about your mouth and the way you taste." He brushed his lips over hers in a light, tantalizing caress. "Kiss me," he demanded again, then took the choice away from her by fastening his mouth on hers, hard, his tongue going deep and again giving her his heady taste. Her eyes closed on a hot swell of pleasure, and her hands clenched his shoulders.

They stood entwined, their mouths greedy and clinging, until Tessa felt light-headed from lack of air and pulled her mouth free; then she bent her head and rested it against his shoulder. The want, the need, that vibrated between them was staggering, and from the pressure of his body she knew that he was strongly aroused, yet he seemed to be waiting for a signal from her. She couldn't give it to him; the act of physical love was an act of commitment for her, and she wasn't certain enough of her feelings on the basis of two meetings to let him have that intimacy. Gently he rubbed the back of her neck, easing the tension in the taut tendons he found there.

"Let's go to bed," he murmured, kissing her temple and the shell of her ear, outlining the rim of her ear with the very tip of his tongue and setting off small ripples of pleasure that flowed over her body. "I know you think it's too soon, but waiting won't change anything. I'm going to have you, and we both know it."

She closed her eyes in an agony of wanting and indecision. He was so warm and strong, and she wanted him so much that she was nothing but an empty ache inside. "I'm afraid I'm going to fall in love with you," she blurted, her voice muffled against his shoulder, and she knew that she lied. She was afraid, yes, because it was far too late for her; she was already so much in love with him that she couldn't pull back now, and no lecture from her common sense was going to change it. She'd been waiting for him all of her life. She could no more halt the tide of her emotions than she could stop breathing.

Brett went very still. Even the hand on the nape of her neck ceased its motion. Love, in the romantic sense, wasn't something that existed for him, and it wasn't something that he wanted. Until she'd said the word, the idea hadn't even occurred to him. He'd taken her out to dinner the first time for a twofold reason: because he wanted to take her to bed, and to question her about the other employees at Carter Engineering. His physical desire had increased until the heat of it seared him, until he couldn't sleep and tossed restlessly on the twisted sheets, his body taut and frustrated. She intrigued him as no other woman had ever done; she was both bold and wary, inviting and resisting at the same time. For the first time in his life, he resented the thought of other men. He didn't want her associating with Sammy Wallace for a reason quite apart from the fact that the man was a suspected embezzler. He wanted all her time to be his, all her kisses to be his, and a primitive possessiveness ate at him. When he thought of the two men she'd been engaged to, he wanted to shake her for allowing them to get close enough to her that she'd even considered marriage.

But he didn't want the entanglements of emotion. Love was greedy and demanding, and he didn't want that sort of emotional intimacy. His mind was always a little aloof, always in control, and he wanted to stay that way; he'd seen too many men make complete fools out of themselves, all in the name of some confused emotional high that they called love.

Already Tessa was intruding into his thoughts, when he should have his mind strictly on business. The image of her sleek, silky body stretched out on white sheets, waiting for him, was one that burned in his mind at all hours, entering his thoughts when he least expected it. She was distracting him from the clandestine cat-and-mouse game he and Evan were playing with a thief, and he wanted to take her, satiate himself with her, so he could put her out of his thoughts and get on with the job at hand.

The thought of her falling in love with him jolted him. What would it be like to have this fancy, flirty woman belonging to him? Could she love, or was she just playing with the word? Had she really loved either of those men she'd been engaged to? What had she said about the one who had been cheating on her? That she didn't love him enough to forgive him? Perhaps it was all just a game to her, to lure a man deeper and deeper into the trap of her charm. But at the same time, the idea tantalized him, much like the subtle perfume she wore that drifted to his nose every so often, then faded elusively.

Tessa correctly read his stillness, and she fiercely blinked back the sudden scalding of tears, taking care to keep her head buried against his shoulder. "Why don't we call a halt to this now?" she whispered. "I don't know if I can keep it under control on my part, and I'd rather walk away from it before I get hurt." More lightly, she said, "We could always remember each other as the one that got away."

He put his hands on her shoulders and pushed her a little away from him so he could see her face, and a frown laced his brows. "No," he said curtly, not wanting to examine too closely his reason for rejecting her suggestion, but there was no way he was going to let her walk away from him. Her laughter would echo in his mind for the rest of his life, and he'd feel the ache of unsatisfied desire.

"Please." Her eyes were very clear and direct. "I told you, I don't sleep around. I don't have casual affairs. I have a lot to give a man; I'm more than just someone for fun and games, and I expect a lot from a man. If you aren't willing to give it, then let me go free."

"What do you expect from a man?" he asked roughly, drawing her closer to him once again, because he couldn't tolerate the distance between them.

"Friendship. Passion. Faith and trust and fidelity."
She moved her head in a quick motion. "Love."

"I'm too old to believe in fairy tales, baby. Love is
just a word that people throw around as an excuse for
making fools of themselves." His hard hands hurt her
shoulders. "I want you, and you want me. Let that be
enough."

She shook her head again, but before she could say
anything he bent his head and kissed her, slow and hard
and deep, and again she was helpless against the black
magic he practiced on her flesh. His hands moved over
her body, touching her breasts and hips and thighs, as
if branding her with his touch. When he pulled away,
his face was full of dark color and his eyes were burning. "Think about that tonight. I'll pick you up tomorrow night at seven."

"There's no point in it," she said weakly, but she
doubted that he heard her. He was already going out the
door, and she stood there in the middle of the floor for
a long time, her head bent, her eyes closed. He wasn't
going to let her play it safe, and she wondered if she'd
be able to survive another failed relationship.

She was torn between the instinctive need to protect herself and the needs of her deeply passionate
heart, which told her to reach out and grab him, to
twine herself about him so tightly that he'd never be
able to get her out of his heart or mind. She had no
chance at all if she was too cowardly to take one.
Love gave, instead of demanded, and she wanted to
give herself to him. Perhaps his mind didn't recognize love, but his body would. She was afraid…but it
was too late for fear.

EVAN RUBBED HIS eyes tiredly, then returned to the stack of computer printout sheets before him. "I'm so tired, none of this is making any sense," he muttered.

Brett checked his watch; it was a little after midnight. He'd welcomed the intense concentration required by their investigation; it took his mind off his frustration, off his empty bed. But he was tired, too, and he had the nagging feeling that he'd been missing something, something that he'd have seen if he hadn't been so tired, if a part of his mind hadn't still been on Tessa. Damn her, why couldn't he stop thinking about her? She was just another woman, despite her laughing eyes and searing kisses. "We're missing something," he muttered. "Something is right here under our noses, and we're passing over it."

"A 747 could be under my nose right now and I'd have a hard time seeing it," Evan yawned, tossing his pencil down. "This guy has to be a real genius. Why don't you just offer him a bonus if he'll tell us how he's doing it?"

"You're pretty sure it's Wallace?" Brett asked, slanting Evan a quick, hard look.

"It's someone who knows how to play hardball with a computer, that's for sure."

"Tessa told me that he has a fortune in electronics in his apartment. He knows all the access codes; he can get into our computers any time he wants."

"I checked the guard's records, and he works late a lot of nights, but damn it, I can't find anything!" Evan said fiercely.

"It's here; we just haven't matched everything up yet." Brett got to his feet, moving restlessly around the hotel room. Damn, but he was getting tired of hotels, of living out of a suitcase. He wanted the crisp, clean air of the mountains, the wood-smoke smell of a roaring fireplace, the surging power of a horse beneath him. He moved his broad shoulders as if flexing against invisible chains, and the irritation of the job ate at him.

Evans rose, too, and stretched his tired muscles. "I'm calling it quits for the night. The weekend is ahead of us. I can do a lot more work then, when I don't have to spend the day pretending to study systems and options. I'm making a quick trip back to San Francisco in the morning, but I'll be back by Saturday morning at the latest. Do you need anything from the office?"

"No," Brett said absently, staring out the window at the sea of lights that stretched as far as he could see. Like New York, Los Angeles never slept. On the ranch, when night came, the livestock bedded down and so did the people.

After Evan had gone to his own room, Brett still stood at the window, but he no longer saw the lights. His body felt the pressure of her soft flesh against him, and his jaw tightened. He wanted her. He didn't even have to think her name; all other women became faceless, without identity, even sexless, when compared with her.

He gave the hotel bed a disgusted look, knowing that he wouldn't be able to sleep when he did finally lie down in it. His bed at the ranch was big and wide, and suddenly he pictured her in it, her soft dark hair spread across his pillow while she slept quietly, with the quilts pulled up over her bare shoulders to protect her from the frosty bite of the early spring morning. He shook his head to dislodge the picture, but it remained with him, and another disturbing image joined it: that of long winter nights, of making love to her in that bed, and knowing that the next night he'd have her again.

He scowled. He wasn't going to let her get to him like that. He'd take her and then forget about her, because in the taking he'd find that she was just like all the other women he'd had and then forgotten.

CHAPTER FOUR

TESSA WAS ALWAYS at her desk a little early, and today Sammy brought in a cup of coffee for her before it was time to start work. "I couldn't remember if you took cream and sugar or not, so I brought both," he said, flushing a little as he dug in his pockets and produced two packets of sugar and a small plastic container of nondairy creamer, with a peel-off top.

She took the coffee gratefully; after lying awake half the night, she'd overslept a little and had missed her usual leisurely breakfast. She felt more than a little bruised, and only the assurance of her mirror had given her the courage to face the day. She looked normal, except for faint circles under her eyes, but she didn't feel normal. "You may have saved my life," she sighed. "Thanks, Sammy. I missed breakfast this morning."

He shifted his weight from one foot to the other. "We've been working on Nelda practically all night. Hillary's really great, isn't she? I don't have to explain things to her; she already knows."

"She's perfect for you," Tessa said firmly. It went right over his head.

"I'd still be putting Nelda together if Hillary hadn't been helping me. She has some contacts who might be able to help us with marketing Nelda, too; she meets all sorts in the bank."

"She's a wonderful girl. Very pretty, too."

He looked a little surprised. "Well, yeah, but the best thing about her is that she's so smart. She wrote the program for Nelda."

Tessa gave up; she'd done everything but propose to him for Hillary. She doubted that any woman held the same degree of fascination for him as Nelda did, but that was Hillary's problem. Right now, Tessa felt that she had a large problem of her own to worry about, and that problem was about six-four with indigo eyes. Hadn't she known from the start that Brett Rutland was more than she could handle?

She caught a movement just past Sammy's shoulder, and she looked up, feeling her heart skip a beat as she met Brett's narrowed eyes. He gave Sammy a hard look, then turned that look on her. "Good morning," he said, but Tessa heard the anger under the cool tones.

"Good morning," she returned evenly. "Mr. Rutland, this is Sammy Wallace, from data processing. Sammy, Brett Rutland."

Sammy thrust out his hand with a quick, awkward movement, and his face lit with eagerness. "Nice to meet you!"

With impeccable control, Brett shook hands. "I've heard a lot about you, Mr. Wallace. You're something of a genius with computers, aren't you?"

Sammy glowed. Before he could say anything, however, Perry Smitherman came rushing over, having spotted Brett. He practically skidded to a stop when he reached them. "Mr. Rutland!" Perry cried with a pleasure so obviously feigned that Tessa winced for him. "May I help you with something, sir?"

"Yes," Brett said curtly. "I'd like to speak with you privately, and I thought I'd stop by on my way up to the office. There's some information I'd like you to get for me."

"Yes, of course, of course," Perry babbled. "Right this way—my office—"

With a nod to both Tessa and Sammy, Brett went into Perry's office, with Perry skittering around him like a nervous poodle.

"Can you believe that?" Sammy asked incredulously. "He's actually *heard* of me." He was beaming with pleasure, his eyes sparkling behind the lenses of his glasses.

Tessa sat very still, but Sammy didn't notice her lack of response; he was too bemused and too pleased to notice anything. It was time for him to be on the job, so he ambled out as casually as he'd ambled in. Tessa turned on her video screen but sat staring at the blinking cursor without really seeing it. Brett had been as controlled as usual, but she was acutely sensitive to his mood, and she'd felt the seething anger beneath his calm exterior. Had something happened this morning to put him in a bad mood, or was he angry because he'd walked in and found her talking with Sammy? He'd expressly ordered her not to see Sammy after working hours, but this was on the job; surely he didn't expect her to go out of her way to avoid the people she worked with? It was ridiculous even to think that he might be jealous of Sammy. Sammy wasn't even in the same class with Brett, and Brett had to know it. She'd also told him that Sammy was just a friend, but he'd been glaring at Sammy as if he'd like to take a swing at him, and poor Sammy wouldn't even have an inkling of what was going on.

Was Brett jealous? The possibility made her almost dizzy with hope. He had no reason to be, but wouldn't jealousy signal that he cared more deeply for her than she'd thought?

Tessa was good enough at her job, and disciplined enough, that she managed to be productive even though she kept one eye on Perry's door, waiting for Brett to reappear. She was jittery and excited, and she smiled a little in amusement at herself, because none of her friends here would ever believe that Tessa Conway could be nervous over a man. The difference was that Brett wasn't just *a* man, he was *the* man, and that was quite a lot of difference. Not even Andrew had ever made her feel the way she felt with Brett, and at the time Tessa had thought herself sincerely in love with Andrew. She was learning that there were many different degrees of love, and that the deep, hungry need she felt for Brett far surpassed anything she'd even imagined.

At last Brett came out of Perry's office, but he passed her without even glancing in her direction. Tessa felt a pang of unreasonable hurt; after all, she'd been the one who'd said that she would feel uncomfortable with office gossip, so Brett was only following her wishes in not making their relationship obvious. But she found that she still wanted something from him: a look, a smile, anything to reassure her that he didn't feel as cold as he looked.

Whatever he'd wanted from Perry, evidently Perry hadn't found it to be a pleasant visit. Through the open door of Perry's office, Tessa could see him pacing back and forth, alternately wringing his hands or shoving his fingers through his thinning hair. She'd heard that

Brett often had that effect on the executives and department heads who had to deal with him. There were two sides to his personality, and she felt a little disoriented because she couldn't quite reconcile the coldly scathing executive who tore strips of hide off anyone who crossed him with the man of burning sensuality who kissed her with such sweet fire.

How could she find herself so helplessly in love with a man she didn't really know? He was a puzzle to her, his personality an intricate maze that she longed to solve, because she felt that her reward for finding the secrets of his personality would be a fiery love that would last a lifetime.

By noon, the fact that Brett Rutland had had a private meeting with Perry was all over the office. "What's going on?" Billie asked eagerly over lunch. "Is Perry in trouble?"

"Not that I know of," Tessa said, startled at the thought.

"Then why did Rutland have a private meeting with him?"

"Now, you know you're always telling me not to get too friendly with people," Tessa said innocently. "What was I supposed to do, go up to the man and say, 'Mr. Rutland, honey, what are you doing in here?'"

"No one would be surprised," Billie grumbled. "And the hell of it is, he'd probably say, 'Miss Conway, honey, why don't I take you out to dinner tonight and tell you all about it?'"

Yes, he might say exactly that, Tessa thought, and smiled. She had to be a blue-ribbon fool, but she longed for the hours to pass so she could see him again, even knowing that he wasn't in the best of moods and that he was hard to handle even when he was feeling good. But she wanted to see him; she wanted to rest her head on his hard chest and soak up his nearness, like a flower soaking up the sun. She'd known him less than a week, but he'd embedded himself so deeply in her thoughts that it was difficult for her to remember how it had been before, when there had been no tall man with tawny hair and navy eyes who overshadowed every other man she'd ever known, who had taken over her dreams in daylight and dark. Was there a moment in her life now when she was actually unconscious of him? She couldn't think of one. Even when she was asleep, he was in her mind, so that she went to sleep thinking of him and woke to a continuation of the same thought, as if he had been there all along.

"You've gone moony-eyed again," Billie said, watching her. "Whoever he is, he must be something else."

Tessa caught her breath. "He is."

"It's Brett Rutland, isn't it? The way you smiled a moment ago, when we were talking about him…I can't describe it."

There was no use in denying it, since Tessa felt that she couldn't control her expression right then, and in any case she wasn't inclined to deny the way she felt about him. She wasn't ashamed of loving him; she felt glorified by it, as if she were more alive now than she'd ever been before in her life. "Yes," she admitted quietly.

Billie was concentrating fiercely. "Did you meet him for the first time this week, in the elevator?"

"Yes. We had dinner that night…and last night."

"You've been out with him twice, and you think

you're in love with him? The Ax-Man? Tessa, there can't be two people any more mismatched than you and Brett Rutland! You're the life of any party, and he… well, picture it yourself. He walks into a room, and it's instant silence."

That was the public Brett; Billie would never comprehend the potent charm he could exert in private, the intense concentration he turned on a woman that demanded the same degree of attention in return. But Tessa had known his kisses, felt the heat of him straining against her, and she would never be able to think of him as the cold, ruthless troubleshooter who reported only to Joshua Carter.

"Will you keep this to yourself?" she asked Billie. "He said that he doesn't mind who knows, but I don't like the thought of everyone gossiping about us."

"Sure," Billie agreed readily, and reached over to pat her hand. "You didn't pick an easy one to fall for, did you?"

"Of course not." Tessa's soft mouth curved wryly. "The easy ones were all too…easy."

Billie felt that she'd been watching out for Tessa ever since the younger woman had moved to Los Angeles, but never before had she felt that Tessa was heading for deep trouble. Even when she'd just begun to adjust to the differences between Tennessee and California, Tessa had always approached everything with high spirits and good humor. But Brett Rutland could break Tessa's bright spirit with his cool ruthlessness if Tessa cared too much and he cared too little. Billie's eyes were troubled as she looked at her friend. "If you need me, all you have to do is pick up the telephone and call me," she offered. "I can always offer you a drink, an extra bed and a shoulder to cry on, singly or in any combination."

"Thanks. I know that you're there for me if I need you." Tessa smiled warmly at her friend. "But don't be so glum! I've always landed on my feet before, haven't I?"

"You haven't been in love before," Billie retorted. "Believe me, love can be hell."

Yes, it could be, and Tessa had already been singed by its fires, but the small flames Andrew had generated were nothing compared to the inferno Brett lit just by walking into the room. Faintly confused, because she'd never before doubted that she'd loved Andrew, she was now beginning to wonder if she'd ever been more than fond of him. There was simply no comparison between the way she'd felt then and the way she felt now about Brett. With Brett, she felt an irresistible compulsion to walk into his arms and never leave them, to simply press herself against him and cling until her flesh had melded with his, until they were no longer two separate beings but a part of each other, eternally linked in flesh and heart and mind. When she wasn't with Brett, she felt…lonely, and she'd never been lonely before in her life. She'd been alone many times, and enjoyed her solitude as much as she enjoyed the company of friends, but now she felt oddly incomplete.

When Brett came to her apartment that night, Tessa had only to look at him to know that he was angry. His anger wasn't violent, but it was all the more potent for his control. Her spine felt chilled as she looked up into his narrowed eyes. "If you don't want to break off with Wallace, all you have to do is say so. I don't like being lied to."

"I haven't lied to you," she replied steadily. "Sammy is a friend, nothing more. We work on the same floor; I'm forever running into him. I can't hide under my desk to keep from seeing him."

There was something primitive in his expression as he looked down at her, and he touched her delicate jaw with hard, lean fingers, a light touch that nevertheless shocked her with its possessiveness. "Don't ever lie to me," he rasped; then he bent down and kissed her.

It seemed as if it had been forever since she'd tasted him, felt his mouth move hungrily on hers, and she raised her hands to his shoulders to cling to him. Shaking slightly, reveling in the delight that crashed through her in response to his lightest touch, she kissed him with all the sweet fire she could give him. Finally, he raised his head, his eyes searing, and a faint film of perspiration had broken out on his forehead.

The tension between them increased as the night grew older. Though she loved seafood, Tessa could do little more than pick at her lobster, because every nerve ending in her body was picking up the signals of his sensual arousal, and a hot, answering need coiled achingly inside her. He made her feel so female that it was as if she'd never before had any concept of her own femininity. With him, she was a primitive, and the intensity of her emotions frightened her, but at the same time she was lured by their power. The time for running away was past; perhaps it had been too late for her from the first moment she'd looked up into the blue beauty of his eyes.

"Spend the day with me tomorrow," he said abruptly, for the first time in his life putting his personal concerns ahead of business. There was a job to be done, but it paled in importance when compared to the urgency he felt to consolidate his relationship with Tessa. When he'd seen Sammy Wallace hovering over her desk that morning, he'd been seized by a cold rage that had made him want to choke the man. He'd never been possessive of a woman before, but women had come to him so easily and so early that he hadn't valued them for anything other than physical pleasure. But Tessa hadn't offered herself to him; she'd enticed him with her teasing smile and laughing eyes, then danced away from his touch. He was a man, and a hunter. He'd have her, and soon.

"Yes," Tessa agreed, though it hadn't been an invitation as much as a command. Her eyes wandered over his hard, rough face, and a tightness in her chest warned her that she'd forgotten to breathe again.

He swore softly, the words a barely audible rasp. There was a soft, drowning look on her face that made his body tighten in need. "Let's get out of here," he rasped, surging to his feet and pulling her from her chair. She didn't protest; she was silent as he paid the bill; then she leaned on him a little on their way out to the car.

The night had turned cool, and Tessa lifted her flushed face to the fresh breeze. She felt heated, as if her internal furnace were burning away at top capacity, and she wanted to remove the clothing that was suddenly too restrictive. He unlocked the car door and opened it, then put her inside, and Tessa drew a deep, shuddering breath. How could she control the wild need inside her? It was burning her up, turning her body into a cauldron of love and wanting. When he got behind the steering wheel, she said, "Brett," in a dazed voice, and reached out for him.

He jerked as her hands touched his chest. "You're driving me out of control," he said in a low, savage tone. "I want to push you down on the car seat and take you right now. Damn it, if that's not what you want, too, then don't tease me now, because you're skating on thin ice."

She was barely in control herself, but she heard the taut warning in his voice, and she moved away from him, clenching her hands in her lap in an effort to resist the need to touch him. Did he really think she was only teasing him? The party girl wasn't laughing now; she loved, and she wanted, and she hurt. Why was love portrayed as the ultimate happiness when it was so painful? Her emotions for him were so powerful and deep that she felt as if the greater part of herself, the essence of her very being, had been taken away from her own control and placed in his hands. Love like that was a sword, and in loving Brett she was balanced precariously on the cutting edge; he wasn't a safe man to love. She risked more than her heart in loving him; she risked her very life, for that was what he meant to her, and if anything happened to him the light would go out of her life, and her laughter would fade away. It was frightening to love anyone like that, but Tessa found that, with Brett, her protective barriers of wit and laughter were useless. He demolished them with his intense masculinity and tapped the deep vein of passion within her. She had always thought herself capable of loving deeply, but until Brett, she hadn't known just how deeply.

He drove a little too fast, and when she glanced at him she saw that his jaw was set, and his sensual mouth was pressed into a grim line. He looked hard and dangerous, not the sort of man a woman should play with. In more primitive times, he would probably have thrown her over his shoulder and carried her off. Tessa glanced at him again, and a shiver ran down her spine, because there was a ruthlessness in his face that frightened her a little.

When they reached her apartment, he silently took the key from her and opened the door, then stepped back for her to enter. Tessa switched on the light and turned to face him, but whatever she'd meant to say was forever lost as he closed the door and locked it. She caught her breath, her eyes lifting to his. His eyelids had drooped sensually, so that only a thin line of navy blue was revealed, but his intent was plain to read. Without a word, he shrugged out of his coat and unknotted his tie, pulling it free from his collar, then tossed the discarded garments over the back of a chair. "Now," he whispered harshly, his eyes never leaving hers, "come here and touch me."

Blindly, Tessa walked into his arms.

His mouth was hungry and hurtful, but her mouth clung to his in a trembling ecstasy that asked for all he could give her. Her ribs were crushed by the almost brutal grip of his arms, but she couldn't get close enough to him. She ached at the hateful separation of their flesh. She heard husky little whimpers, but though she didn't recognize them as her own, Brett heard them, and everything male in him responded to those feminine sounds of pleasure. He bent her over his arm, and his mouth left hers to sear a path down the smooth column of her throat, down even more to the firm jut of her breasts. He fastened his mouth on her flesh, and even through the fabric of her dress she felt his moist heat, and desire so sharp that it was painful sliced through her.

She sagged abruptly against him as her knees wobbled and lost their ability to hold her upright. Just as swiftly, he swung her up in his arms and took the few steps to the closest chair, settling into it with her draped over his lap. Tessa opened her love-drugged eyes, the green depths deep and dreamy as she looked at him. Her hands wound around his strong neck. "I've tried not to love you," she whispered achingly, unable to hold her love secret, "but I can't stop myself."

A strong shudder rolled through him at her words. It didn't matter how many other men had heard the words of love from her luscious mouth. It didn't even matter that he'd never wanted a woman to love him. He'd always been coolly indifferent to any feelings of devotion he might have aroused…until Tessa. She was a challenge like none he'd encountered before. It wasn't the resistance she'd put up against him, because she really hadn't resisted him at all. Rather, she'd eluded him, letting him glimpse her womanly richness, then flitting away out of reach. She was so intensely female that he instinctively wanted her; she was a woman who could match the fierceness of his masculinity. In loving him, she gave herself to him, and he wasn't inclined to let her go free again.

His left arm under her back, he arched her up to meet the hungry possession of his mouth, while with his free hand he began opening the line of tiny buttons that marched down the front of her dress. Tessa trembled in his grasp, but didn't protest. She didn't want him to stop; she wanted him to love her like this forever. She'd learned that there was a time for giving and a time for taking. This was her time to give. She'd give all of herself to the man she loved, freely, with all the loving generosity of her nature. Her heart was slamming against her rib cage so violently that she felt dizzy, and in an effort to get more air she turned her head away from his kiss, exposing the tender, elegant line of her throat to him. He explored it with his hot mouth, and Tessa made a little whimpering sound. She wanted him; she needed him so much that she ached deep inside, and she clutched at him with desperate fingers.

"Slow down, slow down," he murmured, easing the dress off her shoulders. "I want this to last a long time. Let's get this off you, so I can see you; I want to strip you naked and touch you all over."

She pulled her arms out of the sleeves and lay back into the cradle of his arm, letting him look his fill at the way her breasts pushed at the thin silky fabric of the white camisole she wore. She hadn't worn a bra, so the dark pink nubs of her hardened nipples were clearly outlined, the small tips begging for his attention. His breath came harder and faster as he lifted her up and tugged the dress down around her hips, then pushed it down her legs and off. She lay on his lap, and his eyes burned her flesh as they moved slowly over her body. Besides the camisole, her only garments were her matching tap pants, a delicate lace garter belt, silk hosiery and her fragile high-heeled sandals. His hand drifted over her body, learning the contours of her, stroking her silk-clad legs until he reached her ankles. Slowly he removed her shoes and let them drop; then his fingers trailed back up her legs. He fingered the elastic of her garters, and a look of almost brutal desire hardened his face.

"You should be put under lock and key," he said gutturally, never taking his eyes from the path his hand traveled. His fingers curled under the waistband of her tap pants and he pulled them down, revealing the soft little hollow of her navel. He circled it with a gentle finger, then the as-yet uncovered riches of her body lured him on, and his hand moved upward to her breasts. He fondled her, his hand burning her flesh. Tessa twisted on his lap, wanting him to push the camisole away and touch her bare flesh.

"Please," she begged softly, arching up to him.

"What is it you want?" he whispered. "Is it this?" He slid his hand inside the camisole and cupped her breast, his thumb rasping over her taut nipple and setting it on fire.

Tessa moaned, squirming against him. "Yes. Yes." She began trembling so violently that her entire body quaked, and he soothed her, cuddling her closer against his hard frame while his hand continued to stroke her breasts.

"Easy, honey," he crooned. "I'm going to give you what you want. Touch me; tell me what you want me to do to you."

The first part of his instructions was easy to carry out. Her hands were drawn to him anyway, and she put them on his chest, feeling the heat of his body burning through his shirt. But the second part.... How could she tell him, when all she knew was that she wanted him so badly she was dying from the exquisite pain of it? She was surrounded by his power, his sexuality.

"I don't know," she whispered shakily, clinging to him. She drew a deep, wavering breath. "I don't know how to handle you."

His blue eyes were so dark that they were almost black. "Sweetheart, you know exactly how to handle me. You know what I want."

"But that's the problem, I don't." Summoning up all her courage, Tessa gave him a tender, shaky smile. "Or rather, I know what you want, but I don't know how to go about it."

Brett went very still, his eyes burning as they searched hers. He considered the meaning of her words, and because he was so sensually aroused and acutely aware of her every reaction, he went straight to the heart of the matter. "Tessa, haven't you ever had a man before?"

"No." Her hands moved over his face. "I love you, and I want you to be the first."

A curious spasm crossed his face; then he surged to his feet, with her held high in his arms. "I'll show you," he muttered hoarsely. "I'll take care of you, honey. You don't have to be afraid."

He strode swiftly to her bedroom and shouldered the door open, then crossed the room and placed her on the bed. He turned on the bedside lamp, and she stared up at his hard face. He didn't look cool and aloof now. He was burning with desire, all other thoughts wiped out of his mind. Gently he removed the rest of her clothing, leaving her lying nude on her bed, and she made an instinctive move to shield her body from his probing gaze. "No, let me see you," he said, and held her arms above her head while he touched every inch of her with his eyes. Incredible that this lovely, delicate piece of femininity had never lain uncovered before a man's hungry eyes before. Incredible that no other man before him had sheathed himself in her sweet depths. Incredible, but he didn't doubt her for a moment. Her innocence was part of her elusiveness. Her lack of sensual knowledge had enabled her to call a halt to his lovemaking when a more experienced woman, knowing what pleasure was in store for her, would have succumbed to the temptation.

And she was his, his alone. A primordial instinct that he'd never before realized he possessed made him want to brand her as his, so no other man would ever think of trespassing. He straightened and began removing his clothing.

Tessa watched him, her mouth going dry with excitement, her eyes hungry as she watched every stage of his disrobing. She hadn't realized quite how muscular he was. When his shirt was tossed aside, she gaped at the ripple of muscles beneath his smooth, tanned skin. His chest was broad and hard, roped with muscles, and tightly curled dark hair spread across it. His abdomen was flat and hard, and his legs were the powerfully muscled legs of a horseman. He lay down on the bed with her and leaned over her, gathering her close to him, and Tessa's eyes widened as she was overshadowed by the sheer size of him. Being naked in bed with him made her realize acutely the difference in their size and strength. She was helpless against his strength. If she had any control at all in this situation, it was only because he allowed her to have it.

Her eyes filled with the instinctive fear every woman feels when lying down with a man for the first time. Brett saw it, and tenderness filled him. He leaned over her and began kissing her lightly, sweet kisses that didn't reveal the violence of his passion. No matter what it cost him, he wouldn't brutalize her. There would be time later for more urgent possessions, but not this time, not her first time. Still kissing her, he slowly began acquainting her with his touch.

Before long, Tessa was twisting in his arms again, her body on fire from the slow caresses that burned her flesh. He knew all her sweet places, and all of them felt the sorcery of his expert fingers. She dug her nails into his shoulders, her mind clouded with heat. She couldn't think; she couldn't do anything but arch and squirm, trying to find more of the maddening pleasure he was giving her. His hand was between her legs, and he was doing things to her that made tension coil unbearably deep inside of her. Tighter and tighter the coil became, and she sobbed at the unbearably delicious sensation that she was about to explode.

Brett rose above her, and settled himself intimately between her thighs. Catching her hips in his powerful hands, he held her still, and broached her virginity with excruciating slowness.

Tessa cried out as she felt herself being filled, but she wasn't aware that she'd made a sound. She was in the grip of something far more powerful than pain, something that banished everything from her consciousness except her body and the wildness that was crashing through her as he took her. This wasn't a simple, basic physical act. It was an act of possession, the forging of a link between them that wove the very fabric of their beings together. She gave and he took, but in the taking found that the complexion of everything had changed. With every slow thrust he branded her as his, yet the threads that bound her to him also bound him to her. Shuddering with the intensity of his pleasure, every inch of him scalded by her hot sweetness, he paused to gather his slipping control.

Her face in the lamplight was both agonized and exalted, her eyes closed as her breath rushed in and out in a broken rhythm. Something tightened in his chest at the sight of her. "Am I hurting you, love?" he murmured urgently, unaware of the word he'd used for the first time in his life.

"No," she moaned, her body undulating against him. "Yes…I don't know. Brett, I don't think I can stand this….I'm flying apart…."

"Shhh, it's all right," he soothed, beginning again the slow movements that set him on fire. "Let go, baby. I'll catch you; I'll take care of you. Come on, darling, come on." He moved against her, his teeth grinding as he strained to hold himself back, all of his attention focused on her, reading every response she gave him. His nude body gleamed with sweat, and his tawny hair was wet and dark.

Tessa's head rolled back and forth, and she cried out blindly. No words had been invented to describe the great waves of feeling that suddenly began crashing through her insides, making her surge upward. She cried his name. Then no other words were possible, nothing was possible except that she give herself completely to the impossible sensations he'd aroused with his powerful masculinity. Dimly she was aware of the way he was moving now, with urgent power, and she heard his deep, growling cries of completion.

In the quiet aftermath, they lay together in silent exhaustion, his face turned into her throat. Tessa smoothed his hair, gently stroked his back and shoulders, though she was so tired that she felt herself drifting to sleep as she lay there. But before she slept, there was something she had to tell him. "I love you," she murmured drowsily, a gift of words that came from her heart without premeditation. "Brett...love." The two words were synonymous to her. She was immediately asleep, like a child, lying trustingly in his arms.

CHAPTER FIVE

Sleep didn't come so easily for Brett; he shifted his weight away from her, knowing that she was far too delicate to bear his weight on her all night, although he'd have liked nothing better than to have remained where he was. She murmured an inaudible protest, and he eased her into his arms, soothing her with his touch. Her head found his shoulder as naturally as if they'd been sleeping together for years, and she nuzzled against him in her sleep, her silky dark hair spread across his shoulder and arm.

His clear-cut lips were pressed into a thin line as he replayed their lovemaking in his mind. She'd been all he'd expected, and more. No other woman in his life had driven him to such a frenzy of desire, and the fact that she'd been virgin had made it even more special, different in a way that he didn't know how to handle. He wasn't a man to leave anything to chance. When she'd told him that it was her first time, he'd realized that she wouldn't be prepared to protect herself from pregnancy, and he'd taken care of it. He didn't think that she'd even noticed when he'd paused for a moment. But when he'd been making love to her, buried deep inside her, he'd thought of what it would be like if he hadn't taken any precautions, and abruptly he wanted to make her pregnant; he wanted her to bear his child. He'd violently resented the need to be careful. He wanted to give her the essence of his manhood, the joining of their bodies in a miracle that became a baby, his baby.

He'd never before wanted to take a woman to the ranch, but he could see Tessa there as easily as if she'd been there all her life. She'd like the sturdy ranch house with its big fireplace, the vast expanses, the soaring mountains. He could see her riding beside him, her delicate, exotic face flushed with pleasure. And he could see her in his bed.

He smiled faintly. There was no doubt how his father would take to her. Was there a man on earth whom Tessa couldn't charm out of his socks? Given the fact that Tom frankly admitted to a decided weakness for women, Brett knew that he and Tessa would hit it off from the first. She'd have Tom wrapped around her little finger the minute he heard that lazy drawl of hers.

A memory pierced him, and he closed his eyes on a sharp pang of desire. "I love you," she'd said, the words soft and liquid, and he'd never known that they could sound so right.

The things he was thinking and feeling were totally foreign to him, and on some edge of his consciousness he bitterly resented Tessa for making him think them. Why couldn't she be like all the other women he'd taken? Just a good time in bed, a casual good-bye kiss, then he'd walk out of her life as free as he'd been when he'd walked in. That was what he'd expected, but it hadn't worked out like that. She'd given him what he wanted, the use of her sweet, soft body, but somehow in the giving she'd taken things from him that he hadn't wanted to offer.

Finally he shifted, stretching out his arm to snap off the lamp, and sudden darkness closed around him, but still he couldn't sleep. Her warm body against his side felt so good that he wanted to turn and press himself fully against her. Her breathing was barely perceptible, but he felt it fan against his skin. He'd slept with a lot of women, but he hadn't liked sleeping entwined; yet now he didn't want to let her go. A man could get used to this in a hurry.

He'd marry her, he thought coolly. She suited him, more than he'd thought possible. And once they were married, he'd put a final stop to the way she had of flirting with every man in the vicinity. She was his, and he wasn't going to stand by and watch her turn a man on with those slow smiles and that magnolia-and-honey drawl of hers.

A sense of satisfaction came over him as he imagined being married to her. Yes, that was exactly what he wanted. Marriage had never figured in his plans for the future, but Tessa had changed all that. The dissatisfaction he'd been feeling with his present life suddenly crystalized, and he knew what he was going to do. He'd marry Tessa, quit his job with Carter-Marshall and take her to Wyoming. Ranch life was what he wanted, what he liked best, and she'd fit right in. It was time old Tom was a grandfather, anyway. His first thought was of the sons he'd have with Tessa, then his imagination supplied the picture of a baby girl with Tessa's enchanting smile and wide green eyes, and a tumble of dark curls on her head. He broke out in a sweat. Hell, what was he letting himself in for? A daughter of Tessa's would keep him on pins and needles for years, wondering what wild young buck was sniffing around his baby girl, and his baby girl would probably be flirting like mad and encouraging those wild young bucks.

In the dark, an unwilling grin spread over his hard face. Life with Tessa would never be boring. And she'd said that she loved him. She'd marry him without question, whenever he wanted. All in all, it was a very satisfactory plan. He relaxed, hugging Tessa closer to him, her bewitching fragrance tantalizing him as he drifted into sleep.

Tessa woke first the next morning, made restless by the unfamiliar weight and warmth in her bed. When she opened her eyes, she found herself staring at the back of his head. During the night he'd turned over on his stomach and he was sprawled out on the bed, taking up his share of the bed and half of hers. Her breath caught at the sight of his tousled tawny hair, like a shaggy lion's, and her heart actually skipped a beat. Love so powerful that it hurt welled up in her, and she'd reached out a trembling hand to touch him before she realized what she was doing and drew it back. Let him sleep. What should she say to him this morning, anyway? How should she act? Surprised, she realized that she was nervous about facing him the morning after. The compulsive passion they'd shared had made them intimate physically, but she was unsure of where she stood in every other way.

Gingerly, she slid off the bed and grabbed up her robe, quietly leaving the room to take a shower. Her eyes were troubled. She'd told him how she felt about him, but not even in the most passionate moments between them had he indicated that he felt anything for her other than sexual attraction. That was powerful enough, she admitted wryly, standing under the shower head and letting the water hit her full in the face. Her body was tender and achy, reminding her of his strength, reminding her of what had happened between them the night before.

She paused, her thoughts drifting. It had been good, so good that she'd thought she would die from the sharp pleasure of it. So that was what it was like.... She'd never imagined it would be so wanton, and so exalted. So that was what it was like to give herself to the man she loved.

When she finished with her shower, she wrapped herself in the robe and peeked into her bedroom, but Brett was still asleep. She went into the kitchen and put on a pot of coffee and sat down at the table, folding her hands on the tabletop and staring at nothing, her thoughts absorbed by the man in her bed and the lovemaking they'd shared during the night. Despite his passion, she sensed that there was a part of him that remained aloof, untouched, some inner core that watched but didn't become involved. Why did he want so much from her, when he refused to share that part of himself? She didn't want to hold in her emotions; Tessa was too warmly responsive to constantly rein herself in. She wanted to give him everything that she could, but because of his reserve, she felt wary and uncertain of herself. She didn't like the feeling. She'd never been the sort of person to be uncertain. She was generally decisive, knowing immediately what she wanted, though she was equally realistic in estimating her chances of getting it.

She wanted Brett, wanted him with a fierce female

need that she'd never before experienced. He'd become as necessary to her as the air she breathed.

The coffee finished brewing, and as she was pouring herself a cup she heard Brett stirring. Immediately she felt warm all over, and she felt her face flush. Taking a hasty sip of coffee, she burned her tongue, and her hands trembled. She set the cup down before she spilled the coffee all over herself. Stop acting like a teenager! she scolded herself, but not all the scolding in the world could calm her racing heart.

"Tessa."

His early-morning voice was a raspy grumble, and a shiver of response raced down her spine. Slowly she turned her head and looked at him standing in her kitchen doorway wearing only a pair of dark blue briefs. Fascinated by his hard, tough masculinity, her eyes drifted down his body, examining him from head to toe, and not missing an inch in between. Heat began to color her face, caused by a mixture of excitement and embarrassment.

He'd been watching her expressive face, seeing the open admiration in the way she looked at him, and her bold innocence made him want to pick her up and take her back to bed. Then, incredibly, she blushed.

He crossed the floor to her, putting his arms around her and easing her against his chest. "Why the blushes?" he asked gently.

"Last night…I acted so…and the things I said…"

"And the things we did," he finished, smiling a little above her head. "Are you all right?" As much as he wanted to make love to her again, he'd felt the delicacy of her body with its slender, aristocratic bones, and he didn't want to hurt her.

"Yes," she sighed, leaning her head against him. Her hands slid around his taut waist, then began to search over the heavy muscles of his back. "A little achy, that's all."

He kissed the tumble of curls on her forehead, then brushed them back, schooling himself to patience. He could wait; not easily, but he could wait. Remembering his plans of the night before, he felt a sudden urge to begin putting them in motion. The sooner he could have her installed at the ranch, the better. "Next weekend," he murmured, "if I can manage to get free, I'll take you to the ranch."

Her head lifted from his chest, and her eyes sparkled with excitement. "The ranch! I'd like that. But why shouldn't you be able to get free? Even executives usually get an occasional weekend off."

"Usually," he agreed, smiling at her impatience. "But this isn't the usual job—" He broke off, frowning at himself. It wasn't like him to confide in anyone, especially about sensitive matters, but he'd nearly blurted the whole thing out to her. It was one more measure of how close she'd gotten to him, how deeply she'd embedded herself in his thoughts.

Attuned to him as she was, Tessa felt his abrupt tension. Her smile faded. "Brett? Is something wrong here?" Alert now, she remembered snatches of gossip about Brett Rutland. His appearance usually meant trouble, not for him, but for the people who had to deal with him. He was called the Ax-Man. He found the root of any trouble, and the people causing it were fired. And after talking with Brett the day before, Perry Smith-erman had been a basket case. "Perry…is something going on in the bookkeeping department? Is it Perry?"

Instinctively he moved to cover his slip, though he was uneasy at how swiftly she'd picked up the correct thread. "No, nothing like that," he murmured, distract-ing her by bending down to kiss her. He held her mouth under his, leisurely tasting her, until the growing tight-ness of his body warned him to slow things down.

The ploy had worked, almost too well. She was cling-ing to his shoulders, her soft body pliant against him. He could have her now, he realized, and groaned aloud. The temptation was too great. Despite his concern for her, despite the fact that he needed to check in with Evan, he wrapped his arms around her and lifted her off her feet. Instantly her slender arms wound about his neck, and she began kissing him fiercely as he walked back to the bedroom with her dangling from around his neck.

EVAN TRIED BRETT'S hotel room again, and again there was no answer. Frowning, he dropped the receiver back into its cradle. It wasn't like Brett to disappear when there was work to be done, or not to let someone know where to reach him. Brett was a hard man to know, but when it came to work, he was utterly dependable. This was the first time in Evan's memory that Brett Rutland hadn't been there when his job called for him.

Well, there was no point in worrying about it. Brett could take care of himself, and there was work to be done. Evan began going over the computer printouts again, straining his eyes at the difficult print. The rib-bon on the printer needed replacing, too, which made his job that much more difficult. He still had that nagging feeling that he was missing something, something so obvious that he should have seen it from the beginning. One of these accounts was bogus; it had to be. But he'd spent hours tracking the accounts down, and so far every one of them was legitimate; he'd been systematically checking them off his list. It should be getting easier, like the last pieces of a jigsaw puzzle, but it wasn't working that way. Nothing seemed wrong, yet he couldn't shake the feeling that something was, if he could only see it.

Damn! The print swam before his eyes, and he squinted to refocus his gaze. He was going to go blind before this was over.

The phone at his elbow rang, and he snatched it up. "Evan Brady."

"Found anything yet?" Brett's raspy voice growled in his ear.

"Nothing. I was beginning to think someone had taken out a contract on you. I've been trying to get you all day."

"Nothing like that. I'm in my room now; I'll be there in a minute, as soon as I take a shower. Is there any coffee ready?"

Evan reached over and lifted the pot that he'd had brought up some time ago. Nothing sloshed. "I'll call room service."

Brett hurried through his shower, well aware that he'd spent the day making love instead of working as he should have been doing, but he just hadn't been able to walk away from Tessa. She was wildfire, burning through his veins, out of control. The way she responded to him drove everything else out of his mind, until nothing else mattered but having her again, fusing their bodies as tightly as he could, wiping out the separateness of their beings. When he'd left she'd been asleep, curled on her side in exhaustion. He'd straightened the tangled sheets and pulled the covers up over her bare shoulders, fighting the urge to get undressed again and crawl into bed beside her. She was the most powerful distraction he'd ever seen, but he had work to do, even if he was a little late in remembering it.

After putting on khaki pants and a blue pullover knit shirt, he went to Evan's hotel room and rapped on the door with his knuckles.

"It's open; come on in!"

Evan didn't look as tired as he had before, but he was irritable, and the overflowing ashtray on the table was a measure of his tension. The room was filled with stale blue smoke. He didn't question Brett about his extended absence. Evan had worked with Brett long enough to know how far Brett would let anyone probe into his life, and those boundaries didn't stretch very far.

Still, there was something about Brett, and Evan eyed him closely. He looked tired, and he needed to shave, but he looked…almost happy. Strangely satisfied. It wasn't easy to read Brett; he wasn't beaming, but there was a hint of contentment in his eyes, a small relaxation of the line of his mouth. A woman! Evan thought, and had to control a grin. And not just any woman, either. Tessa Conway. It had been a long time coming, and Evan had long ago decided that the woman didn't exist who could get under Brett's skin, but that was before he, and Brett, had met Tessa Conway.

Yawning, Evan got to his feet and stretched his cramped muscles. "I'm going to move around for a while before I become rooted to the chair."

Brett took his place and lifted the sheaf of printouts onto his lap, then stretched his long legs out and propped them on the coffee table in front of him. By the time room service delivered the pot of fresh coffee, Brett was frowning in concentration, everything else wiped out of his mind as he went over the printouts line by line, checking them with a pencil. Evan poured two cups of coffee and set one beside Brett, but he remained on his feet, prowling about the room.

"Stir crazy?" Brett muttered, checking yet another line.

"Yeah. And half-blind, too. The first thing I'm going to do Monday morning is see that that printer has a new ribbon in it."

The print was bad, Brett admitted. Two hours later, he felt as if his eyes were crossing, and he stopped, leaning his head back and pinching his nose at the point between his eyes. "Is the coffee gone?"

"We emptied it about an hour ago."

Brett checked his watch. It was almost midnight, and he wondered if Tessa was still asleep, or if she was restless without him. He wanted to work himself into exhaustion, knowing that he'd toss and turn if he didn't, thinking about her, wanting her again. Sleeping with her the night before had been oddly satisfying, as if holding her in his arms while they slept completed him in some way.

Looking back at the printout sheets, his eyes fell on a name that had recurred frequently in the payout sheets.

What caught his attention was that the name was the same as Tessa's. "What's this Conway, Inc. that so many checks are made out to? What sort of business is it?"

"Supplier," Evan said. "They've been supplying Carter Engineering for years. Basic building materials. I checked it out."

Several minutes later, Brett looked up. "What about Conmay?"

"Weren't you listening? They're a supplier—"

"No, not Conway. Conmay," he said, stressing the last syllable.

"That's what I thought you said." Evan went very still, staring at Brett. "Conmay belongs to two men, Connors and Mayfield."

Brett's eyes were narrowed. "We have checks sent out to both a Conway, Inc., and a Conmay, Inc. Are they both legitimate?"

"I'll be damned if I know," Evan growled, crossing to Brett's side to lean down and squint at the two very similar names. "That slipped by me completely. I thought it was the same account."

Brett began flipping back through the pages they'd already checked, looking for the first entry for Conway, Inc. Instinct told him that they were on the right track. Conway, Inc.... If it hadn't been for the similarity to Tessa's name, he wouldn't have noticed it.

"We need a computer terminal," he said decisively, getting to his feet. "We might as well go to the source." It would be a lot easier to track down that account with access to the central computer.

"Might as well," Even agreed. Like Brett, he sensed success, and that banished his fatigue. They could work as long as they liked, without fear of detection, for it was Saturday night, almost Sunday morning, and the building would be deserted except for the guards.

By three o'clock Sunday morning, they were both certain that they'd found the right thread. All they had to do was follow it back to the embezzler. The computer-made payments to Conway, Inc. had begun a little over a year before, weren't made with any regularity, and were never for an outstandingly large amount; but a few thousand here and there added up before long. All of the checks were on microfilm, but they were unable to get a signature from the canceled checks; they were all stamped with a rubber stamp that said DEPOSIT ONLY, CONWAY, INC. with the account number and bank name beneath it. Brett jotted down the number and bank.

"That's it until we can see the withdrawal slips, or the name on the checks written on that account." He had a headache from hours of staring at the bright green numbers on the display screen. Impatience rose up in him, impatience with both himself and the job, which grated on him increasingly as the days passed. Soon, he promised himself silently. Soon he would be on the ranch, and his fatigue would be the result of good, hard physical work, rather than from sitting hunched over faded computer printouts or working his way through the maze of computer programming, ferreting information out of electronic files.

"Let's pack it up and get some sleep."

Evan was more than willing, and the drive back to the hotel was accomplished in silence. In his room, Brett undressed and sprawled on the bed, almost groaning aloud as his tired muscles relaxed. The end was in his grasp now, and he wanted to get it over and done with; he wanted to put this behind him and get to the ranch. Funny, but years ago, when he'd been in college, the ranch hadn't pulled at him the way it was doing now. It had been home, but there had been an entire world out there that had challenged him, daring him to take his sharp, icy intellect and master it. He'd done it; he'd made a success of himself, using his cool grit and steely determination. He was not only very good at what he did, but he was well paid for it, too, and that had enabled him to invest, to diversify. His financial acumen had put the ranch on solid ground, much better able to weather the vagaries of the beef market than a lot of ranches. Tessa wouldn't be reminded of her youth, spent in a rundown old farmhouse. She'd still be able to wear silk, if she wanted it.

He closed his eyes, but her image filled his mind, and he opened them again, knowing that he wouldn't be able to sleep. His body burned, as if she were still lying against him, her arms and legs twined around him.

It was a hell of a coincidence that the embezzler had used Conway as a name.

His memory was almost photographic; abruptly he recalled Tessa's personnel file, and the dates of her employment. She'd been working at Carter Engineering for fifteen months. The embezzling had begun roughly thirteen months before. She worked in the bookkeeping department. And she was on very friendly terms with Sammy Wallace.

He swore aloud in the darkened room. Hell, what was he thinking? It wouldn't be Tessa; she was all sunlight and laughter. No, it would be Sammy Wallace, who'd probably picked Tessa's last name as some sort of twisted tribute. Like all men, Sammy Wallace could easily make a fool of himself where Tessa was concerned.

But, damn him, why did he have to drag her into his dirty little scheme? Didn't he realize that using her name would automatically make her the first suspect? Brett's mouth tightened. Of course he realized that! Why not try to throw the blame on Tessa? Wallace probably knew well enough that she would be less likely to be prosecuted than anyone else working at Carter Engineering.

He'd like to knock the bastard's teeth down his throat for putting her in jeopardy like that.

He was so tired that his entire body ached, and it was almost dawn, but he couldn't sleep. He kept thinking of Tessa, of the day he'd spent with her…mostly in bed. His good intentions hadn't been worth a damn when faced with the temptation of her body; he couldn't get enough of her. No matter how wild their lovemaking had been, he'd begun wanting her again as soon as it was over. Nothing in his previous experience had prepared him for the deep hunger he felt for her, and the inability to satisfy that hunger. But he'd tried, and she'd been sleeping in exhaustion when he left her, her dark hair spread in a wild tangle across the pillow.

The image haunted him. He turned restlessly on his stomach, bitter resentment rising in him again. He didn't like this compulsive need for her. He liked being in control, and with her he wasn't even in control of his own body, because he couldn't make himself stay away from her. He didn't like the power she had over him. He couldn't get her out of his mind! Even now, when he needed so badly to sleep, he remembered the feel of her silky body beneath him, the clasp of her legs around his hips, the deep, inner heat of her. His flesh stirred, and he swore between his teeth. Even in bed, she'd flirted and teased, laughing at him and moving elusively away from him. He'd been too sexually preoccupied to mention getting married, but soon he'd have to put an end to this damnable situation. When they were married, when he had her in his bed every night, she'd be his for good, and he'd be in control once more. With that on his mind, he went to sleep, but even in his sleep it seemed that he was tortured by the power she had over him, and fought with her for control of their relationship. He'd never felt so strongly about a woman before, and his feelings were both unexpected and unwelcome. In his life, he'd trusted only Tom, but now he had Tessa to deal with, and in her own way she was an enigma to him. She was both delicate and strong, elusive but his for the taking, yet even when he took her, he felt that there was a part of her that escaped him, and she was driving him crazy, even in his dreams.

When he woke, it was late in the afternoon; the first thing he thought was that Tessa must be wondering where the hell he was. He'd already picked up the receiver to call her before resentment rose in him. Damn it, he didn't have to check in with her like some grade-schooler! He dropped the receiver back into its cradle; then frustration with himself got the upper hand and he picked it up again, punching out Evan's room number. Evan answered on the third ring, his voice thick and still sleepy, and Brett knew that, like himself, Evan was catching up on his sleep. "I'm going over to Tessa's," he said brusquely. "You can get in touch with me there if you need me."

"Sure," Evan agreed sleepily, then laughed. "I don't blame you. If I could be with her, I wouldn't be wasting time in a hotel room, either!"

Brett showered and shaved, his lowered eyebrows testimony to his black mood. He was getting damned tired of every man in the country slavering over Tessa like dogs over a juicy bone. She was his. No other man had ever held her naked in his arms as he had done. With his hands and mouth and possessive lovemaking he'd branded her as his, every lovely, silky inch of her. He burned to have her again, to bury himself in her and hold her so close that nothing could get between them, to protect her from the undefined threat that was hanging over her head. He hoped that no one ever told her that she'd been used as a cover to hide an embezzler. She liked Sammy Wallace. She'd be distressed enough when he was arrested without knowing that he'd used her.

Half an hour later he rang her doorbell. Then impatience made him abandon the bell and bang on the door with his fist.

"Hold your horses!" he heard her mutter irritably on the other side of the door, and surprise at her bad mood made his eyebrows lift. "Who is it?"

"Me," he answered shortly.

The door didn't open, and she said just as shortly, "What do you want?"

The surge of anger that shook him was so strong that he ground his teeth in an effort to control it. What sort of game was she playing now? He wasn't going to argue with her through a door. "Tessa, open this door," he said in a controlled voice, then barked, *"Now!"*

She opened it, but blocked his entrance. Her face was cool and blank, but her eyes were spitting green fire. She didn't have any prior experience with love affairs, but she'd known immediately that she didn't like going to bed with her lover, the man she loved, and waking to an empty bed and an empty apartment, with no note to tell her where he was or when he would be back, with no phone call all day long. Brett Rutland was so arrogant that he probably expected her still to be waiting for him in bed where he'd left her.

He took a step forward, towering over her, but she didn't step back to let him in the door. His navy eyes narrowed. Did she expect to block him with her body? The idea was almost laughable, if he'd been in the mood to laugh. She barely reached his shoulder, and he outweighed her by at least a hundred pounds; he was roped with powerful muscles, while she was all soft silk and satin, yet she stood there glaring stubbornly up at him. Why had he never noticed the proud willfulness in her expression? She had a flashfire temper, he suddenly realized, a temper that was usually hidden behind lazy laughter, because she protected herself with indifference and humor. She became angry only when she cared about something.

She cared. Before she realized what he was about, he put his hand on her waist and gently lifted her to eye level with him, holding her suspended in the air. "I worked all night," he explained in a quiet, level tone. "Evan and I went to bed about dawn. When I woke up,

I showered and shaved and came straight over here. I'm not used to anyone having the right to expect an explanation of my whereabouts."

Tessa still glowered at him. If that was supposed to be an apology, he needed a lot of work in that area; but then, it was really only an explanation, and a reluctantly given one at that. Still, in a back-ended way he'd admitted that she had the right to an explanation. The hard edge of her anger evaporated, but she wasn't able to forgive him completely yet.

"Put me down," she finally said, her voice as level as his.

"Kiss me, first."

She stared at him, then blushed. "No. If I do, you'll… we'll…"

A tiny smile of amusement curled his hard mouth. "Baby, I already am, and we will anyway."

She wanted to hit him. "You're not short in the ego department, are you?"

"Or any other department," he whispered, and eased her against him. "Put your legs around me."

Furiously she pushed against him. "Brett, we're standing in an open door! Put me down!"

He took another step forward and kicked the door shut behind him. "Tessa," he growled, and fastened his mouth to hers. Her hands were braced against his heavy shoulders, and she tried again to push herself away from him, again without result. His mouth was hot, moving on hers, opening her lips for the entry of his tongue, and she shuddered at the electric pleasure that jolted her body. With a whispery moan she stopped trying to hold on to her anger. Despite wanting to box his ears, she loved him, and loving him was so much better than fighting with him. He hadn't declared undying love and devotion, but still he'd given her more than any other woman had ever had from him. He'd given her the right to question him. She hadn't chosen a comfortable man to love, but he was all man, and she was going to make him all hers.

His breathing was heavy, his mouth hungry as he moved it down to her throat. Arching her against him with one hard arm clamped around her waist, he closed his other hand over her breast. Her legs parted automatically for him; she lifted them to clamp her thighs on either side of his lean waist, with her ankles locked behind him. "That's right," he rasped against her throat as he pushed himself against the cradle of her body. He kneaded her breast, wringing little cries of pleasure from her and making her writhe against him until he couldn't stand the sweet torment any longer and began walking toward the bedroom, still holding her wrapped tightly around him.

"Tell me that you love me," he demanded in a low, harsh whisper as he placed her on the bed and swiftly stripped away her clothes.

"I love you." She saw the flare of satisfaction in his eyes, satisfaction and something else, something cool and unreadable, and she was suddenly frightened. But then he was naked and he came down on the bed with her, covering her with his hard, heated flesh. He entered her at once, so powerfully that her nails sank into his shoulders. He made love to her with a passion that was almost violent, but always controlled, and he controlled her, too, setting their rhythm and pace, wringing sensations from her. He gave her exquisite pleasure, but even at the peak of her ecstasy, she wondered at the bitter look of resentment he'd given her.

CHAPTER SIX

BRETT STARED AT the microfilm of the checks written on the account of the bogus Conway, Inc. and sweat beaded on his forehead as he fought the urge to vomit. Nothing in his life had ever made him any sicker than he felt at the moment, and he closed his eyes, slumping weakly against the back of his chair. He couldn't take it in; he simply couldn't believe it, couldn't grasp the implications of it. The signature on the bottom of those checks was a very feminine one. An attempt had been made to disguise the handwriting by using a script that was a mixture of printing and writing, but that didn't matter. What mattered, what had hit him with such force that he felt as if he'd been pole-axed, was the name: Tessa Conway. Tessa! God in heaven, how could it be her? How could she cling to him as she had, give herself so fiercely, whisper that she loved him, when all the time she was stealing from the company that it was his job to protect?

He raised a shaking hand to his eyes, as if to shield them from the damning evidence before him, but he couldn't shield himself from his own thoughts, and they grew more bitter as the moments passed. He'd been used, for a motive as old as time. Had she thought that if she forged a relationship with him, he wouldn't be able to prosecute her if her little get-rich-the-easy-way scheme was uncovered? Had she thought that he might even protect her? Damn her, she'd even given him her virginity! She was a smart woman, all right. Few men could cast off the entwined chains of guilt, responsibility and passion.

He'd made a fool of himself with her, he thought bitterly. But at least he hadn't gotten around to asking her to marry him. At least she didn't know just how big a fool he was. That was the only consolation his pride could find: She didn't know. Black rage boiled up in him at the thought that she must be smugly congratulating herself for luring him into her net so easily. It was barely a week since he'd seen her for the first time, and she'd had him tied in knots, ready to quit his job and take her away with him to the ranch, full of stupid dreams about the future with her as his wife, even planning for the children they'd have.

The hell of it was, the signs had been there for him to read, if he hadn't been blinded by his own lust. She had both the skill and the opportunity. Her apartment, though not luxurious, certainly wasn't cheap. She drove a new car; she dressed well. She'd grown up in poverty, so much so that her aunt had had to take them in. Had she seen her thievery merely as insurance against a return to poverty?

The lying little bitch!

He shoved himself out of his chair and stood up, running his hand through his hair. He was shaking with the force of his fury, an anger so powerful that he could feel it burning inside him. No matter what her motive, she was a thief, and he was a fool. He'd been so hot for her that he'd neglected his job, something he'd never done before. It would be a long time before he allowed himself to forget that.

A knock on the door made him jerk around. He knew it would be Evan, so he said, "Come on in," and was amazed at the cool control in his voice.

"I couldn't get away from Ralph," Evan said as he entered and closed the door behind him. Ralph Little was head of data processing. "Did you get the microfilm of the checks?"

Brett indicated his desk. "Take a look."

Evan went over to the desk and looked at the copies of the checks. He was silent a moment, then rubbed the back of his neck. "Oh, hell," he said quietly.

Brett was silent.

Evan began to swear under his breath, a string of oaths that would have done credit to a sailor. He looked up at Brett, his eyes a little stunned. "This makes me sick."

His mouth twisting bitterly, Brett moved over to the window and looked out. "I know the feeling."

"Damn it, I never thought—not even when we caught on to that bogus account. I wrote it off as just a coincidence, or thought that the name had been picked because it was so similiar to Conmay."

"Yeah, so did I." He'd gotten control of himself, now that he was over the first brutal shock.

After a moment, Evan said, "What are you going to do?"

"Get a warrant for her arrest. Prosecute. Do the job I was sent down here to do."

The cold steel of Brett's voice made Evan wince.

"Let's hold off for a few days; maybe if we talk to Mr. Carter—"

"His instructions are to prosecute to the full extent of the law. I intend to do just that."

"Brett, damn it, this is Tessa we're talking about!"

"I know exactly who we're talking about: a thief."

"I can't do it," Evan whispered.

There was nothing any colder than Brett's eyes. The expression in them was an arctic wasteland. "I can," he said.

He had to; he didn't have any choice about it. Nothing would ease the crippling sense of betrayal, the feeling that something vital had been torn out of his insides, but he could at least do the job he'd been sent to Los Angeles to do. He could refuse to make any more of a fool out of himself than he'd already done. In time, he might even be able to feel a little grateful to Tessa. After all, she'd shown him irrefutably that the best course was the one he'd always followed before her: Enjoy a woman, but don't allow her under your guard. He wouldn't make this mistake again. All he had to do now was his job... that, and get through the nights without her, when his body ached for her, when his mind was filled with the burning, erotic memories of making love to her.

Already he felt haunted. He pushed the thoughts of her away and strode to the desk to flick on the intercom. "Helen, get the D.A.'s office for me, please."

"The district attorney?" Helen asked in confirmation, her tone a little puzzled.

"That's right."

He turned the intercom off and met Evan's grim look. "We've got all the evidence we need, though I'm

going to have the handwriting of that signature analyzed, anyway," Evan said. "We can get a conviction, if
that's what you're going after. But for God's sake, don't
have her arrested here at work. Don't do that to her."

Brett's eyes went black. "I wasn't going to," he
snapped. "Do you think I'd humiliate her that way?"
Suddenly pain sliced through him, and he closed his
eyes for a moment. No, he didn't want to publicly humiliate her. He wanted to beat the living daylights out
of her to teach her not to steal; then he wanted to chain
her to his wrist and drag her off to Wyoming and keep
her there for the rest of her life. Even now, even knowing how she'd used him, he wanted her, and admitting
that to himself hurt as much as the knowledge that she'd
been playing with him.

The intercom buzzed. "Mr. Rutland, I have John
Morrison, the district attorney, on line one."

"Thank you, Helen." Brett punched the appropriate line, not even wondering how Helen had gotten the
district attorney himself. He didn't care. All he could
do now was concentrate on getting this done and over
with, and living through it.

When he hung up the phone ten minutes later, he had
a hollow feeling in the pit of his stomach. The wheels
had been set in motion. Sweat beaded on his forehead,
and he wiped it away. "We have to take all of this to
the D.A.'s office," he said, indicating the damning copies of the checks, the piles of computer printouts, the
lists of account numbers, all the methods they'd used
to eliminate the legitimate withdrawals.

"Yeah. I'll do it." Evan's voice was hollow, and his
face was gray. Brett wondered briefly what in hell he

looked like, if Evan looked that bad. Evan knew her only peripherally, while he…God, he'd had her beneath him in bed, writhing in mindless need, her body sweet and hot and clinging, accepting his powerful thrusts with joyous abandon. At least he'd kept his head enough not to risk making her pregnant…. As soon as he had the thought, he went cold. Yesterday afternoon. He remembered standing in the doorway, lifting her up and clasping her to him. He remembered her legs locking around his waist. He'd carried her to bed, and in his urgency to possess her he hadn't thought about protecting her. Perhaps, in the back of his mind, he'd even discounted the need to do so, since he'd planned on marrying her so soon that any pregnancy would have been only a little early. But now…

Was this part of her scheme, too? She'd never even mentioned birth control. Had she deliberately ignored it, hoping that the possibility of her having his baby would force him to protect her if she got caught?

What the hell difference did it make? he wondered, agonized. If she was pregnant, whether it was deliberate or an accident, he'd have to protect her. He couldn't let his child be born in a prison hospital. He'd no longer have the option of quitting his job. He'd be fired for going behind Joshua Carter's back and dropping the charges against her, but he had the legal authority to do it, and he'd use it, if he had to. A bitter smile curved his mouth. It was a measure of how far down the road to madness he was that he found himself actually hoping that she was pregnant, so he'd have an excuse to step in and jerk her out of the mess she'd gotten herself into.

"Brett? Are you all right?"

Evan's reluctantly posed question brought him out of his black thoughts, and he realized that his fists were clenched. Slowly, he forced himself to relax. "I'm all right," he said, but his throat burned on the words, as if he'd screamed them instead. "Get this stuff down to the D.A.'s office, and let's get it over with."

OVER LUNCH WITH Billie that day, Tessa couldn't keep the smile from her lips or the glow from her eyes. She was in love, and after yesterday she was certain that Brett loved her, too, even though he hadn't said it. She realized instinctively that the words would come hard to him; he'd be reluctant to admit his emotional vulnerability. His aloof, controlled character made it difficult for him to allow anyone to get close to him, but she no longer had any doubt that by some bright miracle she'd done exactly that. The thought of having that incredibly tough, sexy man love her made her feel oddly humble, for her life had been almost boringly mundane and normal, and she'd never done anything outstanding or exalted enough to earn his love. She wasn't a high-powered executive or lawyer, or a passionately dedicated doctor, or a brilliantly talented artist. She was a bookkeeper, and content with her position in life, for she lacked intense ambition in her character makeup. Her only gifts were laughter and the ability to enjoy life. Why was that enough to attract a man like him? And did she really care, so long as he *was* attracted? Of course not!

She was so full of happiness that when the waiter rather sloppily served their food, she overflowed with joy and rewarded him with a smile that stopped him in his tracks, and he retreated with a rather stunned look on his face.

"You look happy," Billie understated dryly.

"Do I?" Happy wasn't the way she felt; she felt delirious with joy.

"The waiter's tongue is hanging out." Then Billie laughed. "I take it you had an enjoyable weekend?"

"I never thought it would happen this fast," Tessa mused, answering Billie's question obliquely. "I thought that it would grow gradually, like a building going up brick by brick."

"Brett Rutland doesn't look like the type to have any patience with the brick-by-brick method. I never should have doubted you. The poor guy didn't have a chance. Rather than warning you, I should've been warning him. So when's the wedding?"

"We haven't discussed that," Tessa answered serenely, never doubting that the subject would be discussed before too much longer. "If he can get away this weekend, he's taking me to his ranch in Wyoming."

"Oh, ho! To meet the family?"

"His father, anyway. They own the ranch together. He hasn't mentioned any other family."

"No problem, then. Well, whaddaya know?" Billie sighed in intense satisfaction. "We have great timing. Both of us, in the same weekend."

Surprised, Tessa looked at Billie's bright, smiling face, then glanced quickly at Billie's left hand. A sparkling diamond adorned it. She shrieked, then jumped up to pull Billie out of her chair and hug her. "You sneak!" she chortled. "You didn't even tell me you were getting serious about anyone! Well, who is it? David? Ron? No, I know, don't tell me! I know!"

"You do not," Billie laughed, ignoring the scene they were making in the restaurant.

"Patrick!"

"How did you know?" Billie yelped; then they were hugging each other again.

"This calls for a toast," Tessa proclaimed, picking up her glass of bottled water with the twist of lime that she liked in it. "To Billie and Patrick!"

"To Tessa and Brett!" Billie picked up her teacup, and they clicked cup and glass together, then drank toasts to each other. When they resumed their seats, Billie said, "Well, how did you know?"

"Elementary, my dear Billingsley." Tessa sniffed. "Patrick is obviously smarter than the other two."

Billie had been dating Patrick Hamilton, as well as her other two suitors, for almost a year, but she'd never revealed any partiality to any of them. In Tessa's opinion, though, Patrick was definitely the best man for Billie. He was a civil engineer, more at home in jeans and a hard hat than he'd ever be in a suit, but with a self-assured masculinity that would do wonders to Billie's rather delicate ego.

"Thanks," Billie said softly. "What would I have done without you?"

"Met and married him anyway. I told you, Patrick is smart."

"He'd never even looked at me twice before you came along and stopped me from looking like an escapee from a punk rock concert. I knew what you were doing, but I pretended not to notice," Billie admitted a little shyly. "When Patrick asked me out, I had to pinch myself so I'd know it was real. I mean, look at him! And look at me. I couldn't believe it; I didn't even let myself hope. But this weekend…well, he'll be leaving the country on a job that'll keep him gone for almost two years, and he…he put this ring on my finger and flatly informed me that there was no way in hell—his words—he was going to spend two years without me, so I'd have to quit my job and go to Brazil with him." She grinned. "I almost sprained my tongue, I said yes so fast. I'll be turning in my notice at the end of this month."

They were so caught up in their celebrating that they were almost late getting back to work, and Tessa sailed through the rest of the day on a cloud. Brett hadn't called her to make plans for the night, but somehow she hadn't expected him to. Their relationship had progressed to the point that she felt he knew she wouldn't have any other plans, just as she knew that she'd see him that night. She didn't even feel a twinge of regret when she turned down invitations from two men she liked very much. They simply weren't Brett.

After work, she rushed home and took a pack of beef tips out of the freezer section of the refrigerator, putting it in the sink to thaw. She didn't know what sort of work Brett was doing, but she'd seen the strain of it in his face when he'd shown up yesterday afternoon. He was tired; if he wanted dinner, they'd eat there. And if he had to work, she had to have dinner anyway, she thought philosophically, though she felt lonely at the mere thought of not seeing him that night.

She stopped in the middle of the kitchen floor, her

eyes dreamy, her pulse speeding up. Until she'd met him, she hadn't known she could be so sensual, but all she had to do was look at him to feel her body heating. She wanted him with an intensity that was alarming, because her life had become focused on him to the exclusion of all else. His lovemaking made her go out of her mind with feverish desire. She couldn't control it, didn't even want to control it. She just wanted to lie with him every night for the rest of her life. She wanted to have his children, fight with him, love with him, ride beside him on his ranch, flirt with him until his beautiful navy eyes smoldered with desire and he reached out for her in compulsive need. She couldn't wait to tell Aunt Silver—

Silver! Groaning, Tessa remembered that an airmail letter from Silver had been in her mailbox, but she'd been in such a hurry to get the beef tips out of the freezer that she'd just thrown everything on the couch and gone straight to the kitchen. After retracing her steps to the living room, she sorted through her mail, picking out the letter from Silver and tearing it open.

Smiling, she read the long, newsy letter. The mountains were full of blooms, and the summer crowds had already begun pushing into Gatlinburg. The doll shop was doing so well that Silver had hired extra help, and she'd been approached by a man who wanted to buy the old farm in Sevierville, if Tessa was interested in selling her half.

Silver didn't mention Brett until the last paragraph, but Tessa laughed out loud when she read it. She'd known Silver's instinct would zoom in on him like steel to a magnet. "Bring this Brett Rutland to see me," Silver instructed in her letter. "Your handwriting shook when you wrote his name!"

The doorbell rang, and still chuckling, Tessa laid the letter aside. Her heart had already begun racing when she opened the door, expecting Brett. But it wasn't Brett who stood there. She didn't know the man and woman who faced her. "Teresa Conway?" the woman asked.

"Yes. Can I help you?"

The woman opened the flap of her purse, exhibiting a badge. "I'm Detective Madison, from the L.A.P.D. This is Detective Warnick. We have a warrant for your arrest."

IT WAS LATE that night when Tessa let herself back into her apartment, and she groped her way through the dark to the couch, not even thinking to turn on any lights. She sat down, Silver's discarded letter crinkling under her, and she automatically removed the sheets of paper. Fine tremors shook her entire body, and she couldn't stop them. She'd been shaking for hours, ever since the nightmare had begun. This wasn't happening to her; it couldn't be happening. She hadn't believed Detective Madison, at first. She'd actually laughed, wanting to know who was behind the joke. Detective Warnick had read her her rights, gently but inexorably insisted that she get her purse and come with them, and still Tessa hadn't believed it was anything serious. It wasn't until she was escorted outside and put in the back seat of what was obviously an unmarked police car that she'd been struck with the realization that this was no joke, and it was then that she'd begun shaking.

She'd been arrested for embezzling. She'd understood that much of what they'd told her. They'd told her a lot, but though she'd tried very hard to concentrate, most of it hadn't made any sense. She was too frightened, too stunned to take it in. The police station had been a buzz of activity, with people coming and going and not paying any attention to her, but she'd been taken through the process of being booked with a casual sort of professionalism that chilled her. She'd been fingerprinted, and her picture taken, and both questioned and advised. Someone had given her a tissue to wipe the black ink from her fingertips, and she'd devoted herself to that task. It had been of paramount importance to clean the stain from her hands.

Finally, the thought had been born that she should call Brett. He'd get her out of this nightmare. At the thought of him, she'd become calm. There was nothing that Brett couldn't handle. He'd sort out this mistake, because that was obviously all it was. But what if he weren't at his hotel? What if he were waiting at her apartment, growing more and more furious because she wasn't there? What if he thought she'd gone out with some other man—which she had, in a way. She almost giggled, thinking of the way Detective Warnick had held her arm as they walked out to the car.

But she'd called his hotel anyway, only to be told that Mr. Rutland had given instructions that no calls were to be put through to him. Tessa tried to explain that it was an emergency, but the hotel operator couldn't be budged. In desperation, she asked for Evan Brady's room. He could take a message to Brett, if Brett was tied up with work.

Evan had answered on the second ring, and in a

stumbling rush, Tessa explained who she was and that she needed to talk to Brett. There had been a long pause, then Evan had said evenly, "He knows."

Tessa's fingers had been shaking so much that she'd almost dropped the telephone. "Wh—what?" she stammered. "How…no, that doesn't matter. When will he be here?"

"I…ah…don't think he will."

That didn't make sense. Tessa closed her eyes, fighting down the nausea that had been threatening for some time. "What do you mean? You don't understand what I'm talking about—"

"Yes, I understand." The disembodied voice in her ear became a little rougher. "Miss Conway…Tessa… Brett is the one who filed the charges against you."

Had he said anything after that? She didn't know. She'd simply taken the phone from her ear and sat there with the receiver clutched in her hand so tightly that her fingers had turned white, until Detective Warnick had gently removed the instrument from her grasp and offered, probably against all regulations, to call someone else for her. She'd refused, her mind blank, her emotions numb. Who else was there to call? What did it matter, anyway?

She hadn't seen the faintly concerned glances that passed between Detectives Madison and Warnick. She hadn't seen anything unusual in the Styrofoam cup of very strong, black coffee that was pressed into her grasp. She hadn't drunk it, but had held it, grateful for the warmth it brought to her chilled hands.

She'd been told that the court would appoint an attorney for her, if she couldn't afford one, and she'd frowned in a puzzled manner. "I can afford a lawyer," she said mildly, and gone back to examining the odd swirls of color on top of the black coffee.

She'd been allowed to sign her own bond, and she'd done so, but though she was then free to go, it hadn't seemed very important to her, and she'd continued to sit there in the hard, uncomfortable chair. When Detective Madison's shift had ended at eleven, she'd shepherded Tessa out to her own car, and that was how Tessa had gotten home.

She couldn't think. Unformed words swirled in her mind, but she couldn't grasp them long enough to make anything coherent of them. At last, moving slowly and jerkily, she curled up in a ball on the couch, as if to protect herself from the pain that awaited her if she ever allowed herself to notice it. It was there, hovering just on the edge of her consciousness, like a savage animal crouched in readiness to spring on her and claw her to shreds. If she just didn't let herself look at it, if she didn't admit its presence to herself, she'd be safe. She'd be safe. Telling herself that, she sank into the comforting blackness of sleep.

It was daylight when she woke, and she surged to her feet, her mind thick with sleep but recognizing instinctively that it was late. She had to hurry, or she'd be late to work. Tearing off her wrinkled clothing as she stumbled to the bathroom, not even questioning why she'd been sleeping on the couch, she was actually under the shower before she remembered what had happened the night before. Her lips trembled as she sagged against the wall of the shower. Late for work? The guard probably had express orders not to let her inside the building! If there was anything she could count on, it was that she no longer had a job.

It was then that the first tears came, and she cried helplessly as she automatically soaped and rinsed herself. How had this happened? It didn't make any sense. She'd never stolen anything. Didn't Brett know that? He had to know that! Unless someone had deliberately made it look as if she'd been embezzling—of course, what else could it be? She had to talk to Brett. If he thought she'd been stealing, there had to be some pretty strong evidence against her, but she'd make him believe her.

Rushing now, she turned off the shower and dried off, then wrapped the towel around her and stumbled to the phone, punching out the numbers for Carter Engineering. She was put through to Brett's office without any trouble, and her spirits took a crazy upward swing. But when Helen Weis answered the phone, and Tessa asked for Brett, Helen hesitated.

"I'm sorry," Helen finally said. "Mr. Rutland isn't taking any calls."

"Please," Tessa begged. "This is Tessa Conway. I have to speak to him!"

"I'm sorry," Helen repeated. "He expressly said that he wouldn't take any calls from you."

Tessa was trembling again as she hung up the phone. What was she going to do now? What could she do? Brett wouldn't talk to her, and in the face of that she was lost.

Several minutes later, she took a deep breath and straightened her spine. No, she wasn't lost. She couldn't get through to Brett on the phone. She'd see him in person, at his hotel, this evening. She wasn't going to let him go on thinking that she was a thief. She wouldn't even let herself believe that he'd been the one to press charges against her until he told her so himself. In the meantime, she had to take steps to protect herself. She'd been in shock, but she wasn't helpless, and she wasn't going to let herself be railroaded into prison for something she hadn't done. Her first step was to hire a lawyer, and the best place to find one was the telephone book.

By mid-afternoon, she'd secured the legal services of Calvin R. Stine and had a long meeting with him. He'd turned out to be a sharp-eyed man in his early thirties, just beginning to establish himself as a trial lawyer. He'd taken down a lot of information, most of which had seemed irrelevant to Tessa, but she'd willingly answered all his questions. He'd also told her what to expect. Her case, being a felony, would be brought before a grand jury, who would consider the evidence and decide if the State of California had sufficient evidence against her to warrant a trial. If the grand jury decided that there was insufficient evidence, all charges against her would be dropped.

Tessa pinned her hopes on that. If she had to go on trial…somehow, she didn't think she could stand it.

When she finally left Mr. Stine's office, she felt so weak that she could barely walk, and with faint surprise she realized that she hadn't eaten since lunch the day before, when she and Billie had laughed and toasted each other. How brightly the sun had shone on her barely twenty-four hours before! But everything was gray now, she thought, not noticing the gorgeous Southern Californian spring day.

She had to eat something, but it was getting close to the time when Brett would return to his hotel, and she didn't want to miss him. The best thing to do, she decided, was to go to his hotel and get something to eat in the coffee shop there.

She did exactly that, but when her club sandwich was set before her, she could only pick at it. Every bite she took expanded in her mouth as she chewed it, and it was as tasteless as sawdust. Doggedly she forced herself to swallow a little of it, then picked the lettuce off and ate it a shred at a time while she nursed her glass of mineral water and checked the time every few minutes. Would Brett leave work promptly at five o'clock? She hadn't known him long enough to know his personal habits, she realized with a sharp pang. She hadn't known him long enough for him to believe without question that she wasn't capable of embezzlement.

Finally, when the waitress began giving her suspicious looks, Tessa decided to try her luck. If he wasn't in his room yet, she'd simply wait in the lobby for a while, then try again. Fortunately, she didn't have to ask for his room number; he'd given it to her the week before, in case she'd wanted to get in touch with him.

Her knees were shaking so badly that she had to cling to the rail in the elevator as it rose through the building, and they were still shaking as she searched for his room. When she finally found it, she froze before the blank door. What if he wouldn't let her in? Taking several deep breaths, she rapped sharply on the panel.

Evidently he was expecting someone, for he opened

the door without checking. He went very still, staring down at her, and his rough-hewn face was contemptuous. "Somehow, I didn't expect you to force yourself in here," he said coldly.

"I have to talk to you," Tessa said in desperation, almost crying at the look on his face.

"Is it really necessary?" His voice was laced with boredom. "You won't accomplish anything, except to waste my time."

"I have to talk to you," she repeated, and with a sigh he stepped back, opening the door wider.

"Get it over with, then."

She entered the room, fingering her purse nervously. She'd planned to tell him immediately that she wasn't guilty, but now that she faced him and could see the distaste in his eyes, as if she'd brought a foul smell into the room with her, she couldn't quite do it. He didn't look like a man in pain, a man who'd been forced to do something that had to be almost as traumatic for him as it had been for her. He looked as cool and controlled as he'd ever been. There was no hint in his eyes that he even remembered the hours of lovemaking between them.

She stopped in the middle of the room and forced her hands to cease their nervous movements. "Evan Brady—" Her voice was raw and shaky and she stopped, clearing her throat. "Evan Brady told me that you're the one who pressed charges against me."

"That's right," Brett said easily, moving away from her and settling himself against the edge of the writing desk in front of the windows. He stretched out his long legs, crossing them negligently at the ankle.

"You didn't even warn me—"

He burst out laughing, a cold, contemptuous laugh that flayed her skin, making her wince. "Did you think that just because we had sex together, I'd be so wild about you that I'd let you get away with theft? You're a good lay, honey, I'll give you that, but I had a job to do."

Tessa stared at him, her breathing stopped in her chest, though her heart was pounding so heavily that the sound of it filled her head. He couldn't be saying those things! She was as still and pale as a statue, only her burning eyes alive as she looked at him. Slowly she went over his words, feeling something die inside of her. Her tongue was stiff and didn't want to work, but she forced the words out. "Did you…are you saying that the only reason you asked me out…the only reason…"

"You made our investigation easy," he said, and smiled. "Maybe I shouldn't have taken advantage of the fringe benefits you offered, but you're a sexy little thing, and I wanted you to feel secure enough that you wouldn't bolt." Clenching his jaw with the effort it cost him to smile, he mentally thanked her for giving him the excuse herself. He couldn't let her see that she'd almost brought him to his knees. If nothing else, he had to hang on to his pride. God, she was lovely, and so delicate that it was almost impossible to believe her capable of embezzlement, even though he'd seen the evidence himself.

"One other thing," he said, disguising his bitterness with a casual tone. "You made me lose my head Sunday afternoon, and I forgot to take care of things. It's not likely, but if you're pregnant, let me know. Damn it, even knowing you probably did it deliberately, a pregnancy would change things," he admitted reluctantly.

Tessa hadn't moved an inch. Her face was paper white. "No, I don't think it would change anything at all," she said, and walked out.

CHAPTER SEVEN

TESSA HAD BEEN hurt before, but nothing had ever made her feel as she did when she walked out of Brett's hotel room. It was a pain so deep, so crippling, that she couldn't even imagine the scope of it, yet in a way it was also a blessing, because the shock of it numbed her. He not only didn't love her, but also had been using her all along! She'd thought that they'd had something real, something infinitely precious between them, only to find that he'd sought her out for his investigation. The love she'd been so certain of had existed only in her mind. If he felt anything at all for her, it was only lust. He'd used her body only because she'd offered it, and it had meant nothing to him beyond momentary physical pleasure.

Now, with the wisdom of hindsight, she remembered all the casual questions he'd asked her the first time he'd taken her out to dinner. A harsh laugh tore from her throat. She'd thought he was making conversation, an easy way of getting to know her, but instead he'd been digging for information!

She felt…dirty. The horror of being arrested, of being fingerprinted, hadn't made her feel that way, because she'd known herself to be innocent of the charge they'd made against her, of the charge that *Brett* had filed against her. But now she felt violated, both mentally and physically. She'd given her love to him in every way she knew, openly, trustingly, and he'd used her as casually as any whore had ever been used. He'd turned his back on her, not caring that he'd trampled on her emotions, not caring that she felt soiled and lifeless.

There was a lump in her throat that felt as if it were choking her. She swallowed convulsively, looking around in mild surprise. She was in her own apartment, and she had no remembrance of getting there. She didn't remember anything from the moment she'd left Brett's hotel room, though the clock on the wall told her that so little time had elapsed that she must have come straight home.

There had been times in the past when she'd felt beaten down, but she'd always recovered, always found again the ability to laugh and enjoy life. Perhaps laughter was beyond her now, but there was steel in her, steel that wouldn't allow her to knuckle under. She wasn't going to go tamely to prison for something she hadn't done, even if Brett Rutland had torn her heart out. She'd do whatever she could to prove her innocence. He could break her only if she allowed him to, and she wasn't going to do that. All she had left now was her pride, and the knowledge of her innocence; with that, she'd survive. She had to turn her back on her pain, push Brett out of her mind, because if she allowed her tortured thoughts to dwell on him, she'd go mad.

With that decision, it was as if a door had slammed in her mind. Her face was calm as she went to the phone. She wanted the one person who would never turn against her.

"Honey, it's so nice to hear your voice!" Silver exclaimed happily, hundreds of miles and three time zones away. "I was just thinking about you. Are you calling about wedding plans?"

"No," Tessa said calmly. "Aunt Silver, I've been arrested. I need you."

Five minutes later, when Tessa hung up the phone, it was with Silver's grim reassurance ringing in her ears that she would be there the next day. If Tessa had needed an example of love and trust to compare with Brett's behavior, Silver had given it to her. Her aunt's support had been immediate and unquestioning, and so fierce that if Silver had been able to get her hands on Brett Rutland at that moment, he'd have been mauled before he'd even had the chance to protect himself.

She'd barely hung up the phone when her doorbell rang. Remembering the night before when she'd opened the door to the two detectives, an especially cruel shock when she'd been anticipating Brett's arrival so eagerly, Tessa froze for a moment. Had something gone wrong? Could her bond be rescinded?

"Tessa? Are you all right?"

It was Billie's voice, and she sounded anxious. As Tessa opened the door to her friend, she wondered how much Billie knew, if it was common knowledge at the office yet that she'd been arrested.

Billie's eyes were worried as she stepped into the apartment. "Are you sick?" she asked. "No one knew why you weren't at work today. I tried calling you at lunch, but there wasn't any answer."

"Would you like a cup of coffee?" Tessa offered, her voice calm and flat. Billie had already answered one of her questions: The reason for her absence hadn't been made public yet, though of course it would be, eventually. Gossip had a way of filtering out, like fine dust through the cracks in a floor.

"I'd like an answer, but I'll take a cup of coffee, too," Billie replied testily.

Well, why not? Why should she evade the issue? She hadn't done anything wrong. "I've been fired, I think." A faintly wry smile curved her lips. She hadn't actually received a dismissal, but then a warrant for her arrest had been pretty effective.

Following her into the kitchen, Billie stuttered questions at her. "Fired? Don't be ridiculous— What are you talking about? Why would anyone want to fire you? And what about Brett?"

Taking the coffee can down from the cabinet, Tessa calmly went about the process of making coffee. "Brett had me arrested," she stated from a remote sea of indifference. "For embezzlement. Turns out he was only interested in me from an investigative standpoint."

She turned and watched Billie, wondering if her offhand statement would spell the end of their friendship. At this point, she didn't have much faith in anyone, except Silver.

Billie flushed a dark red. "Are you for real?" she demanded in a harsh tone.

Tessa didn't say anything, but evidently the look on her pale, expressionless face convinced Billie. "Why that blind, conniving bastard!" Billie snarled, her small hands balling into fists. "You're no more a thief than… than my mother is! Where did he get a screwball idea like that? What sort of evidence does he have?"

"I don't know. I hired a lawyer today; I suppose he'll

find out." A part of her frozen heart was warmed by Billie's instant defense, but it was a small part. The greater portion of her heart had died about an hour before.

Billie looked at Tessa, seeing the emptiness in her friend's eyes, and her lips trembled. "Oh, God, I can't stand this," she whispered, reaching out to hug Tessa tightly. "You were so happy, and for him to hit you between the eyes like this...I'm turning in my notice tomorrow! I'm not working for a monster like that!"

"I'll be all right," Tessa said quietly. "I know that I'm innocent; that's the most important thing. There's no need for you to quit because of me. You'll need your salary for all the things you'll have to buy when you and Patrick get married."

"But—"

"Please. It isn't necessary."

She eventually convinced Billie not to quit her job, but Billie's red-headed temper was aroused, and she stormed around the apartment, alternately threatening Brett with dismemberment and feverishly planning any defense Tessa could use. Tessa remained quiet, not really paying attention. She was interested in the future only in an abstract way, because she didn't have a real future anymore. Even if she cleared her name—no, *when* she cleared it—she would still be only half alive, going through the motions of living without feeling any of the joy, an empty shell that held only the echo of laughter.

When Billie calmed down, she and Tessa sat at the table and drank coffee. Billie tried to cheer Tessa up, and Tessa tried to respond, if only to ease Billie's mind, but the subject was like a sore tooth. No matter how they tried to talk about something else, they kept coming back to worry at it.

"There hasn't been a breath of this in the office," Billie said incredulously. "I'd swear that even Perry doesn't know about it."

Her eyes bitter, Tessa said, "I'm not going to try to cover it up. I'm not a thief, and I'm not going to act as if I'm guilty. Perhaps Brett and Evan have their reasons for keeping it quiet, but as far as I'm concerned, let everyone know about it, and let them know that I intend to fight this down to the last pea in the dish."

"You want me to let it out?" Billie asked incredulously.

"Why not? You know the old saw about the best defense—"

"Is a good offense. Gotcha. You're going to give him something to think about, right?"

"I don't care what he thinks. I'm fighting for my life," Tessa said flatly.

When Billie had gone, Tessa very carefully went around the apartment and made certain everything was locked, but even then she felt vulnerable and exposed, as if there were prying eyes looking through the walls. She had a horrible thought: Had the place been bugged? Wildly she looked around, before common sense reassured her that such measures would hardly be employed in her case. She forced herself to shower and get ready for bed, but when she went into the bedroom she stopped in her tracks, staring at the bed. There was no way she could sleep in that bed. Brett had slept in it with her, initiated her into the searing intimacies of lovemaking, held her through the night—and it had all been lies. The love she'd been so certain of had been a mirage, a false image projected to gain her confidence. There had been no security in his arms, only lies.

Shaking, she grabbed an extra blanket and returned to the living room, curling up on the couch as she'd done the night before. Lying there in the dark, staring into the darkness with wide, empty eyes, she wondered when she'd feel the first stirring of anger. Why couldn't she be angry? With anger would come strength, strength that she needed, but the only emotion she could feel was the hollow pain of betrayal, and that pain was too deep even for tears. She'd cried once, that morning in the shower, but somehow that seemed as if it had happened years ago, to someone else. This morning, even though she'd known then that Brett had been involved in her arrest, she'd still given him the benefit of the doubt. She'd hurt, but she'd also thought that he would be hurting, too, that he'd been faced with evidence so strong that he'd been forced to take action against her. Without even consciously thinking about it, she'd already forgiven him, because she loved him so much. This morning, she'd still been able to hope.

Now there was nothing for her except a bleak stretch of years. After Andrew, even in the depths of her bitterness, she'd somehow known that there would be sunny times ahead for her. She hadn't been broken; she'd been furious and hurt, but never broken, because she hadn't loved Andrew deeply enough that his betrayal could slash her heart. Well, the party girl was finally paying off all her old debts to fate. She'd waltzed away relatively unscathed too many times, but she wouldn't waltz away from this one. Even proving her innocence wouldn't change the fact that Brett didn't love her, and had never loved her.

She'd been too certain of her own charms, she realized bitterly; it was poetic justice. She was so used to men falling all over themselves for her that it had never entered her mind that Brett Rutland wasn't going to do the same. All her life, she'd been able to get around men with her slow smile and a flutter of her long lashes, but Brett Rutland was pure steel, and he'd probably smiled coldly to himself as he wound her around his little finger, all the while allowing her to believe that she was the one doing the charming.

But, dear God, she'd never been malicious in her flirting! Had she really deserved this?

It was the blackest night of her life, worse even than the one before. At least then she'd been numb and had eventually slept. There was no sleep for her tonight. She lay awake, chilled even beneath the blanket, and none of the prayers she sent up in any way lightened the darkness in her heart. Her heart beat slowly, heavily, as if it would never again race with joy or pound with excitement at being in the arms of the man she loved.

At dawn, she got up and prepared breakfast, but could force herself to eat only a slice of toast. It was hours yet before Silver's plane was due in, yet she had nothing else to do to pass the time. She dressed and drove to L.A. International, where she sat for hours in a coffee shop drinking cup after cup of coffee until her stomach was upset and she was forced to buy a roll of antacid tablets. Her mind was blank of all thoughts except the most superficial ones as she sat in the uncomfortable seat and waited for Silver's plane.

It landed at one-thirty, and she was waiting when Silver came out of the tunnel. As soon as she saw her aunt, Tessa felt some of the burden ease from her shoulders, and she actually smiled.

"Tessa, honey." Silver's warm, throaty voice, so much like Tessa's own, sounded in her ear as loving arms enveloped her, and the two women hugged each other with the fierceness of family love and loyalty.

"I'm glad you're here," Tessa said simply.

"You knew I'd come, and I'll stay as long as you need me. Gatlinburg can get along without me for a while."

They retrieved Silver's suitcase, and by the time they'd reached the car, Silver was making plans. She wasn't going to let her beloved niece be railroaded into jail without a fight that would make Brett Rutland think he'd caught a wildcat by the tail, with no way to turn it loose. The first thing to do was see this lawyer Tessa had hired and judge for herself if he was capable of fighting as fiercely for Tessa as he should.

By NOON, THERE wasn't a person working for Carter Engineering who didn't know that Tessa Conway had been arrested for embezzlement, and Brett was coldly furious. Damn it, he'd done everything he could to keep it quiet for as long as possible. Despite what she'd done, he wanted to spare Tessa as much as he could. The knowledge that he wouldn't be able to protect her from the worst ate at him, like a gnawing animal inside. He hadn't even been able to keep gossip down for a measly two days. The only person who knew, besides himself, was Evan, though Helen was too smart not to have figured out most of it by now. But when he questioned them, they both denied breathing a word to anyone else. Helen eyed his stony face warily. She'd never before seen a man look so deadly. "I've been asked about it by at least ten different people this morning," she said. "Do you want me to try to track it down? Someone had to tell them."

"Find out," Brett said in a clipped tone.

Helen was competent enough and determined enough that Brett had no doubt that she'd be able to trace the gossip to its source before the day was out, and he only hoped he'd feel calmer by the time he knew the person's identity. But, damn it, who else could know?

He'd never been the most popular guy around. His job made that impossible, and his aloof personality only increased the distance between himself and the people he dealt with. But he'd never before felt himself to be so violently unpopular as he had that morning. People all over the building were glaring at him, including the guard. Tessa's charm had bubbled out and touched everyone she met, blinding them so that they were ready to ignore any evidence and rush to her defense.

Less than an hour later, Martha Billingsley, Tessa's friend, stood in his office with her arms crossed and her face hostile. "I heard that you're trying to find out how the news got out," she said coldly. "I did it."

Brett got to his feet, towering over the small redhead, who nevertheless continued to glare up at him. "I thought you were her friend," he snapped.

"I am. Friend enough that I want everyone to know what a raw deal she got. Tessa never stole a penny in her life. If you don't like what I'm saying, then fire me."

"Who told you about it?" he asked, ignoring her last statement.

"Tessa."

Somehow, he hadn't expected that. He'd have thought Tessa would try to keep it as quiet as she could. "She called you?"

"No. I went to her apartment last night."

His fist slowly clenched. Her face, when she'd left his hotel room, had been white and blank. Her last words had gone around and around in his mind, but still he couldn't pin down her meaning. *No, I don't think it would change anything at all,* she'd said, her voice remote, and she'd turned and quietly left. Did she mean that she thought he'd go through with the prosecution even if she were pregnant? She'd been so pale that he'd started to go after her, but his pride had stopped him. He wouldn't chase after her like a dog after a bitch in heat, not after he knew her for a liar and a thief.

"How was she?" he asked rawly, unable to stop the words.

Billie gave him a scathing look. "What do you care?"

"Damn it, how was she?" he roared, a muscle jerking in his cheek as he felt his control breaking.

It wasn't in Billie's pugnacious character to back down. "If you're so interested, go see for yourself, though I doubt Tessa would let you in the door." She stormed out, and even slammed the door behind her. Brett itched to grab the little red-headed wildcat and shake her, but at the same time he felt a grudging respect for her. Few people stood up to him at all.

Restlessly he paced over to the window. What sort of game was Tessa playing now? Did she think that if

she stirred up enough support in the ranks at Carter Engineering, the charges against her would be dropped?
Who knew what went on in her mind? She was a thief,
a woman skilled enough at deceit that he'd been totally
taken in by her until the evidence had forced him to accept the truth. She was capable of such a high degree of
duplicity that the two images he had of her still warred
in his mind. He simply couldn't blend them together
into a single person.

And he wanted her. Heaven help him, he still wanted
her.

TESSA STRIPPED THE bed and put clean sheets on it. "You
can have the bed," she told Silver calmly. "I'll sleep on
the couch."

"I'll do no such thing," Silver retorted, helping Tessa
smooth the sheets. "I'll take the couch."

"It'll be crowded, with both of us on the couch,"
Tessa said. She didn't look up. "I can't sleep in here.
I've been sleeping on the couch since   "

She broke off, her hands busy, and Silver watched
her niece worriedly. Tessa had changed, and it wasn't
simply that she was distraught at being arrested, though
that was enough to make anyone a nervous wreck. But
Tessa wasn't nervous; she was calm, unnaturally so.
The sparkle that had always lit her from the inside was
gone. Silver didn't want to think that it had been extin-
guished permanently, but she'd never seen Tessa like
this before, not even after Andrew.

Silver looked at the bed, then back at Tessa. "He seduced you, didn't he?"

"At the time, I thought he was making love," Tessa

said, after a silent moment. She smiled at Silver, but the smile didn't reach her eyes. "I'll be all right. At least I'm not pregnant."

"Are you sure?"

"Yes. This morning." Brett didn't have anything to worry about now. He could prosecute her with a clear conscience. Then she shoved him out of her mind, because she couldn't think about him any longer without breaking down, something that she refused to do. She had to keep the pain at bay, or she wouldn't be able to function. To that end, she kept her thoughts concerned only with the present. Rehashing every moment she'd spent with him wouldn't accomplish anything except to undermine her emotionally.

She was tired, very tired after not having slept the night before, but she wondered if the coming night would be any better. Her eyes were burning, yet she felt unable to close them.

The phone rang. Tessa jumped; then her face closed up, her eyes going curiously blank. "You answer it," she told Silver abruptly. "I'll finishing making the bed."

Frowning, Silver went into the living room and picked up the phone. "Hello." Tessa could hear Silver's side of the conversation clearly from the bedroom, and she tensed. What if it was Brett? No, she was being stupid. Brett wasn't going to call her. He'd gone out of his way to make certain she couldn't reach him by phone, so he wasn't likely to try to call her. Quickly she finished smoothing the comforter, then went into the bathroom and closed the door, running the water so she wouldn't be able to hear anything Silver said.

After a few moments, Silver tapped on the bathroom

door, and Tessa hastily shut off the water. "That was your friend Billie."

Tessa opened the door. "Thank you," she said quietly, knowing that no explanations were needed.

Silver thought about passing along everything Billie had told her, but she decided against it. Tessa had already made it clear that she didn't want to discuss Brett Rutland in any way.

Still, it was disquieting that Tessa went immediately to the telephone and unplugged it.

Tessa had a meeting with her lawyer the next day, and Silver went with her. If Calvin Stine didn't approve of having anyone else present, he gave no sign of it. His gray eyes seemed sharper than before as he surveyed Tessa.

"I've talked with John Morrison, the district attorney. He seems to think there's an open-and-shut case against you."

Meeting his eyes, she saw that he didn't believe in her innocence, and her blood chilled. "I didn't take the money," she said, her voice expressionless. "Someone else did."

"Then that someone has done a good job of making it look as if you did it," he pointed out.

"Isn't it your job to find out who that someone is?" Silver broke in, glaring at the man.

He had such cold eyes, Tessa thought. "No, ma'am, that's an investigator's job. My job is to give your niece the best legal counsel and representation in court that I can. My job is to present evidence that contradicts theirs, or to cause the jury to doubt the prosecution's evidence."

"And if the only way of proving my innocence is to find out who is really the guilty one?" Tessa asked softly.

He sighed. "Miss Conway, you've been watching too many 'Perry Mason' reruns. It doesn't work that way. We're dealing with computer theft. There are no marked bills, no fingerprints, no bloody dagger, as it were. Everything is done in an electronic file."

"And my name was used."

"Your name was used," he agreed.

Her back was very straight, her voice as level as his. "Very well, then, where is the money? What have I done with it? Have I spent it? If so, on what? Do you think that an embezzler steals just to stockpile the money somewhere and not use it?"

"It's been known to happen." His eyebrows lifted. "If the money is invested under another name, or simply hidden in a savings account somewhere, an embezzler can expect to serve a fairly short sentence in prison, then collect the money on his or her release and simply disappear."

"So there's no way to prove my innocence unless the real embezzler confesses?"

"That's another unlikely scenario. It doesn't happen."

Tessa got to her feet. "Then I suppose it's up to me," she told him politely. "Thank you for your time."

He got to his feet, frowning slightly. "What do you mean, it's up to you?"

"To prove my innocence, of course."

"How are you going to do that?"

"By tracking down the real embezzler. I know someone who can help."

When they were in the car, Silver said sharply, "Tessa, you don't need him. I think you should hire another lawyer."

"I don't think hiring another lawyer would do any good." Tessa waited for a break in the traffic, then accelerated sharply. "He was being honest with me, and I prefer that to someone who'll only pretend to believe me."

After a moment, Silver nodded. "What are you going to do? Who do you know who can help?"

"I don't know that he will, but I'm going to ask him. His name is Sammy Wallace. He's a genius with computers. If anyone can track down an electronic thief, Sammy can." Then she frowned. "I don't want him to jeopardize his job, though. He works at Carter Engineering, and he'd probably be fired if anyone knew he was trying to help me."

"Ask him anyway," Silver urged. "Let him make his own decision about that. Having to find another job isn't as bad as going to jail!"

For the first time since she'd been arrested, Tessa smiled, really smiled, though it was quickly gone. "No, I guess it isn't." She was faced with prison, something so ghastly that her mind shied away from the thought of it. Suddenly she wondered if she'd be fighting to prove her innocence if she'd only been fired, instead of having charges pressed against her. Would she have accepted the stigma of thief if she didn't have to fight for her freedom as well as her name? She had the shamed feeling that she would have. It would have been the easiest way. But not now. She'd learned the value of honor. Her own sense of honor was all she had left now, that and her freedom, and her freedom was in jeopardy.

Silver bullied her into eating the most substantial meal she'd had since the ordeal had begun; then they cleaned up together and talked about the shop in Gatlinburg, and of the many friends Tessa had in Tennessee. Catching up on the news kept her occupied until the time when she knew Sammy usually got home. He might refuse, of course. Even Sammy had to realize that helping her was a risky business. But all she could do was ask.

She let the phone ring, knowing that if Sammy were tinkering with Nelda, it might take him a while to realize that the phone was ringing. Her patience was rewarded, and on about the twelfth ring he picked up, sounding vaguely surprised as he said, "Hello?" as if his mind were on something else.

"Sammy, this is Tessa."

"Tessa! Where are you? I heard a…well, uh, a rumor, but—"

"It isn't a rumor. I've been arrested for embezzling."

"That's crazy," he said roughly.

"I didn't do it."

"Of course you didn't do it. Did you think you had to tell me?"

"No, of course not," she said gently. "Sammy, I need your help in finding out who really did it. But…it could cost you your job if anyone finds out that you're helping me. So if you don't want to take the risk, I'll understand."

"I'll come over," he said with rare decisiveness. "What's your address?"

She told him, and he hung up. His instant support,

like Billie's, made her eyes sting. If only— No! She broke the thought off before it could be fully formed.

It was an hour before Sammy arrived; his blond hair was rumpled, but his normally vague air was missing. He hugged Tessa, cuddling her against his lanky body for a moment. "Don't worry," he said confidently. "I'll find out who did it and get you out of this mess. You want me to use the computers, don't you?"

"Yes, but it isn't going to be easy," she warned.

He grinned, and she could tell that the prospect of matching his wits against the computer excited him. "Tell me what you know."

She didn't really know anything, but she'd gone over and over it in her mind, and settled on the most likely course. A bogus account had been set up in accounts payable, and the computer had been instructed to issue checks to that account. Those checks had then been deposited in a bank, and withdrawals made from the account. But she didn't know the name of the bogus account, and the lack of that extremely important fact made Sammy frown. "I have to have the name, or I don't have a starting place."

Silver said simply, "Ask someone who knows."

Sammy looked startled, then he grinned. "You mean, walk right up to Mr. Rut—"

"No, don't ask him," Tessa interrupted harshly. "It could mean your job. You can't let anyone know you're doing this."

"No one will know. I can do it without tipping anyone off, but I have to have the name. I'll do some snooping around at work." His brow furrowed, then he said, "They had to be using the computers at work to hunt for the bogus account to begin with. They'd have left tracks like anyone else using the computer. If I can't find out something that way, I'll ask around. Someone will know. Maybe Perry will know. After all, you work in his department."

Worked, her mind corrected him. Past tense. Everything was past tense.

The phone rang, and Silver got up to answer it. Panic flaring in her eyes, Tessa hastily asked Sammy, "How is Hillary doing these days?"

"I don't know. I think she's mad at me, but I can't figure out why she should be."

The habit of looking out for Sammy was hard to break. "Pay more attention to her, and see if that doesn't help," she advised.

"Pay attention to her? You mean like taking her out?"

"Well, why not? Would it hurt? You like her, don't you?"

"Yeah, but Hillary doesn't—"

"Hillary does," Tessa assured him, smiling wanly. "She thinks the sun rises and sets on you. Ask her out."

Silver hung up the phone and came back to sit down, her forehead lined with worry. "Trouble on the home front," she sighed. "I left your number at the shop, in case they needed to get in touch with me."

"What's wrong?" Tessa asked.

"A little of everything, evidently. An order of supplies is late, the roof started leaking during a storm last night and a customer who bought a doll for her granddaughter's birthday left the doll on a chair, and her dog got it and chewed it to pieces. It was a custom-made doll." Silver sighed. "Now she wants another one, by Sunday."

After a moment, Tessa said, "I think you need to go home."

"No, they'll just have to get along without me. I can't leave you now."

"You can always come back," Tessa pointed out. "Nothing will be happening now until the grand jury is called, and that won't be for another two weeks."

Silver hesitated. Her strong practical streak recognized the truth of what Tessa was saying, yet she was still reluctant to leave Tessa. If Tessa had been angry, if she'd cried or called Brett Rutland every name she could think of, Silver wouldn't have worried, but none of that had happened. It was all locked inside Tessa, concealed behind her quiet face and carefully controlled manner, a seething cauldron of pain, outrage and betrayed love. That man had a lot to answer for.

"I'll be all right," Tessa assured her. "Go. Call now and get a flight for tomorrow. You can come back as soon as you've got everything settled, if you'll feel better doing that. Sammy and Billie are here, you know. I won't be alone."

"No. I'll call or come by every day," Sammy promised.

"Well, all right." Silver gave in. "But I'll call you every night, too."

Which meant that she'd have to start answering the phone again, Tessa realized. Well, what did it matter? Brett wasn't going to call her. It was just that she'd developed this silly fear of answering either the phone or the door. She had to get over that, just as she'd have to

get over everything else. But deep down, inside her,
there was a small cry of pain, because Brett wasn't
going to call.

CHAPTER EIGHT

BRETT SAT BOLT upright in bed, sweat streaming from his body, his jaw tight from the effort he'd been making not to yell. Swearing under his breath, he kicked the tangled sheet away from his legs and swung out of bed. His heart was still pounding, and he was breathing as if he'd been running miles. Naked, he paced up and down the too-small confines of the hotel room, running his hand through his already tousled hair.

The dream had been so real, but the real horror of it was that it was likely to come true. Tessa had been convicted, and he'd watched her being led away to prison. She'd been wearing a rough, blue uniform dress of sorts, and she'd been so pale and fragile that he'd been afraid she'd collapse. But she'd walked away from him without looking back, flanked on each side by a burly prison guard, and she'd disappeared into a black tunnel. As she'd gone out of sight, an iron-barred gate had slammed shut and locked, and he'd known that he'd never see her again. That was when he'd woken, his throat aching from the silent roar of protest.

The very image was obscene. In the dark truth of the night, he knew that no matter how much money she'd stolen, that even if she had made a fool of him, he couldn't bear for her to go to prison. Not Tessa, with her flashing smile and twinkling eyes, her slow, liquid drawl, the bright laughter that so effortlessly enchanted. And the hot ecstasy of her body, he thought, closing his eyes as the memory slammed into him with the power of a sledgehammer. Her silky legs clasping his hips. The look of trusting passion in her eyes when he took her. The flirtatious, languid movement of her hips when she walked. The incendiary sweep of her long lashes over eyes that laughed and invited. Everything about her drove him mad, and it was the wine-sweet sort of madness that he knew would linger with him for the rest of his life.

He wanted a drink, but a quick look at the clock told him that it was almost two-thirty in the morning. His mouth twisted wryly. That was definitely a little early…or a little late…to start hitting the bottle. His father would nod his head and smirk and say that he'd always said that a woman could drive a man to drink. The thought of Tom reminded him that he hadn't been able to take Tessa to meet him, as he'd almost promised her he would do, this weekend. But now it was very early Monday morning, and the weekend was over. It had been a week since he'd had Tessa arrested, a week during which he'd been dying a little more each day from the wound caused by her absence.

His emotions had swung from hurt and pain to raw fury; then the anger had changed to outraged pride, and a determination that she would never have the chance to make a fool of him again. Now, however, pride didn't seem very important beside the fact that he'd lose her forever if he let her go to prison. Her guilt no longer mattered. What mattered was that he have her back in his arms again. He'd coddle her and keep her safe for the rest of her life, and make damned sure that she never got in this kind of mess again.

With that inner realization that nothing else meant as much to him as Tessa, he became aware of a growing sense of peace, an easing of the weight on his shoulders. The action he needed to take was abruptly clear. He never thought that it would be easy, but he knew what had to be done. He'd catch the first flight he could get to San Francisco.

He was able to go back to sleep, but he woke early, eager to get things moving. There was no need to pack. He planned to be back that night, even if he had to drive. He showered and shaved, not noticing in the mirror that his face was set in grim determination. After calling the airlines and getting a seat on a flight leaving at nine-twenty, he called Evan.

"I'm going to see Joshua this morning," he said grimly when Evan answered.

"Has something come up?"

"I'm not letting her go to jail."

Evan sighed. "It's about time. What're you going to tell the old man? He was dead set on making an example of the thief."

"I'll handle it." If Joshua didn't decide to make things difficult, he had a plan all worked out, one that would reimburse Joshua and keep Tessa out of jail. If Joshua wouldn't go along with that, Brett knew what he had to do.

"Have you talked to Tessa?"

"No. I don't want her to know anything about it yet." Perhaps it was a little cruel to keep her in the dark, but not as cruel as getting her hopes up and keeping her nerves strung out until she could hear from him again.

"Maybe this will settle things down at work," Evan grunted.

"Maybe." As he hung up, an unwilling grin touched Brett's hard mouth. Tessa didn't lack for support. Everyone was in an uproar, and he was about as welcome as Typhoid Mary. He expected to get a knife in the back at any time from that little red-headed spitfire, and a couple of times he'd had the uneasy feeling that the papers in his office weren't exactly as he'd left them. It didn't matter, because he kept all important papers locked in his briefcase, and all the evidence against Tessa was in the D.A.'s possession, but if he caught anyone in his office they'd be fired on the spot. Even spineless Perry Smitherman had gotten huffy with him, something that had given him a moment of bitter amusement at the incongruity of it.

Shortly before noon, he was striding through the plush dove-gray carpeted corridors of the Carter-Marshall building. Some of the people he passed greeted him; most didn't. The frown on his face was enough to discourage all but the most intrepid.

He entered Joshua Carter's office, and the secretary looked up. A smile lit her pretty face as she recognized him. "This is a surprise. We weren't expecting you, were we?"

"No, we weren't," he growled, but he managed a tight smile for her. Donna had done a lot of favors for him in the past.

"Are you back for good…until the next crisis, that is?"

"Just a flying visit. I need to see Joshua. It's urgent."

Donna pursed her lips, frowning. "Well, he has a luncheon appointment, but I'll stall them. Go on in."

"Thanks. I'll dance at your next wedding."

"Deliver me," she muttered. Donna was currently off men, having just gotten through a messy divorce.

Brett gave the door one hard rap, then opened it. Joshua Carter looked up from his desk, surprise widening his eyes; then he grinned. "Hell, I should've known who it was from the way you came barging in, but I didn't know you were back. Everything sewn up down there?"

Brett put his briefcase on a chair and walked over to the bar that occupied one end of Joshua's office, going behind it to the coffeepot that was always kept full. He poured a steaming cup of coffee, then looked up at his employer. Joshua was of medium height, but bulky from a lifetime of doing hard manual work. His gray hair was thinning, and he had to wear glasses now, but there was still a glint in his hard blue eyes that warned people he was a formidable opponent. Joshua had started out dirt poor, but by his own crafty intelligence and sheer determination he'd built a fortune. He wouldn't be inclined to dismiss charges against someone who'd been stealing from him. In Brett, he'd met his match in willpower, and now they were going to do some hard dealing.

"Let's negotiate," Brett said evenly.

At the tone of Brett's voice, Joshua lifted one gray eyebrow, his blue eyes growing cautious. "Negotiate? This sounds serious. Is some head-hunter stealing you away?"

"No. It's the case in Los Angeles."

"The woman you caught embezzling? What about her?"

"I want to make a deal with her."

"What sort of deal?" Joshua blazed.

"All charges dropped in exchange for full restitution."

Joshua got to his feet and braced his hands on his desk. He drew a deep breath. "There's no way in hell."

Brett sipped the coffee. That was exactly the response he'd expected. "I don't want her in prison," he said coolly.

If there was anything Joshua was, it was shrewd. He looked at Brett for a long, hard minute before he snorted. "But you do want her in your bed, don't you?"

"Exactly."

"I never thought I'd see the day," Joshua muttered. "I think I need some coffee, too." As the older man crossed the room, Brett poured another cup of coffee and set it on the bar. Joshua sat down on one of the stools and picked up the coffee. "I'm not inclined to let her off with a slap on the wrist. How much is missing? Fifty thousand?"

"Fifty-four."

"What did she take it for? Jewelry? A fancy vacation?"

Brett shrugged. He hadn't seen any evidence that she'd spent the money on anything. She dressed well, but not fifty-four thousand dollars worth. "You'll be paid back."

"She still has the money?"

"I don't know. If she doesn't have it, I'll pay you back."

The gray brows drew together. "Brett, that's an expensive woman you're playing with."

"I'm not playing," Brett said laconically.

"Well, I'll be damned." For the first time, a faintly helpless note entered Joshua's voice. He was genuinely fond of Brett, a man made in his own mold, someone who let nothing interfere with getting the job done… or at least, nothing until this woman. "She must be something."

"She's special. The L.A. office is practically in revolt against me for arresting her. Evan's been dragging around like a whipped hound." Brett pushed his fingers through his tawny hair. "And I'm worse than all of them put together," he admitted raggedly.

"Tell me something. Why should I agree to drop charges against her? Why shouldn't she pay for breaking the law?"

"She has paid." Brett's fingers tightened on the cup of coffee as he remembered her white face. It had been a week since he'd seen her, and he was aching to touch her, to whisper to her that everything was going to be all right, that he'd take care of her.

"You're going to marry her? What if she doesn't want to marry you? I don't imagine you're her favorite person, right now," Joshua pointed out.

Brett knew that, but he hadn't let himself think about it. He'd handle that when the time came, after she was no longer in danger of losing her freedom. When he had the charges against her dropped, when she was safe, then he'd deal with her anger. He still had his own anger to work out, and it would probably be a stormy few days before they got everything settled between them, but he wasn't going to let her slip away from him.

"She'll marry me," he said grimly. Then he looked at Joshua, his navy eyes piercing. He might be cutting his own throat by telling Joshua what he was about to say, but he wasn't going to lie to the man. He'd always been aboveboard in his dealings with Joshua, and he wasn't going to change now. "No matter what your decision, I want you to know that I'll be quitting soon. I'm going back to the ranch…and I want to take Tessa with me."

"That's not a smart thing to tell me," Joshua snapped.

"It was honest," Brett snapped back. He'd never toadied to Joshua, which was one of the reasons Joshua prized him. No matter how black the situation or unpleasant the news, he'd always gotten the truth from Brett.

"This woman…Tessa…is she the reason you're quitting?"

"She's only half of it. I've been getting restless, wanting to go back to the ranch. Ranching is what I do best, what I'm most content doing."

"You're damned good at what you're doing now."

"I'm damned good at ranching, too."

Joshua rubbed his jaw, eyeing Brett. He was shrewd enough to realize that the only thing he could do now was make a deal with Brett, which was exactly what Brett had intended all along. He could either deal, or lose Brett entirely. "Why should I drop those charges, when I'll be losing you either way?"

Brett's eyes gleamed. "Negotiate," he said.

Joshua burst out laughing. "Negotiate, hell! You've been herding me to the exact point you've wanted me at from the minute you walked into this office. I can either cooperate with you, or you're quitting completely, whereas if I drop charges against your woman, your... special consultation services...will be available to me—how often?"

"We can work something out," Brett said smoothly.

Sighing, Joshua held out his hand. "Deal," he said, and Brett shook his hand, while relief unknotted the coil of tension in his belly.

THE PHONE RANG, and Tessa paused only fractionally before she turned off the television, which she'd been staring at without realizing what she was watching, and rose to answer the phone. Over the past several days she'd answered calls from Silver and Sammy, while Billie usually came over instead of calling, but still she couldn't stop the shiver that ran down her spine each time she heard a bell peal. Sammy hadn't had any luck, either in finding the account name or any other sort of information that would aid him in a computer search. They were at a dead end, and time was running short on her. The grand jury would meet next week.

The insistent ring reminded her of the phone, and she shook herself to dispel the cold mantle of dread that had settled on her shoulders. She lifted the receiver, expecting to hear Silver's voice again. It was almost ten o'clock in Tennessee, and Silver would be getting ready for bed, but she always called Tessa before turning in for the night.

"Hello."

"Tessa. This is Brett."

She jumped as if she'd been strung, and jerked the

receiver away from her ear. She hadn't needed him to tell her who he was. She'd never forget that voice, so low and raspy. Whimpering, gasping for breath, she slammed the receiver onto the cradle before she could hear anything else. Oh, God, oh, God, why had he called now? She'd had everything under control, she hadn't broken down once, but the simple sound of his voice had shattered her fragile defenses. A high, keening sound assaulted her ears as her knees stiffened, then gave way beneath her. Curling into a tight little ball on the floor, Tessa began to weep. The phone was ringing again, but there was no way she could have answered it, even if she had dared.

All the pain of betrayal, of love offered and scorned, burst out of her in great, tearing sobs that shook her entire body and felt as if they were rupturing her chest, shredding her throat. She would have screamed with the pain of it if she'd been able to draw enough breath, but all she could do was huddle on the floor.

She cried until she thought she couldn't cry any more, until her throat was raw and burning, the tissues swollen from strain, but still the tears ran down her face. At last she managed to stumble to her feet, and she made her way to the bathroom, bent over like someone old, her hand against the wall for support. There she splashed cold water on her face, gasping at the shock of it, but the sudden coldness gave her back a measure of control. She hung over the sink, shuddering with the effort she was making to stop crying, but at last she managed it and slowly straightened. Her reflection in the mirror made her gasp again; her face was red and splotchy, her eyes swollen almost together from the violent siege of weeping that she'd endured. Staring at her face, at the haunted emptiness of her eyes, she wondered if she'd ever be able to forget about him, if she'd ever stop feeling the pain of knowing that he'd never loved her at all.

She drank some water, and almost choked as the liquid ran down her raw, abused throat. Why had he called? To gloat? Hadn't be beaten her down enough?

The telephone was ringing again. Desperately Tessa ran into the living room and unplugged it, but the sudden silence was almost as unnerving as the noise had been. She chewed her lip. Perhaps that had been Silver, or Sammy, but it didn't matter. She simply couldn't take the chance that Brett might be calling again. She couldn't bear it; she just couldn't take any more.

That night too was sleepless, and endless. The strain of it was in her face the next morning. The swelling had subsided, but she was colorless, and dark shadows lay under her eyes. The first thing she had to do was call Silver and reassure her that everything was all right, even though Tessa felt as if nothing would ever be right again. She plugged in the telephone and punched in the numbers, but when Silver answered the phone on the first ring, as if she'd been waiting anxiously, Tessa found that she couldn't say anything.

"Hello? Hello?" Silver said frantically.

With an effort, Tessa cleared her throat, wincing at the raw pain. "Aunt Silver," she croaked.

"Tessa? Is that you? What's wrong?"

Once again Tessa tried to speak, but no sound came out. Swallowing again, she managed, "Sore throat."

"Oh, my goodness, honey, I guess so! Have you been

to a doctor? There wasn't any answer last night, and I've been going out of my mind with worry. When did you get sick?"

"Last night." Each word came a little easier, but her voice was totally alien to her, as hoarse as a frog's and only a little more intelligible. It would only worry Silver to tell her what had happened, so Tessa let her think that she'd come down with something that affected her throat. As a child she'd been prone to sore throats and bouts of laryngitis anyway, so Silver wouldn't think this was unusual.

"Well, take care of yourself, hear? I won't call you while you can't talk, honey, so you call me when you're better. And if you haven't been to a doctor, go to one today. Promise me, now."

Tessa croaked a sound that Silver took for a promise. They hung up, and she promptly unplugged the telephone again. At this rate, she was going to wear the little plastic plug out within a month. If it really mattered, she thought, stricken by the realization that unless Sammy could work a miracle, she wouldn't be needing a telephone for a long time. She should probably have it taken out anyway, to save as much money as she could.

Forcing herself to move, she showered and washed her hair, lingering in the steamy warmth in an effort to soothe her throat until the hot water began to go. Too listless to fool with her hair, she simply towel-dried it and combed it out, to let it finish drying in a straight mass on her shoulders. When she was dressed she poured orange juice over ice and drank that for her breakfast, hoping that the cold would alleviate the swelling in her throat, since the steam in the bathroom hadn't helped any.

It was late in the morning when someone rang her doorbell, then began pounding on the door. Tessa froze, tears stinging her eyes again. There was no way she was going to answer that door.

"Miss Conway! Are you in there? This is Calvin Stine. I need to talk to you immediately."

Her brow knit. Why did he sound so urgent? What had happened? Did this have something to do with Brett calling the night before? She hurried to the door, fumbling with the lock and the safety chain until she could remove them and swing the door open. Calvin Stine stepped inside, smartly dressed in a dark blue suit, his dark brows lowered over his cool, piercing gray eyes.

She closed the door and faced him, her hands clasped together in front of her, her pale face anxious. Her eyes questioned him.

"Please get dressed, as swiftly as you can," he instructed. "I've been trying to call you all morning, but your phone is evidently out of order. The assistant district attorney has called us to a meeting in his office in an hour and a half."

She stood very still, feeling like a small, hunted animal. "Please hurry," he said irritably. "The traffic is a mess this morning. It'll take us at least an hour to get there. By the way, have you reported your phone?"

Tessa shook her head, and moved slowly over to the telephone. Lifting the cord, she showed him that it was unplugged. If he'd been irritated before, he was downright aggravated now.

"That wasn't very smart, Miss Conway. It would've

saved me a trip over here if I could have talked to you on the phone."

Silently she went into her bedroom and closed the door. She dressed mechanically in a white linen suit with a pencil-slim skirt and a short, smart jacket. Perhaps white wasn't the wisest choice, given her own pallor, but she didn't feel capable of the extra effort that changing would require. After slapping on her makeup, she viewed the garish effort in the mirror and seized a tissue to wipe most of it off. She was too pale to look like anything other than a painted clown if she wore the full routine. Her hair was still damp, and lack of time prevented her from doing anything to it, so she twisted it into a knot and pinned it on top of her head. Twenty minutes after she'd walked into the bedroom, she walked out again, her face expressionless, her purse tucked under her arm. No matter what was going on, she wasn't going to break down again. She wouldn't give them the satisfaction. At that point in her thoughts, "them" was everyone except Silver, Billie and Sammy, and that included her own lawyer.

He checked his watch. "That was certainly fast." Then he looked critically at her pale, frozen face. "Don't be so frightened. This is just a meeting."

She nodded slowly, and abruptly he realized that she hadn't spoken a word since he'd entered the apartment. He frowned again. "Miss Conway, are you all right?"

"Yes," she said, forcing out the strained, stifled word. "I'm perfectly all right."

"Are you ill?"

"No." She walked past him. "Shall I drive my car, too, to save you a trip back here?"

He winced at her harsh, barely audible voice. "No, we could be separated in the traffic. Have you taken anything for your throat?"

Why was he so concerned about her throat? She didn't bother to answer, and he followed her out of the apartment, locking the door behind him. He took her elbow, his fingers oddly gentle as he walked her to his car and opened the door for her.

"The assistant district attorney is Owen McCary," he told her during the drive. "I'm optimistic about this meeting. I think they're going to offer to accept a plea-bargain. It's entirely possible that a trial won't be necessary, that you'll be given a suspended sentence and placed on probation."

Was that supposed to thrill her? Tessa looked out the window, feeling cold and distant, a little disoriented. She completely missed the reluctantly worried way that Calvin Stine looked at her, the puzzlement in his eyes.

The traffic was a snarled mess, just as he'd said, but they made it with about five minutes to spare. It took those five minutes to make their way to the district attorney's office, where a pleasant young man took them to a small, private office. As soon as Calvin ushered her into the office with his hand on the small of her back, Tessa saw Brett's dark, controlled face, and her mind mercifully went blank. She was unaware of being seated, or of the reassuring pat that Calvin gave her cold hand.

The wonderful, protective blankness didn't last long. Voices intruded on her consciousness as people were introduced, and she looked slowly around the office in an effort to orient herself, but she was very careful not to look at Brett. Evan Brady was there, of course, his nervous energy practically throwing off sparks. Owen McCary, the assistant district attorney, sat at his desk looking for all the world like the stereotypical California golden blond, except for the weary street wisdom in his eyes. There was another man, a tall, silver-haired man, and he was introduced as Benjamin Stiefel, an attorney for Carter-Marshall.

She could feel the searing power of Brett's eyes on her, feel him willing her to look at him, and she withdrew even deeper into herself. She locked herself away in her mind, sheltering herself in thoughts that took her away from the meeting. Let Calvin handle it. That was what she'd hired him for.

FROM THE MOMENT she'd walked into the room, he'd found breathing difficult, almost impossible. She was so pale, her face so still, and she looked even more fragile than he'd remembered. The wide, mobile, exotic bloom of her mouth was quiet. There was no lovely, enticing smile curling her lips now, though of course he hadn't expected smiles, not yet, anyway. But he had expected her to use her formidable charm, the disarming, enchanting play of lashes over luminous eyes, and instead she sat like a delicate marble statue, never looking at him, even though he willed her to with fierce concentration. He wanted her eyes to meet his. He wanted to reassure her that everything was going to be all right.

She'd hung up on him the night before, and though he'd wanted to shake her for it, he felt that he understood how she felt. She hadn't known then that he was offering her her freedom.

What was she thinking? Her face had always been so expressive, so alive, but now it was as if she wore a mask. Why wouldn't she look at him? When she heard the offer, would she cry? He couldn't stand the idea of her crying, even in relief. He'd take her out of here, to a place where they could be alone together; then he'd dry her tears, and begin the process of cementing their relationship.

If only she'd look at him.

"Miss Conway. Tessa," Calvin Stine said gently, drawing her attention to him. She regarded him somberly, waiting for him to tell her why he'd drawn her from the cocoon of her thoughts.

He took her hand, enfolding it in both of his as if to warm her cold fingers. "Mr. Rutland has proposed, with the approval of the district attorney's office, that the charges against you be dismissed if you agree to sign a statement of guilt, and to repay the money that is missing." He spoke softly, so softly that only she could hear him. The others in the room must think they were conferring, rather than that he was explaining something she should have been listening to herself. But Calvin's gray eyes gentled as they moved over her face. "Tessa, do you understand?"

"Yes, I understand," she whispered.

There was a stunned, haunted expression in her eyes, and instinctively he moved in front of her, shielding her from the view of everyone else in the room. "I advise you to accept their offer," he murmured urgently. "You've been through enough. I can't tell you how risky a trial would be."

Her stifled voice was barely audible. "You don't think I have a chance of acquittal?"

"Only a slim one, I'm afraid. Their evidence is very strong. Don't take the chance. You couldn't survive in prison," he said angrily.

Why was he so angry? He didn't believe in her innocence, hadn't from the beginning. But in the view of the law, even the guilty were entitled to competent legal representation, and that was what he was offering now. He was attempting to give her the best advice he could.

A little sigh escaped her as weariness pulled at her limbs. "I'd have to sign an admission of guilt? A confession?"

"That's what they want, yes."

She smiled now, a slow movement of her pale lips. "But I'm not guilty."

A desperate look came into his eyes. "Don't even think it, Tessa. Take the chance they're offering you and run with it."

"I'd have to run. I certainly couldn't face myself in the mirror in the mornings. My self-respect, my good name, are all I have left, and I wouldn't have those if I signed a confession that isn't true. It would be an act of cowardice." Her voice broke several times, and the sounds were harsh and strained, but she managed to say what she felt.

"My God, this isn't the time for nobility!"

"Oh, I'm not noble at all. I'm desperate." She turned her hand in his until *she* was holding *him*, trying to make him understand. "I won't do it. I'm sorry, but I can't admit to something I didn't do."

He bit off the curses that rose to his lips. He was

pale, too, and sweating. Behind him, the others were shifting restlessly, wondering about the extended conference, the pleading note they had detected in Calvin's hushed voice. Tessa released Calvin's hands and stood up, her eyes on Owen McCary. She didn't dare look anywhere else.

"I refuse to accept the offer," she said, straining her voice to achieve the necessary volume. "I won't admit to something I didn't do."

Brett surged to his feet, uttering a violent oath. Tessa didn't look at him, but she sensed that he moved toward her, and her heart stopped beating. Clinging tightly to Calvin's arm, she walked past Brett as if he were invisible.

The door closed behind them, and in the pool of silence that was left behind, Evan swore shakily. Brett turned to face him, his eyes burning with an emotion that couldn't be named. A feeling of horror was clawing at his insides. "God in heaven, what have I done to her?" he choked. "She's innocent. *She didn't do it!*"

Benjamin Stiefel sighed. "I never expected this."

That was an understatement, Brett thought savagely. Like a wild animal he turned on Owen McCary. "Drop the charges. Completely. Now." He bit the words off like bullets.

McCary was shaken, too, but he said, "Mr. Rutland, the evidence against her is very strong—"

"I know how strong it is," Brett interrupted harshly. "I'm the one who found it. But I didn't look far enough. I didn't find out who set this up to make Tessa take the blame for it. *I'm dropping the charges*, as of right now."

Benjamin Stiefel tried to interject a bit of caution. "Brett, I don't think Mr. Carter will approve—"

"I'm not asking for his approval. I have the authority to withdraw the charges, and I'm doing it. He'll have his thief, all right. I'll bring him to Joshua Carter on a silver platter."

Evan's dark eyes were full of the same anger that burned in Brett. "Ben, we nearly sent an innocent woman to prison. It didn't seem right from the beginning. It just didn't fit in with the type of person she is. We'll keep Mr. Carter posted on what we're doing, and if he doesn't like it"—Evan shrugged his shoulders—"let him fire us."

Brett paced the office like a caged animal, his control shattered by the events that had just taken place. Without thinking it out in a logical progression, he'd known as soon as she'd refused his offer that she was innocent. He'd known it instinctively, and without doubt. He'd driven her to the very edge, hurt her—he winced at the thought of how he must have hurt her. No wonder she wouldn't look at him!

He'd give anything to turn back time, to wipe this past week out of existence for her. Every protective male instinct in him was aroused, and outraged, because he'd almost destroyed the very person he loved most in the world. He had to find the real embezzler now, to clear Tessa's name in everyone's mind as well as on paper. It was the only reparation he could offer her.

CHAPTER NINE

CALVIN DIDN'T WANT to leave her. He took her back to the apartment, but seemed totally incapable of walking away from her. She sat on the couch and watched him as he prowled restlessly around, wondering what he wanted. He kept watching her, too, with a stricken look in his gray eyes, as if he still couldn't believe what she'd done.

Finally his pacing began to wear on her nerves, even through the remote emotional exile she'd placed herself in. "Calvin, I'm sorry," she croaked in as soft a voice as she could manage. "I know you advised me to do the most sensible thing."

"It isn't that." His voice was muffled. "It's just... ah, hell, I've forgotten what it is like to trust someone, to simply be able to take their word on something. I should've trusted you, but I didn't. I was so damned cynical that I thought your guilt or innocence didn't matter to me as a lawyer."

"It doesn't. It can't, or you wouldn't be able to do your job." Why was she trying to comfort him? She was so tired, and she wanted to go to sleep. If he would just leave, she could wrap herself up in a blanket and lie on the couch. She felt as if she wouldn't be able to keep going much longer. Her legs and arms were leaden, and fatigue dragged at her.

Someone beat on the door, and it sounded as if they were using their fist. Calvin looked at her, but Tessa made no move to get up and answer it. She'd gone very still, like a small animal when a hawk flies over, so he answered the door himself. Brett Rutland filled the doorway, his face dark and dangerous, his eyes savage. "How is she?" he barked.

Calvin turned and looked at Tessa, but she stared straight ahead, not looking in their direction. Brett shouldered past him, ignoring Calvin's sharp, "Mr. Rutland, this is highly irregular—"

"I don't give a damn about irregular," Brett snapped, crossing to Tessa and hunkering down in front of her so he could see her face. Her eyes slid away from him to focus blindly on some spot on the wall. He reached out and took her hand, and that small touch electrified him. It had been so long since he'd felt her skin, been close enough to smell her subtle fragrance. He wanted to lift her in his arms and hug her to him, but she was so pale and stiff, withdrawing from him without actually moving. Her hands were icy. He captured her other hand and held both of them in his in an effort to warm them.

"Tessa, I've dropped the charges. Do you understand? You're clear. You don't have to be afraid."

Calvin was galvanized into speech. "What? You've dropped the charges? But why—I don't understand."

"I'll explain it all to you in a minute," Brett said without taking his eyes from Tessa's face. "Tessa, do you understand what I'm telling you?"

"Yes," she whispered, too numb to feel anything, not relief, or surprise, or even curiosity. She didn't want to feel; she didn't want to think. Not now, with Brett so close. Why didn't he go away? Why didn't he let go of her hands?

"What's wrong with your voice?" he asked sharply.

She looked at him then, and he drew in a convulsive breath at the look in her eyes. "Go away."

Something in her eyes, her face, convinced him to let her go. He released her hands and got to his feet, his bronzed features set. "Let's talk in the kitchen," he said to Calvin, and the two men left the room. Tessa remained where she was, alarmed that they were discussing her, but totally unable to go in there when Brett was there. His presence overwhelmed her, brought too much pain for her to handle, for her even to cope with in any way except to admit to its existence. She couldn't examine it; she couldn't face it.

It seemed as if time dragged, that they spent hours in the kitchen. She wanted desperately to lie down and sleep, but she didn't dare, not with Brett so close. What could they be talking about? Surely there weren't any legal difficulties involved in dropping charges against someone? The charges had really been dropped, he'd said. She was free. She no longer had the grim specter of prison hanging over her head. Why didn't it seem real to her?

When they came out of the kitchen, Calvin crossed over to her and clasped her hand. "You'll be okay," he reassured her. "Mr. Rutland is going to take care of everything. I have to get back to the office, but I'll be in touch with you later."

"Wait," Tessa whispered desperately, her eyes darting to Brett. He wasn't going to leave her alone with Brett, was he?

"Mr. Rutland will take care of everything," Calvin repeated; then he dropped her hand and went to the door. Tessa struggled to her feet. She had to stop him; she had to do something. She couldn't stay there with Brett! But Brett moved, his broad shoulders blocking her as he went with Calvin to the door, and Tessa hesitated, not willing to go so close to him. He closed the door behind Calvin, and turned to face her.

Desperation gave her strength. She swallowed, causing her throat to tighten in pain, but she looked straight at him and said hoarsely, "Get out of my apartment."

"What's wrong with your voice?" he asked again, ignoring her order. Before she could evade him, he'd crossed to stand very close to her, and for the first time she noticed that he held a glass in his hand, a glass of clear, yellowish liquid. He put the glass in her hand, wrapping her fingers around it, and it was so hot that she almost couldn't hold it.

"Hot lemonade," he said. "Drink it. It'll be good for your throat."

It felt like heaven to her cold fingers, and because it was a remedy that she'd often been treated with as a child, she raised the glass to her lips and cautiously sipped the hot, tangy mixture of sweet and sour. The taste was a sweet memory on her tongue, and burned on her throat, but it felt good for all of that.

"What's wrong with your voice? Are you sick?"

Why couldn't he just leave her alone? He was going to badger her with the same question over and over until she screamed, or went mad, or both. "No, I'm not sick!" she yelled, but it came out as only a stifled rasp.

"Then what's wrong?"

His persistence ate at her, destroying her control, but then, he was the only man who'd ever been able to make her react in ways she couldn't control. She drew away from him, a fine trembling beginning to shake her body as she stared at him, at the hard, unhandsome face and the stunning blue beauty of his eyes, the same face and eyes that had held her bemused from the first time she'd seen him. She'd loved him, and he'd turned on her. The trembling grew worse, and suddenly she erupted into rage, her face twisting as she hurled the contents of the glass at him. "Damn you! I hate you! I hate you, do you hear?"

The night before, the sound of his voice had shattered the barriers that she'd built around the hurt she felt, and now he'd broken the control she'd had on the seething anger that had been building up inside her. She flew at him, her fists beating at his face, his chest, any part of him that she could reach, screaming wildly in her stifled voice, but the stress on her throat was too much and her voice began to go entirely, until the screams were silent. Tears streamed from her eyes as the hysteria built in her. Brett jerked his head back, protecting his face, but he simply stood there and let her pound at his chest, absorbing the blows and the pain, the rage, his own heart aching at what he'd done to her. When her strength was gone, she sagged weakly against him, and only then did he put his arms around her, stilling her feebly pounding hands.

"Baby, I'd let you throw boiling water at me if it would make you feel better," he said raggedly, brushing his lips against her hair, her forehead, her temples.

"God, if I could only undo it all!" It was a bitter cry
from the depths of his soul.

The feel of his arms around her was so painful that
she almost couldn't bear it, yet she didn't feel able to
push him away. His shirt and suit jacket were sticky
from the lemonade that she'd thrown on him, and it
was making her face and hair sticky, too, yet her head
lay tiredly on the broad expanse of his chest. The lemonade wouldn't ruin the expensive wool, she thought
fuzzily, but she was glad that he'd have the expense of
having it cleaned.

The room swung around her in a dizzy arc as he
lifted her in his arms and carried her into the kitchen,
where he sat her on a chair. He wetted a paper towel
and washed the stickiness from her face, then dabbed at
her hair. Gently he removed the pins from the knot on
top of her head and raked his fingers through her hair,
tumbling the dark mass down around her shoulders.
Then he poured another glass of lemonade for her, and
pressed it into her hand. "Here's the rest of the lemonade. Throw it at me if you want, but it'll do you more
good if you drink it."

Obediently she drank it, too exhausted and empty to
do otherwise, watching him as he took off his coat and
tossed it over the back of a chair, then unbuttoned his
shirt and took it off, too. The sight of his naked, powerful torso made the bottom drop out of her stomach. She
had curled her fingers in the dark hair that covered his
broad chest, had noted that it was several shades darker
than the tawny, sun-streaked brown of the hair on his
head. The memory of the way his body had felt under
her lightly stroking, exploring fingers made her jerk

her eyes away from him to stare blindly at the floor as he washed the lemonade from his chest and shoulders, but she saw in her mind's eye the way the muscles in his arms and back would flex as he moved, his biceps bulging, rippling.

"Come on, finish that," he said gently, and she jumped, because she hadn't realized he'd moved to her side. He was rubbing a towel over his torso, but his attention was on her. She drank the rest of the lemonade, then handed him the empty glass. He rinsed it out and placed it in the dish drainer to dry, then came back to her and bent down, one arm sliding under her knees and the other going around her back. He lifted her, and Tessa made a hoarse sound of protest.

"Shhh," he soothed. "Don't try to talk; you'll only hurt your throat. You're exhausted, and you need to sleep. I'm just going to put you to bed. When you wake up, you'll feel better, and then we'll talk."

He carried her into the bedroom, and panic made her twist in his arms, but all her strength was gone, and he undressed her as easily as he would have a fractious child. When she was naked, he placed her between the cool sheets, then crossed to the window and pulled the shade down, shutting out the bright California sun. She lay frozen, unwilling to get up while he was there, exposing herself to him again, and equally unwilling to lie in that bed. He removed his shoes and socks, then undid his pants and dropped them.

Tessa struggled upright, a silent protest on her lips. "No, don't try to talk," he said sternly, stepping out of his briefs and coming to her totally, gloriously naked. He got into bed with her and forced her back against the pillows. "Just sleep, baby. I'm going to hold you, that's all. I said no talking," he repeated as she tried again to say something. "You've strained your throat, and you're going to have to let it rest." He drew her against him, his nakedness searing her like a furnace, the warmth enveloping her and sinking into her. His arms were living bonds, wrapped around her, and the hollow of his shoulder made a resting place for her head. The urgent thrust of his masculinity made her struggle weakly for a moment, but he made no sexual advances to her, merely held her, and she was so tired that her brief struggles ceased.

"Go to sleep, darling," he whispered, and she did.

Hours later, she woke to total darkness and an urgent need for the bathroom. She fought out of the grasp of his arms and the tangle of the sheets to stumble, still half-asleep, to the bathroom. When she came out he was leaning against the wall in the hallway, waiting. Without a word he took her back to bed and once again settled her in his arms. Tessa burrowed her face against the warm strength of his neck, inhaling the unforgotten, faintly musky scent of his skin, and fell deeply asleep again, the long periods of unconsciousness just what she needed for both body and spirit.

When she woke again, she was alone in the bed, and an inborn sensitivity to the sun and the passage of time told her that it was late in the afternoon, which meant that she'd slept more than twenty-four hours, at least. She felt dopey from sleep, yet stronger than she had in what seemed like an eternity. Was Brett still in the apartment? Oddly, she wasn't alarmed by the possibility that he might be. Well rested, she was capable of facing him now. Getting out of bed, she wrapped herself in a robe, then gathered her clothes and went to the bathroom. A shower was the most urgent thing on her agenda, and she took a long one, letting the briskly cool water finish washing away the cobwebs in her mind.

The little grooming rituals of brushing her teeth and combing her hair were soothing, and made her feel even better than she had before. Finding Brett waiting patiently outside the bathroom door made her entire body quiver in reaction, but the panic was gone now.

"Breakfast is ready," he announced, then smiled faintly, but the smile wasn't reflected in his eyes. "I guess it's still breakfast, even though it is almost four in the afternoon. I figured you had to like oatmeal, otherwise you wouldn't have bought it, and that'll be easiest on your throat. How is your throat? Can you talk?"

"Yes," she said, a little embarrassed at her froglike croak.

His hard, warm hand went to her wrist, and before she could draw away he had bent down and kissed her mouth briefly. "Don't worry, your voice will come back," he comforted, gently urging her toward the kitchen with the pressure of his hand.

She was so rattled by the touch of his mouth on hers that her hands were shaking as she ate her hot oatmeal, which he must have prepared as soon as he heard her stirring. Why had he kissed her? For that matter, why had he bothered to spend the night with her? Certainly not because of love, she thought tiredly. Guilt, probably. Well, that was his cross to bear, because she had her own problems, not the least of which was getting over him. If she ever could. If she'd ever see another day when she didn't think about him, ever wake up in the morning and not wish that he was beside her. Somehow, she just didn't think that day would ever come.

He was wearing different clothes, she noticed, khaki pants and a pullover white cotton shirt that fit loosely, with the sleeves rolled up over his brawny forearms. "When did you go back to the hotel?" she asked hoarsely, indicating the clothes.

"I didn't. I called Evan, and he brought my clothes over. I didn't want to leave you, even for an hour."

She sipped her coffee thoughtfully, and it was a moment before she spoke. "I'm all right. I'm not going to do something stupid, if that's what you're thinking."

"No, that wasn't what I was thinking. I was afraid that you'd wake up while I was gone, and lock me out," he said simply.

She nodded. "Yes," she said.

"I couldn't take that chance. Not now." His voice roughened. "I know I can't make it up to you for what you've been through this past week, but I swear I'm going to spend the rest of my life trying."

Anger stirred in her. "I don't need your guilt! I told you, I'm all right."

He drank his own coffee, not responding to her heated statement. "I called your aunt," he said instead, totally surprising her. "I found her number in your telephone index. By the way, you have it listed under A, instead of S."

"It's Aunt Silver, not Silver Aunt," Tessa muttered distractedly. "Why did you call her?"

"I knew she had to be worried about you, and I wanted her to know that it's over with, at least as far as you're concerned. I still have a thief to catch," he added grimly.

Again, Tessa was startled. "What do you mean?"

"I know you didn't do it."

"You do? What about all of that famous evidence?" she rasped, rising to her feet in agitation.

"I was wrong. You didn't do it."

The steadiness of his gaze had the opposite effect on her; it shook her instead of calming her. She hadn't really thought about the whys and wherefores of it, hadn't wondered about his reason for dropping the charges. She had assumed simply that he felt sorry for her, or perhaps was having an attack of conscience over the fact that he'd seduced her for the purpose of his investigation. To hear him state flatly that he thought she was innocent was almost more than she could take in.

"I don't understand," she said shakily. "Why should you believe me now, when you didn't before? The evidence hasn't changed, has it? Have you learned something else?"

"No. Nothing new had turned up." It would take too long to explain his feelings to her, and she wasn't ready to hear about them anyway. He'd lain awake for hours the night before, holding her in his arms while she slept, examining his sudden strong conviction that he'd wrongly accused her. Part of it had been the staggering realization of her unyielding sense of honor, so strong that she wouldn't betray it even to protect herself. But even more, it had been the way she had loved, the open, unreserved way she'd given herself, and her virginity, to him. She was twenty-five, and she'd been engaged twice before. He certainly hadn't expected her to be a virgin. No one would have. Yet she'd remained a virgin out of a deep sense of self-respect, an inner knowledge that perhaps she wasn't ready yet to commit herself to that sort of intimacy with a man. She hadn't loved her fiancé enough to forgive him his infidelity, and neither had she loved him enough to give him herself.

He felt tension coiling in his gut. Would she love him enough to forgive him? She'd loved him enough to give him the sweetness of her body, but that had been before he'd taken her love and trampled on it. What would he do if she couldn't forgive him?

Tessa stood uncertainly by her chair, the expression on his face making her shy away from the subject. Instead she went back to the previous topic. "What did Aunt Silver say?"

"She cried," Brett said abruptly. She'd also said some things to him that had scorched the telephone lines, but they were between him and Silver only. He'd deserved most of the things she'd said. It wasn't until she had accused him of using Tessa that he'd brought her up short. Silver, at least, now knew exactly what his intentions were concerning Tessa. Convincing Tessa, however, was something else, and he knew he'd have to be patient. Only time would heal the wound he'd dealt her. She wouldn't even listen to him right now if he tried to tell her that he loved her.

"Is she…is she coming back this weekend?"

"No. There's no need for it."

Her head drooped on her slender neck. "Then I think I'll go home." Even as hoarse as her voice was, there was poignancy in the way she said "home." She longed for the peace and splendor of the mountains, bursting with the fresh green miracle of spring. She could go hiking, touring the park as she had done every year until she'd moved to California, letting the solitude ease her bruised spirit. There was certainly nothing left for her here. She'd left Tennessee in an effort to get over Andrew, and she'd succeeded beyond her wildest dreams. Andrew was nothing but a vague memory now, forever burned out of her heart by the fires Brett had ignited. She wanted to go home.

Brett was stunned by the thought that she might simply pack up and leave, and he couldn't follow her, not now. He was bound to stay in Los Angeles until he found the embezzler, so he'd have to keep Tessa with him. If he let her go now, he was afraid he'd never be able to get her back.

"You can't leave now," he said sharply.

Her green eyes widened in fear. "I can't?"

"I need your help," he said, improvising rapidly.

She was wary now. "Help doing what?"

"Finding out who framed you," he said promptly.

"I don't see how I can help."

"No one knows that the charges against you have been dropped. The embezzler has to be feeling pretty safe, but if you leave, that could tip him off. He could grab the money and run."

"He?" Tessa asked, lifting her brows.

"A figure of speech."

After a minute, she said, "I don't care if you catch him or not."

He got to his feet, too, a little angry. "You don't want to catch the person who almost caused you to go to prison?"

Automatically, she stepped back. "I know I should want a criminal to be caught and punished, but right now I just don't care. All I want to do now is forget about this…all of this. Everything."

Including me, he thought furiously. Too bad, because he wasn't going to let it happen. His navy eyes were narrowed angry slits as he reached out for her, his hands gentle despite his anger. She went stiff at his touch, but didn't fight him as he eased her into his arms, holding her against him while he stroked her hair. "You're worn out, and you've been through a bad time," he murmured. "Poor baby, I'll make it up to you. You don't have to worry about a thing now; I'll take care of you."

"I'm not worn out, and I can take care of myself." His big body, pressed against her, reminded her too vividly of the times when he'd held her beneath him, making love to her with shattering intensity. Her protest was automatic, and she might have saved her breath for all the attention he paid her.

"I've missed holding you," he said huskily, moving his lips against her temple. "You smell so sweet. Tell me something, honey. Are you pregnant? Are you going to have my baby?"

A bolt of pain shot through her. Was that why he'd dropped the charges? Was all his talk about believing in her innocence just that—talk? "No," she almost spat, bracing her hands against his stomach and trying to push him away. "No, I'm not. I found out last week."

He pulled her hands from his stomach and gently forced her arms behind her back, anchoring them there with one big hand. He was aware of disappointment that she wasn't going to have his baby, but he knew that it was for the best. He didn't want her to associate the conception of their first child with anything except pleasure, anything except love. She felt so good in his arms, as if part of him had been missing and was now restored. The feel of her firm, round breasts pushing against him made his body stir with arousal, a condition aggravated by the fact that he'd held her naked in his arms all night long, longing to make love to her but knowing that she was exhausted, that she desperately needed sleep.

Tessa could feel what was happening to him, and her throat tightened in mingled fear and remembered ecstasy. The ecstasy was a part of her now, a memory that would never leave her, and she feared him because she was so terribly vulnerable to him. She loved him, and he had hurt her worse than she'd ever imagined she would be hurt. Because she loved him, he could hurt her again, and she had no defenses against him. "Brett, please," she groaned. "I don't want that to happen. I can't handle it, not now. Please."

"I know," he reassured her harshly. "I know. I'm not going to do anything except hold you. You know I won't force you, don't you?"

"Yes." The word breathed out of her. In that, she did trust him. Physically, he'd never been anything but tender with her.

He relaxed fractionally, but he still held her tightly to him, and gradually she relaxed, too. After all, she'd slept naked in his arms the night before, and he hadn't done anything, so she felt safe standing in the kitchen fully clothed.

The doorbell rang, and she jerked out of his arms,

whirling around like a small, startled animal. "Easy," he soothed, frowning at her reaction. "That's probably Evan. I told him to come by late this afternoon and we'd start work."

"Why can't you work in your hotel room?" she demanded, following him into the living room.

"Because I don't have a hotel room," he explained easily, and opened the door to Evan.

Tessa had an alarming feeling that was too certain to be classified as a suspicion. Rather, she *knew*. But their relationship was too tangled and too private for her to pursue the matter with Evan present, which was something Brett had probably been counting on.

Evan greeted her with a friendliness that put her off stride, particularly when Brett rested his arm heavily around her waist and drew her with him to the couch, keeping her by his side as Evan began pulling papers out of his stuffed briefcase. Tessa sat stiffly for a moment, then moved far enough away from Brett that their bodies weren't touching. Did he think she'd fall for his devoted act? That was all it was, an act, and she wasn't fool enough to be taken in twice. At her movement, Brett's head whipped around, and the expression in his eyes was dangerous, but Evan began talking, and Brett had to turn his attention back to the other man.

"I got some interesting information this afternoon," Evan said with controlled excitement. "The handwriting analysis of the signature on the checks."

Brett leaned forward, and Evan passed him the report. Quickly Brett scanned it, his brows knitting in concentration.

"What does it say?" Tessa asked, tilting her head in an effort to read it.

"It says, darling, that the signature on the checks is very similar to yours, but that there are enough differences to make a definite decision impossible. However, the person who wrote those checks is almost certainly a female, and that rules out the one person we've thought all along was the most likely prospect."

She frowned at the easy endearment, but was distracted by his last sentence. "Who did you think it was?"

"Sammy Wallace," Evan said, accepting the report as Brett passed it back to him.

"Impossible," Tessa said immediately.

"We know that now, but he was the most suspicious. According to you, he has a lot of expensive equipment in his apartment, and it had to be paid for in some way."

So he'd been using her to get information on her friends, too! She clenched her hands as her anger surged. From being numb, she had gone on an emotional roller-coaster, with her moods swinging from one extreme to the other, as if, now that they had broken free of the control she'd placed on them, they were reacting wildly.

"Sammy has been trying to help me," she said, and both of them looked startled. "If he has the name or number of the account that was used, he can trace it back to the original entry, the time of day it was made, I think even to the original terminal that was used. But he couldn't get the account name."

A black look crossed Brett's harsh features. "Damn it, I knew someone had been going through the papers in my office!"

She blanched at the thought that she might have gotten Sammy fired. That had been the one thing she had wanted to avoid. "He was only trying to help," she pointed out, and refrained from adding that Sammy had believed her from the beginning.

As if on cue, the doorbell rang. This time she didn't jump, though the sound jangled her nerves. Evan quickly began gathering papers up as Brett went to the door.

Sammy and Billie stood in the doorway, gaping at Brett; then Billie shot to Tessa's defense. "What are you doing here? Get out! How dare you badger her like this!"

"Settle down," Brett advised her coolly. "We're not badgering her. We're trying to find out who set her up."

"What do you mean, set her up?" Billie shot back.

"Just what I said. Well, come on in. This is turning out to be quite a party." He opened the door wider, and Evan came into their view.

"What is this?" Billie asked suspiciously.

Brett jerked his head sideways in silent command, and they both came cautiously into the apartment. "To begin with, we dropped the charges against Tessa yesterday."

Sammy's face brightened, but Billie said, "Is that supposed to make everything all right? You think you can just waltz back in here and take up where you left off?"

A flush pinkened Tessa's wan face, and Brett said grimly, "I should be so lucky. No, that isn't what I think. But someone deliberately made it look as if Tessa was embezzling, and I want to know who it was."

"Billie, please," Tessa interjected, intending to ask

Billie to halt the hostilities, but she didn't get any further.

"What's wrong with your voice? You sound like a frog."

"She strained her throat," Brett said, then deftly changed the subject. "Wallace, I understand that you can trace the account if you have either the name or the number."

Sammy eyed him cautiously. "That's right."

"How long would it take you?"

When it came to computers, Sammy lost all his shyness. He was a master in the field, and his confidence showed. "That depends. If I used the master computer at work, a couple of nights. Maybe less."

"How about if that's all you work on tomorrow?"

"You mean, on company time?"

"That's exactly what I mean."

"I can give you the data on the original entry tomorrow."

"Do it," Brett said.

"What's the account name?"

"Conway, Inc.," Brett said softly, sensing the way Tessa stiffened. "They used her name, all the way through."

"No wonder you thought she did it!" Billie muttered.

Sammy was frowning. "No, that's wrong. It isn't Conway, is it?"

"There's another account, under the name of Conmay, Inc. Only one letter is different, and that letter is so similar that, with a dot matrix printer and a bad ribbon, which is the common state of affairs, it's almost impossible to distinguish between the two when you're checking down a list."

Hearing how she'd been set up almost made Tessa ill. "Then my name was used to sign the checks written on the account that the company funds were deposited into...." The evidence had been over-whelming, and all of it had pointed to her. It didn't seem like a casual choice, but a deliberate effort to incriminate her specifically.

Brett looked sharply at her. "That's right."

"I'll work with you tomorrow," Evan said to Sammy. "With both of us on it, we can do it in half the time. Who knows, Brett and I may save our jobs yet."

Tessa froze momentarily, then turned and looked at Brett, a look that was long and very level. "Did you have the authority to drop the charges against me?" she asked quietly.

Brett gave Evan a cutting glance. "I have the authority," he drawled, daring Evan to say anything else.

"Then let me put it another way: Did you have the authorization to drop the charges?"

"Not exactly," he said with a wolfish smile. He didn't like her questions, but he wasn't going to lie to her, not now. There was a lot of information he wouldn't volunteer, but if she asked him a direct question, he was going to answer it honestly. "I took the responsibility for the decision."

"But you could be fired?"

"It's possible, but not likely. Mr. Carter and I have an agreement about things like this. When an on-the-spot decision is called for, I make it."

There were a lot of questions Tessa wanted to ask

him about that, but not in front of everyone else. She simply added them to her list of things to ask him about when they were alone—and she had no doubt that they would be alone. When the others left, she knew that Brett would be staying.

It wasn't particularly gratifying to find that she was right, but once they were alone again, she turned to face him. She felt far more balanced now than she had in a week, and though she couldn't help feeling grateful to him for taking care of her the day before, when she'd practically been a basket case, it was past time that she faced him. Putting it off wouldn't lessen the hurt.

"Now we talk," she said.

He nodded, a hint of satisfaction in his eyes, as if he'd found it difficult to restrain himself. "Yes, we do. You've managed to evade the question several times, darling, but now you're going to tell me exactly what *is* wrong with your voice," he said very softly.

Their eyes met, and she saw the determination in his. She gave a wry smile. "I cried too much."

Something changed in his face, but before he could speak again, she drew a deep breath and said, "The next question is mine: Where are you staying, now that you've given up your hotel room?"

His eyes moved over her face, and his voice was gentle but implacable when he said, "I'm staying here."

CHAPTER TEN

TESSA PULLED HERSELF up very straight, her gaze unwavering. "I haven't asked you to stay."

"I know," he admitted dryly. "That's why I had to invite myself."

As she stared at him, she realized that he was determined to stay, to wear down her resistance to him. He made her feel hunted, and desperation made her angry. "Damn it, Brett, it's over!"

"Not by a long shot. I'm not giving up, baby. I'm not going to let you go. What we have together is too good to just give up on."

"We never had anything *together*!" she said bitterly. "I had love, while you had your investigation. Now you have your guilt, and I...I just don't want any part of it," she finished in a dull tone.

He flinched at the lash of her words. "Yes, I feel guilty! I should have trusted you, but I didn't. When I saw your signature on those checks, I went crazy, because I thought you'd been using me as a hedge against being prosecuted!"

"What a lovely opinion you have of me!" she flared, her small hands knotting into fists at her sides.

Brett shoved his fingers through his thick hair, groping for an explanation. "I'm a loner, Tessa. I'm not used to trusting anyone, or to letting anyone get close to me.

You got so close to me that you knocked me off balance. That's not much of an excuse, but it's the only one I have. I thought you were using me, and it hurt like hell. It hurt so much that I almost vomited. All I could think of was not to let you know that I was hurting. Damn it, I love you!" he said angrily.

Tears stung her eyes. "Sure you do. You love me so much that you never faced me with the evidence. You didn't even give me a chance to defend myself! Do you have any idea what it's like to be arrested, to be booked and fingerprinted, how humiliating it is? I felt dirty! I tried to call you; I kept thinking that if I could just get in touch with you, everything would be all right, that you'd straighten it all out. Can you even begin to imagine how I felt when I learned that *you* had had me arrested?" Her voice became thickened and strained, almost soundless. "You don't know what love is."

He cursed rawly. This was the first time in his life he'd ever told a woman that he loved her, and she didn't believe him! The hell of it was that he could understand her reasoning. She must think that he was motivated by guilt, that he was taking care of her in an effort to assuage that guilt. And there was nothing he could say that would change her mind; there were no words that could ease her pain. Instead of being betrayed, he had betrayed her. By not trusting her, he had lost *her* trust, and he had hurt her so deeply that she might never recover from it. The thought was so unbearable that he rejected it completely; he would do anything in the world for her, except let her walk out of his life. He would do whatever he had to do to convince her that he loved her, to rekindle the love she felt for him. She was his, and if words weren't enough to convince her of that, then he'd have to use more drastic measures.

Watching him with bitter weariness, Tessa saw his face change, saw his eyes narrow with determination, as a subtle shift of expression hardened his features. Abruptly, he looked more dangerous than a crouching panther.

Slowly he reached out and turned off the lamp. A pool of light spilled into the living room from the kitchen, falling across his face and illuminating half of it, while the other half was shadowed. Tessa caught her breath and instinctively moved back a step, but she couldn't look away from him. She was caught, mesmerized by the burning sensuality of his face as he tugged the white cotton shirt out of his pants and slowly pulled it off over his head, then tossed it to the floor. His bronzed skin gleamed darkly, and the hair on his chest made an even darker shadow against his flesh. "If you won't believe me," he said in a rough whisper, "then I'll have to show you."

Tessa took another backward step, her heart leaping high to lodge in her throat, making breathing difficult. Her eyes were huge and haunted as she stared at him. "What...what are you doing?"

He was stalking her with slow, silent movements, his eyes never leaving her face. "You said that you loved me. Were you lying?"

Whatever she had expected, it wasn't to be questioned. The question demanded her attention, and she stared at him, distracted by the anger building in her. "No, I wasn't lying! Did you think I'm a liar as well as a thief?"

He ignored the last part of her response, moving still another step closer to her. "You were engaged twice before, but you didn't make love with either of them, because you didn't really love them. You love *me*, you went to bed with *me*, and you can't forget what we have any more than I can. No matter what, you still love me, don't you?"

"Will a confession make you feel any better?" she asked raggedly, her body stiff with pain. "Yes, I love you, but I won't waste my life on someone who doesn't love me! I went to you; I wanted to tell you that I loved you, that I was innocent, but you never gave me the chance."

"I was going to pieces on the inside," he rasped. "It nearly drove me crazy, thinking that you'd been using me. Damn it, Tessa, you know how that feels! You thought the same thing about me!"

Her eyes were raw, burning with the hell inside her. "There's a slight difference," she said, flinging the words at him like stones. "I wasn't trying to send you to prison!"

"When I could think straight again, I knew that I couldn't let you go to prison. Damn it, listen to me!" he growled, grabbing her arm as she turned away and pulling her back to face him. "When I called that meeting in the D.A.'s office, I still thought you were guilty, but it didn't matter. What mattered was protecting you. There was no way I was going to let you go to prison."

Tessa pulled against the strength of his hands, but he held her effortlessly, his long fingers wrapped around her upper arms. "Let me go," she choked, panic rising in her. She felt stifled by his size, his overwhelming masculinity, and her tenuous hold on her control was slipping. Deep inside her, an insidious need was undermining her resolve; even now, she wanted him, needed him. She needed his heat to ward off the arctic cold that surrounded her; she needed his strength, because she had none left. She was tired, defeated, and she couldn't take much more. "Please," she whimpered. "Let me go."

"No. Never." He shook her lightly. "Tell me that you love me."

"Let me go!"

Watching the way her lips trembled, Brett knew she was close to breaking. He had an agonized moment of indecision about the wisdom of pushing her, but it was his last desperate gamble; he had to break down the wall of icy remoteness she'd built between them, or he'd never be able to reach her again.

"You love me," he said roughly, holding her as she tried to jerk away from him. "I love you. Tell me that you love me. I want to hear it. Tell me!"

Tessa was shaking wildly, staring up at him with desperate eyes. Love him? She ached for him. She felt as if she would die without him, but she'd learned, this past week, that a human being could be acutely miserable and still live, still function. She would give almost anything if she could turn back the clock and totally erase this past week. At least then she would still be living in her fool's paradise. She wouldn't know what it was like to feel the laughter die.

"Tell me that you love me," he insisted, shaking her again.

The acid burning of tears in her eyes blurred his image, then the tears overflowed and began to roll slowly down her cheeks. "Why are you doing this to me?" she whispered. "Haven't you hurt me enough?"

He wouldn't let up. "Tell me that you love me."

"I love you," she said, defeated, giving him the words that he wanted, but the words were stones taken from the wall she'd built to protect herself, and the gap permitted all the forbidden emotions to come rushing in, battering at her, tearing her down. A sobbing gasp broke from her throat, signaling the end of her control. Her head dropped forward and she stood docilely in his grasp, her body shuddering with the force of her weeping. There was something different in her tears, an acceptance of the grief and pain that she'd been denying.

A muscle twitched in Brett's jaw, and he felt his own lips tremble for a moment before he controlled them. Slowly he released her arms and slid his hard hands down to curve around her waist. He pulled her against him so she could feel every line of his body.

Her eyes blinded by tears, Tessa was nevertheless aware that his warm, bare chest was there for her to lay her head on; his powerfully muscled legs supported hers, his thighs taut and corded. He was holding her up, offering her his strength when she had none of her own. Yet she was afraid to depend on that strength, and she turned away from him, only to have him catch her and pull her back against him, and this time her head did fall back on his chest. "How can I trust you?" she wept, not noticing the irony that now their situations had been reversed, but he noticed, and winced.

"In time, love. In time," he breathed. "Just don't throw it away. Give me another chance to show you how much I love you." She was weak now, leaning on him, just as he'd wanted her to be. For now she was utterly defenseless, and he moved to fortify his newly gained position. He bent his head to nibble at her ear, then slid his mouth down the exposed arch of her neck, knowing how sensitive her skin was there. She shuddered and pressed herself against him, her hands reaching back to curve around his thighs and pull him forward, as if she could meld them together. He bit off a groan, sliding his palms up to cover both her breasts.

She rolled her head against his shoulder, tears still rolling down her cheeks, because she wanted him so much. She was afraid to believe him, but she couldn't pull away from him. She was so empty and cold and alone, and he was the warmth that would keep her from dying.

He did groan aloud then, turning her in his arms and lifting her against his chest. "Don't cry, darling. Please don't cry," he whispered as he carried her to bed. He had wanted her to break, but he hadn't known it would hurt so much. All he wanted to do now was to make everything right in her world.

She wrapped her arms around his neck and clung, her face buried in the hollow between his face and shoulder. "I only cried once, right after I was arrested," she gasped between sobs. "But now I can't seem to stop. Oh, Brett, I was so scared!"

"I know, darling, I know." His face was tortured as he placed her on the bed and began undressing her. "I don't ever want to make you cry again." It wasn't easy, getting her clothes off while she clung to his neck, but he managed it. He wouldn't have torn her arms loose for anything in the world. Then he struggled out of his pants and kicked them away, and got into bed with her.

He just held her while she cried, and his own eyes burned. She was his woman, a part of him; it hurt him that she hurt.

At last her sobs became little gasps, then ceased altogether, but still he held her and made no effort to make love to her. Tessa lay quietly in his arms, feeling the soft rasp of his hairy legs against her smooth ones, the hardness of his stomach and chest, the corded strength of his arms around her. She felt as if a momentous decision was forcing itself on her, and she wasn't ready for it, but neither did she want to force an irrevocable break between them. She had thought the break was already there, and she had been in agony at losing him, yet now that another chance had been offered to her, she was afraid to take it. What if she were wrong again? She wanted his love, not his guilt, and if she ever found that he'd offered only a pale image instead of the reality of love, it would break her. Yet she couldn't send him away, not now, when she was so empty and only he could fill her, bring her back to life.

They lay together while he slowly stroked one hand up and down her slender back, the soothing movement lulling her into a drowsy sense of contentment. At least in this moment he was hers. He felt her relaxing against his body. "Better now?" he whispered into her hair.

Her hand moved over his chest, her fingers sliding through the hair. "Yes," she said sleepily. She didn't think about what she said next; the words came out of her subconscious, out of an inborn need to reach out to the man she loved. "Brett…make love to me, please."

His entire body was suddenly taut, quivering with need, the electricity of his sensuality banishing her drowsiness. "Are you sure?"

"Yes," she breathed. "I need you so much." She needed to be as close to him as she could get, to reaffirm her life and freedom in the mingling of their bodies. This night wouldn't answer her questions, but it would help to banish the week of nightmares and desolation. She needed him to make her whole again.

Without another word he rolled atop her, parted her legs, and slid deeply into her. She cried out wordlessly, at both the shock of his entry and the fierce pleasure she felt at their joining, at the moment when they ceased to be two separate beings. He comforted her with a rough murmur, drawing her legs up to wrap them around his waist.

Their lovemaking wasn't prompted so much by passion as it was by a need to come together, to give and receive comfort, yet before long Tessa was gasping as his slow movements wrung new heights of ecstasy from her body. His hands stroked and soothed and excited, and his kisses were so deep and hungry that she was unable to breathe, but breathing wasn't important any longer. The only thing that mattered to her was the man she loved, and in that moment she didn't care what happened.

"I love you," he groaned against her throat. "Tessa!" He gasped her name urgently and seized her hips, lifting her up to meet him. She cried out, too, shuddering with the force of her pleasure and accepting his.

There was silence afterward, but she was content. He lay heavily in her arms, his body damp with sweat, and instead of moving away he pushed himself closer against her. He turned his face into the softness of her neck, murmured something unintelligible, and went to sleep. Tessa held him in her arms, staring at the ceiling in the darkness, wondering why she had asked for his lovemaking, wondering if it had solved anything at all, or only made her thoughts more complicated.

His heavy weight bore down on her, pinning her to the bed, but she wouldn't have moved him for anything. She couldn't regret inviting his lovemaking. It had soothed a deep, crippling pain in her heart. She had been left lost and bewildered by his sudden desertion, and his passion had reassured her that he had really wanted her. She could trust his physical need for her, if not his emotional one.

With his actions that day he had offered her a clear choice, though he probably hadn't meant to give her any choice at all. Her lips moved in a small, resigned smile. Brett Rutland was an autocratic, arrogant, dominating male. Any woman who lived with him would have a constant struggle to keep their relationship balanced. She wanted to be that woman. She *could* be that woman, because Brett had given her the opportunity— if she made the choice to live with him.

She could either trust him or not trust him, and she still felt too confused, too emotionally battered, to rely on herself to make the correct decision. The only thing she didn't doubt was her love for him. That was odd, because she had always thought that love had a limit, that there was a point in any relationship where love could die. That had certainly been her experience with both Will and Andrew, and at the time she had been certain she loved them. Yet had she? What she felt for Brett so far surpassed anything she'd felt before that it made her doubt her own emotions, or at least her ability to read them. Life hadn't always been easy for her. As a young child she had had to accept her father's desertion, and not so many years later the death of her mother. But somehow she had skated around the edges of those emotional disasters, preferring to look at the sun instead of the shadows. The ultimate party girl, that was her. She hadn't been malicious, but still she had slipped away from any relationship that could have touched her deeply, that could have made her care.

Until she met Brett. His character was so intense and powerful that he had overwhelmed her frothy defenses, and at the same time she had been challenged on a very personal, feminine basis by his cool control. Given their particular personalities, it had been inevitable that she would fall in love with him, truly in love for the first time in her life.

He had hurt her more than she had ever thought she would be able to accept from any man, yet it hadn't killed her love for him. She loved him despite everything, and she wouldn't be getting over it.

Welcome to the big time, Tessa, she told herself in aching realization.

A long time later he stirred in her arms and lifted himself higher against her. Tessa felt awareness tighten his muscles, and gently she stroked her palms over his powerful back.

His voice was a low, sleep-roughened rasp of sound, quiet in the darkness that surrounded them. "Have you slept?"

"No," she murmured, her voice still as rough as his. They were a pair, she thought absently. They both sounded like frogs.

Several minutes passed in silence, while his hand moved slowly, exploringly, over her hip and side. "Any regrets?" he finally asked.

"About this? No," she answered slowly.

"What have you been thinking?"

"That I still love you. That I still hurt. That I still don't know what to do."

He sighed. "It isn't easy, is it? Loving. Hell, I didn't even know what it was."

In the quiet, warm darkness, she felt better able to talk to him than she ever had before. There was only his voice, and the warmth of his body, with no outside distraction to break her concentration. She wanted to concentrate on him, to learn everything she could about this man; she knew him physically, but now she needed to know all the little things that would give her the key to his thoughts. "You love your parents, don't you? Your home? There's your horse, your dog, your first-grade teacher...."

A low laugh rumbled through him. "No, I never loved my first-grade teacher. As for the ranch...I don't know if it's love. The ranch is a part of me. I can't separate myself from it; no matter where I am or what I'm doing, it's there in my head." He paused for a moment, as if considering the matter. "Horses and dogs...I've had my favorites, but I can't say that I've ever loved an animal. My father...yes, I love him. I owe my life to him, and it wasn't easy for him to take care of me."

"Your mother died?" Tessa asked gently.

"I don't know. She gave me away when I was a week old. She may still be alive, but it doesn't much matter. There's no connection between us now, no curiosity, or sense of need. There never has been. Tom is my natural father, but he wasn't married to my mother. He was working in southwest Texas when he met her. She was a rancher's daughter, and he was just a hired hand, a drifter, but she was wild and looking for a way out, trying to kick the traces. They would meet in an old line shack."

Tessa lay spellbound, caught up in the tale he was telling her in a low, slow voice. She felt as if he were finally giving her the key to himself, unlocking a portion of that private part of his mind.

"She got pregnant, of course. I imagine she could have gotten an abortion, if she had wanted to risk the back-alley operations they had then, but she chose to have me. I was probably the ultimate gesture of rebellion. It caused an almighty scandal, but she refused to tell her folks who the father was, refused to go away, refused to hide herself until after I was born. Tom tried to get her to marry him, but she refused that, too. Ranch life was exactly what she was trying to get away from, and that was all he could offer her. It was all he knew."

He was silent then for so long that Tessa feared that he wasn't going to tell her any more. She touched his hair, sliding her fingers through the tousled, tawny silk. "And when you were born?"

"When I was born, she named me, nursed me for a week, then got in touch with Tom and told him to meet her at the line shack. She took me with her to meet him, handed me to him, and walked away. That was the last time he saw or heard from her. She never went back home, just kept on going."

"So your father raised you by himself."

"Yeah. He left Texas that day, too, because he was afraid her parents would take me away from him if they knew she hadn't taken me with her." In the darkness, she could feel his grin against her skin. "Can you imagine a rough ranch hand lugging a week-old baby cross-country, not knowing the first thing about kids? I imagine the wonder is that I survived."

She found herself chuckling. "I feel sorrier for your father than I do for you!"

"Well, we both survived the diaper stage, and he was always there for me. We didn't have anything, but we were together. He worked his way around the country, taking what jobs he could get. I guess I've been fed in more ranch house kitchens that you could count, sort of like a puppy who wandered in. I'd play in the yard and barns, waiting for Tom to come back in at night, until I got old enough to go with him."

"How old was that?"

"Four or five, I guess."

"That's not old enough!"

"It was old enough to stay in a saddle all day long. I can't remember when I couldn't ride. By the time I was six, I was working. I could rope and cut, and though I wasn't strong enough to bulldog, I could still help with the branding and dipping."

"What about school?"

"That's what decided Tom to settle down. I had to go to school, or somebody would eventually notify the authorities and I might have been taken away from him.

We were in Wyoming at the time, so he spent every cent he had on a piece of land, built a shack for us to live in, and started ranching for himself, with two cows and a bull and a lot of pure cussedness. We didn't always have a lot to eat, but we didn't starve. I went to school, and did the chores early in the morning and after school. When I was ten, he legally adopted me, so I could have his name. It was the name I'd always used, but it wasn't my legal name. There wasn't any fuss about it; no one knew where my mother was, and my grandparents were getting on in years. They weren't able to take in and handle a ten-year-old hellion, which is what I was."

Tessa continued stroking his hair long after he stopped talking. No wonder he was so aloof, his emotions so controlled! In all his life, there had been only one person he could rely on. He had spent his earliest years leading a transient way of life, with people and places merely stops along the way. His only constant was his father, yet he would have seen that other children had two parents, with a doting mother and a stable homelife, while his own mother had given him away. He had grown up wary, not allowing anyone to get close to him, because the only person he felt able to trust was his father.

Given his childhood, was it any surprise that he hadn't automatically trusted her? Understanding began to ease her mind, bringing her a measure of peace, though even now she didn't know if she'd ever be able to forgive him. Her fingers sifted through his hair. If only she didn't love him so much!

He lifted himself on his elbow, allowing himself access to her breasts, and his hard fingers moved gently over her soft curves, coaxing her velvety nipples into taut little nubs. "When Tom meets you, he's going to melt into a little puddle on the ground. He's got an uncontrollable weakness when it comes to women, anyway, and he's going to fall in love with my delicious little Southern belle." There was a huskier note in his voice now, and he bent his head to suck leisurely at her excited flesh.

Tessa whimpered at the sudden pleasure that jolted her body. He rolled her nipple around with his tongue, then lifted his head to run his hand over her breast in patent satisfaction. "You're well blessed, as delicate as you are. Your bones are so slim I sometimes feel as if I could snap you in two. But here..." He chuckled richly.

Tessa blushed hotly in the darkness; then he put his mouth on her breasts again and it no longer mattered.

She slept afterward, but soon he woke her to love her again. The rest of the night was like that, with him returning to her time and again, demonstrating to her with his body how much he wanted her. She knew that was his purpose, but she needed that intense attention to boost her self-esteem, to restore her faith in her own femininity, and he devoted himself passionately to that goal.

When she woke for the last time to a brightly sunny day, it was to find him propped on his elbow over her, watching her sleep. Dark stubble roughened his jaw, making him look like a roughneck, but his face bore the relaxation of complete physical contentment. He knew what the hours of his lovemaking had done for her, and his satisfaction was plain in his eyes. Their gazes met, and locked.

"Good morning," he murmured, pushing a strand of hair from her eyes.

She yawned, stretching under his appreciative gaze. "Good morning. Aren't you late for work?"

"I'm not going to work. This part is all up to Evan and Sammy. My part is staying here with you and keeping you satisfied."

She regarded him somberly; she was more sensitive now to everything about him, and she knew he was being evasive. "I promise you I won't bolt. Is that what you're afraid of?"

"The thought occurred to me."

"I'm still confused," she said slowly. "I don't know what to do, but last night…I did a lot of thinking. I still love you, and after hearing all the evidence that pointed to me, I can't blame you for thinking that I took that money. What else could you think? I still can't… I can't quite forgive you, but I can't walk away from you, either."

His face tightened at her words. "I won't let you walk away. Give us time; that's all I'm asking."

"All right. I can afford the time; I don't have anything else to do," she said with a residue of bitterness.

He swung off the bed and restlessly swiped his pants up from the floor, where he'd left them the night before. "Do you want to go back to work?" he asked sharply.

"At Carter Engineering? No, I don't think so, not after this. But I'll have to go to work somewhere, won't I? I have the normal assortment of bills to pay."

"Do me a favor. Don't look for anything yet."

"Why shouldn't I?"

He sighed, thrusting his hand through his hair. "Because we won't be living here."

She got out of bed, too, and put her robe on. "Aren't you taking a lot for granted?" she asked quietly.

"Not as much as I want to," he assured her in a grim tone. "Just don't look for work yet. You don't have to worry about money; I'll take care of everything—and don't get your back up at me, you little wildcat. You've been through a rough time and you need a sort of emotional vacation. And since I've moved in on you, it's only fair that I pay my way."

"You're trying to make me dependent on you."

"Is that so bad? Honey, we're trying to work our way through a rough patch. A lack of trust is what caused the problem to begin with. Let's trust each other for a change, emotionally as well as physically."

"For how long? When do you have to go back to San Francisco?"

His face went abruptly blank, and she could read nothing in that expressionless mask. "There's no rush."

His very calmness alarmed her, and she twisted the ties to her robe. "Evan said you could be fired. Is that it?"

"No. I haven't been fired. You don't have to worry about my job, honey."

There was something he wasn't telling her, but his gaze was so deliberately bland that she knew she would be wasting her time trying to pry the information out of him. How was she supposed to trust him when he was still hiding things from her? Frustrated at the way she kept running into an emotional dead end, she turned away abruptly. "I'm going to take a shower."

"That sounds…interesting," he drawled. "I was going to take one myself."

"Fine. You can have the bathroom when I'm finished."

Still naked, totally relaxed, he watched her gather her underwear. "I take it that I'm not invited." He made the words a statement rather than a question.

"No, you're not. It won't take me long. Why don't you start breakfast? Then I'll take over and you can shower. It should be ready by the time you're finished."

He gave in easily. "All right, if that's what you want."

"It is."

She was uneasy, wondering if he might join her anyway, but he was as good as his word. When she left the shower she smelled the delightful aroma of fresh coffee, and the scent made her realize how hungry she was. She dressed hurriedly, then rushed to the kitchen to take over the breakfast preparations. She stopped in the doorway, momentarily stunned at having a tall, powerfully muscled man standing stark naked in her kitchen, whistling through his teeth as he assembled the ingredients for pancakes.

"Why didn't you put on some clothes?" she asked weakly.

"Just letting you get a good look at what you turned down," he explained with dead-level calm as he walked past her.

He'd done that, all right. Her palms were moist, her breathing a little fast, as she mixed the pancake batter and poured it in small circles on the grill. He knew exactly what he'd done to her, because he had taught her, trained her responses until his lightest touch could arouse her.

Right on time, he came back into the kitchen, decently attired in jeans and an open-necked shirt, but still the sight of him made her mouth go dry. He had certainly known what he was doing by moving in with her, she thought dimly. He probably planned on keeping her so drunk on sex that she'd do anything he wanted.

She tensed as she realized what she was thinking. She was automatically attributing ulterior motives to his actions, rather than making an effort to trust him. But you couldn't just make an arbitrary decision to start trusting someone; trust had to be learned, and earned. He had taken very good care of her, and with his lovemaking he had gone a long way toward helping her recover her equilibrium, but a part of her remained wary of him. She didn't want it to be that way. She wanted to simply walk into his arms and forget everything that had happened, but she just couldn't do it. She was still afraid.

"Eat," he said gently, making her realize that she was sitting at the table with her fork motionless in her hand.

"I can't decide," she explained in a low tone, and he knew exactly what she was talking about.

"You don't have to decide now. We have time. Let it ride."

"I do love you," she said achingly.

"I know," he said.

He was restless after they had cleaned the dishes, and he prowled around her small apartment. Several times she started to suggest that he go to work, since he was obviously bored, but there was a growing edge to his temper that made her reluctant to suggest anything to him. She had been depressed and listless, and had let her normal chores slide, but her old energy was back, and she had plenty to do in cleaning and catching up on her laundry, so she generally ignored him and let him prowl. When the telephone rang early in the afternoon, and he leaped for it, she suddenly realized that he'd been waiting for the call.

Hurrying to his side, she tried to piece together the conversation from his noncommittal responses, but he was a master at one-word answers. His eyes were flinty, his mouth a hard line as he listened.

"Okay. I'll be right there," he said, and hung up.

"What is it?" she asked anxiously, dogging his footsteps as he went into the bedroom and began pulling off his clothes. "Have they found out who did it?"

"Maybe," he grunted. He was in slacks and a dress shirt before she realized that he wasn't going to tell her anything else, and as he began capably knotting a tie around his neck, her brows snapped together.

"Oh, no you don't, Brett Rutland! You're not leaving me here without telling me anything!" She kicked off her shoes and wiggled out of her jeans. "I'm coming with you."

"No, you're not." He hooked his jacket over one finger and seized her by the nape of the neck, holding her still while he bent and kissed her roughly. "It could get dirty, and I don't want you hurt, not any more than you already have been. See you later."

"Brett!" she yelled furiously at his back, and her voice cracked.

He stopped at the door and looked over his shoulder

at her. For the first time, she saw the murderous look in his eyes, and she shivered, suddenly glad that that look wasn't directed at her. "I'll be back," he said evenly.

The apartment was silent and empty without him, and her nerves crawled when she remembered the way he had looked. If that look had been meant for her, she'd have died of fright on the spot. He was always controlled. She couldn't imagine him in a rage, yet she sensed that he had been holding on to his control by only the narrowest of margins. He knew who had done the embezzling, who had deliberately blamed it on her, but he hadn't told her. Who could have done it, that he would hesitate to reveal the embezzler's identity to her? Someone she trusted?

She had been too frightened to really wonder about the identity of the criminal, even though she realized the necessity of discovering who it had been. Whoever it was had to hate her, and again Tessa's conception of herself was shaken. What had she done to deserve such hatred, such vindictiveness?

Her thoughts tumbled about like a mad squirrel, trying to recall every woman who worked at Carter Engineering, trying desperately to think of something she had done, but nothing came to mind. She hadn't stolen anyone's lover, or broken up a relationship. She couldn't remember doing anything that would earn her an enemy, yet she had.

Tortured by her inability to find a reason for what had happened, she began to cry, soft, soundless sobs that were full of misery. Where was Brett when she needed him? Didn't he know how painful it was to be so totally in the dark? No, how could he know? Brett had never been in the dark; he was always in control, always on top of the situation. She had reached out to him during the night trying, almost in spite of herself, to mend the rift between them. She loved him; she wanted to trust him with her love, and she wanted to be certain that he loved her in return. Yet he had left her alone with her thoughts, knowing that she must be wild with anxiety and uncertainty. Was that love? Had he walked out to give her the chance to make her decision, taking the chance that, when he returned, she wouldn't be there?

The afternoon became night, and Tessa's nerves were so jittery that she jumped and stifled a small cry when a key turned in the lock and Brett entered, his face tired and lined. Sammy was with him, looking as pale and tired as Tessa felt, but his presence barely registered on her consciousness. She stared at the key in Brett's hand. "You took my house key," she said numbly.

He looked at the key in his hand and grimaced. "Yeah," he said, putting the key back into his pocket. Coming over to her, he looked down at her critically, examining every inch of her. "You've been crying again, damn it," he said fiercely.

"Did you…find out anything?"

Instead of answering, Brett asked, "Is there any fresh coffee? I need something to keep me going."

"No, there isn't. Brett, answer me!"

"I'll make a pot."

She stormed to her feet. "I'm going to throw the pot at you if you don't answer my question!"

An unwilling grin twisted his mouth and brought a gleam to his eyes. "Hellcat," he said with tender affection. "Sammy is going to tell you what's going on."

Tessa whirled on Sammy, who stood with his hands shoved deep in his pockets. His blue eyes were miserable. "It's my fault," he said grimly. He had always seemed so boyish, even though he was older than she, but he looked as if he had aged ten years overnight.

She shook her head. That didn't make any sense at all. "How could it be your fault? You're not the embezzler."

"It's Hillary. She did it for me."

It was as if someone had drawn a curtain aside. Tessa stared at him in horrified realization, immediately seeing the whole of it. All of it was there. Poor Hillary, so shy and unsure of herself, and so much in love with Sammy. Sammy had needed money to develop his electronic ideas; Hillary had gotten it for him. She had had all the opportunity she could want: She worked in a bank; she worked with Sammy, and through him had access to the computers at Carter Engineering; and she was smart enough to know how to do it. Even choosing Tessa as the scapegoat made sense, because Sammy so obviously admired Tessa, because Tessa was bright and charming and confident, relaxed with men, while Hillary froze with shyness.

She looked at Sammy, her eyes brimming with sympathetic tears.

"I traced it," he said hoarsely. "She accessed the computer several times from my apartment. She has a key.... She came and went anytime she wanted. My God, I practically set it up for her! Tessa, I traced it back to my own number!"

He was shaking; she went to him and put her arms

around him, and they clung together. "What happened?" she whispered, aching for him.

"We met her when she got off work at the bank, Mr. Rutland and Evan and I. She saw us and just…started crying. She knew."

"Has he had her arrested yet?" Tessa asked shakily.

"No, I haven't. I wanted to talk to you first," Brett interrupted coolly. He had been leaning, unnoticed, in the doorway. Now he straightened and walked over to Tessa. "My first instinct is to lock her away, for what she did to you more than for taking the money. But I don't want revenge to be my motive for doing anything, so everything's on hold. Evan is with her now, babysitting and waiting for my call."

Appalled, Tessa stared at him. He was asking her to decide the fate of another human being. It was up to her whether he prosecuted Hillary, or let her go. Why was he so certain that revenge wouldn't color *her* thinking? She was human, too! "Brett, don't do this to me."

"I know what I'm asking," he said flatly, not taking his eyes from her. "But you see, baby, I trust your judgment."

CHAPTER ELEVEN

TESSA TREMBLED ALL over as she stood there staring at him, her eyes begging him. She was hurting, he knew; she was acutely sensitive now, reacting to every nuance in the air. This had changed her. Where before she had been effervescent, sparkling like a vintage champagne, now she was quieter, the laughter stilled. He hoped it hadn't gone forever. The charm of that joyous laughter had been what first lured him, yet he loved her anyway; he loved the woman, and her gift of joyousness had been only a part of the reason why he loved her. If she gave him the chance, he intended to devote his life to bringing that sparkle back into her eyes, but first he had to get over the agony of a decision that was only hers to make. Not even Joshua Carter's interest in this matched Tessa's because she was the one who had suffered the most.

"Let her go," she said.

Her voice was faint, but Brett heard her. He went to her and put his hand on her arm, steadying her. "Are you sure?"

Tessa nodded, and Brett eased her down onto the couch. Sammy dropped into a chair as if he'd suddenly gone boneless, and maybe he had.

She clutched at Brett's hands, holding them as if they were lifelines. "Hillary loves him. She did it because she loves him. I can understand that, because I'd go to any lengths for you—" She broke off, afraid that she was saying too much, but her shaky, tumbling words were all he'd hoped to hear, and more. He had the feeling that Tessa did understand, that she knew more than they did, even though she had been told only the bare bones of it.

Tessa looked desperately at Sammy. "Sammy, she loves you. You know that, don't you?"

He looked stunned and exhausted. "I can't take it in. She didn't have any reason to be jealous of you! If anything, you were always trying to get us together."

"But she didn't know that, did she? And that's only part of it. She believed in you, in what you were doing."

"Chewing on it won't do any good," Brett said quietly, the authority in his voice making both of them fall silent. "And wallowing in guilt won't do any good, either. I know. I've already tried it. What we have to do now is work out a solution that Mr. Carter will accept. He's due total reimbursement, if nothing else. The money has been spent. What do you suggest?"

Sammy chewed on his lip. "Nelda is marketable. I've thought of selling her to a computer company, but if that won't work…"

"If you say the computer is marketable, I'll take your word on it. Since you had already planned to sell it anyway, I don't feel that we'll be taking anything away from you, except the amount of money that was stolen."

Relief was plain on Sammy's face. "Do you mean it? It won't be any more complicated than that?"

"It'll be complicated by the time a lawyer gets through with it," Brett said dryly. "And I can't promise that Mr. Carter will go for it, though I think he will. It's the same terms I twisted his arm to get for Tessa, so he shouldn't kick too much about it."

"Will it take very long to get it settled?"

"Nelda will have to be sold, and that could take some time, because you'll want to wait for the best offer, but the legal paperwork won't take that long."

Leaving Tessa, he walked Sammy to the door. Tessa was watching them, and she saw the worried frown on Sammy's face. "I don't know what to do about Hillary," he muttered. "I was trying to get up enough nerve to ask her to marry me, but now..."

"Do what I was going to do," Brett advised sharply. "Put her over your knee and whale the living daylights out of her. That's the least of what she deserves."

He closed the door on Sammy and came back to Tessa's side. He was tenderness itself as he sat down beside her and hugged her against him, his eyes worried. Gently he brushed her hair back from her forehead. "Are you all right? It's over now, really over."

She didn't feel as if *finis* had been written to the episode; when she looked at him, she knew that there were still problems to be solved, but now didn't seem to be the time to go into them. "You don't have to treat me like china," she said with a faint smile. "It was a shock, but I'm not going to break."

"I hated to do that to you, but I couldn't trust myself to make a rational decision. No matter which way I went, I knew I'd always doubt my reasons for doing it."

"And if I had wanted her prosecuted?"

The hard, flinty expression came back into his eyes. "You would have wanted what I wanted."

He was a little frightening, a hard man who wouldn't tolerate any threat against anything or anyone he considered his. The realization, instead of frightening her, made her eyes widen. He felt that way about her. It wasn't guilt, but an expression of something she had sensed the first time he had made love to her. The act had not been one of casual pleasure, but one of possession, in the most basic way. She had become his, which was why he had lashed out at her when he thought she had betrayed him and his trust. Yet even before he knew her to be innocent, he had begun working for her release. Her innocence or guilt hadn't mattered; she was his, and he would have handled it. That was why he had given Sammy that rather primitive advice.

"Were you going to beat me?" she asked, giving him a hard look.

He made no apologies. "I was planning on it. I doubt I'd ever have done it, because I couldn't deliberately hurt you, but thinking about it made me feel better. Now, with Sammy…that girl may get the spanking of her life. When the quiet ones get angry, there's no stopping them. Do you care? Are you really that forgiving?"

"No, I'm not. I'm far more human than that," she replied with a flash of spirit. "I'd like to punch her out. But this has gone on long enough, and I want it to end. Let Sammy take care of her. I just want to put it behind me and forget about it. Besides, if you had prosecuted, Sammy would have been hurt, too, and he didn't deserve it."

He gave a soft sigh, and removed his arm from around her, leaving her feeling faintly chilled. His expression was grim as he leaned forward, resting his

forearms on his thighs. "If you're so generous with a
stranger, why can't you be that generous with me? Why
can't you forgive me and give me a second chance? I'm
not asking for time, but for a real second chance." He
drew a deep breath, waiting for her reaction.

Tessa stared at him, stricken by what he had said,
because it was nothing less than the truth. She *had* been
more generous with a stranger than she had been with
him, and she loved him more than she'd ever thought it
was possible to love anyone or anything. But precisely
because she did love him so much, his lack of trust had
cut her far more deeply than Hillary's treacherous actions. Hillary didn't mean anything to her at all, except
as someone important to one of her friends.

So this was love, she thought painfully. It wasn't only
forgiving, it was taking a chance that her love was returned. He had lashed out at her only when he thought
she'd betrayed him first, and even then, when his first
pain had faded, he had moved swiftly to protect her.
Even thinking that she was guilty, he had forgiven her
and reached out for her.

It was love, and she really didn't have a choice about
trusting him, because she had no life without him.

She had been silent for a long time, and Brett's mouth
had firmed into a grim line. He had one more card to
play, one more chance at convincing her that he loved
her, that he'd do whatever he had to do to protect her.
If she misunderstood his motives now, he didn't know
what he would do, because he was playing his last card.
"Tessa, I've resigned my job."

She made a sharp movement, and the color washed

out of her face. "But…but you told me that you didn't have to worry about your job!"

"I don't. Because I don't have one. I resigned Monday, effective whenever this was finished. The deal I made with Joshua," he said carefully, "was that in exchange for you, I would continue to do the occasional consulting job for him. That's what he called it, anyway. It means I'll get the easy jobs like negotiating the settlement of a strike, or industrial espionage, things like that. But for the most part, I intend to be on the ranch with you, raising kids and cattle."

Her heart was doing crazy things in her chest, interfering with her breathing. "Is that a proposal?" she demanded.

"I guess it is. I intend to be the father of your children, and I'd like for it to be legal." His entire world hinged on her answer, and he couldn't read her expression at all. He started to sweat. "Do you love me enough to forgive me?"

She got to her feet, propelled by a sudden need for action, anything to give herself something to do. "It was never a matter of forgiving," she said jerkily. "I love you so much I think I can forgive you anything. That doesn't mean I'd let you get away with it," she added, in case he got the wrong idea. "It just means I'd forgive you for it."

Something was changing in his face; his navy eyes were lighting, as if fired from the inside. "After you threw hot lemonade on me? Or hit me over the head with something?"

"Or kicked you out of our bed."

"Whoa, honey, you're talking nasty now. If there's

one place I'm going to be, it's in bed with you. But if you forgive me, what was the problem?"

"I was trying to decide if I should take you without being sure you loved me, or wait until I was sure," she said baldly.

He surged to his feet, towering over her, his shoulders so broad that they blocked out the light. "Would you like a demonstration of what it's like to be a rancher's wife?"

Suddenly she was the old Tessa again, her long lashes sweeping down languidly to hide the vibrant sparkle in her green eyes. "Why, I believe I would," she said in her slowest, most wicked drawl, the one that made Brett's loins turn to molten lava. With a low growl, he tossed her over his shoulder and carried her off to bed.

SOME MEN DIDN'T know when they were well off, he thought an hour later. She was turning the charm on him, enticing him and teasing him and generally driving him crazy, and even though he knew he was being managed, there wasn't a damn thing he could do to help himself.

She lay propped above him, her lovely breasts nestled into the hair that covered his chest and doing a good job of distracting him. She was winding one finger through the curls of hair, then she moved it on to his ear, his mouth, his throat, across his shoulder and down his arm, over to his side, down his hip…. What she did with that one finger was amazing. He shifted restlessly, considering tossing her over on her back and finishing what she'd started, but she was still talking.

"I want to get married in Tennessee," she murmured,

nipping at his chin with her white teeth, then kissing the slight sting away. "In our old church in Sevierville, with Aunt Silver there. You do want your father to be best man, don't you?"

"I don't care," he muttered in raw frustration, sitting up abruptly and dumping her off his chest. As he reached for her she drew away, but she caught his hand and carried his fingers to her lips, where she nibbled and sucked at each of his fingertips in turn.

Her voice was dreamy. "I want to show you the farm, and the old country roads. Gatlinburg is best in the spring and summer, I think. We can go into all the old-time crafts stores on Glades Road, and walk in the mountains. I want to show you the whole park. We can go to the Chimneys, and Cade's Cove, and Grandfather Mountain. And I want to see *Unto These Hills* one last time—"

He put his hand over her mouth, stifling the flow of words. "Tessa, darling, *yes*! I'll agree to anything you want. I'll marry you anywhere you want, in front of as many people as you want, and I'll hike from Tennessee to Wyoming with you, if that's what you want. Now, does that cover everything?"

A suspicious sound came from behind his hand, and he looked into green eyes that were brimming with laughter, sparkling in the way that he loved. She'd been playing with him, he realized, deliberately driving him mad with frustration, and loving her feminine power to do so. If he hadn't been so certain of her intention of fully satisfying him, he'd have erupted into rage, but all he could do was fall back on the bed, his chest heaving with his heavy breathing.

He'd asked for it. She was just what he wanted, every devilish, delicious inch of her. He had to be crazy, considering what a chase she was going to lead him on for the rest of their lives. Then he chuckled, and before she could evade him again, he had reached out a brawny arm and toppled her onto the bed. Quickly he covered her, parting her legs and taking her. "This is what you get for teasing me," he said, kissing her hungrily.

An expression of delight spread across her lovely, exotic face, radiant now with his love. "Really?" she drawled. "Oh, good."

THE MOONLIGHT SPILLED across the big bed, lighting a room with polished wooden floors covered by a hand-woven rug. The bed was long and wide, big enough to accommodate the length of the man who sprawled in it. Tessa sat up in the bed, folding her arms and resting them on top of her knees, and putting her chin on top of her arms. They had been married only that morning, and Brett had barely given her time to pack before he'd whisked her to Knoxville to catch a plane. She had hugged Aunt Silver and cried, knowing that this time she was truly leaving. Her home would be in Wyoming now, not in Tennessee. Silver had cried, too, until Tom, Brett's father, had snatched her up in his brawny arms and kissed her until she'd forgotten about crying.

"Come visit," he'd growled to the astonished woman in his arms. "I'd love to have you." His deep voice had given the words another meaning, probably his real meaning, because Tom was a big, hard, battle-scarred old tomcat of a man.

The flight had been a long one, from Knoxville to

Chicago to Denver, then to Cheyenne, and they had flown the last leg of the journey in their own plane. By then Tessa had been exhausted, curled up in her seat sound asleep. Brett had shaken her awake only when the plane was on the ground at the ranch. The drive from the dirt airstrip to the ranch house had been a short one, but she'd been fully awake by the time they reached the house. Brett had carried her inside and straight up to his room, and a grinning Tom had brought their suitcases in.

"We have a private bathroom," Brett had said, opening a door off the bedroom. "Are you hungry, or would you rather take a bath and go to bed?"

Tessa had stretched and yawned. "Why don't I take a bath, then get something to eat, then go to bed? How does that sound?"

"Too damned long," he muttered. He looked longingly at the big bed.

"Poor baby, are you tired?" she'd purred.

"No."

"Hungry?"

"Yes."

It had been obvious that her man wasn't concerned with his stomach. She had slowly unbuttoned her blouse and drawn it off, then unhooked her bra and dropped it. "Why don't you take a shower with me?" she'd suggested innocently. "That would save time."

His eyes had narrowed, and his hands had gone to the buttons of his shirt. "I hope you're not really hungry, darling, because it could be a while before you have dinner. As a matter of fact, we'll probably have to call it breakfast."

"You can take me down for a midnight snack," she had said, stepping out of her skirt.

"Deal."

Now she really was hungry, and it was long after midnight. His hand touched her back, but she wasn't startled. Gently his long fingers moved down her spine.

"I fantasized about this, the first night I made love to you." His smoky, whiskey-rough voice was low, and it rubbed over her like a caress. "I held you after you'd gone to sleep, and I thought of how it would be to make love to you in this bed, and hold you when the loving was finished. I decided then that I was going to marry you."

She turned and went into his arms, rubbing her face into the hair on his chest. "Was it as good as your fantasy?"

He laughed. "It was better. You were awake this time."

"Good enough that you'd like to do it again?"

"Now, that's a foolish question if I've ever heard one."

"There's a purpose to it. I was about to point out that if you want to keep my strength up, you're going to have to feed me."

"All right, Mrs. Rutland, hint taken." He got out of bed and pulled on his pants. He began zipping them, then looked up at her as she tried to straighten the tangle of her nightgown. Even in the moonlight he could tell that her lips were sweetly swollen, her hair mussed. She wore the look of a woman in love, and a woman who had been thoroughly loved.

"I'm glad you're my wife," he said simply.

Tessa discarded the nightgown and made do with her robe, tying the belt securely around her slender waist. "I am, too," she said, and went into his arms. The horrible, nightmarish week was gone now, in the past where it belonged. She had changed, yes, but so had he. They had both let their barriers down, because there was no room for barriers between them. How could she not trust this man? Not only was her life safe in his hands, but also her love.

* * * * *

WHITE LIES

CHAPTER ONE

IN RANKING THE worst days of her life, this one probably wasn't number one, but it was definitely in the top three.

Jay Granger had held her temper all day, rigidly controlling herself until her head was throbbing and her stomach burning. Not even during the jolting ride in a succession of crowded buses had she allowed her control to crack. All day long she had forced herself to stay calm despite the pent-up frustration and rage that filled her, and now she felt as if she couldn't relax her own mental restraints. She just wanted to be alone.

So she silently endured having her toes stepped on, her ribs relocated by careless elbows, and her nostrils assailed by close-packed humanity. It began to rain just before she got off the last bus, a slow, cold rain that had chilled her to the bone by the time she walked the two blocks to her apartment building. Naturally she didn't have an umbrella with her; it was supposed to have been a sunny day. The clouds hadn't cleared all day long.

But at last she reached her apartment, where she was safe from curious eyes, either sympathetic or jeering. She was alone, blessedly alone. A sigh of relief broke from her lips as she started to close the door; then her control cracked and she slammed the door with every ounce of strength in her arm. It crashed against the frame with a resounding thud, but the small act of violence didn't release her tension. Trashing her entire office building might help, or choking Farrell Wordlaw, but both those actions were denied her.

When she thought of the way she had worked for the past five years, the fourteen- and sixteen-hour days, the work she had brought home on the weekends, she wanted to scream. She wanted to throw something. Yes, she definitely wanted to choke Farrell Wordlaw. But that wasn't *appropriate* behavior for a professional woman, a chic and sophisticated executive in a prestigious investment-banking firm. On the other hand, it was entirely appropriate for someone who had just joined the ranks of the unemployed.

Damn them.

For five years she had dedicated herself to her job, ruthlessly stifling those parts of her personality that didn't fit the image. At first it had been mostly because she needed the job and the money, but Jay was too intense to do anything by half measures. Soon she had become caught up in the teeming rat race—the constant striving for success, for new triumphs, bigger and better deals—and that world had been her life for five years. Today she had been kicked out of it.

It wasn't that she hadn't been successful; she had. Maybe too successful. Some people hadn't liked dealing with her because she was a woman. Realizing that, Jay had tried to be as straightforward and aggressive as any man, to reassure her clients that she would take care of them as well as a man could. To that end she had changed her habits of speech, her wardrobe, never let even a hint of a tear sparkle in her eyes, never giggled, and learned how to drink Scotch, though she had never learned to enjoy it. She had paid for such rigid control with headaches and a constant burning in her stomach, but nevertheless she had thrown herself into the role because, for all its stresses, she had enjoyed the challenge. It was an exciting job, with the lure of a fast trip up the corporate ladder, and for the time being, she had been willing to pay the price.

Well, it was over, by decree of Farrell Wordlaw. He was very sorry, but her style just wasn't "compatible" with the image Wordlaw, Wilson & Trusler wanted to project. He deeply appreciated her efforts, et cetera, et cetera, and would certainly give her a glowing reference, as well as two weeks' notice to get her affairs in order. None of that changed the truth, and she knew it as well as he. She was being pushed out to make room for Duncan Wordlaw, Farrell's son, who had joined the firm the year before and whose performance always ranked second, behind Jay's. She was showing up the senior partner's son, so she had to go. Instead of the promotion she'd been expecting, she'd been handed a pink slip.

She was furious, with no way to express it. It would give her the greatest satisfaction to walk out now and leave Wordlaw scrambling to handle her pending work, but the cold, hard fact was that she needed her salary for those two weeks. If she didn't find another well-paying job immediately, she would lose her apartment. She had lived within her means, but as her salary had gone up so had her standard of living, and she had very little in savings. She certainly hadn't expected to lose her job because Duncan Wordlaw was an underachiever!

Whenever Steve had lost a job, he'd just shrugged and laughed, telling her not to sweat it, he'd find another. And he always had, too. Jobs hadn't been that important to Steve; neither had security. Jay gave a tight little laugh as she opened a bottle of antacid tablets and shook two of them into her hand. Steve! She hadn't thought about him in years. One thing was certain, she would never be as uncaring about unemployment as he had been. She liked knowing where her next meal was coming from; Steve liked excitement. He'd needed the hot flow of adrenaline more than he'd needed her, and finally that had ended their marriage.

But at least Steve would never be this strung out on nerves, she thought as she chewed the chalky tablets and waited for them to ease the burning in her stomach. Steve would have snapped his fingers at Farrell Wordlaw and told him what he could do with his two weeks' notice, then walked out whistling. Maybe Steve's attitude was irresponsible, but he would never let a mere job get the best of him.

Well, that was Steve's personality, not hers. He'd been fun, but in the end their differences had been greater than the attraction between them. They had parted on a friendly basis, though she'd been exasperated, as well. Steve would never grow up.

Why was she thinking of him now? Was it because she associated unemployment with his name? She began to laugh, realizing she'd done exactly that. Still chuckling, she ran water into a glass and lifted it in a toast. "To the good times," she said. They'd had a lot of good times, laughing and playing like the two healthy young animals they'd been, but it hadn't lasted.

Then she forgot about him as worry surged into her mind again. She had to find another job immediately, a well-paying job, but she didn't trust Farrell to give her a glowing recommendation. He might praise her to the skies in writing, but then he would spread the word around the New York investment-banking community that she didn't "fit in." Maybe she should try something else. But her experience was in investment banking, and she didn't have the financial reserves to train for another field.

With a sudden feeling of panic, she realized that she was thirty years old and had no idea what she was going to do with her life. She didn't want to spend the rest of it making deals while living on her nerves and an endless supply of antacid tablets, spending all her free time resting in an effort to build up her flagging energy. In reacting against Steve's let-tomorrow-take-care-of-itself-while-I-have-fun-today philosophy, she had gone to the opposite extreme and cut fun out of her life.

She had opened the refrigerator door and was looking at her supply of frozen microwave dinners with an expression of distaste when the doorman buzzed. Deciding to forget about dinner, something she'd done too often lately, she depressed the switch. "Yes, Dennis?"

"Mr. Payne and Mr. McCoy are here to see you, Ms. Granger," Dennis said smoothly. "From the FBI."

"What?" Jay asked, startled, sure she'd misunderstood.

Dennis repeated the message, but the words remained the same.

She was totally dumbfounded. "Send them up," she said, because she didn't know what else to do. FBI? What on earth? Unless slamming your apartment door was somehow against federal law, the worst she could be accused of was tearing the tags off her mattress and pillows. Well, why not? This was a perfectly rotten end to a perfectly rotten day.

The doorbell rang a moment later, and she hurried to open the door, her face still a picture of confusion. The rather nondescript, modestly suited men who stood there both presented badges and identification for her inspection.

"I'm Frank Payne," the older of the two men said. "This is Gilbert McCoy. We'd like to talk to you, if we may."

Jay gestured them into the apartment. "I'm at a total loss," she confessed. "Please sit down. Would you like coffee?"

A look of relief passed over Frank Payne's pleasant face. "Please," he said with heartfelt sincerity. "It's been a long day."

Jay went into the kitchen and hurriedly put on a pot of coffee; then, to be on the safe side, she chewed two more antacid tablets. Finally she took a deep breath and walked out to where the two men were comfortably ensconced on her soft, chic, gray-blue sofa. "What have I done?" she asked, only half-joking.

Both men smiled. "Nothing," McCoy assured her, grinning. "We just want to talk to you about a former acquaintance."

She sank down in the matching gray-blue chair, sighing in relief. The burning in her stomach subsided a little. "Which former acquaintance?" Maybe they were after Farrell Wordlaw; maybe there was justice in the world, after all.

Frank Payne took a small notebook out of his inner coat pocket and opened it, evidently consulting his notes. "Are you Janet Jean Granger, formerly married to Steve Crossfield?"

"Yes." So this had something to do with Steve. She should have known. Still, she was amazed, as if she'd somehow conjured up these two men just by thinking of Steve earlier, something she almost never did. He was so far removed from her life now that she couldn't even form a clear picture in her mind of how he'd looked. But what had he gotten himself into, with his driving need for excitement?

"Does your ex-husband have any relatives? Anyone who might be close to him?"

Slowly Jay shook her head. "Steve is an orphan. He was raised in a series of foster homes, and as far as I know, he didn't stay in touch with any of his foster parents. As for any close friends—" she shrugged "—I haven't seen or heard from him since our divorce five years ago, so I don't have any idea who his friends might be."

Payne frowned, rubbing the deep lines between his brows. "Would you remember the name of a dentist he used while you were married, or perhaps a doctor?"

Jay shook her head, staring at him. "No. Steve was disgustingly healthy."

The two men looked at each other, frowning. McCoy

said quietly, "Damn, this isn't going to be easy. We're running into one dead end after another."

Payne's face was deeply lined with fatigue, and something else. He looked back at Jay, his eyes worried. "Do you think that coffee's ready yet, Ms. Granger?"

"It should be. I'll be right back." Without knowing why, Jay felt shaken as she went into the kitchen and began putting cups, cream and sugar on a tray. The coffee had finished brewing, and she transferred the pot to the tray, but then just stood there, staring down at the wafting steam. Steve had to be in serious trouble, really serious, and she regretted it even though there was nothing she could do. It had been inevitable, though. He'd always been chasing after adventure, and unfortunately adventure often went hand in hand with trouble. It had been only a matter of time before the odds caught up with him.

She carried the tray into the living room and placed it on the low table in front of the sofa, her brow furrowed into a worried frown. "What has Steve done?"

"Nothing illegal, that we know of," Payne said hastily. "It's just that he was involved in a…sensitive situation."

Steve hadn't done anything illegal, but the FBI was investigating him? Jay's frown deepened as she poured three cups of coffee. "What sort of sensitive situation?"

Payne looked at her with a troubled expression, and suddenly she noticed that he had very nice eyes, clear and strangely sympathetic. Gentle eyes. Not at all the kind of eyes she would have expected an FBI agent to possess. He cleared his throat. "Very sensitive. We don't even know why he was there. But we need, very badly, to find someone who can make a positive identification of him."

Jay went white, the ramifications of that quiet, sinister statement burning in her mind. Steve was dead. Even though the love she'd felt for him had long since faded away, she knew a piercing grief for what had been. He'd been so much fun, always laughing, his brown eyes lit with devilish merriment. It was as if part of her own childhood had died, to know that his laughter had been stilled. "He's dead," she said dully, staring at the cup in her hand as it began to shake, sloshing the coffee back and forth.

Payne quickly reached out and took the cup from her, placing it on the tray. "We don't know," he said, his face even more troubled. "There was an explosion; one man survived. We think it's Crossfield, but we aren't certain, and it's critical that we know. I can't explain more than that."

It had been a long, terrible day, and it wasn't getting any better. She put her shaking hands to her temples and pressed hard, trying to make sense of what he'd told her. "Wasn't there any identification on him?"

"No," Payne said.

"Then why do you think it's Steve?"

"We know he was there. Part of his driver's license was found."

"Why can't you just look at him and tell who he is?" she cried. "Why can't you identify the others and find out who he is by process of elimination?"

McCoy looked away. Payne's gentle eyes darkened. "There wasn't enough left to identify. Nothing."

She didn't want to hear any more, didn't want to

know any of the details, though she could guess at the horrible carnage. She was suddenly cold, as if her blood had stopped pumping. "Steve?" she asked faintly.

"The man who survived is in critical condition, but the doctors are what they call 'cautiously optimistic.' He has a chance. Two days ago, they were certain he wouldn't last through the night."

"Why is it so important that you know right now who he is? If he lives, you can ask him. If he dies—" She halted abruptly. She couldn't say the words, but she thought them. If he died, it wouldn't matter. There would be no survivors, and they would close their files.

"I can't tell you anything except that we need to know who this man is. We need to know who died, so certain steps can be taken. Ms. Granger, I *can* tell you that my agency isn't directly involved in the situation. We're merely cooperating with others, because this concerns national security."

Suddenly Jay knew what they wanted from her. They would have been glad if she could have helped them locate any dental or medical records on Steve, but that wasn't their prime objective. They wanted her to go with them, to personally identify the injured man as Steve.

In a dull voice she asked, "Can't they tell if this man matches the general description of any of their own people? Surely they have measurements, fingerprints, that sort of thing?"

She was looking down, so she didn't see the quick wariness in Payne's eyes. He cleared his throat again. "Your husband—ex-husband—and our man are… were…the same general size. Fingerprints aren't possible; his hands are burned. But you know more about him than anyone else we can find. There might be something about him that you recognize, some little birthmark or scar that you remember."

It still confused her; she couldn't understand why they wouldn't be able to recognize their own man, unless he was so horribly mutilated... Shivering, she didn't let herself complete the thought, didn't let the picture form in her mind. What if it *was* Steve? She didn't hate him, had never hated him. He was a rascal, but he'd never been cruel or meanhearted; even after she had stopped loving him, she had still been fond of him, in an exasperated way.

"You want me to go with you," she said, making it a statement instead of a question.

"Please," Payne replied quietly.

She didn't want to, but he had made it seem like her patriotic duty. "All right. I'll get my coat. Where is he?"

Payne cleared his throat again and Jay tensed. She'd already learned that he did that whenever he had to tell her something awkward or unpleasant. "He's at Bethesda Naval Hospital in D.C. You'll need to pack a small suitcase. We have a private jet waiting for us at Kennedy."

Things were moving too fast for her to understand; she felt as if all she could do was follow the path of least resistance. Too much had happened today. First she had been fired, a brutal blow in itself, and now this. The security she had worked so hard to attain for herself had vanished in a few short minutes in Farrell Wordlaw's office, leaving her spinning helplessly, unable to get her feet back on the ground. Her life had been so *quiet* for the past five years; how could all this have happened so quickly?

Numbly she packed two dresses that traveled well, then collected her cosmetics from the bathroom. As she shoved what she needed into a small zippered plastic bag, she was stunned by her own reflection in the mirror. She looked so white and strained, and thin. Unhealthily thin. Her eyes were hollow and her cheekbones too prominent, the result of working long hours and living on antacid tablets. As soon as she returned to the city she would have to begin looking for another job, as well as working out her notice, which would mean more skipped meals.

Then she felt ashamed of herself. Why was she worrying about a job when Steve—or someone—was lying in a hospital bed fighting for his life? Steve had always told her that she worried too much about work, that she couldn't enjoy today because she was always worried about tomorrow. Maybe he was right.

Steve! Sudden tears blurred her eyes as she stuffed the cosmetic bag into her small overnighter. She hoped he would be all right.

At the last moment she remembered to pack fresh underwear. She was rattled, oddly disorganized, but finally she zipped the case and got her purse. "I'm ready," she said as she stepped out of the bedroom.

Gratefully she saw that one of the men had carried the coffee things into the kitchen. McCoy took the case from her hand, and she got her coat from the closet; Payne silently helped her into it. She looked around to make certain all the lights were off; then the three of them stepped into the hallway, and she locked the door behind her, wondering why she felt as if she would never be back.

SHE SLEPT ON the plane. She hadn't meant to, but almost as soon as they were airborne and she relaxed in the comfortable leather seat, her eyelids became too heavy to keep open. She didn't feel Payne spread a light blanket over her.

Payne sat across from her, watching her broodingly. He wasn't quite comfortable with what he was doing, dragging an innocent woman into this mess. Not even McCoy knew how much of a mess it was, how complicated it had become; as far as the other man knew, the situation was exactly the way he'd outlined it to Jay Granger: a simple matter of identification. Only a handful of people knew that it was more; maybe only two others besides himself. Maybe only one other, but that one carried a lot of power. When *he* wanted something done, it was done. Payne had known him for years, but had never managed to be comfortable in his presence.

She looked tired and oddly frail. She was too thin. She was about five-six, but he doubted she weighed much over a hundred pounds, and something about her made him think such thinness wasn't normal for her. He wondered if she was strong enough to be used as a shield.

She was probably very pretty when she was rested, and when she had some meat on her bones. Her hair was nice, a kind of honey brown, as thick and sleek as an otter's coat, and her eyes were dark blue. But now she just looked tired. It hadn't been an easy day for her.

Still, she had asked some questions that had made him uncomfortable. If she hadn't been so tired and upset she might have pinned him down on some things he didn't want to discuss, asked questions in front of McCoy that he didn't want raised. It was essential to the plan that everything be taken at face value. There could be no doubt at all.

THE FLIGHT FROM New York to Bethesda was a short one, but the nap refreshed her, gave her back a sense of balance. The only thing was, the more alert she felt, the more unreal this entire situation seemed. She checked her watch as Payne and McCoy escorted her off the private jet when they landed at Washington National and into a government car waiting on the tarmac for them, and was startled to see that it was only nine o'clock. Only a few hours had passed, yet her life had been turned upside down.

"Why Bethesda?" she murmured to Payne as the car purred down the street, a few flakes of snow drifting down like flower petals on a light breeze. She stared at the snowflakes, wondering absently if an early-winter snowstorm would keep her from getting home. "Why not a civilian hospital?"

"Security." Payne's quiet voice barely reached her ears. "Don't worry. The best trauma experts were called in to work on him, civilian and military. We're doing the best we can for your husband."

"Ex-husband," Jay said faintly.

"Yes. Sorry."

As they turned onto Wisconsin Avenue, which would eventually take them to the Naval Medical Center, the snow became a little heavier. Payne was glad she hadn't asked any more questions about why the man was in a military hospital instead of, say, Georgetown University Hospital. Of course, he'd told her the truth, as far as it went. Security *was* the reason he was at Bethesda. It just wasn't the only reason. He watched the snow swirling down and wondered if all the loose threads could possibly be woven into a believable whole.

When they reached the medical center, only Payne got out of the car with her; McCoy nodded briefly in farewell and drove away. Snowflakes quickly silvered their hair as Payne took her elbow and hurried her inside, where the welcome warmth just as quickly melted the lacy flakes. No one paid them any attention as they took an elevator upward.

When the elevator doors opened, they stepped out into a quiet corridor. "This is the ICU floor," Payne said. "His room is this way."

They turned to the left, where double doors were guarded by two stern young men in uniform, both of whom wore pistols. Payne must have been known on sight, for one of the guards quickly opened a door for them. "Thank you," Payne said courteously as they passed.

The unit was deserted, except for the nurses who monitored all the life-support systems and continually checked on the patients, but still Jay sensed a quiet hum that pervaded every corner of the unit—the sound of the machines that kept the patients alive or aided in their recovery. For the first time it struck her that Steve must be hooked up to one or more of those machines, unable to move, and her steps faltered. It was just so hard to take in.

Payne's hand remained under her elbow, unobtrusively providing her with support. He stopped before a door and turned to her, his clear gray eyes full of concern. "I want to prepare you a little. He's badly injured. His skull was fractured, and the bones in his face were crushed. He's breathing through a trach tube. Don't expect him to look like the man you remember." He waited a moment, watching her, but she didn't say anything, and finally he opened the door.

Jay stepped into the room, and for a split second both her heart and lungs seemed to stop functioning. Then her heart lurched into rhythm again, and she drew a deep, painful breath. Tears sprang to her eyes as she stared at the inert form on the white hospital bed, and his name trembled soundlessly on her lips. It didn't seem possible that this...*this* could be Steve.

The man on the bed was almost literally a mummy. Both legs were broken and encased in pristine plaster casts, supported by a network of pulleys and slings. His hands were wrapped in bandages that extended almost to his elbows. His head and face were swathed in gauze, with extra-thick pads over his eyes; only his lips, chin and jaw were visible, and they were swollen and discolored. His breath whistled faintly but regularly from the tube in his throat, and various other tubes ran into his body. Monitors overhead recorded every detail of his bodily functions. And he was still. He was so still.

Her throat was so dry that speaking was painful. "How can I possibly identify him?" she asked rawly. "You *knew* I couldn't. You knew how he looks!"

Payne was watching her with sympathy. "I'm sorry, I know it's a shock. But we need for you to try. You were married to Steve Crossfield. You know him better than any other person on earth. Maybe there's some little detail you remember, a scar or a mole, a birthmark. Anything. Take your time and look at him. I'll be just outside."

He went out and closed the door behind him, leaving her alone in the room with that motionless figure and the quiet beeping of the monitors, the weak whistle of his breathing. Her hands knotted into fists, and tears blurred her eyes again. Whether this man was Steve or not, a pity so acute it was painful filled her.

Somehow her feet carried her closer to the bed. She carefully avoided the tubes and wires while never looking away from his face—or as much of his face as she could see. Steve? Was this really Steve?

She knew what Payne wanted. He hadn't actually spelled it out, but he hadn't needed to. He wanted her to lift the sheet away and study this man while he lay there unconscious and helpless, naked except for the bandages over his wounds. He thought she would have a wife's intimate knowledge of her husband's body, but five years is a long time. She could remember Steve's grin, and the devilish sparkle in his chocolaty brown eyes, but other details had long since faded from her mind.

It wouldn't matter to this man if she stripped back the sheet and looked at him. He was unconscious; he might well die, even now, with all these miracle machines hooked up to his body. He would never know. And as Payne would say, she would be doing her country a service if she could somehow identify this man as Steve Crossfield, or as definitely not.

She couldn't stop looking at him. He was so badly hurt. How could anyone be injured this critically and still live? If he were granted a lucid moment, right now, would he even want to live? Would he be able to walk again? Use his hands? See? Think? Or would he take stock of his injuries and tell the doctors, "Thanks, guys, but I think I'll take my chances at the Pearly Gates."

But perhaps he had a tremendous will to live. Perhaps that was what had kept him alive this long, an unconscious, deep-seated will to *be*. Fierce determination could move mountains.

Hesitantly she stretched out her hand and touched his right arm, just above the bandages that covered his burns. His skin was hot to the touch, and she jerked her fingers back in surprise. Somehow she had thought he would be cold. This intense heat was another sign of how brightly life still burned inside him, despite his stillness. Slowly her hand returned to his arm, lightly resting on the smooth skin just below the inside of his elbow, taking care not to disturb the IV needle that dripped a clear liquid into a vein.

He was warm. He was alive.

Her heart was pounding in her chest, some intense emotion welling up in her until she thought she would burst from the effort of trying to control it. It staggered her to think of what he had been through, yet he was still fighting, defying the odds, his spirit too fierce and proud to just let go. If she could have, she would have suffered the pain in his place.

And his body had been invaded enough. Needles

pierced his veins; wire and electrodes picked up and broadcast his every heartbeat. As if he didn't have enough wounds already, the doctors had made more to insert drainage tubes in his chest and side, and there were other tubes, as well. Every day a host of strangers looked at him and treated him as if he were nothing but a slab of meat, all to save his life.

But she wouldn't invade his privacy, not in this manner. Modesty might not mean anything to him, but it was still his choice to make.

All her attention was focused on him; nothing else in the world existed in this moment except the man lying so still in the hospital bed. Was this Steve? Would she feel some sense of familiarity, despite the disfiguring swelling and the bandages that swathed him? She tried to remember.

Had Steve been this muscular? Had his arms been this thick, his chest this deep? He could have changed, gained weight, done a lot of physical work that would have developed his shoulders and arms more, so she couldn't go by that. Men got heavier in the chest as they matured.

His chest had been shaved. She looked at the dark stubble of body hair. Steve had had chest hair, though not a lot of it.

His beard? She looked at his jaw, what she could see of it, but his face was so swollen that she couldn't find anything familiar. Even his lips were swollen.

Something wet trickled down her cheek, and in surprise she dashed her hand across her face. She hadn't even realized she was crying.

Payne reentered the room and silently offered her his

handkerchief. When she had wiped her face he led her away from the bedside, his arm warm and comforting around her waist, letting her lean on him. "I'm sorry," he finally offered. "I know it isn't easy."

She shook her head, feeling like a fool for breaking down like that, especially in light of what she had to tell him. "I don't know. I'm sorry, but I can't tell if he's Steve, or not. I just...can't."

"Do you think he could be?" Payne asked insistently.

Jay rubbed her temples. "I suppose so. I can't *tell*. There are so many bandages—"

"I understand. I know how difficult it is. But I need something to tell my superiors. Was your husband that tall? Was there anything at all familiar about him?"

If he understood, why did he keep pushing? Her headache was getting worse by the second. "I just don't know!" she cried. "I guess Steve is that tall, but it's hard to tell when he's lying down. Steve has dark hair and brown eyes, but I can't even tell that much about this man!"

Payne looked down at her. "It's on his medical sheet," he said quietly. "Brown hair and brown eyes."

For a moment the import of that didn't register; then her eyes widened. She hadn't felt any sense of recognition for the man at all, but she was still dazed by the storm of emotion he *had* caused in her: pity, yes, but also awe, that he was still alive and fighting, and an almost staggering respect for the determination and sheer guts he must have.

Very faintly, her face white, she said, "Then he must be Steve, mustn't he?"

A flash of relief crossed Payne's face, then was gone

before she could be certain it was there. He nodded.
"I'll notify our people that you've verified his identity.
He's Steve Crossfield."

CHAPTER TWO

WHEN JAY AWOKE the next morning she lay very still in the bed, staring around the unfamiliar hotel room and trying to orient herself. The events of the previous day were mostly a blur, except for the crystal-clear memory she had of the injured man in the hospital. Steve. That man was Steve.

She should have recognized him. Even though it had been five years, she had once loved him. *Something* about him should have been familiar, despite the disfiguring bruises and swelling. An odd feeling of guilt assailed her, though she knew it was ridiculous, but it was as if she had let him down somehow, reduced him to the level of being too unimportant in her life for her to remember how he looked.

Grimacing, Jay got out of bed. There she went again, letting things matter too much to her. Steve had constantly told her to lighten up, and his tone had sometimes been full of impatience. That was another area where they had been incompatible. She was too intense, too involved with everyday life and the world around her, while Steve had skated blithely on the surface.

She was free to return to New York that morning, but she was reluctant to do so. It was only Saturday; there was no hurry as long as she returned in time to go to work Monday morning. She didn't want to sit in her apartment all weekend long and brood about being unemployed, and she wanted to see Steve again. That seemed to be what Payne wanted, too. He hadn't mentioned making arrangements for her return to New York.

She had been so exhausted that for once she had slept deeply, and as a result the shadows beneath her eyes weren't as dark as they usually were. She stared into the bathroom mirror, wondering if being fired might have been a blessing in disguise. The way she had been pushing herself had been hard on her health, burning away weight she couldn't afford to lose, drawing the skin tightly over her facial bones so that she looked both haggard and emaciated, especially without makeup. She made a face at herself in the mirror. She'd never been a beauty and never would be, but she had once been pretty. Her dark blue eyes and swath of sleek, heavy, golden-honey-brown hair were her best features, though the rest of her face could be described as ordinary.

What would Steve say if he could see her now? Would he be disappointed, and bluntly say so?

Why couldn't she get him out of her mind? It was natural to be concerned about him, to feel sharp sympathy because of his terrible injuries, but she couldn't stop herself from wondering what he would think, what he would say, about her. Not the Steve he had been before, that charming but unreliable will-o'-the-wisp, but the man he was now: harder, stronger, with the fierce will to survive that had kept him alive in the face of overwhelming odds. What would that man think of her? Would he still want her?

The thought made her face flame, and she jerked away from the mirror to turn on the shower. She must be going mad! He was an invalid. Even now, it wasn't by any means certain that he would survive, despite his fighting nature. And even if he did, he might not function as well as he had before. The surgery to save his sight might not have worked; they wouldn't know until the bandages came off. He might have brain damage. He might not be able to walk, talk or feed himself.

Helplessly she felt hot tears begin to slide down her cheeks again. Why should she cry for him now? Why couldn't she stop crying for him? Every time she thought of him she started crying, which was ridiculous, when she hadn't even been able to recognize him.

Payne was calling for her at ten, so she forced herself to stop crying and get ready. She managed that with plenty of time to spare, then found, surprisingly, that she was hungry. She usually didn't eat breakfast, sustaining herself with an endless supply of coffee until lunch, when her stomach would be burning and she wouldn't be able to eat much. But already the strain of her job was fading away, and she wanted food.

She ordered breakfast from room service and received it in a startlingly short length of time. Falling on the tray like a famine victim, she devoured the omelet and toast in record time; when Payne knocked on her door, she had been finished for almost half an hour.

Without seeming to, Payne studied her face with sharp eyes that noted and analyzed every detail. She'd been crying. This was really getting to her, and though that was exactly what they wanted, he still regretted that she had to be hurt. She also looked immeasurably better this morning, with a bit of color in her face. Her marvelous eyes were bigger and brighter than he had remembered, but part of that was the result of her tears. He only hoped she wouldn't have to shed too many more.

"I've already called to check on his condition," he reported, taking her arm. "Good news. His vital signs are improving. He's still unconscious, but his brain waves are increasing in activity and the doctors are more optimistic than they've been. He's really done better than anyone expected."

She didn't point out that they had expected him to die, so anything was better than that. She didn't want to think about how close he had come to dying. In some way she didn't understand, Steve had become too important to her during those minutes when she had stood beside his bed and touched his arm.

The big white naval hospital was much busier that morning than it had been the night before, and two different guards stood at the doors to the ICU wing where Steve's room was located. Again they seemed to know Payne on sight. Jay wondered how many times he had been here to see Steve, and why he would have felt it necessary to be there at all. As he had that morning, he could have checked on Steve's condition by phone. Whatever Steve had gotten himself into must be extremely important, and Payne wanted to be on hand the instant he recovered consciousness, if ever.

Payne left her to enter the room on her own, saying he wanted to talk to someone. Jay nodded absently, her attention already focused on Steve. She pushed open the door and walked in, leaving Payne standing in the hall practically in midsentence. A wry, faintly regretful smile touched his mouth as he looked at the closed door; then he turned and walked briskly down the hall.

Jay stared at the man in the bed. Steve. Now that she was seeing him again, it was a little hard to accept that he *was* Steve. She had known Steve as vibrant, burning with energy; he was so still now that it threw her off balance.

He was still in the same position he'd been in the night before; the machines were still quietly humming and beeping, and fluids were still being fed into his veins through needles. The strong scent of hospital antiseptic burned her nose, and suddenly she wondered if, in some corner of his mind, he was aware of the smell. Could he hear people talking, though he was unable to respond?

She walked to the bed and touched his arm as she had the night before. The heat of his skin tingled against her fingertips despite the coolness of the controlled temperature. The mummylike expanse of bandages robbed him of individuality, and his lips were so swollen they looked more like caricatures than the lips of the man she had once kissed, loved, married, fought with and finally divorced. Only the hot bare skin of his arm made him real to her.

Did he feel anything? Was he aware of her touch?

"Steve?" she whispered, her voice trembling. It felt so funny to talk to a motionless mummy, knowing that he was probably so deep in his coma that he was unaware of everything, and that even if by some miracle he could hear her, he wouldn't be able to respond. But even knowing all that, something inside compelled her to try. "I…it's Jay." Sometimes he'd called her Jay-bird, and when he'd really wanted to aggravate her he'd called her Janet Jean. Her nickname had evolved when she'd been a very young child. Her parents had called her Janet Jean, but her elder brother, Wilson, had shortened it to J.J., which had naturally become Jay. By the time she'd started school, her name was, irrevocably, Jay.

"You've been hurt," she told Steve, still stroking his arm. "But you're going to be all right. Your legs have been broken, and they're both in casts. That's why you can't move them. They have a tube in your throat, help-ing you to breathe, and that's why you can't talk. You can't see because you have bandages over your eyes. Don't worry about anything. They're taking good care of you here."

Was it a lie that he was going to be all right? Yet she didn't know what else to tell him. If he could hear her, she had to reassure him, not give him something else to worry about.

Clearing her throat, she began telling him about the past five years, what she'd been doing since the di-vorce. She even told him about being fired, and how badly she'd wanted to punch Farrell Wordlaw right in the nose. How badly she still wanted to punch him in the nose.

THE VOICE WAS CALM and infinitely tender. He didn't un-derstand the words, because unconsciousness still wrapped his mind in layers of blackness, but he heard the voice, felt it, like something warm touching his skin. It made him feel less alone, that tiny, dim con-

tact. Something hard and vital in him focused on the contact, yearning toward it, forcing him upward out of the blackness, even though he sensed the fanged monsters that waited for him, waiting to tear at his flesh with hot knives and brutal teeth. He would have to endure that before he could reach the voice, and he was very weak. He might not make it. Yet the voice reached out to him, pulling at him like a magnet, lifting him out of the deep senselessness that had held him.

"I REMEMBER THE doll I got for Christmas when I was four years old," Jay said, talking automatically now. Her voice was low and dreamy. "She was soft and floppy, like a real baby, and she had curly brown hair and big brown eyes, with inch-long lashes that closed when I laid her down. I named her Chrissy, for my very best friend in the world. I lugged that doll around until she was so ragged she looked like a miniature bag lady. I slept with her, I put her on the chair beside me when I ate, and I rode miles around and around the house on my tricycle with her on the seat in front of me. Then I began to grow up, and I lost interest in Chrissy. I put her on the shelf with my other dolls and forgot about her. But the first time I saw you, Steve, I thought, 'He's got Chrissy eyes.' That's what I used to call brown eyes when I was little and didn't know my colors. You have Chrissy eyes."

His breathing seemed to be slower, deeper. She couldn't be certain, but she thought there was a different rhythm to the rise and fall of his chest. The sound of his breathing whistled in and out through the tube in his throat. Her fingers gently rubbed his arm, maintaining the small contact even though something inside her actually hurt from touching his skin.

"I almost told you a couple of times that you have Chrissy eyes, but I didn't think you'd like it." She laughed, the sound warm in the room filled with impersonal, humming machines. "You were always so protective of your macho image. A devil-may-care adventurer shouldn't have Chrissy eyes, should he?"

Suddenly his arm twitched, and the movement so startled her that she jerked her hand away, her face pale. Except for breathing, it was the first time he'd moved, even though she knew it was probably an involuntary muscle spasm. Her eyes flew to his face but there was nothing to see there. Bandages covered the upper two-thirds of his head, and his bruised lips were immobile. Slowly she reached out and touched his arm again, but he lay still under her touch, and after a moment she resumed talking to him, rambling on as she dragged up childhood memories.

Frank Payne silently opened the door and stopped in his tracks, listening to her low murmurings. She still stood by the bed; hell, she probably hadn't moved an inch from the man's side, and she had been in here—he checked his watch—almost three hours. If she had been the guy's wife, he could have understood it, but she was his *ex*-wife, and she was the one who had ended the marriage. Yet there she stood, her attention locked on him as if she were *willing* him to get better.

"How about some coffee?" he asked softly, not wanting to startle her, but her head jerked around anyway, her eyes wide.

Then she smiled. "That sounds good." She walked

away from the bed, then stopped and looked back, a frown knitting her brows together. "I hate to leave him alone. If he understands anything at all, it must be awful to just lie there, trapped and hurting and not knowing why, thinking he's all alone."

"He doesn't know anything," Payne assured her, wishing it was different. "He's in a coma, and right now it's better that he stays in it."

"Yes," Jay agreed, knowing he was right. If Steve were conscious now, he would be in terrible pain.

THAT FIRST FAINT glimmer of awareness had faded; the warm voice had gone away and left him without direction. Without that to guide him, he sank back into the blackness, into nothingness.

FRANK LINGERED OVER the bad cafeteria food and the surprisingly good coffee. It wasn't great coffee; it truly wasn't even good coffee, but it was better than he'd expected. The next batch might not be as good, so he wanted to enjoy this one as long as he could. Not only that, he didn't know exactly how to bring up the subject he'd been skating around all during lunch, but he had to do it. The Man had made it plain: Jay Granger had to stay. He didn't want her to identify the patient and leave; he wanted her to become emotionally involved, at least enough to stay. And what the Man wanted, he got.

Frank had sighed. "What if she falls in love with him? Hell, you know what he's like. He has women crawling all over him. They can't resist him."

"She may be hurt," the Man had conceded, though the steel never left his voice. "But his life is on the line, and our options are limited. For whatever reason, Steve Crossfield was there when it went down. We know it, and they know it. We don't have a list of possibilities to choose from. Crossfield is the *only* choice."

He hadn't needed to say more. Since Crossfield was the only choice, his ex-wife was also the only choice by reason of being the only person who could identify him.

"Did McCoy buy it?" the Man had asked abruptly.

"The whole nine yards." Then Frank's voice had sharpened. "You don't think Gilbert McCoy is—"

The Man interrupted. "No. I know he isn't. But McCoy's a damned sharp agent. If he bought it, that means we're doing a good job of making things look the way we want."

"What happens if she's with him when he wakes up?"

"It doesn't matter. The doctors say he'll be too confused and disoriented to make sense. They're monitoring him, and they'll let us know when they start bringing him out of it. We can't keep her out of his room without it looking suspicious, but watch it. If he starts making sense, get her out of the room fast, until we can talk to him. But there's not too much danger of that happening."

"You're stirring that coffee to death." Jay's voice broke in on his thoughts, and he looked up at her, then down at the coffee. He'd been stirring it so long that it had cooled. He grimaced at the waste of not-bad coffee.

"I've been trying to think of how to ask something of you," he admitted.

Jay gave him a puzzled look. "There's only one way. Just ask."

"All right." He took a deep breath. "Don't go back to New York tomorrow. Will you stay here with Steve? He needs you. He's going to need you even more."

The words hit her hard. Steve had never needed her. She had been too intense, wanting more from him, from their relationship, than he had in him to give. He'd always wanted a slight distance between them, mentally and emotionally, claiming that she "smothered" him. She remembered the time he'd shouted those words at her; then she thought of the man lying so still in the hospital bed, and again she felt that unnerving sense of unreality.

Slowly she shook her head. "Steve is a loner. You should know that from the information you have on him. He doesn't need me now, won't need me when he wakes up, and probably won't like the idea of anyone taking care of him, least of all his ex-wife."

"He'll be very confused when he wakes up. You'll be a lifeline to him, the only face he knows, someone he can trust, someone who'll reassure him. He's in a drug-induced coma…the doctors can tell you more about it than I can. But they've said he'll be very confused and agitated, maybe even delirious. It'll help if someone he knows is there."

Practicality made her shake her head again. "I'm sorry, Mr. Payne. I don't think he'd want me there, but I wouldn't stay anyway, if I could. I was fired from my job yesterday. I have two weeks' notice to work out. I can't afford not to work those two weeks, and I have to find another job."

He whistled through his teeth. "You had a bitch of a day, didn't you?"

She had to laugh, in spite of the seriousness of the situation. "That's a good description of it, yes." The longer she knew Frank Payne, the more she liked him. There was nothing outstanding about him: he was of medium height, medium weight, with graying brown hair and clear gray eyes. His face was pleasant, but not memorable. Yet there was a steadiness in him that she sensed and trusted.

He looked thoughtful. "It's possible we can do something about your situation. Let me check into it before you book a flight back. Would you like a chance to tell your boss to go take a flying leap?"

Jay gave him a very sweet smile, and this time he was the one who laughed.

It wasn't until later that she realized the request meant they were certain Steve would live. She was back in Steve's room, standing by his bed, and she gently squeezed his arm as relief filled her. "You're going to make it," she whispered. It was almost sundown, and she had spent most of the day standing beside his bed. Several times a nurse or an orderly had requested that she step outside, but except for that and the time she had spent with Frank at lunch, she had been with Steve. She had talked until her throat was dry, talked until she couldn't think of anything else to say and silence had fallen again, but even then she had kept her hand on his arm. Maybe he knew she was there.

A nurse came in and gave Jay a curious look but didn't ask her to leave the room. Instead she checked the monitors and made notes on a pad. "It's odd," she murmured. "But maybe not. Somehow I think our boy knows when you're here. His heartbeat is stronger and his respiration rate settles down if you're here with him. When you left for lunch his vital signs deteriorated, then picked back up when you returned. I've noticed the same thing happen every time we've asked you to leave the room. Major Lunning is going to be interested in these charts."

Jay stared at the nurse, then at Steve. "He *knows* I'm here?"

"Not consciously," the nurse said hastily. "He isn't going to wake up and talk to you, not with the barbiturate dose he's getting. But who knows what he senses? You've been talking to him all day, haven't you? Part of it must be getting through, on some level. You must be really important to him, for him to respond to you like this."

The nurse left the room. Stunned, Jay looked back at Steve. Even if he somehow sensed her presence, why would it affect him like that? Yet she couldn't ignore the nurse's theory, because she had noticed herself that the rhythm of his breathing had changed. It was almost impossible for her to believe, because Steve had never needed her in any way. He had enjoyed her for a time, but something in him had kept her at a small but significant distance. Because he couldn't return love of any depth, he hadn't allowed himself to accept a deep love. All Steve had ever wanted was a superficial sort of relationship, a light, playful love that could end with no regrets. Theirs had ended in just that way, and she had seldom thought of him after they had parted. Why should she be important to him now?

Then she gave a low laugh as understanding came to her. Steve wasn't responding to *her*; he was responding to a touch and a voice meant for him personally, rather than the impartial, automatic touches and words of the healers surrounding him. Anyone else would have done just as well. Frank Payne could have stood there and talked to him with the same result.

She said as much an hour later, when Major Lunning studied the charts and stroked his jaw, occasionally glancing at her with a thoughtful expression. Frank stood to one side, careful to keep his face blank, but his sharp gaze didn't miss anything.

Major Lunning was one of the top military doctors, a man devoted to both healing and the military. He wasn't stationed at Bethesda, but he hadn't questioned the orders that had gotten him up in the middle of the night and brought him there. He and several other doctors had been given the task of saving this man's life. At the time they hadn't even known his name. Now there was a name on his chart, but they still had no inkling why he was so important to the powers that be. It didn't make any difference; Major Lunning would use whatever weapon or procedure he could find to help his patient. Right now, one of those weapons was this too-thin young woman with dark blue eyes and a full, passionate-looking mouth.

"I don't think we can ignore the pattern, Ms. Granger," the Major said frankly. "It's your voice he responds to, not mine, not Mr. Payne's, not any of the nurses'. Mr. Crossfield isn't in a deep coma. He's breathing on his own and still has reflexes. It isn't unreasonable to think that he can hear you. He may not understand and he certainly can't respond, but it's entirely possible that he hears."

"But I understood that his coma is drug-induced," Jay protested. "When people are drugged, aren't they totally unconscious?"

"There are different levels of consciousness. Let me explain his injuries more completely. He has simple fractures of both legs, nothing that will prevent him from walking normally. He has second-degree burns on his hands and arms, but the worst of the burns are on his palms and fingers, as if he grabbed a hot pipe, or perhaps put his hands up to shield his face. His spleen was ruptured, and we removed it. One lung was punctured and collapsed. But the worst of his injuries were to his head and face. His skull was fractured, and his facial bones were simply shattered.

"We performed surgery immediately to repair the damage, but to control the swelling of the brain and prevent further damage, we have to administer large doses of barbiturates. That keeps him in a coma. Now, the deeper the coma, the less the brain functions. In a deep coma the patient may not even be able to breathe for himself. The level of the coma depends in part on the patient's tolerance for the drugs, which varies from person to person. Mr. Crossfield's tolerance seems to be a bit higher than usual, so his coma isn't as deep as it could be. We haven't increased the dosage, because it hasn't been necessary. In time we'll gradually decrease the dosage and bring him out of the coma. He's going to make it on his own, but I'll tell you frankly, he definitely does better when you're with him. There's still a lot we don't know about the mind and how it affects the body, but we know it does."

"Are you saying he'll get well faster if I'm here?"

The Major grinned. "That's it in a nutshell."

Jay felt tired and confused, as if she'd spent hours in a house of mirrors trying to find her way out but instead finding only one deceitful reflection after another. It wasn't just these people, all insisting that she stay; part of it was inside. Something happened when she touched Steve, something she didn't understand. She certainly hadn't felt it before, even when they'd been married. It was as if he were more than he had been, somehow different in ways she sensed but couldn't define.

She wished they hadn't put this responsibility on her. She didn't want to stay. This strange feeling she had for Steve made her feel threatened. If she left now, it wouldn't have a chance to develop. But if she stayed... She hadn't been devastated by their divorce, five years earlier, because their love had never grown, never gone any deeper. In the end it had simply faded away. But Steve was different now; he'd changed in those five years, into a man whose power she could feel even when he was unconscious. If she fell in love with him again, she might never get over it.

But if she left, she would feel guilty because she hadn't helped him.

She needed to find another job. She had to get back to New York and begin doing something to keep her life from disintegrating. But she was tired of the frantic pushing and maneuvering, the constant dealing. She didn't want to go, but she was afraid to stay.

Frank saw the tension in her face, felt it vibrating through her. "Let's walk down to the lounge," he said, stepping forward to take her arm. "You need a break. See you later, Major."

Major Lunning nodded. "Try to talk her into staying. This guy really needs her."

Out in the hall, Jay murmured, "I hate it when people talk around me, as if I'm not there. I'm tired of being maneuvered." She was thinking of her job when she said that, but Frank gave her a sharp look.

"I don't mean to put you in a difficult position," he said diplomatically. "It's just that we badly need to talk to your husband…sorry, ex-husband. I keep forgetting. At any rate, we're willing to do whatever is possible to aid in his recovery."

Jay put her hands in her pockets, slowing her steps as she considered something. "Is Steve going to be arrested because of what he was doing, whatever it was?"

Frank didn't have any hesitation on that score. "No," he said with absolute certainty. The man was going to get nothing but the best medicine and best protection his country could provide him; Frank only wished he could tell Jay why, but that wasn't possible. "We think he was simply in the wrong place at the wrong time, an innocent bystander, if you will. But given his background, we think it likely he would have picked up on the situation. It's even possible he was trying to help when everything blew up in his face."

"Literally."

"Yes, unfortunately. Anything he can remember will help us."

They reached the lounge and he opened the door so she could precede him. They were alone, thank heavens. He went over to the coffee machine and fed coins into it. "Coffee?"

"No, thank you," Jay replied tiredly as she sat down.

Her stomach was blessedly calm, and she didn't want to upset it now with the noxious brew that usually came from those machines. She hadn't noticed before how tired she was, but now fatigue was washing over her in great waves that made her feel giddy.

Frank sat down opposite her, cradling the Styrofoam cup in his hands. "I talked to my superior, explained your situation," he began. "Would you stay if you didn't have to worry about finding another job?"

She let her eyelids droop as she rubbed her forehead in an effort to force herself to concentrate on what he'd said. She couldn't remember ever having been as tired as she was now, as if all energy had drained from her. Even her mind felt numb. All day long she had focused so fiercely on Steve that everything else had blurred, and now that she had let herself relax, exhaustion had crashed in on her, a deep lassitude that was mental as well as physical.

"I don't understand," she murmured. "I have to work at a job to make money. And even if you've somehow lined one up for me, I can't work and stay here, too."

"Staying here would be your job," Frank explained, wishing he didn't have to push her. She looked as if it were all she could do to sit erect. But maybe she would be more easily convinced now, with fatigue dulling her mind. "We'll take care of your apartment and living expenses. It's that important to us."

Her eyelids lifted and she stared at him incredulously. "You'd *pay* me to stay here?"

"Yes."

"But I don't want money to stay with him! I *want* to help him, don't you understand that?"

"But you can't, because of your financial position," Frank said, nodding. "What we're offering to do is take care of that for you. If you were independently wealthy, would you hesitate to stay?"

"Of course not! I'll do whatever I can to help him, but the idea of taking money for it is ugly."

"We aren't paying you to stay with him, we're paying you so you *can* stay with him. Do you see the difference?"

She had to be going mad, because she did see the difference between the two halves of the hair he had just split. And his eyes were so kind that she instinctively trusted him, even though she sensed a lot going on that she didn't understand.

"We'll get an apartment for you close by, so you can spend more time with him," Frank continued, his voice soothing and reasonable. "We'll also keep your New York apartment for you, so you'll have that to go back to. If you give me the word now, we can have a place here ready for you to move into on Monday."

There had to be arguments she could use, but she couldn't think of any. Frank was sweeping all obstacles out of the way; it would make her feel mean and petty if she refused to do what he wanted, when he had gone to so much trouble and they—whoever *they* were—so badly wanted her to remain.

"I'll have to go home," she said helplessly. "To New York, that is. I need more clothes, and I'll have to quit my job." Suddenly she laughed. "If it's possible to quit a job you've already been fired from."

"I'll make the travel arrangements for you."

"How long do you think I'll be here?" She was estimating a two- or three-week stay, but she wanted to be certain. She would have to do something about her mail and utilities.

Frank's gaze was level. "A couple of months, at least. Maybe longer."

"Months!"

"He'll have to have therapy."

"But he'll be conscious then. I thought you only wanted me to stay until the worst was over!"

He cleared his throat. "We'd like you to stay until he's dismissed from the hospital, at least." He had been trying to break the idea to her gradually, first by just getting her here, then convincing her that Steve needed her, then talking her into staying for the duration. He only hoped it would work.

"But why?"

"He'll need you. He'll be in pain. I haven't told you before, but he needs more surgery on his eyes. It will probably be six to eight weeks before he'll get the bandages off his eyes for good. He's going to be confused, in pain, and they'll put him through more pain in therapy. To top it all off, he won't be able to see. Jay, you're going to be his lifeline."

She sat there numbly, staring at him. It looked as if, after all this time and now that it was too late, Steve was going to need her more than either of them had ever thought.

CHAPTER THREE

IT FELT STRANGE to be back in New York. Jay had flown back on Sunday afternoon and had spent the hours packing her clothes and other personal possessions, but even her apartment had felt strange, as if she no longer belonged there. She packed automatically, her mind on the hospital room in Bethesda. How was he doing? She had spent the morning with him, constantly talking and stroking his arm, yet she felt frantic at spending such a long time away from him.

On Monday morning she dressed for work for the last time, and was conscious of a deep sense of relief. Until it had been lifted, she hadn't been aware what a burden that job had been, how desperately she had been driving herself to compete. Competition was a fine thing, but not at the expense of her health, though part of it could be blamed on her own intensity. She had channeled all her temper, interests and energy into that job, leaving nothing as an escape valve. She was lucky she hadn't developed an ulcer, rather than the less severe stress symptoms of a nervous stomach, constant headaches and disturbed sleep.

When she reached her office in the high-rise office building that housed many such firms, she scrounged around until she located a cardboard box, then swiftly cleaned out her desk, depositing all her personal items in the carton. There weren't many: a tube of lipstick, an extra pair of panty hose, a small pack of tissues, an expensive gold ballpoint pen, two small prints from the wall. She had just finished and was reaching for the phone to call Farrell Wordlaw to request a meeting when the intercom buzzed.

"Mr. Clements with EchoSystems on line three, Ms. Granger."

Jay depressed the button. "Please transfer all my calls to Duncan Wordlaw."

"Yes, Ms. Granger."

Taking a deep breath, Jay dialed Farrell on the inter-office line. Two minutes later she walked purposefully into his office.

He smiled benignly at her, as if he hadn't cut her off at the knees three days before. "You're looking well, Jay," he said smoothly. "Is something on your mind?"

"Not much," she replied. "I just wanted to let you know that I won't be able to work out the two weeks' notice you gave me. I came in this morning to clean out my desk, and I left instructions for all my calls to be transferred to Duncan."

It gave her a measure of satisfaction to see him blanch. "That's very unprofessional!" he snapped, surging to his feet. "We were counting on you to tie up the loose ends—"

"And train Duncan how to do my job," she interrupted, her voice ironic.

His tone was threatening. "Under these circumstances, I don't see how I can give you the positive recommendation I had planned. You won't work again in investment banking, not without a favorable reference."

Her dark blue eyes were steady and cold as she stared at him. "I don't plan to work in investment banking, thank you."

From that he decided she must already have another job, which took away the leverage he had been planning to use on her. Jay watched him, practically seeing the wheels turning as he considered his options. She was really leaving them in the lurch, and it was his fault, because he had fired her. "Well, perhaps I was too hasty," he said, forcing his voice to show warm paternalism. "It will certainly leave a black eye on this firm, and on you, if the matters on your desk aren't handled properly. Perhaps if I add two weeks' salary as severance pay, you'll reconsider leaving us so precipitately?"

She was supposed to fall back in line when he waved the magic carrot of money in front of her nose. "Thank you, but no," she declined. "It isn't possible. I won't be in town."

Panic began to edge into his face. If the deals she had been handling fell through, it would cost the firm millions of dollars in fees. "But you can't do that! Where will you be?"

Already Jay could imagine panicky phone calls from Duncan. She gave Farrell a cool smile. "Bethesda Naval Hospital, but I won't be accepting any calls."

He looked absolutely stunned. "The…the naval hospital?" he croaked.

"It's a family emergency," she explained as she walked out the door.

When she was outside again with the small cardboard box tucked under her arm, she laughed out loud from the sheer joy of being unemployed, of being able to put that look of panic in Farrell Wordlaw's eyes. It was almost as good as if she had been able to strangle him. And now she was free to return to Steve, drawn by the powerful compulsion to be with him that she could neither understand nor resist.

She had come up on a commuter flight, but because of the amount of luggage and personal furnishings she was taking back to D.C., Frank had arranged for her to take a charter flight back, and she was pleasantly surprised when he met her at the airport. "I didn't know you were going to be here!" she exclaimed.

He couldn't help smiling at her. Her eyes were sparkling like the ocean, and the lines of tension were gone from her face. She looked as if she had thoroughly enjoyed walking out of her job, and he said as much.

"It was…satisfying," she admitted, smiling at him. "How is Steve today?"

Frank shrugged. "Not as well as he was before you left." It was damned strange, but it was true. His pulse was weaker and faster, his breathing shallow and ragged. Even though he was unconscious, the man needed Jay.

Her eyes darkened with worry and she bit her lip. The urge to get back to Steve grew more intense, like invisible chains pulling at her.

But first she had to get settled in the apartment Frank had gotten for her, something that took up too much time and ate at her patience. The apartment was about half the size of her place in New York, really only two rooms—the living room and bedroom. The kitchen was a cubbyhole in a corner, and there was a crowded little alcove for dining. But the apartment was comfortable, especially since she planned to spend most of her time at the hospital, anyway. This was simply a place to sleep and have a few meals.

"I've arranged for you to have a car," Frank said as he carried in the last case. He grinned at her surprised look. "This isn't New York. You'll need a way to get around." He produced the keys from his pocket and dropped them on the table. "You can come and go at the hospital as you like. You have clearance to see Steve at any hour. I won't be around all the time, the way I have been, but whenever I'm gone another agent will be on hand."

"Are you going to the hospital with me now?"

"Now?" he asked, looking surprised in turn. "Aren't you going to unpack?"

"I can unpack later tonight. I'd rather see Steve now."

"All right." Privately he thought the plan was working a little too well, but that couldn't be helped. "Why don't you follow me in your car, so you can get used to the streets and learn the way to the hospital? Uh... you do drive, don't you?"

Smiling, she nodded. "I've only lived in New York for the past five years. Everywhere else I've lived, I needed a car. But I warn you, I haven't driven very much in that time, so give me a chance to get used to it again."

Actually, driving a car was a lot like riding a bicycle: once you had learned, the skill wasn't forgotten. After taking a moment to familiarize herself with the instrumentation, Jay followed Frank's car without difficulty. She had always been a steady, deliberate driver; Steve had been the daredevil, driving too fast, taking chances.

It wasn't until she stepped into his hospital room and approached the bed that she felt a knot of tension deep inside begin to loosen. She stared down at his bandaged head, with only his bruised, swollen lips and jaw visible, and her heart slammed painfully against her ribs. With infinite care she laid her fingers on his arm and began talking.

"I'm here. I had to go back to New York yesterday to pack my things and quit my job. Remind me to tell you about that someday. Anyway, I'm going to be staying here with you until you're better."

THE VOICE WAS BACK. Slowly it penetrated the black layers that shrouded his mind, forming a tiny link with his consciousness. He still didn't understand the words, but he wasn't aware that he didn't understand. The voice simply was, like light where before there had been nothing. Sometimes the voice was calm and sometimes it rippled with amusement. He wasn't aware of the amusement, only of the change in tone.

He wanted more. He needed to get closer to the sound, and he began trying to fight his way out of the dark fog in his mind. But every time he tried, a vicious, burning pain that permeated his entire body began gnawing at him, and he would withdraw, back into the protecting blackness. Then the voice would lure him out again, until the beast attacked once more and he had to retreat.

HIS ARM TWITCHED the way it had once before, and again the movement startled Jay into jerking her hand away. She stopped talking and stared at him. Then, with only

a slight pause, she replaced her hand on his arm and resumed what she had been saying. Her heart was pounding. It had to be an involuntary twitching of muscles
forced into one position for too long. He couldn't be trying to respond, because the barbiturates they were feeding him literally shut down most of his brain functions.
Most, but not all, Major Lunning had said. If Steve
was aware of her, could he be trying to communicate?

"Are you awake?" she asked softly. "Can you twitch
your arm again?"

His arm was motionless under her fingers, and with
a sigh she again took up her rambling discourse. For
a moment the feeling had been so strong that she had
been convinced he was awake, despite everything they
had told her.

SHE WAS BACK at the hospital the next morning before
the sun was little more than a graying of the eastern
sky. She hadn't slept well, partly because of the unfamiliar surroundings, but she couldn't place all the
blame on being in a strange apartment. She had lain
awake in the darkness, her mind churning as she tried
to analyze and diminish her absurd conviction that, for
a moment, Steve had actually been trying to reach out
to her in the only way he could. But, for all her analyzing, logic meant nothing whenever she remembered
the feeling that had burned through her.

Stop it! she scoffed at herself as she rode the elevator up to the ICU. Her imagination was running away
with her, fueled by her own characteristic tendency to
totally immerse herself in her interests. She had never
been one of those cool, aloof people who could dole

out their emotions in careful measure, though she had nearly wrecked her health by trying to be that way. Because she so badly wanted Steve to recover, she was imagining responses where there were none.

His room was bright with lights, despite the hour, since light or darkness hardly mattered to him in his condition. She supposed the nurses left the lights on for convenience. She closed the door, enclosing them in a private cocoon, then walked to his bed. She touched his arm. "I'm here," she said softly.

He drew a deep breath, his chest shuddering slightly.

It hit her hard, jerking at her like a rope that had suddenly been pulled taut. That deep sense of mutual awareness stretching between them, a communication that went beyond logic, beyond speech, was there again, stronger this time. He knew she was there. Somehow he recognized her. And he was fighting to reach her.

"Can you hear me?" she whispered shakily, her eyes locked on him. "Or do you somehow sense my touch? Is that what it is? Can you feel it when I touch your arm? You must be scared and confused, because you don't know what happened and you're trying to reach out, but you can't seem to make anything work. You're going to be all right, I promise you, but it's going to take time."

The voice. Something in it drew him, despite the pain that waited to claw him whenever he left the darkness. He feared the pain, but he wanted the warmth of the voice more. He wanted to be closer to it...to her. At some point too dim for him to remember or even comprehend, he had realized it was a woman's voice. It held tenderness and the only hint of security in the black swirling emptiness of his mind and world. He knew very little, but he knew that voice; some primal instinct in him recognized it and yearned for it, giving him the strength to fight the pain and the darkness. He wanted her to know he was there.

HIS ARM TWITCHED, the movement somehow too slow to be an involuntary spasm of cramped muscles. This time Jay didn't jerk her hand away. Instead she rubbed her fingertips over his skin, while her eyes fastened on his face.

"Steve? Did you mean to jerk your arm? Can you do it again?"

ODD. SOME OF THE WORDS made sense. Others made no sense at all. But she was there, closer, the voice clearer. He could see only darkness, as if the world had never been, but she was much nearer now. Pain racked his body, great waves of it that made sweat bead on his skin, but he didn't want to let go after getting this far, didn't want to fall back down into the black void.

His arm? Yes. She wanted him to move his arm. He didn't know if he could. It hurt so damned bad he didn't know if he could hold on, if he could try anymore. Would she go away if he didn't move his arm? He couldn't bear being left alone again, where everything was so cold and dark and empty, not after getting this close to her warmth.

He tried to scream, and couldn't. The pain was incredible, tearing him apart like a wild animal with fangs and claws, ripping at him.

He moved his arm.

THE MOVEMENT WAS barely there, a twitch so light she would have missed it if her hand hadn't been on his arm. He had broken out in a sweat, his chest and shoulders glistening under the bright fluorescent lights. Her heart was pounding as she leaned closer to him, her gaze riveted on his lips.

"Steve, can you hear me? It's Jay. You can't talk because you have a tube in your throat. But I'm right here. I won't leave you."

Slowly his bruised lips parted, as if he were trying to form words that refused to take shape. Jay hung over him, breathing suspended, her chest aching, as he struggled to force his lips and tongue through the motions of speech. She felt the force of both his desperation and dogged determination as, against all logic, he fought pain and drugs to be able to say one word. It was as if he *couldn't* give up, no matter what it cost him. Something in him wouldn't let him give up.

Again he tried, his swollen, discolored lips moving in agonized deliberation. His tongue moved, doing its part to shape the word that would remain soundless:

"Hurt."

The pain in her chest became acute, and abruptly she gulped in deep breaths of air. She didn't feel the tears sliding down her cheeks. Gently she patted his arm. "I'll be right back. They'll give you something so you won't hurt any longer. I'm only leaving you for a minute, and I promise I'll be back."

She flew to the door and jerked it open, stumbling into the hall. She must have been there a lot longer than it seemed, because the third shift had gone home and the first shift was back on duty. Frank and Major

Lunning were standing at the nurses' station, talking in low, urgent voices that didn't carry; both men looked up as she ran toward them, and a sort of disbelieving horror filled Frank's eyes.

"He's awake!" she choked. "He said that he hurts. Please, you have to give him something—"

They bolted past her, practically shoving her to the side. Frank said, "This wasn't supposed to happen," in a voice so hard she wasn't certain it was his.

But it had to be, even though the words didn't make any sense. What wasn't supposed to happen? Steve wasn't supposed to wake up? Had they lied to her? Had they expected him to die after all? No, that couldn't be it, or Frank wouldn't have gone to so much trouble to get her to stay.

Nurses were scurrying into Steve's room, but when Jay tried to enter she was firmly escorted back into the hallway. She stood outside, listening to the muted furor of voices inside, chewing on her bottom lip and wiping the slow-welling tears from her cheeks. She should be in there. Steve needed her.

Inside the room, Frank watched as Major Lunning swiftly checked Steve's vital signs and brain-wave activity. "No doubt about it," the major confirmed absently as he worked. "He's coming out of it."

"He's on barbiturates, for God's sake!" Frank protested. "How can he come out of it until you lessen the dosage?"

"He's fighting it off. He's got one hell of a constitution, and that woman out there in the hall has a strong effect on him. Adrenaline is a powerful stimulant. Enough of it, and people perform superhuman feats of strength and endurance. His blood pressure is up and his cardiac output has increased, all signs of adrenaline stimulation."

"Are you going to increase the dosage?"

"No. The coma was to keep his brain from swelling and causing more damage. I was almost ready to begin bringing him out of it anyway. He's just moved up the timetable a little. We'll have to keep him on drugs for the pain, but he won't be in a coma. He'll be able to wake up."

"Jay thought he said that he hurt. Can he feel pain, as drugged as he is?"

"If he was conscious enough to communicate, he was conscious enough to feel pain."

"Can he understand what we're saying?"

"It's possible. I'd say he definitely hears us. Understanding is something else entirely."

"How long will it be before we can question him?"

Major Lunning gave him a severe look. "Not until the swelling in his face and throat subside enough for me to remove the trach tube. I'd say another week. And don't expect him to be a fount of information. He may never remember what happened to him, and even if he eventually does, it could be months in the future."

"Is there any danger that he might reveal some classified information to Jay?" Frank didn't want to say too much. Major Lunning knew that Steve was a very important patient, but he didn't know any of the details.

"It isn't likely. He'll be too dazed and confused, maybe even delirious, and at any rate, he still isn't able to talk. I promise you, you'll be the first to see him when we take the trach tube out."

Frank stared at the still form on the bed; he had been unconscious for so long, it was hard to accept that he could hear or feel, that he had even made an attempt to communicate. But knowing what he knew about the man, Frank realized he should have been prepared for something like this. The man never gave up, never stopped fighting, even when the odds were so strong against him that anyone else would have walked away, and because of that he had survived in many instances when others wouldn't, just as he had this time. Most people never saw past the easy grin to that enormous, fearsome determination.

"What's the likelihood of permanent brain damage?" he asked quietly, remembering that Steve could hear, and there was no way of telling how much he could understand.

Major Lunning sighed. "I don't know. He received excellent, immediate care, and that counts for a lot. It may be so minimal that you won't be able to tell the difference, but I wouldn't put my money on anything right now. I simply can't tell. The fact that he woke up and responded to Ms. Granger is totally out of the expected range. He leapfrogged over several stages of recovery. I've never seen anything like it before. Normally the stages are stupor, where it would take vigorous stimulation to rouse him at all, then delirium and extreme agitation, as if the electrical processes of his brain had gone wild. Then he would become quieter, but he'd be very confused. In the next stage he would be like an automaton. He'd be able to answer questions, but unable to perform any but the simplest physical tasks. The higher brain functions return gradually."

"And the stage he's at now?"

"He was able to communicate, as if he were in the automaton stage, but I think he's lapsed back now. It must have taken a tremendous effort for him to do that much."

"As you cut down on the barbiturates, he'll be able to communicate more?"

"Perhaps. This one incident may not be repeated. He may revert to the more classical stages of recovery."

Exasperated, Frank said, "Is there *anything* you're certain of?"

Major Lunning gave him a long, level look. "Yes. I'm certain that his recovery depends on Ms. Granger. Keep her around. He'll need her."

"Is it safe for her to be with him while you bring him off the drugs?"

"I insist on it. She may keep him calm. I sure as hell don't want him thrashing around with that tube in his chest. Will she be able to take it?"

Frank lifted his brows. "She's stronger than she looks." And Jay was oddly devoted to Steve in a way that he hadn't expected and could not quite understand. It was as if something pulled her to him, but there wasn't any basis for that kind of attraction. Maybe later, when he was awake—his effect on women had always had his superiors shaking their heads in disbelief. But he was little more than a mummy now, unable to use the charm for which he was famous, so it had to be something else.

He had to let the Man know what had happened.

Suddenly the door was shoved open and Jay entered, giving them a hard, bright look that dared them to throw her out again. "I'm staying," she said flatly, moving to Steve's side and putting her hand on his arm. Her chin lifted stubbornly. "He needs me, and I'm going to be here."

Major Lunning looked from her to Steve, then at Frank. "She's staying," he said mildly, then consulted the file in his hand. "Okay, I'm going to begin decreasing the barbiturates now, to completely bring him out of the coma. It will take from twenty-four to thirty-six hours, and I don't know how he's going to react, so I want him under full-time observation." He glanced up at Jay. "Ms. Granger—may I call you Jay?"

"Please," she murmured.

"A nurse will be in here with him most of the time until he's completely off the drugs. His reaction may be unpredictable. If anything happens, it's important that you move away from the bed and not hinder anything we have to do. Do you understand?"

"Yes."

"Can I trust you not to faint and get in the way?"

"Yes."

"All right. I'll hold you to that." His stern military gaze measured her, and he must have been reassured by what he saw, because he gave an abrupt nod of approval. "It won't be easy, but I think you'll hold up."

Jay turned her attention back to Steve, dismissing everyone else in the room as if they no longer existed. She couldn't help it. He crowded everyone else out of her consciousness, flattening them into one-dimensional cartoon characters. Nothing mattered except him, and since his agonized attempt to talk to her, the feeling was even stronger than before. It shattered her and terrified her, because it was so far outside her previous experience, but she couldn't fight it. It was so strange; Steve was exerting far more power over her now than he ever had before, when he'd had full use of his senses and body, and his full range of charm. He was motionless and, for the most part, insensate, but something deep and primal pulled her to him. Just being in the same room with him made her heart settle into a stronger rhythm, heating her flesh as her blood raced through her veins, energizing her.

"I'm back," she murmured, touching his arm. "You can go to sleep now. Don't worry, don't fight the pain... just let it go. I'm here with you, and I won't leave. I'll watch over you, and I'll be here when you wake up again."

Slowly his breathing settled into an easier rhythm and his pulse rate dropped. His blood pressure lowered. Air hissed from the tube in his throat in what would have been a faint sigh had the tube not been in place. Jay stood by his bed, her fingers lightly stroking his arm as he slept.

WHERE ARE YOU? He came awake, screaming silently as he clawed his way through the shrouding darkness and pain into an even greater horror. The pain was like being eaten alive, but he could bear that because despite its force, it was secondary to the horrible emptiness. God, was he buried alive? He couldn't move, couldn't see, couldn't make a sound, as if his body had died but his mind had remained alive. Terrified, he tried again to scream and couldn't.

Where was he? What had happened?

He didn't know. God help him, he didn't know!

"I'm here," the voice crooned soothingly. "I know you're frightened and don't understand, but I'm here. I'll stay with you."

The voice. It was familiar. It had been in his dreams. No, not dreams. Something deeper than that. It was in his guts, his bones, his cells, his genes, his chromosomes. It was part of him, and he focused on it with an intense, almost painful recognition. Yet it was oddly alien, connected to nothing his conscious mind could produce.

"The doctors say you're probably very confused," the voice continued. It was a calm, tender voice, with a slightly husky catch in it, as if she had been crying. She. Yes. It was definitely a woman. He had a vague memory of that voice calling to him, pulling him out of a strange, suffocating darkness.

She began reciting a litany of injuries, and he listened to her voice with fierce concentration, only gradually realizing that she was talking about him. He was injured. Not dead, not buried alive.

The tidal wave of relief exhausted him.

She was still there the next time he surfaced, and this time the initial terror was of shorter duration. Fractionally more alert, he decided she was hoarse rather than teary.

She was always there. He had no concept of time, only of pain and darkness, but gradually he became aware that there were two darknesses. One was in his mind, paralyzing his thoughts, but he could fight it. Slowly that darkness was becoming less. Then there was the other darkness, the absence of light, the inability to see. Again he would have panicked if she hadn't been there. Over and over she explained, as if she knew he would only gradually comprehend her words. He wasn't blind; there were bandages over his eyes, but he wasn't blind. His legs were broken, but he would walk again. His hands were burned, but he would use them again. There was a tube in his throat to help him breathe; soon the tube would be removed and he would talk again.

He believed her. He didn't know her, but he trusted her.

He tried to think, but words boomeranged around in his head until he couldn't make sense of them. He didn't know... There was so much he didn't know. He didn't know anything. But he couldn't catch the words and arrange them in proper order so he'd know what it was he didn't know. It just didn't make sense, and he was too tired to fight.

Finally he woke to find that his thoughts were clearer, the confusion different, because the words made sense even though nothing else did. She was there. He could feel her hand on his arm, could hear her slightly hoarse voice. Did she stay with him all the time? How long had it been? It seemed forever, and it nagged at him, because he felt as if he should know exactly.

There was so much he wanted to know, and he couldn't ask. Frustration ate at him, and his arm flexed beneath her fingers. God, what would happen to him if she left? She was the one link he had to the world outside the prison of his own body, his link to sanity, the only window in his world of darkness. And suddenly the need to know coalesced inside him into a single thought, a single word: *Who?*

His lips formed the word and gave birth to it in silence. Yes, that was the word he'd wanted. Everything he wanted to know was summed up in that one small word.

Jay gently laid her fingers over his swollen lips. "Don't try to talk," she whispered. "Let's use a spelling system. I'll recite the alphabet, and whenever I get to the letter you want, twitch your arm. I'll do the alphabet over and over until we've spelled out whatever you want to say. Can you do that? One twitch for yes, two twitches for no."

She was exhausted; it had been two days since the first time he had woken up, and she had been with him for most of that time. She had talked until her voice was almost gone, her words giving him a bridge out of his coma into reality. She knew when he was awake, sensed that he was terrified, felt his struggle to understand what had happened. But this was the first time his lips had moved, and she was so tired she hadn't been able to grasp what he'd been trying to say. The alphabet game was the only way she could think of for them to communicate, but she didn't know if he'd be able to concentrate enough for it to work.

His arm twitched. Just once.

She drew a deep breath, forcing her exhaustion away. "All right. Here we go. A…B…C…D…"

She began to give up hope as she slowly ran through the alphabet and his arm lay motionless under her hand. It had been a long shot, anyway. Major Lunning had said it could be days before Steve's mind would be clear enough for him to really understand what was going on around him. Then she said "W," and his arm twitched.

She stopped. "W?"

His arm twitched. Once, for "Yes."

Joy shot through her. "Okay, W is the first letter. Let's go for the second one. A...B..."

His arm twitched on the H.

And again on the O.

He stopped there.

Jay was astounded. "*Who?* Is that it? You want to know who I am?"

His arm twitched. *Yes.*

He didn't know; he really didn't know. She couldn't remember if she had mentioned who she was, except when she had first begun talking to him. Had she thought he would remember her voice after not seeing her for five years?

"I'm Jay," she said gently. "Your ex-wife."

CHAPTER FOUR

HE WAS VERY STILL. Jay had the impression that she could feel him withdrawing, though he didn't move a muscle. A surprisingly sharp pain bloomed inside, and she chided herself for it. What had she expected? He couldn't get up and hug her, he couldn't speak, and he was probably exhausted. She knew all that, yet she still had the feeling that he was pulling back from her. Did he resent being so dependent on her? Steve had always been aloof in a curious sort of way, holding people away from him. Or maybe he resented the fact that she was here with him now, rather than some impersonal nurse. After all, a certain degree of independence remained when the service was detached, done because it was a job. Personal service carried a price that couldn't be paid in dollars, and Steve wouldn't like that.

She schooled her voice to a calmness she didn't feel. "Do you have any more questions?"

Two twitches. *No.*

She had been pushed away so many times that she recognized it now, even as subtle and unspoken as the message was. It hurt. She closed her eyes, fighting for the control that would let her speak again. It was a moment before she managed it. "Do you want me to stay in here with you?"

He was still for a long moment. Then his arm twitched. And twitched again. *No.*

"All right. I won't bother you again." Her control was shot, her voice thin and taut. She didn't wait to see if he made any response, but turned and walked out. She felt almost sick. Even now, it was an effort to walk out and leave him alone. She wanted to stay with him, protect him, fight for him. God, she would even take his pain on herself if she could. But he didn't want her. He didn't need her. She had been right all along in thinking that he wouldn't appreciate her efforts on his behalf, but the pull she thought she had felt between them had been so strong that she had ignored her own good sense and let Frank talk her into staying.

Well, at least she should let Frank know that her sojourn here was over, and that she would be leaving. Her problems hadn't changed; she still had to find a new job. Digging a coin out of her purse, she found a pay phone and called the number Frank had given her. He hadn't spent as much time at the hospital these past two days as he had before; in fact, he hadn't been there at all that day.

He answered promptly, and hearing his calm voice helped. "This is Jay. I wanted you to know that my job is over. Steve doesn't want me to stay with him anymore."

"What?" He sounded startled. "How do you know?"

"He told me."

"How in blue blazes did he do that? He can't talk, and he can't write. Major Lunning said he should still be pretty confused, anyway."

"He's a lot better this morning. We worked out a

system," she explained tiredly. "I recite the alphabet, and he signals with his arm when I get to the letter he wants. He can spell out words and answer questions. One twitch means 'Yes' and two twitches means 'No.'"

"Have you told Major Lunning?" Frank asked sharply.

"No, I haven't seen him. I just wanted to let you know that Steve doesn't want me with him."

"Have Lunning paged. I want to talk to him. Now."

For such a pleasant man, Frank could be commanding when he chose, Jay thought as she went to the nurses' station and requested that Major Lunning be paged. It was five minutes before he appeared, looking tired and rumpled, and dressed in surgicals. He listened to Jay, then, without a word, walked to the pay phone and talked quietly to Frank. She couldn't make out what he was saying, but when he hung up he called a nurse and went directly into Steve's room.

Jay waited in the hallway, struggling to handle her feelings. Though she knew Steve and had expected this, it still hurt. It hurt more now than it had when they had divorced. She felt oddly…betrayed, and bereft, as if she had lost part of herself, and she hadn't felt that way before. She hadn't felt so strongly connected to him before. Well, this was just another classic example of her own intensity leading her to read things into a situation that simply weren't there. Would she ever learn?

Major Lunning was in Steve's room a long time, and a phalanx of nurses came and went. Within half an hour Frank arrived, his face taut and set. He squeezed Jay's arm comfortingly as he went past, but he didn't stop to talk. He, too, disappeared into Steve's room, as if something dreadfully important were going on in there.

Jay moved to the visitors' lounge, sitting quietly with her hands folded in her lap while she tried to plan what she should do next. Return to New York, obviously, and get a job. But the idea of hurling herself back into the business world left her cold. She didn't want to go back. She didn't want to leave Steve. Even now, she didn't want to leave him.

Almost an hour later Frank found her in the lounge. He looked at her sharply before going to the coffee machine and buying two cups. Jay looked up and managed a smile for him as he approached. "Do I really look as if I need that?" she asked wryly, nodding toward the coffee.

He extended a cup toward her. "I know. It tastes worse than it looks. Drink it anyway. If you don't need it now, you will in a minute."

She took the cup and sipped the hot liquid, grimacing at the taste. It was a mystery how anyone could take simple water and coffee and make them taste so horrible. "Why will I need it in a minute? It's over, isn't it? Steve told me to go away. It's obvious that he doesn't want me here, so my presence will only upset him and slow his recovery."

"It isn't over," Frank said, looking down at his own coffee, and his flat tone made Jay look at him sharply. He looked haggard, with worry etching new lines into his face.

A cold chill ran down her spine and she sat up straight. "What's wrong?" she asked. "Has he relapsed?"

"No."

"Then what's wrong?"

"He doesn't remember," Frank said simply. "Anything. He has amnesia."

FRANK HAD BEEN RIGHT; she did need the coffee. She drank that cup, then got another one. Her head was reeling, and she felt as if she'd been punched in the stomach. "What else can go wrong?" she asked, talking mostly to herself, but Frank knew what she meant.

He sighed. They hadn't counted on this. They had needed him awake, able to talk, able to understand what needed to be done. This latest development had thrown a monkey wrench into the whole plan. He didn't even know who he was! How could he protect himself if he didn't know who he had to be on guard against? He couldn't recognize friends or enemies.

"He's been asking for you," Frank said, taking her hand. She started, already rising to her feet, but he tugged on her hand and she sank back into her chair. "We've been asking him a lot of questions," he continued. "We used your system, though it takes a while. When you told him you were his ex-wife, it confused him, scared him. He couldn't remember you, and he didn't know what to do. Remember, he's still easily confused. It's hard for him to concentrate, though he's getting better fast."

"Are you certain he's asking for me?" Jay asked, her heart pounding. Out of everything he had said, her emotions had centered on his first sentence.

"Yes. He spelled out your name over and over."

The instinct to go to him was so strong it was almost painful. She forced herself to sit still, to understand more. "He has total amnesia? He doesn't remember anything?"

"He doesn't even know his own name." Frank sighed again, a heavy sound. "He doesn't remember anything about the explosion or why he was there. Nothing. A total blank. Damn it!" The last expressed his helpless frustration.

"What does Major Lunning think?"

"He said total amnesia is extremely rare. More often it's a sort of spot amnesia that blocks out the accident itself and anything that happened a short while before it. With the head trauma Steve suffered, amnesia wasn't that unexpected, but this..." He made a helpless gesture.

She tried to think of what she had read about amnesia, but all that came to mind was the dramatic use often made of it on soap operas. Invariably the amnesiac recovered his full memory during a highly dramatic moment, just in time to prevent a murder or keep from being murdered himself. It was good melodrama, but that was all it was.

"Will he regain his memory?"

"Probably. Part of it, at least. There's no way to be certain. It might start coming back almost immediately, or it could take months before he begins remembering anything. Major Lunning said that his memory will come back in bits and pieces, usually the oldest memories first."

Might. Probably. Could. Usually. What it all added up to was that they simply didn't know. In the meantime Steve lay in his bed, unable to talk, unable to see, unable to move. All he could do was hear and think.

What would it be like to be so cut adrift from everything familiar, even himself? He had no point of reference for anything. The thought of the inner terror he
must be feeling squeezed her heart.

"Are you still willing to stay?" Frank asked, his clear
eyes filled with concern. "Knowing that it might take
months or even years?"

"Years?" she echoed faintly. "But you only wanted
me to stay until the surgery on his eyes was completed."

"We didn't know then that he wouldn't remember
anything. Major Lunning said that being around familiar things and people would help stimulate his memory,
give him a feeling of stability."

"You want me to stay until he regains his memory,"
Jay stated, putting it into words. The idea frightened
her. The longer she stayed with Steve, the more strongly
she reacted to him. What would happen to her if she
fell in love with him far more deeply than she had the
first time, only to lose him again when he returned to
his footloose life? She was afraid that she already cared
too much to simply walk away. How could she walk
away when he needed her?

"He needs you," Frank said, echoing her thoughts.
"He's asking for you. He responds to you so strongly
that he keeps confounding Major Lunning's predic-
tions. And we need you, Jay. We need you to help him
in any way you can, because we need to know what
he knows."

"If sentiment won't get me, try patriotism?" she
asked tiredly, leaning her head back against the pad-
ded orange vinyl chair. "It wasn't necessary. I won't
leave him. I don't know what's going to happen, or

how we'll handle it if he doesn't get his memory back soon, but I won't leave him."

She got up and walked out, and Frank sat there for a moment staring at the cup still in his hands. From what she'd just said, he knew that Jay sensed she was being manipulated, but she was willing to let them do it because Steve was so important to her. He had to talk to the Man about this latest development, and he wondered what would happen. They had counted on Steve's willing participation, on his talents and skills. Now they had to let him walk out on the streets as helpless as a baby because he couldn't recognize the dangers, or take the risk of telling him things that could set back his recovery. Major Lunning had been adamant that upsetting him would be the worst thing they could do. He needed quiet and tranquillity, a stable emotional base, his memory would return faster under those conditions. No matter what decision the Man reached, Steve was at risk. And if Steve was at risk, so was Jay.

It was hard for Jay to enter Steve's room after the emotional battering she had taken. She needed time to get herself under control, but she felt the pull between them again; it was growing so strong she no longer had to be in the room with him, touching him. He needed her right now, far more than she needed time. She opened the door and felt his attention center on her, though not even his head moved. It was as if he were holding his breath.

"I'm back," she said quietly, walking to his bed and putting her hand on his arm. "It seems I can't stay away."

His arm twitched urgently, several times, and she got the message. "All right," she said, and began reciting the alphabet.

Sorry.

What could she say? Deny that she'd been upset? He would know better. He felt the pull just as she did, because he was on the other end of that invisible rope. He turned his face slightly toward her, his bruised lips parted as he waited for her answer.

"It's all right," she said. "I didn't realize what a shock I had just given you."

Yes.

It was odd how much expression he could put in a single motion, but she felt his wryness and sensed that he was still shocked. Shocked, but in control. His control was astounding.

She began spelling again.

Afraid.

The admission hit her hard; it was something the old Steve never would have admitted, but the man he had become was so much stronger that he could admit it and lose nothing of his strength. "I know, but I'll stay with you as long as you want me," she promised.

What happened? He made it a question by a slight upward movement of his arm.

Keeping her voice calm, Jay told him about the explosion but didn't give him any of the details. Let him think that he'd simply been in an accident.

Eyes?

So he hadn't understood everything she'd told him before and needed reassuring. "You'll have more surgery on your eyes, but the prognosis is good. You'll see again, I promise."

Paralyzed?

"No! You've broken both legs and they're in casts. That's why you can't move them."

Toes.

"Your toes?" she asked in bewilderment. "They're still there."

His lips moved in a very slight, painful smile. *Touch them.*

She bit her lip. "Okay." He wanted her to touch his toes so he'd know he still had feeling in them, as a reassurance that he wasn't paralyzed. She walked to the foot of the bed and firmly folded her hands over his bare toes, letting his cool flesh absorb the heat from her palms. Then she returned to his side and touched his arm. "Did you feel that?"

Yes. Again he gave that painful fraction of a smile.

"Anything else?"

Hands.

"They're burned, and in bandages, but they're not third-degree burns. Your hands will be fine."

Chest. Hurts.

"You have a collapsed lung, and a tube in your chest. Don't do any tossing around."

Funny.

She laughed. "I didn't know anyone could be silent and sarcastic at the same time."

Throat.

"You have a trach tube because you weren't breathing well."

Face broken?

She sighed. He wanted to know, not be protected. "Yes, some bones in your face were broken. You aren't disfigured, but the swelling made it hard for you to breathe. As soon as the swelling goes down, they'll take the trach tube out."

Lift the sheet and check my—

"I will not!" she said indignantly, halting her spelling when she realized where his words were heading. Then she had to laugh because he actually managed to look impatient. "Everything is still there, believe me."

Functional?

"You'll have to find that out on your own!"

Prissy.

"I'm not prissy, and you behave or I'll have a nurse change your tube. Then you'll find out the hard way what you want to know." As soon as she said the words she felt herself blushing, and it didn't help that he was smiling again. She hadn't meant to sound the way she had.

The effort of concentrating for so long had tired him, and after a minute he spelled *Sleep.*

"I didn't mean to tire you out," she murmured. "Go to sleep."

Stay?

"Yes, I'm staying. I won't go back to my apartment without telling you." Her throat felt thick at his need for reassurance, and she stood by the bed with her hand on his arm until his breathing changed into the deep, steady rhythm of sleep.

Even then she was reluctant to take her hand away, and she stood beside him for a long time. A smile kept curving her lips. His personality was so strong that it came through despite his limited means of communication. He wanted the truth about his condition, not vague promises or medical double-talk. He might not know his name, but that hadn't changed the man he was. He was strong, much stronger than he had been before. Whatever had happened to him in the past five years had tempered him, like steel subjected to the hottest fires. He was harder, stronger, tougher, his willpower so fierce it was like an energy field emanating from him. Oh, he had been a charming rascal before, devilishly reckless and daring, with a glint in his eye that had turned many feminine heads. But now he was… dangerous.

The word startled her, but when she examined it, she realized that it described exactly the man he had become. He was a dangerous man. She didn't feel threatened by him, but danger didn't necessarily constitute a threat. He was dangerous because of his steely, implacable will; when this man decided to do something, it wasn't safe to get in his way. At some time in the past five years, something had drastically changed him and she wasn't sure she wanted to know what it was. It must have been something cataclysmic, something awful, to have so focused his character and determination. It was as if he had been stripped down to the bare essentials of human existence, forced to discard all his personality traits that weren't necessary to survival and adopt new ones that were. What was left was hard and pure, unbreakable and curiously resilient. This was a man who wouldn't admit defeat; he didn't know what it was.

Her heart was beating heavily as she stood looking down at him, her attention so focused on him that they might have been the only two people in the world. He awed her, and he attracted her so strongly that she jerked her hand away from his arm as soon as the thought formed. Dear God! She would be a fool to let herself get caught in that trap again. Even more now than before, Steve was essentially alone, his personality so honed that he was complete unto himself. She had walked away relatively unscathed before, but what would happen to her this time if she let herself care too much? She felt scared, not only because she was teetering on the edge of heartbreak, but because she was even daring to think of getting too close to him. It was like watching a panther in a cage, standing outside the bars and knowing you were safe, but feeling the danger that was barely restrained.

Making love with him before had been...fun, passionate in a playful way. What would it be like now? Was the playfulness gone? She thought it must be. His lovemaking would be intense and elemental now, as he was, like getting caught up in a storm.

She became aware that she could barely breathe, and she forced herself to walk away from his bed. She didn't want him to mean that much to her. And she was very much afraid that he already did.

"WHAT DO WE DO?" Frank asked quietly, his clear eyes meeting shuttered black ones.

"We play out the hand," the Man answered just as quietly. "We have to. If we do anything out of the ordinary now, it could tip someone off, and he isn't able to recognize his enemies."

"Any luck in tracing Piggot?"

"We lost him in Beirut, but we know he hooked up with his old pals. He'll surface again, and we'll be waiting."

"We just have to keep our guy alive until we can neutralize Piggot," Frank said, his tone turning glum.

"We'll do it. One way or the other, we have to keep Piggot's cutthroats from getting their hands on him."

"When he gets his memory back, he isn't going to like what we've done."

A brief smile touched the Man's hard mouth. "He'll raise mortal hell, won't he? But I'm not taking any chance with the protected-witness program until he's able to look out for himself, and maybe not even then. It's been penetrated before, and could be again. Everything hinges on getting Piggot."

"You ever wish you were back in the field, so you could hunt him yourself?"

The Man leaned back, hooking his hands behind his head. "No. I've gotten domesticated. I like going home at night to Rachel and the kids. I like not having to watch my back."

Frank nodded, thinking of the time when the Man's back had been a target for every hit man and terrorist in the business. He was safe now, out of the mainstream...as far as was generally known. A very small group of people knew otherwise. The Man officially didn't exist; even the people who followed his orders didn't know the orders came from him. He was buried so deeply in the bowels of bureaucracy, protected by so many twists and turns, that there was no way to connect him to the job he actually did. The President knew about him, but Frank doubted the vice president did, or any department secretary, the Chiefs of Staff or the head of the agency that employed him. Whoever was President next might not know about him. The Man decided for himself whom he could trust; Frank was one of those people. And so was the man in Bethesda Naval Hospital.

TWO DAYS LATER, they took the tube out of Steve's chest because his collapsed lung had healed and reinflated. When they let Jay into his room again she hung over the side of his bed, stroking his arm and shoulder until his breathing settled down and the fine mist of perspiration on his body began to dry.

"It's over, it's over," she murmured.

He moved his arm, a signal that he wanted to spell, and she began reciting the alphabet.

Not fun.

"No," she agreed.

More tubes?

"There's one in your stomach, for feeding you." She felt his muscles tense as if in anticipation of the pain he knew would come, and he spelled out a terse expletive. Her hand moved over his chest in sympathy, feeling the coarseness of his hair as it grew out, and avoiding the wound where the tube had entered his body.

He took a deep breath and forced himself to slowly relax. *Raise head.*

It took her a few seconds to figure that one out. He must be incredibly sore from lying flat for so long, unable to shift his legs or lift his arms. The only time his arms were moved was when the bandages were changed. She pressed the control that raised the head of the bed, lifting him only an inch or so at a time, keeping her hand on his arm so he could signal her when he wanted her to stop. He took several more deep breaths as his weight shifted to his hips and lower back, then moved his arm to halt her. His lips moved in silent curse, his muscles tightening against the pain, but after a moment he adjusted and began to relax again.

Jay watched him, her deep blue eyes mirroring the pain he felt, but he was improving daily, and seeing the improvements filled her with heady joy. The swelling in his face was subsiding; his lips were almost normal again, though dark bruises still stained his jaw and throat.

She could almost feel his impatience. He wanted to talk, he wanted to see, he wanted to walk, to be able to shift his own weight in the bed. He was imprisoned in his body and he didn't like it. She thought it must be close to hell to be cut off from his own identity as he was, as well as being so completely constrained by his injuries. But he wasn't giving in; he asked more questions every day, trying to fill the void of memories by making new ones, maybe hoping that some magic word would take him back to himself. Jay talked to him even when he didn't ask questions, idle conversation that, she hoped, gave him basic information and perspective. Even if it just filled the silence, that was something. If he didn't want her to talk he would tell her.

A movement of his arm alerted her, and she began the alphabet.

When married?

She caught her breath. It was the first personal question he'd asked her, the first time he'd wanted to know about their past relationship. "We were married for three years," she managed to say calmly. "We divorced five years ago."

Why?

"It wasn't a hostile divorce," she mused. "Or a hostile marriage. I guess we simply wanted different things out of life. We grew apart, and finally the divorce seemed more like a formality than any wrenching change in our lives."

What did you want?

Now that was a twenty-thousand-dollar question. What did she want? She had been certain of her life up until the Friday when she had been fired and Frank Payne had brought Steve back into her life. Now she wasn't certain at all; too many changes had happened all at once, jolting her life onto a different track entirely. She looked at Steve and felt him waiting patiently for her answer.

"Stability, I guess. I wanted to settle down more than you did. We had fun together, but we weren't really suited to each other."

Children?

The thought startled her. Oddly, when they had been married, she hadn't been in any hurry to start a family. "No, no children." She hadn't been able to visualize having Steve's children. Now…oh God, now the idea shook her to the bones.

Remarried?

"No, I've never remarried. I don't think you have, either. When Frank notified me of your accident, he asked if you had any other relatives or close friends, so you must have stayed single."

He'd been listening closely, but his interest suddenly sharpened. She could feel it, like a touch against her skin. *No family?*

"No. Your parents are dead, and if you had any relatives, I never knew about them." She skated around telling him that he'd been orphaned at an early age and raised in foster homes. Not having a family seemed to disturb him, though he'd never given any indication that it bothered him while they had been married.

He lay very still and the line of his mouth was grim. She sensed there was a lot he wanted to ask her, but the very complexity of his questions stymied him. To get his mind off the questions he couldn't ask and the answers he wouldn't like, she began to tell him about how they had met, and slowly his mouth relaxed.

"…and since it was our first date, I was a little stiff. More than a little stiff, if you want the truth. First dates are torment, aren't they? It had been raining off and on all day, and water was standing in the streets. We walked out to your car, and a passing truck hit this huge puddle just as we reached the curb. We were both drenched, from the head down. And we stood there laughing at each other like complete fools. I don't even want to think what I looked like, but you had muddy water dripping off your nose."

His lips were twitching, as if it hurt him to smile but he couldn't stop the movement. *What did we do?*

She chuckled. "There wasn't a lot we could do, looking the way we did. We went back to my apartment, and while our clothes were washing we watched television and talked. We never did make it to the party we'd been going to. One date led to another, and five months later we were married."

He asked one question after another, like a child listening to fairy tales and wanting more. Knowing that he was reaching for the part of himself that was lost due to the blankness of his memory, she tirelessly recounted places they had gone and the things they'd done, people they had known, hoping that some little detail would provide the spark needed to bring it all back. Her voice began to grow hoarse, and finally he managed a small shake of his head.

Sorry.

She pressed his arms, understanding. "Don't worry," she said softly. "It will all come back. It will just take time."

But the days passed and still his memory didn't return—not even a glimmer of a link to the past. She could feel his intense concentration on every word she uttered, as if he were willing himself to remember. Even now, his control was phenomenal; he never allowed himself to become frustrated or lose his temper. He just kept trying, keeping his feelings under control as if he sensed that any emotional upheaval could set his recovery back. Total recovery was his aim, and he worked toward it with a single-minded concentration that never wavered.

Frank was there the day they took the trach tube from Steve's throat, and he waited in the hall with Jay, holding her hand. She looked at him questioningly, but he merely shook his head. Several minutes later a hoarse cry of pain from Steve's room made her jerk, and Frank's hand tightened on hers. "You can't go in there," he said softly. "They're removing his stomach tube, too."

The cry had been Steve's; the first sound he'd made had been one of pain. She began to tremble, every instinct she had screaming at her to go to him, but Frank held her still. There were no other sounds from the room, and finally the door opened and the doctors and nurses exited. Major Lunning was last, and he paused to talk to Jay.

"He's all right," he said, smiling a little at her tense face. "He's breathing just fine, and talking. I won't tell you what his first words were. But I want to warn you that his speaking voice won't be the way you remember it; his larynx was damaged, and his voice will always sound hoarse. It will improve some, but he'll never sound the way he did before."

"I'd like to talk to him now," Frank said, looking down at Jay, and she understood that there were things he wanted to tell Steve, even though Steve didn't remember what had happened.

"Good luck," Major Lunning said, smiling wryly at Frank. "He doesn't want you, he wants Jay, and he was pretty autocratic about it."

Knowing just how autocratic he could be, Frank wasn't surprised. But he still needed to ask Steve some questions, and if this was his lucky day, the questions just might trigger some return of memory. Patting Jay's hand again, he went into Steve's room and firmly closed the door behind him.

Less than a minute later, he opened the door and looked at Jay, his expression both frustrated and amused. "He wants you, and he isn't cooperating until he gets you."

"Did you think I would?" a raspy voice demanded behind him. "Jay, come here."

She began trembling again at the sound of that rough, deep voice, so much rougher and deeper than she remembered. It was almost gravelly, and it was wonderful. Her knees felt rubbery as she crossed the room to him, but she wasn't aware of actually walking. She was just there, somehow, clinging to the railing of his bed in an effort to hold herself upright. "I'm here," she whispered.

He was silent a moment; then he said, "I want a drink of water."

She almost laughed aloud, because it was such a mundane request that could have been made of anyone, but then she saw the tension in his jaw and lips and realized that, again, he was checking out his condition, and he wanted her with him. She turned to the small Styrofoam pitcher that was kept full of crushed ice, which she used to keep his lips moist. The ice had melted enough that she was able to pour the glass half full of water. She stuck a straw into it and held it to his lips.

Gingerly he sucked the liquid into his mouth and held it for a moment, as if letting it soak into his membranes. Then, slowly, he swallowed, and after a minute he relaxed. "Thank God," he muttered hoarsely. "My throat still feels swollen. I wasn't sure I could swallow, and I sure as hell didn't want that damned tube back."

Behind Jay, Frank turned a s.
a cough.

"Anything else?" she asked.

"Yes. Kiss me."

CHAPTER FIVE

WHEN SHE OPENED the door to Steve's room the next morning, he turned his head on the pillow and said, "Jay." His voice was harsh, almost guttural, and she wondered if he'd just awakened.

She paused, her attention caught as she stared at his bandaged eyes. "How did you know?" The nurses were in and out, so how could he have guessed her identity?

"I don't know," he said slowly. "Maybe your smell, or just the feel of you in the room. Maybe I recognize the rhythm of your walk."

"My smell?" she asked blankly. "I'm not using perfume, so if you smell me from that distance something's wrong!"

His lips curved in a smile. "It's a fresh, faintly sweet smell. I like it. Do I get a good-morning kiss?"

Her heart gave a giant leap, just as it had the day before when he'd demanded that she kiss him. She had given him a light, tender kiss, barely brushing her lips against his, while Frank, in the background, had pretended to be invisible; but it had taken her pulse a good ten minutes to settle down afterward. Now, even while her mind shouted at her to be cautious, she crossed the room to him and bent down to give him another light kiss, letting her lips linger for only a second. But when she started to draw away, he increased the pressure, his mouth molding itself to hers, and her heart slammed wildly against her rib cage as excitement shot through her.

"You taste like coffee," she managed to say when she finally forced herself to stand upright again, breaking the contact.

His lips had been slightly parted, with a disturbing sensuality, but at her words they took on a smug line. "They wanted me to drink tea or apple juice—" he made it sound like hemlock "—but I talked them into letting me have coffee."

"Oh?" she asked dryly. "How? By refusing to drink anything until you had your coffee?"

"It worked," he said, not sounding at all repentant. She could imagine how helpless the nurses were against his relentless will.

Despite the fact that she no longer needed to communicate with him in their old way, her hand went to his arm in habit, and she was so used to the contact that she didn't notice it. "How are you feeling?" she asked, then winced at the triteness of the question, but she was still rattled from the effects of his kiss.

"Like hell."

"Oh."

"How long have I been here?"

To her surprise, she had to stop and count the days. She had become so involved with him that time had ceased to mean anything, and it was difficult to recall. "Three weeks."

"Then I have three more weeks in these casts?"

"I think so, yes."

"All right." He said it as if giving his permission, and

she felt that he would give them three weeks and not one day longer, or he would take the casts off himself. He lifted his left arm. "I'm minus a couple of needles today. They took the IVs out about an hour ago."

"I hadn't even noticed!" she exclaimed, smiling a little at the note of pride in his ruined voice. She wondered if she would ever get used to its harshness, but at the same time tiny shivers went down her spine every time she heard it.

"And I refused the pain medication. I want my head clear. There were a lot of questions I wanted to ask before, but it took so much time and effort, and my brain was so foggy from the drugs, that it was just too much trouble. Now I want to know what's going on. Where am I? I've heard you call the doctor Major, so I know I'm in a military hospital. The question is, why?"

"You're in Bethesda," she said.

"A naval hospital?" Astonishment roughened his voice even more.

"Frank said you were brought here for security reasons. There are guards posted at every entrance to this wing. And this was a central location for all the surgeons they pulled in for you."

"Major Lunning isn't navy," he said sharply.

"No." It was astonishing that he could lose the most basic of memories, those of himself, yet retain the knowledge that Bethesda was a naval hospital and that major wasn't a navy rank. She watched the stillness of his mouth as he studied the implications of what she had just told him.

"Then someone with a lot of influence wanted me here. Langley, probably."

"Who?"

"Company headquarters, baby. CIA." She felt a chill of dread as he continued, "Maybe the White House, but Langley is the most likely bet. What about Frank Payne?"

"He's FBI. I trust him," she said steadily.

"Damn, this is getting deep," he muttered. "All these different departments and military branches coordinating just isn't normal. What's going on? Tell me about the explosion."

"Didn't Frank tell you?"

"I didn't ask for or volunteer any information. I didn't know him."

Yes, that was like Steve. He had always held back, watching cautiously, though she had already married him before she began noticing that particular trait. He used his charm like a shield, so that most people would have described him as outgoing and spontaneous, when in fact he was just the opposite. He had held people away, not trusting them and not allowing anyone close to him, but they never noticed, because he was such an actor. Now she sensed that the shield was gone. People could take him as he was or leave him; he didn't care. It was a hard attitude, but she found that she liked it better. It was real, without pretense or subterfuge. And for the first time, he was letting her get close to him. He needed her, trusted her. Perhaps it was only because of the extenuating circumstances, but it was happening, and it stunned her.

"Jay?" he prompted.

"I don't know exactly what happened," she explained. "I don't know why you were there. They don't know either."

"Who is 'they'?"

"Frank. The FBI."

"And whoever else he's working for," he added dryly. "Go on."

"Frank told me that you weren't doing anything illegal that they know of. Perhaps you were only an innocent bystander, but you have a reputation for sniffing out trouble, and they think you might know something about what happened to their operation. They had set up a sting, or whatever you want to call it, but someone had planted a bomb at the meeting site. You were the only survivor."

"What kind of sting?"

"I don't know. All Frank has said is that it involved national security."

"And they're afraid their guy's cover was blown, but they don't know, because the players on the other side were disintegrated, too," he said, as if to himself. "It could have been a double double-cross, and the bomb was meant for the others. Damn! No wonder they want me to get my memory back! But all that doesn't explain one thing. Why are you involved?"

"They brought me here to identify you," she said, absently stroking his arm as she had for so many hours.

"Identify me? Didn't they know?"

"Not for certain. Part of your driver's license was found, but they still weren't certain if you were…you, or their agent. Apparently you and the agent were about the same height and weight, and your hands were burned, so they weren't able to get your fingerprints for identification." She paused as something nagged at her memory, but she couldn't bring the elusive detail into focus. For a moment it was close; then Steve's next question splintered her concentration.

"Why did they ask you? Wasn't there anyone else who could identify me? Or did we stay close after our divorce?"

"No, we didn't. It was the first time I'd seen you in five years. You've always been pretty much a loner. You weren't the type for bosom buddies. And you don't have any family, so that left me."

He moved restlessly, his mouth drawing into a hard line as he uttered a brief, explicit curse. "I'm trying to get a handle on this," he said tersely. "And I keep running into this damned blank wall. Some of what you tell me seems so familiar, and I think, yeah, that's me. Then part of it is as if you're telling me about some stranger, and I wonder if I really know. Hell, how *can* I know?" he finished with raw frustration.

Her fingers glided over his arm, giving him what comfort she could. She didn't waste her breath mouthing platitudes because she sensed they would only make him furious. As it was, he had already used up his small store of energy with the questions he had asked her, and he lay there in silence for several minutes, his chest rising and falling too quickly. Finally the rhythm of his breathing slowed, and he muttered, "I'm tired."

"You've pushed yourself too far. It's only been three weeks, you know."

"Jay."

"What?"

"Stay with me."

"I will. You know I will."

"It's…strange. I can't even picture your face in my mind, but part of me knows you. Maybe biblical knowledge goes deeper than mere memory."

His harsh voice gave rough edges to the words, but Jay felt as if an electrical charge had hit her body, making her skin tingle. Her mind filled with images, but not those of memory; her imagination manufactured new ones—of this man with his harder soul and ruined voice, bending over her, taking her in his arms, moving between her legs in a more complete possession than she had ever known before. Her own breath shortened as her breasts grew tight and achy, and her insides turned liquid. Another tingle jolted her, making her feel as if she were on the verge of physical ecstasy, and merely from his words, his voice. The violence of her response shocked her, scared her, and she jerked away from his bed before she could control the motion.

"Jay?" He was concerned, even a little alarmed, as he felt her move away from him.

"Go to sleep," she managed to say, her voice almost under control. "You need the rest. I'll be here when you wake up."

He lifted his bandaged hand. "How about holding my hand?"

"I can't do that. It would hurt you."

"It would blend in with all the other pain," he said groggily. He was losing strength rapidly. "Just touch me until I go to sleep, all right?"

Jay felt his request go straight through her heart. That he should ask anything of her still staggered her, but his need to be touched was almost more than she could bear. She stepped back to the bed, folding her hand over his arm. At the first touch she felt him begin to relax, and within two minutes he was asleep.

She stepped outside, feeling the need to escape, though she wasn't certain exactly what she was escaping from. It was Steve, and yet it was something else, something inside her that was growing more and more powerful. It scared her; she didn't want it, yet she was helpless to stop it. She had never responded to him like that before, not even in the first wild, heady days of their marriage. It's just the situation, she told herself, trying to find comfort in the thought. It was just her tendency to throw herself wholly into something, concentrating on it too intensely, that made her feel like this. But comfort eluded her and despair welled in her heart, because analyzing her emotions didn't change them. God help her, she was falling in love with him again, with even less reason than she'd had the first time. For most of the past three weeks he'd been little more than a mummy, incapable of movement or speech, yet she had felt drawn to him, tied to him; and loving him now was much more dangerous than it had been before. He was a different, stronger, harder man. Even when he'd been unconscious, she had felt his fierce inner power, and her need to know what had happened to him to cause that change was so strong it almost hurt.

A nurse, the one who had first noticed Steve's unconscious reaction to Jay's presence, stopped beside her. "How is he? He refused his pain medication this morning."

"He's asleep now. He tires very easily."

The nurse nodded, her bright blue eyes meeting Jay's

darker ones. "He has the most incredible constitution I've ever seen. He's still in a great deal of pain, but he just seems to ignore it. Normally it would be at least another week before we began tapering off the pain medication." Admiration filled her voice. "Did the coffee upset his stomach?"

Jay had to laugh. "No. He was rather smug about it."

"He was certainly determined to get that coffee. Maybe we can start him on a soft diet tomorrow, so he can begin regaining his strength."

"Do you know when he'll be transferred out of intensive care?"

"I really don't know. Major Lunning will have to make that decision." The nurse smiled as she took her leave, returning to the central station.

Jay walked to the visitors' lounge to buy a soft drink, and she took advantage of the room's emptiness to give herself some much-needed privacy. She was filled with a vague uneasiness, and she couldn't pinpoint the reason. Or reasons, she thought. Part of it was Steve, of course, and her own unruly emotional response to him. She didn't want to love him again, but she didn't know how to fight it, only that she had to. She *could not* love him again. It was too risky. She knew that, fiercely told herself over and over that she wouldn't allow it to happen, even as she acknowledged that it might already be too late.

The other part of her uneasiness was also tied to Steve, but she wasn't certain why. That aggravating sense of having missed something kept nagging at her, something that she should have seen but hadn't. Perhaps Steve sensed it too, judging by all the questions

he'd asked; he didn't quite trust Frank, though she supposed that was to be expected, given Steve's situation.
But Jay knew that she would trust Frank with her life,
and with Steve's. So why did she keep feeling that she
should know more than she did? Was Steve in danger
because of what he had witnessed? Had Steve actually
been involved in the deal? She would have had to be
naive not to realize that the vast majority of the facts
had been kept from her, but she didn't expect Frank to
spout out everything he knew. No, it wasn't that. It was
something that she should have seen, something that
was obvious, and she'd missed it entirely. It was some
little detail that didn't fit, and until she could pinpoint
what it was, she wouldn't be able to get rid of that nagging uneasiness.

STEVE WAS TAKEN out of intensive care two days later
and moved to a private room, and the navy guards
shifted location. The new room had a television, something the ICU room had lacked, and Steve insisted on
listening to every news program he could, as if he
were searching for clues that would tie all the missing
pieces together for him again. The problem was that
he seemed to be interested in all the world situations
and could discuss the politics of others nations as easily as domestic issues. That disturbed Jay; Steve had
never been particularly political, and the depth of his
current knowledge revealed that he had become deeply
involved. Given that, it became more likely that he had
also been more involved in the situation that had nearly
killed him than perhaps even Frank knew. Or perhaps
Frank did know, after all. He had had several long,

private conversations with Steve, but Steve remained guarded. Only with Jay did he lose his wariness.

His various injuries kept him bed-bound much longer than he should have been, but he wasn't able to negotiate with crutches due to his burned hands. His physical inactivity ate at him, eroding his patience and good humor. He quickly decided which television shows he liked, discarding all game shows and soap operas, but even the ones he liked lacked something, since so much of the action was visual. Merely being able to listen frustrated him, and soon he wanted the set on only for the news. Jay did everything she could think of to entertain him; he liked it when she read the newspaper to him, but for the most part he just wanted to talk.

"Tell me what you look like," he said one morning.

The demand flustered her. It was oddly embarrassing to be asked to describe oneself. "Well, I have brown hair," she began hesitantly.

"What shade of brown? Reddish? Gold?"

"Gold, I guess, but on the dark side. Honey-colored."

"Is it long?"

"No. It's almost to my shoulders, and very straight."

"What color are your eyes?"

"Blue."

"Come on," he chided after a minute when she didn't add anything. "How tall are you?"

"Medium. Five-six."

"How tall am I? Did we fit together well?"

The thought made her throat tighten. "You're six feet, and yes, we did dance well together."

He turned his bandaged eyes toward her. "I wasn't

talking about dancing, but so what? When I get out of these casts, let's go dancing again. Maybe I haven't forgotten how."

She didn't know if she could stand being in his arms again, not with her responses running wild every time she heard his harsh, cracked voice. But he was waiting for her to answer, so she said lightly, "It's a date."

He lifted his hands. "The bandages come off tomorrow. Next week I have the final surgery on my eyes. The casts come off in two weeks. Give me a month to build up my strength. By then the bandages should be off my eyes, and we'll do the town."

"You're only giving yourself a month to get your strength back? Isn't that a little ambitious?"

"I've done it before," he said, then went very still. Jay held her breath as she watched him, but after a minute he swore softly. "Damn it, I *know* things, but I can't remember them. I know what foods I like, I know the name of every head of state of every nation mentioned in the news, I can even recall what they look like, but I don't know my own face. I know who won the last World Series, but not where I was when it was played. I know the smell of the canals in Venice, but I can't remember ever being there." He paused a minute, then said very quietly, "Sometimes I want to take this place apart with my bare hands."

"Major Lunning told you what to expect," Jay said, still shaken by what he'd said. How deeply had he involved himself in the gray world Frank had hinted at? She was very much afraid that Steve was no longer an adventurer, but a player. "Stop feeling sorry for yourself. He said your memory would probably come back in dribbles."

A slow grin touched his lips, deepening the lines that bracketed his mouth and drawing her helpless, fascinated gaze. His lips seemed firmer, fuller, as if they were still slightly swollen, or perhaps it was because his face was thinner and older. "Sorry," he said. "I'll have to watch that."

His wry humor, especially when he had good reason to occasionally feel sorry for himself, only reminded her again of his hard inner strength and was one more blow against the shaky guard she had set up around her heart. She had to laugh at him, just as she had years before, but there was a difference now. Before, Steve had used humor as a wall to hide behind; now the wall was gone, and she could see the real man.

She was with him the next morning when the bandages came off his burned hands for good. She had been in there before when the bandages were changed, so she had seen the raw blisters on his palms and fingers when they had looked much worse than they did now. Patches of reddened skin were still visible all the way to his elbows, but his hands had caught the worst of it. Now that the danger of infection was past, the new, tender skin would heal faster without the bandages, but his hands would be too painful for him to use them much for a while.

When she compared how he looked now to the way he had looked the first time she had seen him, hooked to all those machines and monitors, with so many tubes running into his body, it seemed nothing short of a miracle. It had been only four weeks, but he had been little more than a vegetable then, and now he exerted the force of his personality over everyone who entered his room, even the doctors. His face had been swollen and bruised before; now the hard line of his jaw and the precise cut of his lips fascinated her. She knew that plastic surgeons had rebuilt his shattered face, and she wondered about the changes she would see when the bandages were completely gone and she was able to truly see him for the first time. His jaw was a little different, a little squarer, leaner, but that was to be expected, since he had lost so much weight after he'd been injured. His beard seemed darker, because he was so pale. She was very well acquainted with his jaw and beard, since she had to shave him every morning. The nurses had done it until he became conscious and made it known he wanted Jay to shave him, and no one else.

He no longer had a thick swath of gauze wrapped around his skull. There was a big, jagged white scar that ran diagonally from the top of his head, at a point directly above his right ear, to the back and left of his skull, but his hair was already longer than that of the average military recruit in boot camp, and it was beginning to cover the scar. The new hair was dark and glossy, having never been exposed to the sun. His eyes were still covered with bandages, but though the gauze pads and wrapping were much smaller now than they had been before, the upper bridge of his nose and the curve of his cheekbones were still covered. The bandages tantalized her; she wanted to see his new face, to judge for herself how well the plastic surgeon had done his job. She wanted to be able to apply his identity to his face, to look into his dark eyes and see all the things she'd looked for in their marriage and hadn't been able to find.

"Your hands are tender," the doctor who'd been caring for Steve's burns said as he cut away the last of the bandages and signaled for a nurse to clean them. "Be careful with them until all this new skin has toughened. They're stiff right now, but use them, exercise them. You don't have any tendon or ligament damage, so in time you'll have full use of them again."

Slowly, painfully, Steve flexed his fingers, wincing as he did so. He waited until the doctor and nurses had left the room, then said, "Jay?"

"I'm here."

"How do they look?"

"Red," she answered honestly.

He flexed them again, then cautiously rubbed the fingers of his right hand over his left one, then reversed the procedure. "It feels strange," he said, smiling a little. "They're damned tender, like he said, but the skin feels as smooth as a baby's butt. I don't have any calluses now." The smile faded abruptly, replaced with a frown. "I had callused hands." Again he explored his hands, as if trying to find something familiar in the touch, slowly rubbing his fingertips together.

She laughed softly. "One summer, you played so much sandlot baseball that your hands were as tough as leather. You had calluses on your calluses."

He still looked thoughtful; then his mood changed and he said, "Come sit by me, on the bed."

Curious, she did as he said, sitting facing him. The head of his bed had been raised to an upright position, so he was sitting erect and they were on the same level.

Abruptly she noticed how much she had to look up at him. His bare shoulders and chest, despite the weight he had lost, still dwarfed her, and again she wondered what sort of work he had done that had developed his torso to that degree.

Tentatively he reached out, and his hand touched her hair. Realizing why he had wanted her to sit there, she remained still while his fingers sifted through the strands. He didn't say anything. He lifted his other hand, and his palms cupped her face, his fingers gliding lightly over her forehead and brow, down the bridge of her nose, over her lips and jaw and chin before sliding down the length of her throat.

Her breath had stopped, but she hadn't noticed. Slowly he laced his fingers around her neck as if measuring it, then traced the hollows of her collarbones out to her shoulders. "You're too thin," he murmured, cupping the balls of her shoulders in his palms. "Don't you eat enough?"

"Actually, I've gained a little weight," she whispered, beginning to shake at his warm touch.

Calmly, deliberately, he moved his hands down to her breasts and molded his fingers over them. Jay inhaled sharply, and he said, "Easy, easy," as he stroked the soft mounds.

"Steve, no." But her eyes were closing as warm pleasure built in her, her blood beating slowly and powerfully through her veins. His thumbs rubbed over her nipples and she quivered, her breasts beginning to tighten.

"You're so soft." His voice roughened even more.

"God, how I've wanted to touch you. Come here, sweetheart."

He ignored the pain in his hands as he pulled her against him, and he wrapped his arms around her as he had dreamed of doing so many times since her voice had charmed him out of the darkness. He felt her slenderness, her softness, her warmth, and the gut-wrenching pleasure of her breasts flattening against the hard planes of his chest. He smelled the sweetness of her skin, felt the thick silk of her hair, and with a harsh, muffled sound of want, of need, he sought her mouth.

He already knew her mouth. He would beg, cajole, insist until she would give him a kiss in the morning and again at night before she left. He knew it was wide and full and soft, and that her lips trembled each time she kissed him. Now he slanted his mouth to cover hers, pressing hard until her lips parted and gave him the entrance he sought. He could feel her shaking in his arms as he moved his tongue into her mouth and tasted her sweetness. Damn, how had he been fool enough to let her get away from him five years before? Not being able to remember making love to her made him furious because he wanted to know what she liked, how it felt to be inside her, if they had been as good together as every instinct he possessed told them they would be. She belonged to him; he knew it, felt it, as if they were tied together. He deepened the kiss, forcing her to respond to him the way he knew she could, the way he knew she wanted to. Finally she shivered convulsively, and her tongue met his as her arms crept up around his neck.

He shouldn't be this strong, Jay thought dimly, not

after all he's been through. But his arms were hard, and so tight around her that her ribs were being squeezed. Steve had never been this aggressive before; he certainly hadn't been a passive man, but now he was kissing her with naked demand, forcing their relationship into an intimacy that frightened her. He wanted her more than he ever had during their marriage, but now his attention was intensely focused on her because of the circumstances.

"We shouldn't do this," she managed to say, turning her head aside to free her mouth from the hungry pressure of his. She brought her hands down and pushed lightly at his shoulders.

"Why not?" he murmured, taking advantage of the vulnerability of her throat with slow kisses. His tongue touched the sensitive hollow below her ear, and her hands tightened on his shoulders as wonderful little ripples of pleasure radiated over her skin. His lack of sight didn't hinder him; he knew his way around a woman's body. Instinct went deeper than memory.

Both conscience and her sense of self-protection made Jay push at his shoulders again, and this time he slowly released her. "We can't let ourselves get involved again," she said in a low voice.

"We're both free," he pointed out.

"As far as we know. Steve, you could have met someone in the past five years who you really care about. Someone could be waiting for you to come home. Until you get your memory back, you can't be certain that you're free. And...and I think we should be cautious about jumping back into a relationship without knowing more than we do."

"No one's waiting for me," he said with harsh certainty.

Her movements were jerky with agitation as she slid off the bed and walked to the window. The morning sky was a leaden color, and snow flurries were drifting aimlessly on the light wind. "You can't know that," she insisted, and turned back to look at him.

His face was turned toward her even though he couldn't see her, and the hard line of his mouth told her he was angry. The sheet was around his waist, baring his broad shoulders and chest, as he had disdained both pajamas and a hospital gown, though he had finally consented to wear the pajama bottoms with the legs cut off and the seams slit so they would fit over the casts on his legs. He was thin, pale and weak from what he'd been through, but somehow the impression he gave was one of power. Nor was he all that weak, not if the strength she had just felt in him was any measure. He must have been incredibly strong before the accident. Those five years when she hadn't seen him were becoming even more of a mystery.

"So you've stayed here with me all this time just because you have a Florence Nightingale complex?" he asked sharply. It was the first time she had refused him anything, and he didn't like it at all. If he could have walked, he would have come after her, sightless or not, weak or not, even though he was still in pain most of the time. None of that would have stopped him, and for the first time she was grateful for his broken legs.

"I never hated you," she tried to explain, knowing that she owed him at least the effort. "I don't think we were all that deeply in love, certainly not enough to make our marriage work. Frank asked me to stay because he thought you would need me, given your condition. Even Major Lunning said it would help if you were around someone familiar, someone you knew before the accident. So...I stayed."

"Don't give me that crap." Her attempt to explain had made him even more furious, and it was a type of anger she hadn't seen before. He was very still and controlled, his guttural voice little more than a whisper. Chills ran up her spine because she could feel his temper like both ice and fire, lashing out at her even though he hadn't moved. "Do you think that because I can't see, I couldn't tell you were turned on just now? Try again, sweetheart."

Jay began to get angry at the harsh demand in his voice. "All right, if you want the truth, here it is. I don't trust you. You were always too restless to settle down and try to build a life together. You were always leaving on another of your 'adventures,' looking for something I couldn't give you. Well, I don't want to go through that again. I don't want to get involved with you again. You want me now, and you may need me a little, but what happens when you're well? Another pat on the head and a kiss on the cheek while I get to watch you ride off into the sunset? Thanks, but no thanks. I have more sense now than I did before."

"Is that why you start shaking every time I touch you? You want to get involved again, all right, but you're afraid."

"I said I don't trust you. I didn't say I was afraid of you. Why should I trust you? You were still looking for trouble when that explosion almost killed you!"

Abruptly she realized that she was all but yelling at him, while his voice hadn't risen at all. She turned and walked out, then leaned against the wall outside his door until both the temper and the shaking subsided. She felt sick, not because of their argument, but because he was right. She *was* afraid. She was terrified. And it was too late to do anything about it, because she was in love with him again, despite all her warnings and lectures to herself against it. She didn't know him anymore. He had changed; he was harder, rougher, far more dangerous. He was still a leaver, probably far more involved in the situation than Frank had wanted her to know.

But it didn't make any difference. She had loved him before when it had gone against her better judgement, and she loved him now when it made even less sense. God help her, she had left herself wide open for a lot of pain, and there was nothing she could do.

CHAPTER SIX

STEVE LAY QUIETLY, forcing the lingering cloudiness of anesthesia from his mind. He was instinctively still, like an animal in the jungle, until he was aware enough to know what was going on. A man could lose his life by moving before he knew where his enemies were. If they thought he was dead, he gained the advantage of surprise by lying still and not letting them know he was still alive until he could recover enough to make his move. He tried to open his eyes, but something covered them. They had him blindfolded. But that didn't make sense; why blindfold someone they thought was dead?

He listened, trying to locate his captors. The usual jungle sounds were absent, and gradually he realized that he was too cold to be in a jungle. The smell was all wrong, too; it was a sharp, medicinal odor, like disinfectant. This place smelled like a hospital.

The realization was like a curtain going up, and abruptly he knew where he was and what had happened, and at the same time the hazy recollection of the steamy jungle swiftly faded. The final surgery on his eyes was over, and he was in Recovery. "Jay!" It took an incredible amount of effort to call for her, and his voice sounded strange, even worse than usual, so deep and hoarse it was almost like an animal's cry. "Jay!"

"Everything's all right, Mr. Crossfield," a calm voice

said soothingly. "You've had your surgery, and everything is just fine. Lie still, and we'll have you back in your room in a few minutes."

It wasn't Jay's voice. It was a nice voice, but it wasn't what he wanted. His throat was dry; he swallowed, and winced a little because his throat was so raw and sore. That's right; they'd had a tube down it. "Where's Jay?" he croaked, like a frog.

"Is Jay your wife, Mr. Crossfield?"

"Yes." Ex-wife, if they wanted to get technical. He didn't care about the labels. Jay was his.

"She's probably waiting for you in your room."

"Take me there."

"Let's wait a few more minutes—"

"Now." The single word was guttural, the steely command naked. He didn't try to dress it up in polite phrases, because it was all he could do to say a few words at a time. He was still groggy, but he fixed his thoughts on Jay with single-minded determination. He began groping for the rail on the side of the bed.

"Mr. Crossfield, wait! You're going to pull the IV out of your arm!"

"Good," he muttered.

"Calm down, we're going to take you to your room. Just lie still while I get an orderly."

A minute later he felt the bed begin to move. It was a curiously relaxing movement, and he began to go to sleep again but forced himself to stay alert. He couldn't afford to relax until Jay was with him; there was damned little he knew about who he was or what was going on, but Jay was the one constant in his life, the one person he trusted. She had been there from the beginning, as far back as his memory reached, and further.

"Here we are," the nurse said cheerfully. "He couldn't wait to get back to his room, Mrs. Crossfield. He was asking for you and kicking up a fuss."

"I'm here, Steve," Jay said, and he thought she sounded anxious. He noticed that she didn't correct the nurse about her name, and fierce satisfaction filled him. The name didn't mean much to him, but it was a name he'd once shared with Jay, one of the links that bound her to him.

He was lifted onto his bed, and he could feel them fussing around him for a few more minutes. It was getting harder to stay awake. "Jay!"

"I'm here."

He reached out with his left hand toward her voice, and her slim, cool fingers touched him. Her hand felt so small and fragile in his.

"The doctor said everything went perfectly," she said, her voice somewhere above him in the darkness. "You'll get the bandages off for good in about two weeks."

"Then I'm outta here," he murmured. His hand tightened around hers, and he gave in to the lingering effects of the anesthesia.

When he woke again, it was without the initial confusion, but he was still groggy. Impatiently he forced his mind out of lethargy, and it was so habitual now to ignore the pain in his mending body that he truthfully didn't even notice it. At some unknown point in his life he had learned that the human body could be forced to superhuman feats if the brain knew how to ignore pain. Evidently he had learned that lesson so well that it was second nature to him now.

Now that he was more awake, he didn't have to call for Jay to know she was in the room. He could hear her breathing, hear the pages of a magazine turning as she sat by the bed. He could smell the faint, sweet scent of her skin, a scent that identified her immediately to him whenever she entered the room. Then there was that other awareness, the physical awareness that was like an electrical charge, making his skin tingle with pleasure and excitement at her closeness, or even at the mere thought of her.

He hadn't kissed her since their argument the week before, but he was only biding his time. She had been upset, and he didn't want that, didn't want to push her. Maybe he hadn't been much of a prize before, but she still felt something for him, or she wouldn't be here now, and when the time came he would capitalize on those feelings. She was his; he knew it with a bone-deep sense of possession that overrode everything else.

He wanted her. The strength of his sexual need for her surprised him, given his current physical condition, but the stirring in his loins every time she touched him was proof that certain instincts were stronger than pain. Every day the pain was a little less, and every day he wanted her a little more. It was basic. Whenever two people were attracted to each other, the urge to mate became overwhelming; it was nature's way of propagating the species. Intense physical desire and hot, frequent lovemaking reinforced the bond between two people. They became a couple, because back in the human species' first primitive days, it took two people to provide care for their helpless young. In current times one parent could raise a child quite well, and modern medicine had made it possible for a woman not to become pregnant if she didn't want to, but the old instincts were still there. The sexual drive was still there, a man's need to make love to his woman and make certain she knew she was his. He understood the basis of the biological need programmed into his genes, but understanding didn't lessen its power.

Amnesia was a curious thing. When he examined it unemotionally, he was interested in its oddities. He had lost all conscious knowledge of whatever had happened to him before he'd come out of the coma, but a lot of unconscious knowledge evidently hadn't been affected. He could remember different World Series and Super Bowls, and how Niagara Falls looked. That wasn't important. Interesting, but not important.

Equally interesting, and far more important, were the things he knew about both obscure Third World nations and major powers without remembering how he came by the knowledge. He couldn't bring his own face to mind, but somehow that didn't negate what he knew was fact. He knew the desert, the hot, dry heat and blood-sizzling sun. He also knew the jungle, the stifling heat and humidity, the insects and reptiles, the leeches, the shrieking birds, the stench of rotting vegetation.

Taking those bits and pieces of himself that he could recognize, he was able to piece together part of the puzzle. The jungle part was easy. Jay had told him that he was thirty-seven; he was just the right age to have been in Vietnam during the height of the war in the late sixties. The rest of it, all added together, could have only one logical explanation: he was far more involved in the situation than Jay had been told.

He had wondered if scopolamine or Pentothal would be successful on an amnesia victim, or if the amnesia effectively sealed off his memories even from the powerful drugs available today. If what he might know was important enough for him to warrant this kind of red-carpet treatment, then it would have been worth Frank Payne's effort to at least have tried the drugs. They hadn't tried, and that told him something else: Payne knew Steve had been indoctrinated to resist any chemical prying into his brain. Therefore he must be a trained field operative.

Jay didn't know. She really thought he had simply been in the wrong place at the wrong time. She had said that when they had been married, he had constantly been taking off on one "adventure" after another, so he must have kept her in the dark and just let her think that he was footloose, rather than worrying her with the knowledge of just how dangerous his work was, and that the odds were even he wouldn't return from any given trip.

He had fitted that many pieces of the puzzle together, but there were still a lot of little things that didn't make sense to him. He had noticed, as soon as the bandages were taken off his hands, that his fingertips were oddly smooth. It wasn't the smoothness of scar tissue; his hands were so sensitive, with their new, healing skin, that he could tell the difference between the burned areas and his fingertips. He was positive his fingertips hadn't been burned; rather, his fingerprints had been altered or removed altogether, probably the latter. Recently, too, most likely here in this hospital. The question was: Why? Who were they hiding his identity from? They knew who he was, and he was evidently on good terms with them, or they wouldn't have gone to such extraordinary lengths to save his life. Jay knew who he was. Was someone out there hunting for him? And, if so, was Jay in danger simply because she was with him?

Too many questions, and he didn't know the answers to any of them. He could ask Payne, but he wasn't certain he'd get a straight answer from the man. Payne was hiding something. Steve didn't know what it was, but he could hear a faint note of guilt in the man's voice, especially when he spoke to Jay. What had they gotten Jay involved in?

He heard the door to his room open and he lay motionless, wanting to know the identity of his visitor without them knowing he was awake. He had noticed that cautiousness in himself before; it fit in with what he had deduced.

"Is he awake yet?"

It was Frank Payne's quiet voice, and that special note was there again, the guilt and the…affection. Yeah, that's what it was. Payne liked Jay and worried about her, but he was still using her. It made Steve feel even less inclined to cooperate. It made him mad, to think they could be putting Jay in any danger.

"He went to sleep as soon as they got him in bed, and he hasn't stirred since. Have you talked to the doctor?"

"No, not yet. How did it go?"

"Wonderfully. The doctor doesn't think there's any

permanent damage. He has to lie as quietly as possible for a few days, and his eyes may be sensitive to bright light after the bandages come off, but he probably won't even need glasses."

"That's good. He should be leaving here in another couple of weeks, if everything goes all right."

"It's hard to think of not coming here every day," Jay mused. "It won't seem normal. What happens when he's released?"

"I need to talk to him about that," Payne answered. "It can wait a few days, until he's more active."

Steve could hear the worry in Jay's voice and wondered at it. Did she know something, after all? Why else would she worry about what happened to him when he left the hospital? He had news for her, though; wherever she went, that was where he intended to go, and Frank Payne could take those ideas of his and become real friendly with them.

Two more weeks of biding his time. He didn't know if he could do it. It was hard to force himself to exercise the patience he needed to allow his body to heal, and there were still weeks of rehabilitation ahead before he regained his full strength. He'd have to push himself harder than the therapists would, but he could sense his own limits, and he knew they were more elastic than the therapists could guess. It was just one more piece of the puzzle.

He decided to let himself "wake up" and began shifting restlessly. The IV needle tugged at his hand. "Jay?" he called in a groggy tone, then cleared his throat and tried again. "Jay?" He never quite got used to hearing his own voice the way it was now, so harsh and strained, gravelly in texture. Another little oddity. He couldn't remember his own voice, but he knew this one wasn't right.

"I'm here." Her cool fingers touched his arm.

How many times had he heard those two words, and how many times had they provided him with a link to consciousness? They seemed embedded in his mind, as if they were his one memory. Hell, they probably were. He reached for her with his free hand. "Thirsty."

He heard the sound of water pouring; then a straw touched his lips and he gratefully sucked the cold liquid into his dry mouth and down his raw throat. She took the straw away after only a couple of swallows. "Not too much at first," she said in that calm way of hers. "The anesthesia may make you sick."

He moved his hand and felt the needle tugging at it again. Swift irritation filled him. "Get a nurse to take this damned needle out."

"You need glucose after surgery to keep from going into shock," she argued. "And it probably has an antibiotic in it—"

"Then they can give me pills," he rasped. "I don't like being restricted like this." It was bad enough that his legs were still in casts; he'd had enough of having to lie still to last him a lifetime.

She was silent for a moment, and he could sense her understanding. Sometimes it was as if they didn't need words, as if there were a link between them that transcended the verbal. She knew exactly how frustrated it made him to have to lie in bed day after day; it was not only boring, it went against every survival instinct he possessed. "All right," she finally said, her cool fingers drifting against his arm. "I'll get a nurse."

He listened as she left the room, then lay quietly, waiting to see if Frank Payne would identify himself. It was a subtle game; he didn't even know why he was playing it. But Payne was hiding something, and Steve didn't trust him. He'd do anything he could to gain an edge, even if it was something so trivial as pretending to sleep while he eavesdropped. He hadn't even learned anything, other than that Payne had "plans" for him.

"Are you in any pain?" Frank asked.

Steve cautiously turned his head. "Frank?" Another part of the game, pretending he didn't recognize the other man's voice.

"Yes."

"No, not much pain. Groggy." That much was true; the anesthesia made him feel limp and sleepy. But he could force himself to mental alertness, and that was the important part. He would rather be in pain than be so doped up he didn't know what was going on around him. The barbiturate coma had been a nightmare of darkness, of *nothingness*, which he didn't want to experience again, even in a mild form. Even amnesia was better than that total lack of self.

"That's the last of it. No more surgery, no more tubes, no more needles. When the casts come off your legs, you can start getting back to your old shape." Frank had a quiet voice, and there was often a note of familiarity in it, as if they had known each other well.

His words touched a chord of recognition in Steve; his old shape hadn't been bulky muscles, but rather speed and stamina, a steely core of strength that kept him going when other men would have collapsed.

"Is Jay in any danger?" he asked, cutting through the cautious maneuvering to what was most important to him.

"Because of what you may have seen?"

"Yes."

"We don't anticipate any danger," Frank replied, his voice cautious. "You are important to us only because we need to know exactly what happened, and you might provide us with some answers."

Steve smiled wryly. "Yeah, I know. Important enough to cut through red tape and coordinate two, maybe three, separate agencies, as well as pulling in people from different branches of the service and from the private sector. I'm just an innocent bystander, aren't I? Jay may buy that, but I don't. So cut the crap and give me a yes or no answer. Is Jay in any danger?"

"No," Frank said firmly, and after a second Steve gave a fractional nod, all he could manage. Regardless of what Frank was hiding, he was still fond of Jay and protective of her. Jay was safe enough. Steve could deal with the rest later; Jay was what mattered now.

HIS LEGS WERE thin and weak after having been encased in plaster for six weeks; he ran his hands down them, getting himself accustomed to their peculiar lightness. He could move them, but his movements were jerky and uncontrolled. For the past couple of days he had been sitting in a wheelchair or in the bedside chair, letting his body adjust to movement and different postures. His hands had healed enough that he had been able to stand, using a walker for support, for a few minutes each day. His store of knowledge was increasing all the time. He now knew that even when he was bent forward to hold the walker, he was several inches taller than Jay. He wanted to take her in his arms and hold her against him, to feel her soft body adjust to his size as he bent his head to kiss her. He'd been holding off, taking it slow, but now that was at an end.

Jay watched him massage his thighs and calves, his long fingers kneading the muscles with sure strokes. He was scheduled for a session in physical therapy that afternoon, but he wasn't waiting for someone else to do the work for him. He had been like a coiled spring since the surgery on his eyes: tense, waiting, but under iron control. It had been a month and a half since the explosion, and perhaps lesser people would still have been lying in bed and taking pills for the pain, but Steve had been pushing himself from the moment he'd regained consciousness. His hands had to be tender, but he used them and never winced. His ribs and legs had to hurt, but he didn't let that stop him. He never complained of a headache, though Major Lunning had told Jay he would probably have headaches for several months.

She glanced at her watch. He'd been massaging his legs for half an hour. "I think that's enough," she said firmly. "Don't you want to go back to bed?"

He straightened up in the wheelchair and his teeth flashed in a grin. "Baby, I'm so tired of that bed, the only way you could get me back in it would be if you crawled in there with me."

He looked so wickedly masculine that she felt herself weakening even as she tried to warn herself against his

charm. He wasn't above using his appeal as a wounded
warrior to get to her, blast his hide. She couldn't even
look at him without getting wobbly kneed, and sometimes the way she felt about him welled up in her like
a flood tide, pleasure and pain so sharply mingled that
she would almost moan aloud. Every day he was stronger; every day he conquered new territory, exerted his
will over another aspect of his life. It was both amazing
and frightening to watch him and to realize the extent
of his willpower as he dealt with his situation. He was
so fiercely controlled and determined that it was almost
inhuman, but at the same time he let her see how very
human he was; he depended on her now more than she
had ever imagined possible, and the vulnerability he
revealed to her was all the more shattering because she
knew how rare it was.

"Get the walker for me," he ordered now, turning
his bandaged eyes toward her expectantly, as if waiting for her to protest.

Jay pursed her lips, looking at him, then shrugged
and placed the walker in front of him. If he suffered a
setback, it would be his own fault for refusing to accept his limitations. "All right," she said calmly. "Go
ahead and fall. Break your legs again, crack your head
open again and spend a few more months in here. I'm
sure that will thrill the nurses."

He chuckled at her acerbity, a reaction that was becoming more frequent as he healed. He regarded it as
a measure of his recovery; while he had been ill and
helpless, she hadn't refused him anything. He liked
finding this bite to her personality. A passive woman

wouldn't suit him at all, but Jay suited him in every way, at all times.

"I won't fall," he assured her, levering himself into an upright position. He had to support most of his weight on his arms, but his feet moved when he told them to. Jerkily, true, but on command.

"And heee's offf aaand *stumbling*!" Jay cried in dry imitation of a racetrack announcer, her irritation plain.

He gave a shout of laughter and did stumble, but caught himself with the walker. "You're supposed to guide me, not make fun of me."

"I refuse to help you push yourself too hard. If you fall, it will be your own fault."

A crooked smile twisted his lips and her heart speeded up at the roguish charm it gave his face. "Ah, baby," he cajoled. "I'm not pushing too hard, I promise. I know how much I can do. Come on, guide me down the hall."

"No," she said firmly.

Two minutes later she was walking slowly by his side as he maneuvered the walker, and his reluctant legs, down the hall. At the end of the corridor, the Navy guard watched alertly, examining everyone and everything. It was like that every time Steve left his room, though he didn't realize he was guarded so closely. Jay felt a chill as her eyes met those of the guard and he nodded politely; no matter how calm everything seemed, the guards' presence reminded her that Steve had been involved in something highly dangerous. Wouldn't his amnesia put him in even more danger? He didn't even know he was being threatened or by whom. No wonder those guards were necessary! But realizing just how necessary they were terrified her. This was all part of the large gray area Frank hadn't explained, but she knew it was there.

"This is far enough," Steve said, and cautiously turned around. He turned exactly 180 degrees and took two steps before stopping, his head turning back to her. "Jay?"

"Sorry." Hastily she moved to his side. How had he known how far to turn? Why wasn't he more uncertain of his movements? He walked slowly, still supporting most of his weight on his arms and hands, but he seemed deliberate and sure. He was slowed by his injuries but not thwarted. He wouldn't let himself give in; he didn't look on his injuries as something to be recovered from, but rather as something to be conquered. He would handle this on his own terms, and win, because he wouldn't accept anything less.

She saw even more of his determination in the following days as he sweated through physical therapy. The therapist tried to restrain him but Steve insisted on setting his own pace. He swam laps, guiding himself by Jay's voice, and walked endlessly on a treadmill. By the third day of therapy he had discarded the walker permanently and replaced it with Jay. Grinning as he put his arm around her shoulder, he explained that at least she'd cushion him if he fell.

He had gained weight rapidly since the tube had been taken out of his throat, and now he regained his strength just as rapidly. Jay felt as if she could see a difference in him from one day to the next. Except for the bandages over his eyes, he seemed almost normal, but she knew every scar hidden by the comfortable sweats

Frank had brought him to wear. His hands were still
pink from the burns, and his ruined voice would never
be much better. Nor was his memory showing any sign
of returning. There were no flashes of memory or glim-
mers of recognition. It was as if he had been born when
he had fought his way out of unconsciousness to respond to her voice, and nothing existed before that.

Sometimes, watching him as he exercised with that
frightening relentlessness of his, she caught herself
hoping that his memory *wouldn't* return, and then guilt
would eat at her. But he depended on her so much now,
and if he began to remember, the closeness between
them would fade. Even as she tried to protect herself
from that closeness, she treasured every moment and
wanted more. She was caught on the horns of her own
dilemma and couldn't decide how to get free. She could
protect herself and walk away, or she could grab for
whatever she could get, but she couldn't decide to do
either. All she could do was wait, and watch over him
with increasing fierceness.

The day the bandages were supposed to come off his
eyes, he got up at dawn and prowled restlessly around
the hospital room. Jay had gotten there early, feeling
as anxious as he did, but she forced herself to sit still.
Finally he turned on the television and listened intently
to the morning news, a frown knitting his brow.

"Why the hell doesn't that damn doctor hurry up?"
he muttered.

Jay looked at her watch. "It's still early. You haven't
even had breakfast yet."

He swore under his breath and raked his fingers
through his hair. It was still shorter than was fashion-

able, but long enough to cover the scar that bisected his skull, and it was dark and shiny, undulled by sunlight, and beginning to show a hint of waviness. He prowled some more, then stopped by the window and drummed his fingers on the sill. "It's a sunny day, isn't it?"

Jay looked out the window at the blue sky. "Yes, and not too cold, but the weather forecast says we could have some snow by the weekend."

"What's the date?"

"January 29."

His fingers continued to tap against the sill. "Where are we going?"

Jay felt blank. "Going?"

"When they release me. Where are we going?"

She felt a shock like a slap in the face as she realized he would be released from the hospital within a few hours if everything was all right with his eyes. The apartment Frank had rented for her was tiny, only one bedroom, but that wasn't what alarmed her. What if Frank intended to whisk Steve away from her? Granted, he had once said something about her staying with Steve until his memory returned, but it hadn't been mentioned since. Was that still his plan? If so, where did he intend for Steve to live?

"I don't know where we'll go," she replied faintly. "They may want to send you somewhere...." Her voice trailed off into miserable silence.

"Too damn bad if they do." He turned from the window, and there was something lethal in his movement, a predator's grace and power. She stared at him, silhouetted against the bright window, and her throat contracted. He was so much harder than he had been that it almost frightened her, but at the same time, everything about him excited her. She loved him so much that it hurt, deep inside her chest, and it was getting worse.

A nurse brought in his breakfast tray, then winked at Jay. "I noticed you were here early, so I had an extra tray sent up. I won't tell if you won't." She brought in another breakfast tray, smiling as Jay thanked her. "This is the big day," the nurse said cheerfully. "Call this a sort of precelebration meal."

Steve grinned. "Are you that anxious to get rid of me?"

"You've been an absolute angel. We're going to miss those buns of yours, but hey, easy come, easy go."

A slow flush reddened Steve's cheeks, and the nurse laughed heartily as she left the room. Jay snickered as she unwrapped his silverware and arranged everything on the tray as he was accustomed to finding it.

"Bring your gorgeous buns over here and eat your breakfast," she ordered, still snickering.

"If you like them, get a good view," he invited, turning around and lifting his arms so she did indeed have an excellent view of his tight, muscular buttocks. "I'll even let you touch."

"Thank you, but food wins out over your backside. Aren't you hungry?"

"Starved."

They made short work of the meal, and soon he was again prowling about the small room, his restlessness making it seem even smaller. His impatience was a palpable force, bristling around him. He had spent too many weeks flat on his back, totally helpless and blind, unable even to feed himself. Now he had his mobil-

ity back, and in an unknown number of minutes he'd
know if his sight had been restored. The doctor was
certain of the surgery's success, but until the bandages
were off and he could actually *see*, Steve wouldn't let
himself believe it. It was the waiting and the lack of
certainty that ate at him. He wanted to see. He wanted
to know what Jay looked like; he wanted to be able to
put a face to the voice. If he never saw anything else,
he needed to see her face, if only for a moment. Every
cell in his body knew her, could sense her presence;
but even though she had described herself to him, he
needed to have her face in his mind. The rest of his vanished memory didn't haunt him nearly as much as the
knowledge of Jay that he'd lost, and the most piercing
of all was that he couldn't remember her face. It was
as if he'd lost a part of himself.

His head came up like a wary animal's as he heard
the door open, and the eye surgeon laughed. "I half expected you to have taken the bandages off yourself."

"I didn't want to steal your thunder," Steve said. He
was standing very still.

Jay was just as still, tension coiling in her as she
watched the surgeon, a nurse, Major Lunning and
Frank all enter the room. Frank was carrying a bag
with the name of a local department store on it, and he
placed it on the bed. Without asking, Jay knew it contained street clothes for Steve, and she was vaguely
grateful to Frank for thinking of it, because she hadn't.

"Sit down here, with your back to the window,"
the surgeon said, directing Steve to a chair. When
Steve was seated, the doctor took a pair of scissors,
cut through the gauze and tape at Steve's temple and

carefully removed the outer bandage in order not to disturb the pads over his eyes or let the tape pull at his skin. "Tilt your head back a little," he instructed.

Jay's nails were digging into her palms and her chest hurt. For the first time she was seeing his face without bandages; even the relatively small swathe of gauze that had anchored the pads to his eyes had covered his temples and eyebrows, as well as his cheekbones and the bridge of his nose. He had been a handsome man, but he wasn't handsome any longer. His nose wasn't quite straight, and they had made the bridge a little higher than it had been before the explosion. His cheekbones looked more prominent. All in all, his face had more angles than it had before; the battering he'd taken was evident.

Slowly the doctor removed the gauze pads, then wiped Steve's eyes with some sort of solution. Steve's lids looked a little bruised and his eyes were deeper set than before.

"Pull the curtains," the doctor said quietly, and the nurse pulled them across the window, darkening the room. Then he turned on the dim light over the bed.

"All right, now you can open your eyes. Slowly. Let them get accustomed to the light. Then blink until they focus."

Steve opened his eyes to mere slits and blinked. He tried it again.

"Damn, that light's bright," he said. Then he opened his eyes completely, blinked until they were focused and turned his head toward Jay.

She sat frozen in place and her breath stopped. It was like looking into an eagle's eyes, meeting the fierce gaze of a raptor, a high-soaring predator. They were the eyes of the man she loved so much she ached with it, and terror chilled her blood. She remembered velvety, chocolate-brown eyes, but these eyes were a dark yellowish brown, glittering like amber crystal. An eagle's eyes.

He was the man she loved, but she didn't know who he was, only who he wasn't.

He wasn't Steve Crossfield.

CHAPTER SEVEN

HIS HEART ALMOST stopped in his chest. Jay. The face to go with the name and the voice, the gentle touch, the sweet and elusive scent. Her description of herself had been accurate, yet it was far from reality. The reality of Jay was a heavy mane of honey-brown hair, eyes of deep-ocean blue and a wide, soft, vulnerable mouth. God, her mouth. It was red and full, as luscious as a ripe plum. It was the most passionate mouth he'd ever seen, and thinking of kissing it, of having those lips touch his body, made a hard ache settle in his loins. She was immobile, her face colorless except for the deep pools of her eyes and that wonderful, exotic mouth. She stared at him as if mesmerized, unable to look away.

"How does everything look?" the surgeon asked. "Do you see halos of light, or are the edges fuzzy?"

He ignored the doctor and stood, his gaze never wavering from Jay. He would never get enough of looking at her. Four steps took him to her, and her eyes widened even more in her utterly white face as she stared up at him. He tried to make his hands gentle as he caught her arms and pulled her to her feet, but anticipation and arousal were riding him hard, and he knew his fingers bit into her soft flesh. She made an incoherent sound; then his mouth covered hers and the erotic feel of her full lips made him want to groan. He wanted to be alone with her. She was shaking in his arms, her hands clutching the front of his shirt as she leaned against him as if afraid she might fall.

"Well, your sense of direction is good," Frank said wryly, and Steve lifted his head from Jay's, though he kept her tight against him, her head pressed into his shoulder. She was still trembling violently.

"I'd say his priorities are in order, too," Major Lunning put in, grinning as he looked at his patient with a deep sense of satisfaction. It hadn't been too many weeks since he'd had serious doubts that Steve would live. To see him now, like this, was almost miraculous. Not that he was fully recovered. He still hadn't regained his full strength, nor had his memory shown any signs of returning. But he was alive, and well on the road to good health.

"I can see everything just fine," Steve said, his voice raspier than usual as he looked around the hospital room that had been home to him for more days than he cared to remember. Even it looked good. He'd disciplined himself to picture everything in his mind, to form a sense of spatial relations so that he always knew where he was in the room, and his mental picture had been remarkably correct. The colors were oddly shocking, though; he hadn't pictured colors, only physical presences.

The surgeon cleared his throat. "Ah…if you could sit down for a moment, Mr. Crossfield?"

Steve released Jay, and she shakily sat down, gripping the arms of the chair so tightly that her knuckles were white. They were wrong! He wasn't Steve Crossfield! Shock had kept her mute, but as she watched the surgeon examine Steve—no, *not* Steve!—control returned and she opened her mouth to tell him what a horrible mistake had been made.

Then Frank moved, tilting his head to watch the surgeon, and the movement caught her attention. Ice spread in her veins, freezing her brain again, but one thought still formed: if she told them that she'd made a mistake, that this man wasn't her ex-husband, they would have no use for her. He would be whisked away, and she would never see him again.

She began to shiver convulsively. She loved him. She didn't know who he was but she loved him, and she couldn't give him up. She needed to think this through, but she couldn't right now. She needed to be alone, away from watching eyes, so she could deal with the shock of realizing that Steve…dear God, Steve was dead! And this man in his place was a stranger.

She stood so abruptly that her chair tilted back on two legs before clattering forward again. Five startled faces turned to her as she edged toward the door like a prisoner trying to escape. "I…I just need some coffee," she gasped in a strained voice. She darted out the door, ignoring Steve's hoarse call.

He wasn't Steve. He wasn't Steve. The simple fact was devastating, rocking her to the core.

She ran down the hall to the visitors' lounge and huddled on one of the uncomfortable seats. She felt both cold and numb, and faintly sick, as if she were on the verge of throwing up.

Who was he? Taking deep breaths, she tried to think coherently. He wasn't Steve, so he had to be the American agent Frank had been so concerned about. That meant he had been deeply embroiled in the situation, the one man in the world who knew what had happened, if only he regained his memory. Could he be in danger if anyone—perhaps the person or persons who had set off the explosion that had already almost killed him—knew he was still alive? Until he recovered his memory, he couldn't recognize his enemies; his best protection now was the false identity he wore. She couldn't put him in more danger, nor could she give him up.

It was wrong to pretend he was someone he wasn't. By keeping this secret she was betraying Frank, whom she liked, but most of all she was betraying Steve... *damn*, she hated calling him that, but what else could she call him? She had to continue thinking of him as Steve. She was betraying him by putting him in a life that wasn't his, perhaps even hindering his complete recovery. He would never forgive her when he knew, if he ever regained his memory. He would know she had lied to him, that she had forced him to live a lie by putting him in her ex-husband's place. But she couldn't put him at risk. She just couldn't. She loved him too much. No matter what it cost her, she had to lie to protect him.

"Jay."

It was *his* voice, the raw, gravelly voice that haunted her at night in the sweetest of dreams. Numbly she turned her head and looked at him, still so shocked that she couldn't guard her expression. She loved him. Loving Steve, with his need for excitement that she couldn't give him, had been bad enough; what had she done, letting herself love this man whose life consisted of danger? She had walked off an emotional cliff and was now in a free fall, unable to help herself.

He filled the doorway of the lounge. Now that she knew, she saw the differences. He was a little taller than Steve had been, broader of shoulder and deeper of chest, more muscular. His jaw was squarer, his lips fuller. She should have known just by his mouth, the shape of which hadn't been changed by surgery. A funny kind of pain filled her as she realized that she didn't know what he had looked like before. Had his cheekbones been that high and prominent, his eyes that deep set, his nose slightly off center? His face was battered and rough now, but had it been drastically changed?

"What's wrong, baby?" he asked in a low tone, squatting down in front of her and taking her hands in his. His thick, level brows descended in a frown as he felt the iciness of her fingers.

She swallowed, and fine tremors shook her body. Even hunkered down, he was on a level with her. The sense of power, of danger, about him was overwhelming. It had been partially disguised while his eyes had been bandaged, but now, with his fierce will glittering in those yellow-brown eyes, she felt the full force of his personality.

"I'm all right," she managed to say. "It just got to me all of a sudden. I've been so worried...."

He released her hands and slid his palms up her arms. "I wanted to see you so badly I didn't have time to worry," he murmured. The stroking of his big hands warmed her arms, and she felt the heat of his legs as they pressed against hers. "You told me about your blue eyes, but you didn't tell me about your mouth."

He was looking at her mouth. She felt her lips begin to tremble. "What about my mouth?"

"How erotic it is," he said under his breath, and leaned forward. This time his kiss was hard, seeking, forcing her to give way under his onslaught and open her lips for his tongue. Pleasure shuddered through her muscles even though a dim alarm began to sound. While he had been recovering and needed her support so badly, he had been supplicant, asking for her kisses and the intimacy of her touch. Now he wasn't asking, and she realized that he had been holding back all along. He wanted her, and he was coming after her with the full intention of getting what he wanted.

He stood, his strong grip drawing her up, too, without breaking contact with her mouth. He kissed her with the forceful intimacy of a man who intends to take his woman to bed, loosening the reins of control, demanding more. Jay clung to his shoulders, her senses swimming at the hard pressure of his body against hers. He moved his hips, seeking the cradle of hers, and groaned harshly in his throat when his swollen flesh found the warm notch at the apex of her thighs. She would have groaned, too, if she'd had the breath. A wild, hot madness was swirling through her veins, tempting her to forget everything in the demanding urge to satisfy the longings he'd aroused.

A man and woman entered the lounge; the man walked past without more than a sidelong look, but the woman stopped and blushed before looking away and hurrying past. Steve lifted his head, his hands loosening as a crooked smile quirked his mouth. "I think we need to go home," he said.

She panicked all over again. Home? Were they expecting her to take him to the small one-bedroom apartment she'd been using for the past two months? Or would they take him away from her after all, to finish recuperating in some unknown place?

They left the lounge to find Frank leaning patiently against the wall, waiting for them. He straightened and smiled, but his eyes were sympathetic as he looked at Jay. "Feeling better now?"

She took a deep breath. "I don't know. Tell me what's going to happen, then I'll tell you how I feel."

Steve put his arm around her waist. "Don't worry, sweetheart. They're not sending me anywhere without you. Are you, Frank?" He asked the question mildly, but there was steel underlying his tone, and his yellow-brown eyes narrowed.

Frank looked back at him with wry humor. "It never even crossed my mind. Let's step back into your room and we'll talk."

When they were once again behind a closed door, Frank walked over to the window, opened the curtains and looked out, blinking a little at the brightness of the winter sun. "First, you have to let the surgeon finish his examination of your eyes," he said, and glanced back at Steve. "And you'll need a follow-up exam next week, but I'll arrange that."

Steve made an impatient gesture, one that Frank read perfectly. He held up both hands, palms out in a delaying motion. "I'm getting to that. We'd like to keep you safe, but accessible to us. If you agree, we plan to move you to a safe house in Colorado."

Jay's head spun, and she sat down abruptly. Colorado? Her life had been turned upside down in the past two months, so the thought of such a drastic change shouldn't have stunned her, but it did. How could she go off to Colorado? Then she looked at Steve and knew she would go anywhere if it meant she could be with him. It was ironic. When she had been married, the most important thing in her life had been to establish some sort of stability on which to build her relationship with Steve, and the marriage hadn't survived. Now she had to pretend this man was Steve, but she was willing to walk away from everything and everyone she knew just to be with him. Painful sadness filled her, because this pointed out so clearly that she hadn't truly loved the real Steve Crossfield, though she had wanted to. He had held her away, walked his path alone and died alone without anyone ever really being close to him.

"Denver?" Steve guessed.

"No. The closest town is forty miles from the cabin by road, about fifteen air miles. It's a quiet, peaceful place, with no one to put any pressure on you."

"It's really nice of you folks to do all of this, just for the chance to talk to me when I get my memory back," he drawled, watching Frank with a hard gleam in his eyes.

Frank laughed, thinking that some things never changed. Even without his memory, he was so sharp he'd already put part of the puzzle together. "Why don't you go to the apartment and start packing?" Frank suggested to Jay, then lifted his brows in question. "If you want to go, that is."

"She's going," Steve said flatly, crossing his arms as he leaned against the bed. "Or I don't go."

Because she desperately needed the chance to be alone and think, Jay said yes. She slipped from the room without looking at either man, afraid they would see the terror in her eyes.

Steve regarded Frank in silence for a moment before growling, "You told me there wasn't any danger. Why the safe house?"

"So far as we know, you aren't in any danger—"

"Look, you can cut the crap," he interrupted. "I was an agent. I know all of this—" he gestured at the hospital surrounding him "—wasn't done out of the goodness of the government's heart. I know those guards aren't out there for decoration. I also know you wouldn't go to the expense of hiding me away in a safe house unless there was some threat to me, and unless you very badly need some information I may have."

Frank looked interested. "How did you know the guards were there?"

"I heard them," Steve replied shortly.

Now what? Frank looked at the man who had been his friend for over a decade and wondered how much to tell him. Not all of it, for damned certain. Until the Man nailed Piggot, the masquerade had to continue because it was Steve's best protection against any more attacks on his life. He knew too much for them to leave anything about his security to chance, and for the masquerade to be complete, it had to include Jay. The Man didn't take chances with his agents, or his friends, and Steve was both.

"You're right," Frank said. "You're an agent. A very highly trained agent, and we think the information you got on your last assignment is critical."

"Why the safe house?" Steve asked again, not letting up.

"Because the guy who tried to blow you to kingdom come went underground and hasn't surfaced yet. Until we get him, we want to make certain you're safe."

Like a burst of lightning, fury turned his eyes to yellow. "And you dragged Jay into this?"

Frank watched him warily, knowing how fast he could move. "Piggot doesn't know anyone survived the explosion. We just don't want to take any chances with you."

The yellow eyes flickered at the mention of Piggot's name. "Piggot. What's his first name?"

"Geoffrey."

Again there was that flicker in Steve's eyes and Frank watched closely, wondering if the mention of Piggot's name would trigger any real memory. But if it did, Steve kept it to himself. "I want to see the file you have on him," he said.

"I'll see if I can get clearance."

"But don't expect it, right? I'm a security risk now."

"That's the way it's played."

"Yeah. Now tell me why you had to bring Jay into the game. She doesn't know I'm an agent, does she?"

"No. We brought her in to identify you. It's as simple as that. And once she was here…you responded to her voice so strongly that the doctors decided it would help you to have her around. So she stayed." That was the truth, as far as it went. Frank just hoped Steve wouldn't ask too many more questions. He'd told him about all he could without clearance from the Man.

Steve rubbed his jaw as he mentally cataloged what Frank had told him. If he'd felt his presence was endangering Jay, he would have walked away from her that minute, but he felt Frank's sincerity. The other man thought they were safe enough. The deciding factor was the thought of living in an isolated house with Jay, just the two of them. He would have another chance. He would learn again what pleased her, and what made her angry. They would have another first time together. After he got all his strength and stamina back, they would lie in bed on cold, snowy mornings and make love until their bodies were damp with sweat even in the chilled air, and she would give him all the fiercely passionate love he could sense inside her. She presented a calm, controlled facade to the world, but perhaps because he hadn't been able to see her and had been forced to rely on his other faculties, he'd sensed the depth of her emotions behind that cool control. Maybe he'd been fool enough to let her slip away from him before, but not again.

"Okay," he said, exhaling slowly. "So we go to this safe house. What kind of security and communications does it have?"

"Bulletproof windows, reinforced steel doors. The cabin is isolated, built on a high meadow. There aren't any roads going up there, so a four-wheel-drive vehicle will be made available to you. The cabin has its own generator, so there aren't any public utility records.

You're connected to a satellite-dish antenna for communication and entertainment, with both computer and radio-sending capabilities."

Steve's expression was remote as he concentrated, considering the angles. "Are there any active security systems, or just the passive precautions?"

"Just the passive."

"Why not thermal or motion sensors?"

"To begin with, this cabin is so safe it isn't even on file. And there's a lot of wildlife in the area, which would constantly trigger the alarms. We could set up a perimeter of thermal sensors and program the system to sound the alarm only at a large heat source, but a deer would still set it off."

"How inaccessible is this place?"

"There's just one track leading to it, and I'm being kind by calling it a track. It winds from the cabin across the meadow and down a mountain before it hits a dirt road, then it's twenty more miles before the dirt road runs into a paved secondary road."

"Then a laser across the track would alert us to most visitors, while almost eliminating alarms triggered by wildlife, by covering only a thin strip of the track."

Frank grinned. "You know, don't you, that a bunny is going to hop through that light beam and set off the alarm? All right, I'll have a laser alarm system set up. Do you want an audible or visual alarm?"

"Audible, but a quiet one. And I want a portable beeper to carry with me when we have to leave the house."

"For someone with amnesia, you sure remember a

lot," Frank murmured as he took a small pad from his inside coat pocket and began making notes.

"I remember the names of the heads of state of just about every country in the world, too," Steve replied. "I've had a lot of time to play mind games with myself, putting together pieces of the puzzle by cataloging the things I know. I lost everything personal, but I kept a lot of the things related to my job."

"Your job meant a lot to you. It does that, sometimes, takes over so much that the personal side of life kind of fades away."

"Has it done that for you?"

"It did once, a long time ago. Not now."

"How did you get involved in this? You're FBI, and this sure as hell isn't a Bureau operation."

"You're right about that. A lot of strings were pulled, but there are a few people with the power to manage it."

"Very few. So I'm CIA?"

Frank smiled. "No," he said calmly. "Not exactly."

"What the hell does that mean, 'not exactly'? I'm either CIA or I'm not. There's a shortage of alternatives."

"You're affiliated. That's all I can say, other than to assure you that you're perfectly legal. When you recover your memory you'll know why I can't say more."

"All right." Steve shrugged his acceptance. It didn't really matter. Until he regained his memory, the knowledge wouldn't do him any good.

Frank indicated the bag he had brought in with him. "I brought street clothes for you to change into, but first let me get the surgeon in here to finish your exam. After that, I guess you'll be released."

"I'll need more clothes before we go to Colorado. By the way, where did I live?"

"You have an apartment in Maryland. I've arranged for your clothes to be packed and carried to the plane, but they won't fit until you've gained back the weight you've lost. You'll need new clothes until then."

Steve grinned, feeling suddenly light-spirited. "Jay and I will both need new clothes. The snow in Colorado is probably ass-deep to a giraffe."

Frank threw back his head and laughed.

JAY SAT ON the bed in the cramped apartment she'd been using for the past two months. Her heart was pounding and chills kept racing up and down her spine. The implications, and complications, of the situation terrified her.

Now she knew what it was that had been bothering her off and on for two months; what she had never been able to put her finger on before. When she had been brought here and asked to identify the man in the bed, she hadn't been able to positively say he was Steve Crossfield. Then Frank had said that the man had brown eyes, and she had based her identification on that, because Steve had had dark, velvety eyes, "Chrissy eyes." Probably to a man, or on a vital statistics sheet, brown eyes were simply brown eyes. They didn't allow for chocolate brown, hazel brown or fierce yellow-brown. *But Frank had known that the man had brown eyes!*

She pressed her hands to her temples and closed her eyes. Frank must have known the color of his own agent's eyes, and he had known that Steve's eyes were brown, so it followed that Frank had also realized she couldn't base her identification simply on eye color, yet he had led her to do exactly that. She realized now that he had gently maneuvered her into declaring the man to be Steve Crossfield. He must have known there was at least a fifty-percent chance that the man wasn't Steve, so why had he done it?

The only answer she could come up with, and the one that terrified her, was that Frank had known all along that the man was the American agent and not Steve. He had taken Steve's identity and given it to the man, and given the tale substance by having Steve Crossfield's ex-wife confirm the identity, then maneuvered her into a bedside vigil that would have convinced anyone.

So Steve, the real Steve, was dead, and the agent had been given his identity for…protection?

It all fit. The plastic surgery on his face to alter his appearance; the bandaged hands to prevent fingerprints being taken. Had they done surgery to alter his fingerprints, too? Horrible thought: had they also deliberately damaged his larynx to change his voice? No, surely not. She couldn't believe that. All the doctors had fought so hard for his life, and Frank had been so anxious. No wonder. The man was probably Frank's friend!

But was the amnesia real? Or was the man faking it so he wouldn't have to "remember" any of the details of their supposed life together? Amnesia would be a convenient excuse.

She had to believe the amnesia was real, or she would go mad. She had to believe that "Steve" was as much in the dark as she was, maybe even more so.

And Frank had been sincerely distressed when Major Lunning had told them about the amnesia.

So that left her back at the beginning. If she told Frank she knew Steve wasn't really Steve, the game would be up and they would have no more use for her. She was a screen, useful only to provide incontrovertible proof that the man who had survived the explosion was Steve Crossfield.

So she had to go along with the deception and continue pretending he was Steve, because she loved him. She had fallen in love with him before she even knew what he looked like; she had loved his relentless will, his refusal to give in to pain, to stop fighting. She loved the uncomplaining way he went about recovery and rehabilitation. Except for occasional frustration at his lack of memory, he hadn't let anything get him down. She had fallen in love with the man while he was stripped down to his basic character, without any of the camouflaging layers added by society.

She couldn't give him up now. Yet neither could she take him as hers; she was as caught in the web of circumstance as he was. He trusted her, but she was being forced to lie to him about something as basic as his identity. She knew the man, but she still knew nothing about his life. Dear God, what if he were married?

No, he couldn't be. Whatever game they were playing, they wouldn't tell a woman that she was now a widow, then give her husband another identity. Jay simply couldn't believe that of Frank. But there could still be a woman in Steve's life, someone he cared for, someone who cared for him, even though they weren't married. Was there such a woman waiting for him now,

weeping because he'd been gone for so long, and she
was terrified that he would never come back?

Jay felt sick; her only choices were twin prongs of
the devil's pitchfork, and either would be pure torment.
She could either tell him the truth and lose him, very
possibly throwing him into danger, or she could lie
to him and protect him. For the first time in her life
she loved someone with the full force of her nature,
with nothing held back, and her emotions propelled
her toward the only choice she *could* make. Because
she loved him, she could do nothing but protect him,
no matter what the cost to herself.

Finally she got up and threw her clothing haphaz-
ardly into suitcases, not caring about wrinkles. Two
months ago she had stepped into a hall of mirrors, and
she had no way of knowing if the reflections she saw
were accurate or a carefully constructed illusion. She
thought of her chic apartment in New York and how
much she had worried about losing it when she'd lost
her job, but she couldn't think now why it had seemed
so important to her. Her entire life had been thrown
off kilter, and now it rotated on a different axis. Steve
was the center of her life, not an apartment or a job, or
the security she had fought so hard to win. After years
of struggle she was throwing it all away just to be with
him, and she had no regrets or moments of longing for
that life. She loved him. Steve, yet not Steve. His name,
but another man. Whoever he was, whatever he was,
she loved him.

She found a box and dumped into it the few personal
articles such as books and pictures that she'd brought

to Washington. It had taken her less than an hour to get ready to leave forever.

As she went back and forth, loading things into the car, she looked around carefully, wondering if any of the people she could see supposedly going about their own business were in reality watching her. Maybe she was getting paranoid, but too much had happened for her to take anything for granted, even the appearance of normalcy. That very morning she had looked into fierce, golden eyes and realized that everything that had happened during the past two months had been a lie. The blinders of trust had been stripped from her eyes, making her wary.

Suddenly she felt a driving need to be with him again; uncertainty made her desperate for him. He was no longer a patient in need of her care and attention, but a man who, in spite of his memory loss, would be more surefooted than she was in this world of shifting reality. The instincts and reactions she had wondered about were now explained, as was the scope of his knowledge of world politics. He had lost his identity, but his training had remained with him.

He and Frank were lounging in the hospital room, patiently waiting for her. Jay barely managed a greeting for them; her eyes were on Steve. He had changed into khaki pants and a white shirt with the sleeves rolled back over his forearms. Even as lean as he was, he still gave the impression of power. His shoulders and chest strained at the cotton shirt. With the bandages gone from his eyes, he had shed the last semblance of being in need of care. He looked her over from head to foot and his eyes narrowed in a look of sexual intent as old as time. Jay felt it like a touch, stroking over her body, and she felt both warm and alarmed.

He got to his feet with lazy grace and came to her side, sliding his arm around her waist in a possessive gesture. "That was fast. You must not have packed much."

"It wasn't actually packing," she explained ruefully. "It was more like wadding and stuffing."

"You didn't have to be in such a hurry. I wasn't going anywhere without you," he drawled.

"Both of you have to go shopping, anyway," Frank added. "I didn't think of it, but Steve pointed out that neither of you has clothes suited to a Colorado winter."

Jay looked at Frank, at his clear, calm eyes and friendly face. He'd been a rock for her to lean on these past two months, smoothing the way for her, doing what he could to make her comfortable, and all the time he'd been lying to her. Even knowing that, she simply couldn't believe he'd done it for any reason other than to protect Steve, and because of that she forgave him completely. She was willing to do the same thing, so how could she hold it against him?

"There's no point in shopping here," Steve said. "Or even in Denver. If we go to a city, we'll have to get what some department-store buyer thinks is stylish for a winter vacation. We'll stop at some small-town general store and buy what the locals buy, but not at the town closest to the cabin. Maybe one about a hundred miles from it."

Frank nodded at that impeccable logic, as well as the ring of command in Steve's raspy voice. He was taking over the show, but then, they hadn't expected anything else; amnesia didn't change basic character traits, and Steve was an expert at logistics. He knew what to do and how to get it done.

Jay didn't exhibit any surprise at the precautions. Her deep blue eyes were calm. Having made her decision, she was ready for whatever happened. "Will we need any sort of weapon?" she asked. "After all, we'll be pretty isolated." She had the urbanite's distaste for guns and violence, but the thought of living on a remote mountain put things in a different light. There were times when guns were practical.

Steve looked down at her, and his arm tightened around her. He'd already discussed weapons with Frank. "A rifle wouldn't be a bad idea."

"You'll have to show me how to shoot. I've never handled a gun."

Frank checked the time. "I'll make a call and we'll get started. By the time we get to the airport, the plane will be ready."

"Which airport are we using?"

"National. We'll be flying in to Colorado Springs, then driving the rest of the way." Satisfied with the way things had turned out, Frank went to make his call. Actually he had to make two calls: one to the airport to have the plane readied, and another to the Man to bring him up-to-date.

CHAPTER EIGHT

AFTER A SERIES of small delays, it was midafternoon before the private jet actually took off from Washington National Airport, and the sun was already low in the pale winter sky. There was no way they could make it to the cabin that night, so Frank had already made arrangements for them to stay overnight in Colorado Springs. Jay sat by a window, her muscles tense as she looked down at the monochromatic scenery without really seeing it. She had the sensation of stepping out of one life and into another, with no bridge by which to return. She hadn't even told her family where she was going; though they weren't a close-knit group, they did usually know everyone's location. She hadn't seen any of them at Christmas because she had remained at the hospital with Steve, and now it was as if a tie had been severed.

Steve sat beside her, his long legs stretched out as he lounged in the comfortable seat and pored over several current news magazines. He was totally absorbed, as if he'd been starved for the written word. Abruptly he snorted and tossed his magazine aside. "I'd forgotten how slanted news coverage can be," he muttered, then gave a short laugh at his own phrasing. "Along with everything else."

His wry tone splintered her distracted mood and she

chuckled. Smiling, he turned his head to watch her, rubbing his eyes to focus them. "Unless my vision settles down, I may need glasses to read."

"Are your eyes bothering you?" she asked, concerned. He'd worn sunglasses since leaving the hospital, but had taken them off when they had boarded the plane.

"They're tired, and the light is still too bright. It's a little hard to focus on close objects, but the surgeon told me that might clear up in a few days."

"Might?"

"There's a fifty-percent chance I'll need reading glasses." He reached over and took her hand, rubbing his thumb over her palm. "Will you still love me if I have to wear glasses?"

Her breath caught and she looked away. Silence thickened between them. Then he squeezed her hand and whispered roughly, "All right, I won't push. Not right now. We'll have time to get everything settled."

So he intended to push later, when they were alone in the cabin. She wondered exactly what he wanted from her: an emotional commitment, or just the physical enjoyment of her body? After all, it had been at least two months since he'd had sex. Then she wondered who had been the last woman to lie in bed with him, and jealousy seared her, mingled with pain. Did that woman mean anything to him? Was she waiting for him, crying herself to sleep at night because he didn't call?

They spent the night at a motel in Colorado Springs. Jay was surprised to find there was only a light dusting of snow on the ground, instead of the several feet she had expected, but random flakes were swirling softly out of the black sky with the promise of more snow by morning. The cold pierced her coat, and she shivered as she turned the collar up around her ears. She would be glad to get something more suitable to wear.

Steve was tired from his first day out of the hospital, and she was exhausted, too; it had been a hard day for both of them. She lay down across the bed in her room and dozed while Frank went to get hamburgers for dinner. They ate in Frank's room, and she excused herself immediately afterward. All she wanted was to relax and gather her thoughts. To that end she took a long, hot shower, letting the water beat the tension out of her muscles, but it was still hard to think coherently. The risk she was taking frightened her, yet she knew she couldn't go back. Couldn't—and wouldn't.

She tied the belt of her robe securely and opened the bathroom door, then froze. Steve was stretched out on her bed, his arms behind his head as he stared at the television. The picture was on, but the sound was off. She looked at him, then at the door to her room, her brows puckered in confusion. "I thought I locked the door."

"You did. I picked the lock."

She didn't move any closer. "A little something you remembered?"

He looked at her, then swung his legs off the bed and sat up. "No, I didn't remember it. I just knew how to do it."

Good Lord, what other suspicious talents did he have? He looked lean and dangerous, his battered face hard, his yellow eyes narrow and gleaming; he was probably capable of things that would give her

nightmares, but she didn't fe[...]
much; she had loved him from t[...]
touched his arm and felt his will to [...]
But her nerves jangled as he stood [...]
steps he needed to reach her. He was s[...]
she had to look up to see his face; she c[...] [...]ne
heat emanating from his body, smell the wa[...] [...]nusky
male scent of his skin.

He cupped her cheek in his palm, his thumb rubbing
lightly over the shadows fatigue had smudged under
her eyes, making their blueness seem even deeper. She
was pale and jittery, her body trembling. She had taken
care of him for months, spending all day, every day,
at his bedside, willing him to live and pulling him out
of the darkness. She had filled his whole life to the
point that even the shock of having amnesia paled in
comparison. She had gotten him through hell. Now
the strain was telling on her, and he was the stronger
one. He could feel the tension in her, vibrating like a
string at the point of breaking. He slid his arm around
her waist and pulled her forward until her body rested
against his. His other hand moved from her cheek into
her heavy brown hair, exerting just enough pressure
to bring her head against his shoulder.

"I don't think this is a good idea," she whispered,
the sound muffled in his shirt.

"It *feels* like a damned good idea," he muttered.
Every muscle in his body was tightening, his loins
growing heavy with desire. God, he wanted her. His
hands moved over her slender body. "Jay," he whispered
roughly, and bent his head to hers.

The hot, needful pressure of his mouth made her

...e stroking of his tongue against hers made her ...ghten inside with pleasure so piercing it was almost unbearable. Her hands lifted to the back of his neck, clinging as all strength washed out of her legs. She barely noticed as he turned with her still in his arms and forced her backward until the bed nudged against the backs of her knees. She lost her sense of balance, but his arms supported her as she fell back, and then his hard weight came down on top of her.

She had forgotten how the pressure of a man's body felt, and she inhaled sharply as quick response flooded her veins. The wide expanse of his chest flattened her breasts, and the swollen ridge of his manhood pushed against her feminine mound, his thighs controlling the restless movement of her legs. He kissed her again and again, barely letting her catch her breath before his mouth returned to take it away once more. Feverishly they strained together, wanting more. He pulled at the belt of her robe until the knot gave and the fabric parted, exposing the thinner fabric of her nightgown. He made a rough sound of frustration at this additional barrier, but for the moment he was too impatient to deal with it. His hand closed over her breast, kneading the soft flesh, his thumb making circles on her nipple until it tightened into a nub.

She whimpered softly into his mouth. "We can't," she cried, desperation and desire tearing her apart.

"The hell we can't," he rasped, taking her hand and moving it down his body to where his flesh strained at the fabric of his pants. Her fingers jerked at the contact; then a spasm of pain crossed her pale face, and her hand lingered involuntarily, exploring the dimensions of his arousal. He caught his breath. "Jay, baby, don't stop me now!"

She was stunned at how quickly passion had exploded between them; one kiss and they were falling on the bed. Her lips trembled as she stared up at him. She didn't even know his name! Tears burned her eyes and she blinked them away.

He groaned at the liquid sheen welling in her eyes and kissed her again with rough passion. "Don't cry. I know this is fast, but everything's going to be okay. We'll get married as soon as we can, and this time we'll make a go of it."

Shocked, she swallowed convulsively and barely managed to speak. "Married? Are you serious?"

"As serious as a heart attack, baby," he said, and grinned roguishly.

The tears burned again, and again she forced them back. Misery filled her. She wanted nothing more than to marry him, but she couldn't. She would be marrying him under false pretenses, pretending he was someone he wasn't. Such a marriage probably wouldn't even be legal. "We can't," she whispered, and a tear rolled out the corner of her eye before she could catch it.

He rubbed the wetness from her temple with his thumb. "Why can't we?" he asked with rough tenderness. "We did it before. We should be able to do better this time around, with our prior experience."

"What if you've remarried?" She gulped back a sob as she frantically thought up excuses. "Even if you haven't, what if there's someone else? Until you get your memory back, we won't *know*!"

He froze above her; then, with a sigh, he rolled off

her to lie on his back, staring at the ceiling. He swore with a precise, Anglo-Saxon explicitness that was all the more jarring for the control in his voice. "All right," he finally said. "We'll get Frank to check it out. Hell, Jay, he's already checked it out! Isn't that why they had to get you to identify me?"

Too late she saw the trap, and saw also that he wasn't going to give up; with his usual steamroller determination, he was flattening the obstacles in his path. "You could still have some…someone who loves you, someone waiting for you."

"I can't promise you I don't," he said, turning his head to watch her with his predatory golden eyes. "But that's not a legal deterrent. I won't let you get away from me because some unknown woman somewhere may be in love with me."

"Until you get your memory back, you can't know that *you* aren't in love with someone else!"

"I *know*," he snapped, propping himself up on his elbow and leaning over her. "You keep coming up with excuses, but the real reason is that you're afraid of me, aren't you? Why? Damn it, I know you love me, so what's the problem?"

He was so arrogantly sure of her devotion that her own temper flared, but only for a moment. It was true. She had revealed it in a thousand different ways. She admitted shakily, "I do love you." There was nothing to be gained from denying it, and actually saying it aloud held its own painful sweetness.

His face softened and he put his free hand on her breasts, gently cupping them. "Then why shouldn't we get married?"

It was hard to concentrate with his palm burning her flesh through the thin cotton of her gown, and her body quickened again. She wanted him just as much as he wanted her, and denying him was the hardest thing she'd ever done, but she had no choice. Until his memory returned, she was in limbo. She couldn't take advantage of him now by marrying him under false pretenses.

"Well?" he demanded impatiently.

"I love you," she said again. Her lips trembled. "Ask me again when your memory has returned, and I'll say yes. Until then, until we're both certain it's what you want, I...I just can't."

His face hardened. "Damn it, Jay, I know what I want."

"We've been thrown together because of the circumstances! We don't know each other under normal conditions. You're not the same man I married—" how true that was! "—and I'm not the same woman. We need time! When your memory returns—"

"That's not guaranteed," he interrupted, his voice harsh with frustration. "What if my memory never returns? What if there's permanent brain damage? Then what? Are you still going to be saying no this time next year? Five years from now?"

"I don't think you have brain damage," she said shakily. "You recovered your speech and motor functions too easily."

"That's beside the damned point!" He was furious. Before she could move, he rolled onto her and pinned her hands to the bed. He was so close that she could see the yellow flecks in his irises, his curling black lashes, and a tiny scar in his left eyebrow she hadn't noticed before. He took a deep breath and slowly relaxed, the anger fading from him as he moved against the softness of her body, letting her feel his hardness. "I won't wait forever," he said in soft warning. "I'm going to have you. If not now, then later."

Then he rolled off her and was gone, moving with a peculiar silent grace that had become far more evident since the bandages had been removed from his eyes. There had been signs of it before, manifested in the superb control he had over his movements, but now it was striking. He didn't just move, he flowed, his muscles rippling with liquid power. Jay lay quietly on the bed, her body burning from frustration and the lingering sensation of contact with his, her eyes on the door he had closed behind him.

Who was he? Terror washed over her again, but it was terror for him. He was an agent, obviously, but not just any agent. He had clearly had extensive training; he was valuable enough that the government was willing to spend a fortune protecting him, as well as setting up this elaborate charade with her as an unsuspecting partner. If it hadn't been for his eyes, she might never have suspected a thing. But if he was that valuable to his own government, then logic told her he was of at least equal value to his enemies. All things were in proportion; whatever lengths had been taken to protect him, his enemies would be willing to go to equal lengths to find and destroy him.

As each new part of him was revealed, the stakes seemed to get higher. Now she knew that he was skilled at clandestine forced entry. She had picked up some of the lingo at Bethesda; what had she heard it called? Light entry? No, soft entry. They called it a soft entry. Going in hard was an attack with weapons. Maybe the lock on the motel door wasn't the sturdiest model available, but she knew that picking it was beyond the average citizen. A good burglar wouldn't have any trouble with it, though…or a good agent.

And the way he moved. He was as controlled and graceful as a dancer, but a dancer's moves were poetic, while Steve's were evocative of silent danger.

His mind. No detail escaped him. He was trained to notice and use everything. Already Frank was deferring to him, another sign of his importance.

And he was in danger. Perhaps not immediate danger, but she knew it was there waiting for him.

THE PHONE RANG at two in the morning in Frank's room, and he muttered a sleepy curse as he fumbled for the receiver. It was second nature to him not to turn on a light, which could alert any outside observers that he was awake. Nor did he have to ask who it was, because only one man knew where they were.

"Yes," he said, and yawned.

"Piggot surfaced," the Man said. "East Berlin. We couldn't get to him in time, but we did find out that he's learned there was a survivor of the explosion and has made inquiries."

"Did the cover hold?"

"If Piggot asked at all, there has to be some doubt. Make certain your trail is covered. I don't want anyone other than the two of us to know where they are. How is he doing?"

"Better than I would have, if this had been my first day out of the hospital in two months. He's stronger than I expected. One other thing: I never would have believed it, but I think he's falling in love with her. It isn't just that he's been dependent on her, I think he's really serious."

"Good God," the Man said, startled. He laughed. "Well, it happens to the best of us. I have the final medical report on him here. His brain damage, if any, is minimal. He's a walking miracle, especially the speed of his recovery. He should regain his full memory but it may take a trigger of some sort to release it. We may have to bring his family in, or take him home, but not until we find Piggot. Until then, he stays hidden."

"The day we get Piggot, we tell him—and Jay—what's going on?"

The Man sighed. He sounded tired. "I hope he's recovered his memory by then. Damn it, we need to know what happened over there, and what he found out. But with his memory or without it, he has to stay there until we get Piggot. He has to be Steve Crossfield."

STEVE WOKE EARLY and lay in bed, feeling the fatigue that still weighted his body, as well as the sexual frustration that had been plaguing him for several weeks. He had tried, but even the rigorous exercise he'd been taking hadn't rebuilt his strength to the point he would have liked. Yesterday had exhausted him. He grinned sourly, thinking that it had probably been a good thing Jay had turned him down, because there was a good chance he would have collapsed on her in the middle of making love. Damn it.

He didn't intend to let her refusal stand in his way, but his lack of strength was something else. He had to get back in shape. It wasn't just that he was dissatisfied with his lack of strength and his physical limitations; he had a nagging feeling that he needed to be in top shape just in case...*what*? He didn't know what he expected to happen, but he had an uneasy feeling. If anything came up, he had to be in shape to protect Jay and handle the situation.

After getting out of bed, he first took the pistol that had been on the bedside table and placed it on the floor, within easy reach. Then he dropped down and began doing push-ups, counting silently. Thirty was his limit. Already panting, he rolled over and hooked his feet under the bed, his hands behind his head, and did sit-ups. The new scars on his abdomen throbbed at the strain he was putting on them, and sweat broke out on his brow. He had to stop at seventeen. Swearing in disgust, he looked down at his body. He was in pitiful shape. Before, he'd been able to do a hundred push-ups and sit-ups without even breathing hard—

He went still, waiting for the half memory to become full-blown, waiting for the mental door to open, but nothing happened. Just for a second he'd had a glimpse of what his life had been before; then the door had closed again. The doctor had told him not to try to force it, but that blank door taunted him. There was something he needed to know, and rage built inside him because he couldn't force his way past the block.

Suddenly he heard footsteps outside the room, and he rolled, grabbing the pistol as he did so. Stretched out prone on the carpet, he aimed the pistol at the door and waited. The footsteps halted and a grumpy voice said, "June, come *on*. We need to get an early start and you've wasted enough time."

"Will the town be gone if we get there at four instead of three?" an equally grumpy female voice returned.

Steve let out his breath and climbed to his feet, staring at the pistol in his hand. It fit his palm as if he'd been born holding it. It was a Browning automatic, high caliber, and loaded with hollow-tip bullets that would make a hell of a hole going in and an even bigger one coming out. Frank had given it to him at the hospital while they were waiting for Jay to return and had told him to keep it on him, just as a precaution. When Steve had reached to take it, it was as if part of him had slipped back into focus. He hadn't realized how unusual it had been not to be armed, until the pistol was in his hand.

His reactions just now said a lot about the type of life he'd been living; it had been second nature for him to place the pistol within reach even while exercising, and second nature to regard those approaching footsteps as a possible danger. Maybe Jay had been smart to divorce him the first time. Maybe he wasn't doing her a favor by forcing his way back into her life, considering the dangers of *his*.

The pistol in his hand was a fine piece of hardware, but it couldn't compare to the feel of Jay's body. If he had to choose between Jay and his work, the job had just lost. He'd been a damned fool the first time, but he wasn't going to foul up this second chance. Whoever he worked for would just have to reassign him, bring him in, or he'd get out completely. No more clandestine meetings, no more assassins after him. Hell, it was time he settled down and let the Young Turks have their chance. He was thirty-seven, long past the age when most other men had wives and families.

But he wouldn't tell him until his memory returned, he thought cynically as he showered. Until then, he couldn't afford to totally trust anyone, except Jay.

THEY BOUGHT BOOTS, socks and insulated underwear in Colorado Springs, jeans and flannel shirts in another town, hats and shearling coats in another. Jay also bought a thick down jacket with a hood, and a supply of long flannel gowns. The two vehicles Frank had obtained were four-wheel-drive Jeeps with snow tires, so they made good time, even though the snow became deeper the farther west they went.

Frank drove the lead Jeep, with Steve and Jay in the one behind. Jay had never driven a stick shift before, so the driving was left up to Steve. At first Jay worried about his legs, but he didn't seem to have any difficulty with the clutching and braking, so after a time she stopped worrying and began paying attention to the magnificent scenery as they drove west on U.S. 24. The sky, which had been clear, gradually became leaden with clouds, and occasional snowflakes began to drift down. The weather didn't worsen beyond that, and they continued to make good time even after they turned off onto a state highway. Then they left the state highway for a secondary road with much less traffic and a lot more snow, necessitating a slower speed. After that Frank took a dirt road that wound through the mountains for what seemed like hours, and finally he made another turnoff. Jay could see no discernible road or even a trail; they were simply driving up a mountain by the route of least resistance.

"I wonder if he knows where he's going," she muttered, clinging to the seat as the Jeep jolted to one side.

"He knows. Frank's a good agent," Steve returned absently, downshifting to climb a particularly steep rise. Once they reached the top, they seemed to be in a high, wide meadow that stretched and dipped for miles in front of them. They drove along the edge of the tree line until the meadow abruptly ended, and then they descended sharply down the side of the mountain. Next they climbed up another mountain, where there was a stretch of track barely wide enough to accommodate the Jeeps. On one side was the rock face, and on the other, nothing but an increasing distance to the bottom. Then they crested that mountain, too, and reached another rolling meadow. As the sun dipped behind the western peaks, Steve squinted his eyes at the tree line to their left. "That must be the cabin."

"Where?" Jay asked, sitting up eagerly. Just the thought of being able to get out of the Jeep and stretch her legs was pure heaven.

"In that stand of pines, just to the left."

Then she saw it and sighed in relief. It was just an ordinary cabin, but it was as welcome as a luxury hotel. It was tucked just under the trees, visible only from the front. Because it was built on a slope, the front was higher than the back; there were six wooden steps leading up to a porch that ran all the way across. Built onto the cabin at the back was a lean-to for the Jeeps, and thirty yards to the rear was a shed.

They parked under the lean-to and stiffly got out, arching their backs to stretch aching muscles. The air was so cold and crisp that it almost hurt to inhale, but the setting sun was painting the snowy peaks and ridges in shades of red, gold and purple, and Jay stood motionless, entranced, until Steve nudged her into motion.

It took several trips to carry everything in; then Frank took Steve to the shed to show him how the generator worked. Evidently someone had already been up to turn it on, because the electric lights worked and the refrigerator was humming. Jay checked the small pantry and refrigerator, and found them fully stocked with canned goods and frozen meats.

She gave herself a short tour of the cabin. Next to the kitchen was a small utility-mudroom with a modern washer and dryer. There was no dining room, only a round wooden table and four chairs in one corner of the kitchen. The living room was comfortably furnished in sturdy Early American, with brown corduroy upholstery. A brown-and-blue hooked rug covered the wooden floor, and one wall was almost entirely taken up by an enormous rock fireplace. There were two bedrooms of equal size, connected by the cabin's lone bathroom. Jay stared at the connecting door, her heart beating a little faster at the thought of sharing a bathroom with him. She knew the intimacy of damp towels hanging side by side, toiletries becoming jumbled together, a shared tube of toothpaste. His whiskers would be in the sink, his razor on the side. The small details of living together were at least as seductive as physical intimacies, meshing their lives at every moment of the day.

The back door slammed, and Steve called, "Where are you?" His rough voice was even raspier than usual from breathing the cold air.

"Exploring," she replied, leaving the bathroom and crossing to the bedroom door. "Any objections if I take the front bedroom? It has the best view."

A fire had already been laid in the fireplace. He bent down and struck a match on the hearth, then held it to the paper and kindling under the logs, not answering until he'd straightened. "Let me look at them."

Vaguely surprised, Jay stepped aside and let him enter. He examined the location of the windows and their locks, opened the closet and looked at it, then stepped into the adjoining bath.

"It's a connecting bath," she pointed out.

He grunted and opened the door into the second bedroom. The windows in both rooms were on the side walls, but because the rear of the cabin was closer to the ground than the front was, the windows in the second bedroom were more accessible from the outside. "All right," he said, checking the locks on his windows, too. "But I want it understood that if you hear anything at all during the night, you wake me. Okay?"

"Yes," she said, her throat constricting. All this was second nature to him. He must think there was some danger, too, despite all the precautions Frank had taken. She had wanted to think they were safe here, but perhaps they weren't. The best thing she could do was not argue with him.

He glanced at her, and his rough face softened a bit. "Sorry. I guess I'm overreacting to a strange situation. I didn't mean to scare you." Because the tension didn't fade from her eyes, he walked over to her, cupped her face in his hands, then kissed her. Her wonderfully full, lush, exotic mouth opened for him and his tongue teased at hers. Jay put her hands on his shoulders and luxuriated in the heat of his body against her. The cabin wasn't icy, but it was far from warm.

He held her against him for a moment, then reluctantly let her go. "Let's see what this place has in the way of grub. If I don't eat soon, I'm going to fall down." He wasn't exaggerating, she realized. She could feel a faint tremor in his muscles, a sign of the enormous strain he'd put on his body that day.

Casually she put her arm around his waist as they walked back to the living room. "I've already checked the food. We can have almost anything our hearts desire, as long as our hearts desire plain cuisine. If you want lobster or truffles, you're out of luck."

"I'd settle for a can of soup," he said tiredly, and groaned as he sank down into one of the comfortable chairs. He stretched his legs out, absently rubbing his thighs.

"We can do better than that," Frank said as he brought in an armload of wood, having caught Steve's last comment. He stacked the wood on the hearth and dusted his hands. "I think. I'm not much of a cook." He looked hopefully at Jay, and she laughed.

"I'll see what I can do. I'm a real whiz with microwave dinners, but I didn't see a microwave oven, so I'm a little lost."

She was too tired to do much, but it didn't take a lot of effort to open two large cans of beef stew and heat them, or to brown buttered rolls in the gas oven.

They were almost silent as they ate, and after Frank had helped her clean up the few dishes, they all took turns in the shower. By eight o'clock they were asleep, Jay and Steve in their respective bedrooms and Frank rolled in a blanket on the couch.

They rose early the next morning, and after a hearty breakfast Frank and Steve walked around in the snow. The gas stove and hot-water heater operated on butane gas, and the large tank had been filled; it shouldn't need refilling until spring. The fuel tank for the generator would need replenishing, but all Steve had to do was contact Frank by computer, and fuel would be brought in by helicopter. They didn't want a delivery to the cabin by any commercial business or utility, and, at any rate, the cabin was too difficult for an ordinary fuel truck to reach. It was a complicated setup, but it was meant to be an ultrasafe lodging, unlisted in any files. All in all, the place was stocked for a long-term stay, though Frank couldn't help wishing Steve would recover his memory soon and put an end to all this, or that Piggot would be caught.

"The nearest town is Black Bull, population one hundred thirty-three," Frank said. "Go down to the dirt road and turn right, and you'll eventually get there. It has a general store for basic food and supplies. If you want anything fancier, you'll have to find a larger town, but keep a low profile. You should have enough cash to last a couple of months, but let me know if you need more."

Steve looked out over the white meadow. The air was so clear, the early-morning sun so bright on the spotless snow, that it hurt his eyes. The cold burned his lungs. The land was so damned big and empty that it gave him an eerie feeling, but at the same time he was almost content. He was impatient for Frank to leave so he would finally be alone, completely alone, with Jay.

"You're safe here," Frank added. "The Man uses it sometimes." He glanced up at the cabin. "I wouldn't have brought Jay here if it wasn't safe. She's a civilian, so take good care of her, pal."

A tingle, a heightened awareness, had seized Steve when Frank mentioned the Man. It wasn't a sense of danger but a sort of excitement. The memory was there, but blocked from his consciousness by the lingering effects of the explosion. The Man was another piece of the puzzle.

He shook Frank's hand, and their eyes met in the comradeship of men who have been in danger together. "You probably won't see me again until this is over, but I'll be in touch," Frank said. "I'd better get moving. It's supposed to start snowing again this afternoon."

They went inside and Frank got his gear, then told Jay goodbye. She hugged him, her eyes suspiciously bright. Frank had been her rock for two months, and she would miss him. He had also been a buffer between her and Steve; when he left, there would be only the two of them.

She glanced at Steve, to find him watching her intently. His pale brown eyes were glowing, yellower than they had moments before, like those of a raptor that had sighted its prey.

CHAPTER NINE

JAY HAD EXPECTED Steve to pounce on her, but to her relief he seemed to have other things on his mind. For the next week he spent the daylight hours prowling around the cabin and shed and exploring their high meadow, as tense and wary as a cat in unfamiliar surroundings. The hours passed tromping through the snow tired him, and as often as not he would go to sleep soon after eating dinner. Jay worried, until she realized that it was a natural part of his recovery. The rehabilitation he'd had in the hospital had given him a start, but he was still a long way from full strength, and the many hours of walking served two purposes: to acquaint him with his new territory, and to rebuild his stamina. It was the end of the week before he began to relax, but every day he still walked a perimeter around the cabin, watching, checking for any intrusion.

They seemed so isolated that she couldn't understand his caution, but she supposed it was ingrained in him. Watching him gave her an even greater insight into the man he was. He was so superbly suited to his occupation! He knew what to do by instinct, without needing to rely on memory.

When he was stronger, he began chopping wood to keep a good supply for the fireplace. They used the hearth for most of their heat, to conserve fuel. The cabin was so snugly built and insulated that it held heat well, and a good fire was sufficient to keep the entire place comfortable. At first his hands were sore and blistered, despite the gloves he wore, but gradually they toughened. After a while he added jogging to his activities, but he didn't jog in the meadow, where it was clear. He ran through the trees, up and down the hills, deliberately picking the roughest path, and every day his legs were a little stronger, his breathing a little easier, so he would push himself further.

Jay loved those first days in the cabin, high in the vast, silent meadow. Sometimes the only sound was that of the wind stirring the trees. Having been accustomed her entire life to the bustle of cities, the space and silence made her feel as if she'd been reborn in a new world. The last remnants of tension from her old life relaxed and faded away. She was alone in the mountains with the man she loved, and they were safe.

He began teaching her how to drive a stick shift. To Jay, it was fun, bouncing in the Jeep over the meadow. To Steve, it was a precaution, against the possibility that something could happen to him and Jay would have to do the driving. It might come down to a matter of saving her life.

There was a heavy snow the third week they were there. Jay woke early to a world where every sound had been muffled. She got up to peek out the window at the deep drifts of new snow, then tumbled back into her warm bed and fell instantly asleep again. When she woke the second time it was almost ten, and she felt wonderfully rested, as well as starving.

She dressed hurriedly and brushed her hair, wonder-

ing why the cabin was so silent. Where was Steve? She
looked into his room, but it was empty. There was a
pot of coffee in the kitchen, and she drank a cup while
standing at the window, searching the tree line for some
sign of him. Nothing.

Curious, she finished the coffee and returned to her
room to stamp her feet into warm boots; then she put
on her shearling coat and pulled a thick knit cap over
her hair. It was unusual for Steve to go out without telling her where he would be and how long he'd be gone.
She wondered what he was doing, and why he hadn't
woken her. Could he have hurt himself?

Anxious now, she went down the back steps.
"Steve?" she called softly, a little afraid to raise her
voice. The meadow was so silent, and for the first time
its isolation felt threatening, instead of safe. Was there
someone else out there?

His footprints were plainly visible in the new snow.
He'd evidently made several trips to the woodpile to
replenish the supply in the house, because there was
a worn trail between them; then he'd walked up the
slope into the forest. Jay dug her gloves out of her coat
pocket and put them on, and wished she'd wrapped a
scarf around her nose and mouth. It was so cold that
the air felt brittle. She turned the collar of the coat up
around her neck and began following Steve's trail, carefully stepping in his tracks because that was easier than
breaking through the snow herself.

The snow wasn't as deep under the trees, making
the walking easier, but Jay kept to the prints Steve had
made. The thickly-growing evergreens, their branches
weighted down with snow, blanketed noise and muffled

it out of existence. She could barely hear herself breathe or the snow crunching under her boots. She wanted to call Steve's name again but somehow didn't dare, as if it would be sacrilege in this silent white, black and green cathedral.

If anything, she tried to be even quieter, picking her way from tree to tree, trying to become part of the forest. Then, suddenly, she lost Steve's tracks. She stood under the drooping limbs of a spruce and looked around, but there were no more tracks to follow. It was as if he'd vanished. It was impossible to walk in the snow without leaving tracks! But there were no tracks under the trees. She looked up, wondering if he'd climbed a tree and was sitting there laughing at her. Nothing.

Common sense told her that he'd played some sort of trick, but his tracks would have to pick up somewhere. She thought a minute, then began walking in a slow, constantly enlarging circle. She would have to cross his path somewhere.

Fifteen minutes later, she was angry. Damn him! He was playing games with her, unfair games, considering his training. She was getting cold, and she was already starving. Let him play Daniel Boone; she was going back to the cabin to cook breakfast—for *one*!

Just to be perverse, she backtracked as cautiously as she'd come; maybe she could leave him in here, sneaking around and hiding from her while she was already back at the cabin, snug and warm and eating a hot breakfast. He'd show up after a while, all innocence, and he could damn well cook his own breakfast! Show-off!

She crept back toward the cabin, sidling as close to the tree trunks as she could, stopping often to listen for any betraying sound before moving to the next tree, and looking in all directions before moving again. Her indignation grew, and she began to think what she could do in the way of revenge, but most of her ideas seemed both petty and paltry. What she really wanted to do was hit him. Hard. Twice.

She had just begun to creep around a tree when the skin on the back of her neck prickled and she froze, her heart leaping in fear at the ancient warning of danger. She couldn't hear or see anything, but she could feel someone, or some*thing*, close by. Were there wolves in the mountains? Or bears? Motionless except for her eyes, she looked around for something to use as a weapon, and finally she saw the outline of a sturdy-looking stick, buried under the snow. A fraction of an inch at a time, she bent to reach for the stick, her senses raw and screaming.

Something hard and heavy hit her in the middle of the back, and another blow numbed her forearm. She was knocked facedown in the snow, her lungs straining for air, her arm useless. She couldn't even scream. She was jerked roughly onto her back, and there was a flash of shiny metal as a knife was laid against her throat.

Stunned, terrified, unable to breathe, she stared up into narrowed, deadly eyes as yellow as an eagle's.

His eyes widened as he recognized her, then narrowed again with rage. He jabbed the wicked-looking knife back into its scabbard and took his knee off her chest. "Damn it, woman, I could've killed you!" he roared, his voice like rusty metal. "What in hell are you doing?"

Jay could only gasp and writhe on the ground, wondering if she might die from lack of air. Her entire chest was burning and her vision was wavering.

Steve jerked her to a sitting position and whacked her on the back several times, hard enough to hurt, but at least the air rushed back into her body. She almost choked as her lungs expanded again, and tears sprang to her eyes. She gagged and coughed, and Steve patted her on the back but his tone was hard: "You'll be all right. It's less than you deserve, and a hell of a lot less than what could have happened."

She didn't plan it. She saw the stick out of the corner of her eye, the one she'd been reaching for when he'd hit her, and the next thing she knew it was in her hand. Red mist fogged her vision as she swung at him with all the strength her fury had given her. He dodged under the first blow, cursing, and leaped back to escape the second one. She moved to the left, trying to back him against a tree so he wouldn't be able to escape so easily, and swung again. He tried to grab the stick, and she caught him on the wrist with a solid *thunk*! then wound up for another blow. Cursing again, he bent low and rushed her. She hit him on the back with the stick just as his shoulder jammed into her stomach with enough force to knock her sprawling again.

"Damn it!" he yelled, kneeling astride her and pinning her wrists to the ground. "Settle down! Damn it, Jay! What in hell's wrong with you?"

She twisted and bucked beneath him, trying to throw him off. He tightened his knees on her sides, forestalling that effort, and his hands bit into her wrists so tightly there was no way she could free them. Finally she stopped struggling and glared impotently at him, her eyes like blue fire. "Get off me!"

"So you can brain me with that damn stick? Fat chance!"

She took a deep, shuddering breath and forced her voice to a relatively calm tone. "I won't hit you with the stick."

"Damn straight you won't," he grunted, releasing her hand to grab the stick and hurl it away from them. Jay used her free hand to wipe the snow out of her face, and slowly Steve eased his weight off her chest. She sat up and pulled the knit cap off her head to shake it free of snow.

Kneeling on one knee beside her, Steve brushed off her back. "Now suppose you explain just what you thought you were doing," he snapped.

Fury burst in her again and she swung at him. He jerked his head back in time to escape her fist, but the wet cap she held in her hand swiped his face with enough force to sting. Like a stroke of lightning she was flat on her back again. From between gritted teeth he said, "One more time and you'll eat standing up for a month!"

She blazed back at him: "You just try it! When I woke up and couldn't find you, I was worried you might be hurt, so I came looking for you. Then you started showing off with your Super Spy tricks, not letting me find you, until I got fed up and started back to the cabin. *Then* you knocked me down and pulled a knife on me, *and* yelled at me! You deserved to get hit with a stick!"

He glared down at her, taking in her tumbled hair and fierce blue eyes, and the stubborn set of those luscious lips. He swore under his breath and thrust his fingers into the honey-brown strands, holding her still while he ground his mouth against hers. His kiss was half angry and half starving. He was suddenly wild to feel her lips, to put his tongue inside her mouth and taste her. She kicked at him, and he moved swiftly, kneeing her legs apart and settling himself between them, his weight crushing her into the snow.

Jay groaned, and his tongue thrust into her mouth. Suddenly she felt on fire, as her fury turned into a different, white-hot passion. Her hands were in his hair, digging into his scalp as she returned his kiss as fiercely as he gave it. His hips rubbed against her in primal rhythm, thrusting as if to deny the sturdy denim between them, and her blood felt like lava.

Roughly he opened her thick coat and shoved the edges aside, his hands covering her breasts, but still she was protected from him by her shirt and bra, and the contact wasn't enough. He jerked at her shirt, popping three of the buttons off to be lost in the snow, and opened it, too. The cold air rushed at her and she cried out, but the sound was caught in his mouth. Her bra had a front hook; he handled it easily and peeled the thin cups away from her white, swollen breasts. Her nipples were hard and tight from the cold, stabbing into his palms when he put his hands over them.

He lifted his head. "Let me inside you," he rasped. "Now." The need was riding him hard, just the way he wanted to ride her. He put his hot mouth over a pouting nipple and sucked strongly at it, rolling it around with his tongue and listening to the incoherent sounds of pleasure she made.

Jay thought she might die from wanting him, even though he had scared her and hurt her; even though he'd made her angrier than she could ever remember feeling at another human being. He'd loosed the passion that had always been in her nature, torn it out of her control. Her hands were shaking, her entire body was shaking, and she wanted more.

He lifted his mouth from her breast, and the shock of the cold air on her wet flesh was so painful she whimpered. Their eyes met, hers wide and dazed with the sudden passion, his narrow and burning, and she knew what he wanted, knew he was silently waiting for her permission. She knew that if she made the slightest sign of acquiescence he would take her there, in the cold and snow, and her entire body throbbed with the need to let him do just that. She started to whisper his name; then terror washed over her like freezing water and she stared up at his hard face as he waited for her answer. *She didn't know his name!* She could call him Steve, but he wasn't Steve. His face wasn't Steve's. She knew him and loved him, but he was a stranger.

He found his answer in the sudden rigidity of her body beneath him. He swore viciously as he got to his feet, one hand rubbing the back of his neck as if that could relieve his physical tension. Jay fumbled with her shirt, trying to draw the edges together, but the buttons were gone and her hands were shaking too badly, so finally she just fastened her coat and got to her feet. She had been burning up only moments before, but now she was freezing. She was covered with snow. She shook it out of her hair and dusted it off her jeans and coat as best she could, then retrieved her knit cap, but it had snow on it both inside and out, and would be worse than wearing nothing at all. Without a word, unable to look at him, she started toward the cabin.

He caught her roughly by the shoulder and swung her around. "Tell me why, damn it," he rasped.

Jay swallowed. She hadn't meant to stop him, and she couldn't explain the dreadful fear she lived with every moment, every day. "I've told you before," she finally managed. "They're good reasons." A single tear tracked down her cheek and formed frozen salt crystals before it reached her chin.

His face changed, some of the angry frustration leaving him, and he wiped at the tear with his gloved hand. "Are they? Your reasons don't make much sense to me. It's natural to want each other. How much longer do you think I can live like a monk? How much longer can you live like a nun? That's not my calling, baby, and damn it all to hell and back in a little red wagon, it's not as if it'll be the first time!"

She thought she would scream. She wanted to cry and she wanted to laugh, but neither would make sense. She wanted to tell him the truth, but the biggest fear she had was of losing him. So finally she did tell him the truth, or at least part of it. "It *will* be the first time," she croaked, strangling on the words. "This time. And it scares me."

She walked away again, and he let her go. She was shaking with cold by the time she got back to the cabin, and she took a long hot shower, then dressed in dry clothing. The smell of fresh coffee came from the kitchen, and she followed her nose to find him frying bacon and whipping eggs in a bowl. He had changed clothes, too, and she faltered under both his physical impact and a sudden realization. He was tall and muscular, as powerful as a puma, his shoulders and chest straining the seams of his shirt. In the weeks they had been there he'd gained weight and muscle, and his hair had grown enough that now it was a trifle long. He looked uncivilized and dangerous, and so utterly male that she quivered instinctively. He was no longer a patient. He had recovered both his health and his strength. She had followed him because she had been worried, but in her mind he had still been a wounded warrior. Now she knew that he wasn't. Her subconscious had recognized it earlier, when she had fought him. She never would have done that before.

He looked up at her, his gaze assessing. "I made fresh coffee. Drink a cup. You still look a little shaky. Does the thought of making it with me scare you that much?"

"*You* scare me." She couldn't stop the words. "Who you are. What you are."

An icy motionlessness seized him as he realized that she had guessed. "You said I was using Super Spy tricks."

"Yes," she whispered, and decided she did need that cup of coffee. She poured it and watched the steam rise for a moment before sipping. Why had she said that? She hadn't meant to. She was in agony, afraid that it would trigger his memory and he would leave, and equally afraid that he might never get his memory back. She was caught, trapped, because she couldn't call him hers until he regained his memory and *chose* her. If he would. He might just walk away, to his real life.

"I didn't think you knew," he said flatly.

Her head jerked up. "Do you mean you did?"

"There had to be more to it than the possibility that I had seen something before the explosion. The government doesn't work that way. I guessed, and Frank confirmed it."

"What did he say?" Her voice was thin.

His smile was equally thin, and a little savage. "That's about it. He can't tell me more because of the circumstances. I'm a security risk right now. How did you guess?"

"The same. There just had to be more to it."

"Is what I am the real reason you turned me down?"

"No," she whispered, an aching, needing expression in her eyes as she watched him. How could loving a man hurt so much? But it did, when the man was this one.

His entire body was taut, his mouth twisted. His voice was harsh. "Stop looking at me like that. It's all I can do to keep myself from pulling your pants off and laying you down on that table, and that isn't the way I want to take you. Not this time. So stop looking at me as if you'd melt if I touched you."

But I would, she thought, though she turned her eyes away. His words made her feel hot and shivery, thinking of the act he'd described, the scene forming in her mind. It would be raw and hot, and purely sexual. If he touched her, they would burn each other up.

He spent most of the day outside, but the tension between them didn't ease; it hung there, as thick and heavy as fog. When darkness finally drove him inside, his eyes burned her every time he looked at her. Instincts she hadn't known she possessed pulled her toward him, despite the reasons her mind presented for not letting their relationship progress. She lay alone in her bed that night, aching with the need to go to him and spend the long, dark hours in his arms. He was right; what did her reasons matter? It was already too late. She already loved him, for good or bad. That was the real danger, and it had been too late for a long time now. Keeping herself from him wouldn't lessen the pain if the worst happened and she lost him.

But she didn't go to him. Things often seemed different in daylight than when lying alone in the darkness, but caution wasn't what kept her in her own bed. Circumstances were hard enough; she had to call him by a name that wasn't his own, had to pretend he was someone else, but she wanted to be able to see his eyes when they made love. More than anything she wanted to know his real name, to be able to call him by it in her heart; failing that, she wanted to see his eyes, for they were his own.

A chinook blew in during the night, chasing away the weather system that had covered them with new snow. Mother Nature must have chuckled to herself as she promptly began melting the high white drifts with her hot winds, teasing them with a hint of a spring that was still over a month away. The melting snow dripped from the trees with a sound like rain, and there were crashes in the night as limbs dropped their white burdens.

The rise in temperature made Jay even more restless,

and she was up at dawn. She could barely believe what she saw when she looked out. The hot wind had turned their winter wonderland into a wet, brown meadow dotted with shrinking patches of snow. The melting snow still dripped off the roof, and the heated air made her feel as if her skin would explode. How could it have happened so fast?

"A chinook," Steve said behind her, and she whirled, her heart jumping. She hadn't heard him approach, but he moved like a cat. He looked so ill-tempered that she almost stepped back. His eyes were hard and frosty, and a day's growth of beard darkened his jaw. He glanced from her to the window. "Enjoy it while you can. It'll feel like spring while we have it, and then it'll be gone, and the snow will come back."

They ate breakfast in silence, and he left the cabin immediately afterward. Later on in the morning, Jay heard the solid bite of the ax into wood, and she peeked out at him from the kitchen window. He had taken off his coat and was working in his shirt sleeves, which were rolled up over his forearms. Incredibly, sweat had left dark stains under his arms and down the center of his back. Was it that warm?

She walked out onto the front porch and lifted her face to the warm, sweet wind. It was incredible! Her skin tingled. The temperature was at least forty degrees higher than the day before, and the sun burned down from a cloudless blue sky. Suddenly her jeans and flannel shirt were much too heavy, and her skin began to glisten with moisture.

Like a child made giddy by spring, she hurried to her bedroom and stripped off her heavy, restricting clothes. She couldn't stand them another minute. She wanted to feel the air on her bare arms; she wanted to feel fresh and free, like the chinook. So what if winter could come back at any time? Right now, it was spring!

She pulled her favorite sundress from the closet and slipped it on over her head. It was white cotton, sleeveless, with a scoop neck, and far too flimsy for the temperature, which was probably only in the fifties, but it suited her mood perfectly. Some things were just meant for celebrating; this chinook was one of them.

She hummed as she began the preparations for lunch; it was a while before she noticed that Steve was no longer at the woodpile. If he'd gone off just at lunchtime, she would eat alone and he could do without! She still hadn't quite forgiven him for the day before.

Then she heard a slight noise from out front, and she removed the soup from the stove before walking to the front door. He'd pulled the Jeep around and was washing it. It was such a domestic scene that it lured her onto the porch, and she sat down on the top step to watch him.

He glanced up at her, and his eyes flickered over the dress. "Pushing it a little, aren't you?"

"I'm comfortable," she said, and she was. The crisp air was both chilly and warm, and the sun beating down on her was a delicious sensation. He'd given in to the rising temperature, too, by unbuttoning his shirt and pulling it out of his jeans.

She watched as he alternately scrubbed and rinsed, each time having to stop washing to take up the hose and spray the soap off the Jeep. Finally she went down to pick up the hose from where he'd dropped it. "You wash, I'll rinse."

He grunted. "Do you expect the same deal with the dishes?"

"Sounds fair to me. After all, I'm doing the cooking."

"Yeah, but I'm having to eat all that food so it won't go to waste."

She gave him an awful look. "Poor baby. I'll see what I can do to take that burden off you."

"Just like a woman. Tease her a little bit and she turns nasty. Some people just can't take a joke."

Jay turned the hose on the section of Jeep he'd just washed, but he didn't have time to step back, and the water hit the Jeep full blast, spraying back into his face and onto his clothes. He leaped back, swearing. "Damn it, watch what you're doing!"

"Some people just can't take a joke," Jay said sweetly, and turned the hose on him.

He yelled from the shock of the cold water hitting him and started toward her, holding his hands up to deflect the stream from his face. Jay chortled and darted around the Jeep, then got him again when he looked around at her.

He pushed his wet hair back and his light brown eyes took on that unholy yellow gleam. "You're going to get it now," he said, beginning to grin, and with one bound leaped onto the hood of the Jeep. Jay shrieked and ran to the rear, but the hose caught on the tires as she dragged it after her. She tugged frantically as Steve jumped lightly to the ground. He laughed in a way that made her scream again, and she threw the hose down as she ran for safety.

He grabbed the hose and reversed direction, running back around the front of the Jeep, to free it. He met Jay almost head-on.

"Wait," she said, laughing and begging at the same time as she held up her hand. "It's lunchtime. I came out to tell you. The soup's ready—" A blast of water hit her in the face.

The water was almost unbearably cold. She screamed and tried to run for safety, but he was there every time she turned, and the water soaked her from head to foot. Finally her only means of defense was attack, so she ran straight at him. He was laughing like a maniac, a sound that ceased abruptly when she twisted the nozzle up so the water hit him right in the mouth. They wrestled for control of the nozzle, both of them laughing and yelling as the icy water sprayed all over them.

"Truce, truce!" she yelled, backing away. There was no way she could have gotten any wetter, but then, neither could he. She felt a sense of satisfaction that it had turned out so evenly.

"Are you giving up?" he demanded.

She hooted. "What's to give up? We're both half drowned."

He thought about that and nodded. Then he walked over to the spigot to turn it off and began coiling the hose. "You fight dirty. I like that in a woman."

"That's right, butter me up. You just want to make certain I don't stop cooking."

"The situation being what ... from you I can get."

Abruptly the humor was gone ... He dropped the hose and straightened as he looked at her.

Jay felt her breath catch. He had never ... ore beautiful to her than he was at that moment, soaking wet, his hair plastered to his skull, badly in need of a shave, and his eyes glittering with masculine intent. Slowly he let his gaze move over her face, then down her body, taking his time as he traced the outline of her form.

Then she realized that he could see more than the outline. The white cotton dress was almost transparent, plastered to her body the way it was. She couldn't stop herself from looking down. Her nipples were hard and erect, plainly visible under the wet cotton, and the fabric was molded to her hips and thighs. With the sun shining through the material, she might as well have been naked for all the protection the dress gave her.

She looked back up at him and froze in place at the look on his face. He was staring at her with such savage male hunger that her heart leaped, making the blood surge through her veins. Her legs trembled as she felt herself begin to grow warm and moist in response, and she inhaled sharply.

His head jerked up. For another moment he was motionless. Her lips were parted slightly, trembling. Her eyes looked heavy. Her nipples were hard little circles plainly visible through the wet dress, her arms limp at her sides as she let him look. He shuddered, and his control snapped.

couldn't move. He walked toward her without taking his gaze from her, without seeing or hearing anything else, a primal male animal intent on mating. He was breathing hard and deep, his nostrils flaring. Water dripped off him as he moved. She waited, shaking with need and fear, because he was out of control and she knew it. It was an exhilarating terror, freezing her but at the same time filling her with an anticipation so acute she was almost in pain.

Then his hands were on her, and she moaned aloud from the sudden release of tension.

She didn't have time to respond. She had expected to be swept up in his arms and carried to bed, but he had gone far beyond paying attention to niceties. Nothing mattered to him but to have her, right then. He bore her down to the cold, wet earth, which, despite the chinook, still held the long freeze of winter. Jay cried out at the iciness against her back, involuntarily arching upward to escape it. Steve's hard hands pressed her back, and he covered her, his weight pinning her down. He jerked at her dress, pulling the skirt to her waist. "Spread your legs," he said gutturally, though he was already kneeing her thighs apart.

Excitement speared through her. "Yes," she whispered, her hands digging into his shoulders. She wanted him so much that she didn't care where they were or how urgent he was. There would be time for seduction later, as well as worry. Right now there was only this quick, primitive mating.

There was no foreplay, no leisurely petting or stroking. For months there had been too much between them while the final intimacy had been denied, and suddenly the walls were down. He disposed of her panties by the simple means of tearing them apart, then unfastened his pants and shoved them down only as far as was necessary. He pushed her legs wider apart and lowered himself onto her.

She made a little sound of pain as he tried to enter her and couldn't. He swiftly adjusted his position and pushed again, this time sliding deep into her. Shock reverberated through her body as she tried to adjust to his girth, and this time she groaned.

He braced himself on his elbows, and Jay looked up at him dazedly. His yellowish eyes were fierce, his face hard and intent, his neck corded as he drove into her. She arched up to accept him, her heart almost exploding with love. This was what she had wanted, to see his face, to see his eagle-fierce eyes, to imprint his image on her mind and heart even as he imprinted his touch on her body. With the icy earth beneath her and the pure blue sky above, with the bright sun on his face, they were as pure and primitive as their surroundings. No matter what his name or what he did, he was her love, her man.

This was for him. She lifted her hips to meet his thrusts, her flesh quivering under his pounding force. He groaned unintelligibly and slid his arms beneath her to lift her up even more, as if he could grind their bodies so tightly together that they would mesh, then convulsed in release.

She held him tightly, her legs around his hips, her arms about his shoulders as he heaved into her, groaning and shivering. "I love you," she said over and over again, though her lips moved soundlessly and only the warm winds heard her. She closed her eyes, feeling that warm wind on her cheek and his heavy weight both on her and in her, and knew that no matter what happened when he regained his memory, this hard, fast possession had made her his in a way that could never be shattered.

CHAPTER TEN

THEY LAY TOGETHER, motionless, the only movement that of the wind stirring their hair, the only sound that of the trees rustling together, sighing. Jay felt dazed by what had just happened, her senses buffeted as if she had just weathered a storm. She was totally incapable of action.

Then he braced his hands and lifted his weight off her, staring down at her with an expression so fierce that she almost cringed from it, without knowing why. He swore, his voice low and gravelly, as he disengaged their bodies and shifted to a kneeling position. Uncertainty paralyzed her as her sluggish mind began trying to grasp the reason for his anger.

He pulled his pants up but didn't bother fastening them; instead he tugged her up and into his arms, lifting her from the ground and rising to his feet with a lithe grace that belied the strength necessary to do it. He climbed the steps and strode into the house without saying a word, then carried her into the bathroom. After carefully standing her on the rug, he bent to turn on the water, then straightened and turned back to her. Her dress was unfastened and gently pulled over her head, leaving her naked and shivering from both chill and reaction. She stood docilely, her arms limp at her sides, her eyes wide and dazed and a little frightened as she watched him. What was *wrong*?

He hurriedly stripped, then lifted her into the tub and stepped in beside her, pulling the shower door closed. Jay moved back, a little bemused by how much room he took up, and watched the rippling muscles in his back as he adjusted the water, then turned on the shower. Warm water blasted out of the shower head, immediately filling the small area with steam. Steve pulled her under the water and held her there even when she gasped a protest, because the water was stinging her cold skin.

"No, you need to get warm," he said roughly, rubbing his hands up and down her arms and shoulders. "Turn around and let me wash your hair."

Numbly she did so, realizing that they must have gotten mud all over them. His hands were gentle as he lathered and rinsed her hair, then washed her all over. She began to feel very warm from the combination of water and the stroking of his soapy hands, first over her breasts and abdomen, then her legs and buttocks, and finally between her legs. Her breathing began to hasten as heat built in her.

His touch slowed, and a spasm twitched his tight facial muscles. Her breathing halted altogether as he probed tantalizingly at the entrance to her body, his fingertips barely stroking, one finger barely entering. She caught at his shoulders, her nails digging into his sleek, wet skin. Her breasts were tight and aching as she hung there in an agony of anticipation, waiting for that small invasion, wanting so much more. She felt

him hardening against her hip, and a g
pleasure shook her.

He muttered something, but the sound was so r
she couldn't understand it; then she was in his arms,
and his mouth was bruising hers. She yielded to his urgency, sliding her hands to the back of his neck. Their
water-slick bodies rubbed together, his abrasive chest
hair rasping at her nipples, his muscled stomach rippling against the softness of hers, his hardness pushing at her. "Yes," she whimpered.

"I'm sorry, baby," he said, the words rough and frantic and urgent. He slid his mouth down her throat, biting at the sensitive arch, licking the small hollow at the
base, where her pulse throbbed visibly. "I didn't mean
to be that rough."

So that was why he was angry, not at her, but at
himself. But even that wasn't enough to keep him from
having her again. She could feel the hunger in his big,
powerful body, and again his loss of control thrilled
her in a deeply primitive way. She had been married,
but Steve had always kept his cool, kept part of himself securely locked away from her, and the passionate
part of her had been hurt, because she'd needed more.
The man in her arms now was savage in his hunger,
driven out of control by his need for her, and his wildness matched the fierce passion of her own nature. All
her life she had needed this answering intensity to balance her; without it, she had withdrawn behind a shell
of rigid control, and only now was she being freed.

She clung to him like a vine, her wet body undulating against him. "I love you," she groaned, because that

...her throat, his face so close
...gaze was all she could see. "I

...it. "Yes," she said, and fitted her
...ngue delicately probing. His arms
tighte... ...lsively that she couldn't breathe, but
breathing d... matter. Kissing him mattered. Loving
him mattered.

But finally he did find some remnant of control,
enough to allow him to turn off the water and haul her
out of the tub. She never released her hold on his neck
as he swept her up and carried her, both of them dripping wet, to his bed. She didn't care about the sheets.
All she cared about was his hot mouth on her breasts,
the rasp of his slightly roughened fingertips on her silky
skin, and finally his powerful invasion of her body. It
was still such a shock to her senses that she cried out,
instinctively trying to close her thighs. But her legs
tightened on his muscled thighs and the movement only
drew him deeper.

He ground his teeth together, trying to force himself to stillness when every instinct told him to move.
The need was so urgent that it smothered everything
else in the world except the woman he held in his arms,
the woman whose slim body clasped him so tightly and
pushed him to the edge of insanity. But for her sake he
managed to hold still until she was more comfortable
with him. Lying propped on his elbows so his weight
wouldn't crush her, he looked down at her and shuddered with pleasure at the intense, absorbed look on

her face as she lifted her hips slightly, tentatively, to accept all of him. A deep groan tore from his chest. He knew he'd been too rough and urgent to allow her time to enjoy it before, but this time she was with him.

Her lips parted slightly in a smile so female it took his breath away, and her deep blue eyes beckoned him, dared him. Once again her hips lifted. "What are you waiting for?" she breathed.

"For you," he answered, and even as he lost himself in the mindless ecstasy of making love to her, the truth of that remained. He'd waited for her forever.

He was a light sleeper, so much so that even in the heavy-limbed aftermath he was disturbed by the damp sheets, a discomfort they hadn't noticed before. Jay lay in his arms, exhausted and deeply asleep; he didn't want to disturb her, but neither did he want her to become chilled from the wetness. He eased from the bed and lifted her light weight in his arms, then carried her into the other bedroom to place her on the dry bed. She made a disgruntled noise as he jostled her, then relaxed again, and her breathing evened out as he stroked her back. He joined her on the bed, and she snuggled closer, into his hard, possessive embrace.

The way he felt about her was so intense it edged into pain. Even without his memory, he knew no other woman had ever shattered his control as she did. He'd never desired another woman so intensely, never would have waited as long as he'd waited for her. She overshadowed every other concern. Because of her, he hadn't dwelled on his loss of memory, beyond a peculiar irritation and a certain detached interest in the curiosities of what he had retained. His past life didn't matter, because Jay was here in the present. They were linked in a way that went beyond memory.

A slight frown creased his brow as he held her, his rough hand sliding from the curve of her hip to the warmly resilient mound of her breast. Of all the knowledge he'd kept, why wasn't any of it of Jay? Those were the memories he resented losing. He wanted to remember every minute he'd spent with her, and he wanted to remember why he'd let her slip away from him. He wanted to remember their wedding, the first time he'd made love to her, and the total lack of those memories ate at him. She was the core of his life; why hadn't *something* been familiar? Why hadn't he felt some deep-seated recognition of the silkiness of her skin, the rounded curves of her high breasts or the rose-brown of her small nipples? Why hadn't there been some sense of familiarity in the tight sheath of her body as he entered her?

But everything had been new.

She moved slightly against him, and he stilled his stroking hand, content to simply hold her. They would be married as soon as he could talk her into it, and now he had a very powerful weapon at his disposal.

The scene exploded in his mind. There was a laughing bride and a groom looking excited, proud, wary and impatient all at once. The groom shook his head, beaming, and the bride hugged him tightly. "You made it!" she said exultantly. "I knew you would!"

An older woman and man hugged him just as tightly. "I'm glad you're back, son," the man said, and the woman cried a little even as she smiled at him, the smile full of love. Then there was a rush of other people to shake his hand and hug him and clap him on the back, and the scene dissolved in a confusion of voices.

He lay rigidly, his jaw clenched with the effort required not to jackknife out of bed. Where in hell had *that* memory come from? The man had called him "son," but that could as easily have been a title of affection as one denoting a relationship. He didn't have a family, so they must have been close friends, but Jay had said he'd always been a loner. Who were they? Did they worry about him? Did Jay know anything about them?

Hell, was it even something that had really happened, or a scene from a movie he'd watched?

Movie. Just thinking the word triggered another flashback, but this one was complete with rolling credits. It was a television special on Afghanistan. Then it became another movie, starring a widely acclaimed actor. It was a good movie. Then, in slow motion, the scene shifted. He was standing on a rooftop with the same actor when the man pulled a .45 automatic and pointed it at him. Serious business, a .45. It could have a major impact on a man's future. But the guy was too close, and too rattled. Steve saw himself lash out with his foot, sending the gun flying. The actor staggered back and tripped, fell over the low wall and screamed as he dropped the full seven stories to the ground.

Steve stared at the bedroom ceiling, feeling sweat run down his ribs. Was that another movie? Of all the things he could remember, why a series of films? And why were they so realistic, as if he had stepped into the action? He'd have to ask the doctor about that, but at least it was a sign his memory was returning, just as they'd told him it probably would. He needed to make the trip anyway, to have his eyes checked; it was a real strain to read, and the strain hadn't lessened. He definitely needed glasses. Glasses...

An elderly man smiled benignly at him and removed his glasses, placing them on the desk. "Congratulations, Mr. Stone," he said.

He stifled a curse as the scene faded. This was weird; why would that old guy call him "Mr. Stone" unless he'd been using an assumed name? Yeah, that made sense, unless it was just another scene out of another movie. It could just be something he'd watched rather than something that had actually happened.

Jay stirred in his arms and abruptly woke, lifting her head to stare at him in alarm. "What's wrong?"

She had sensed his tension, just as she had from the beginning. He managed a smile and touched her cheek with the backs of his fingers, a different kind of tension taking over his muscles. "Nothing," he assured her. She looked sleepy and sensual, her eyes heavy-lidded, her luscious mouth swollen from contact with his firmer lips.

She looked around. "We're in my room," she said in bewilderment.

"Mmm. The sheets on my bed were wet, so I brought you in here."

Warm color tinted her cheeks as she thought of how the sheets had gotten so wet, but her smile was both secret and content. She lifted her hand and touched his face, much as he had touched hers; her dark blue eyes drifted over his features with aching tenderness, examining each line and plane, feeding the need in her heart. She was unaware of her expression, but he saw it, and his chest constricted. He wanted to say, "Don't love me like that," but he didn't, because it was essential to him that she love him exactly like that.

He cleared his throat. "We have a choice."

"We do? Of course we do. Of what?"

"We can get up and eat the lunch you were cooking—" he broke off to lift his head and look at the clock "—three hours ago, or we can try to wreck this bed, too."

She considered it. "I think we'd better have lunch, or I won't have the energy to help you wreck the bed."

"Good thinking." He hugged her, reluctant to get up despite his own hunger, and found his hands stroking down her sides in sensual enjoyment. Then he paused and moved his hand around to her stomach. "Unless you want to get married this weekend, we'd better do something about birth control."

Jay's heart felt as if it had abruptly swollen so large that it filled her entire chest. For a few glorious hours she'd forgotten how hemmed in she was by this tortuous maze of deception. She wanted nothing more than to simply say "Yes, let's get married," but she didn't dare. Not until he knew who he was—and *she* knew who he was—and he still said he wanted to marry her. So she ignored the first part of his statement and merely answered the second. "We don't have to worry about birth control. I'm on the Pill. My doctor put me on it seven months ago, because my periods had gotten so erratic."

His eyes narrowed a little and his hand lay heavier on her stomach. "Is something wrong?"

"No. It was just stress from my job. I could probably do without them now." Then she smiled and turned her face into his shoulder. "Except for a sudden development."

He grunted. "Sudden, hell. I've been hard for two months. But we could still get married this weekend."

She eased out of his embrace and got up, her face troubled as she put on fresh underwear and got a sweater from the closet, pulling it over her head.

He watched her from the bed. His voice was very soft and raspy when he spoke. "I want an answer."

Harried, she pushed her tangled hair out of her eyes. "Steve—" She stopped, almost cringing at the necessity of calling him by that name. Now more than ever, she wanted, needed, to know her lover's name. "I can't marry you until you've gotten your memory back."

He threw the sheet back and stood, magnificently naked. Jay's pulse rate skittered as she looked at him. All the miles he'd run and the wood he'd chopped had corded his body with muscles. He didn't look as if he'd ever been injured, except for his scars. Her heart settled into a slow, heavy beat. She had cradled his weight, taken his pounding invasion, returned his fire with her own. As tender as she felt now in different parts of her body, she could still feel herself grow warm and liquid as she looked at him.

"What difference does my memory make?" he snapped, and she jerked her gaze upward, realizing that he was angry. "No other woman has a claim on me, and you know it, so don't bring up that crap again. Why should we wait?"

"I want you to be certain," she said, her voice troubled.

"Damn it, I am certain!"

"How can you be, when you don't know what's happened? I just don't want you to regret marrying me when everything comes back to you." She tried a smile, and it only wobbled a little. "We're together, and we have time. That will have to be enough for now."

Steve forced himself to be content with that, and in many ways it was enough. They lived together in the truest sense of the word, as partners, friends and lovers. It was a week before the snows came again, and in that week they explored every inch of their high meadow. He showed her the laser-beam sensor he'd installed across the trail and demonstrated how to operate both the radio and the computer. It was a relief not to have to hide from her how deeply he'd been involved in espionage, though she got a little huffy with him because all the equipment had been hidden from her in the shed and only now had he gotten around to telling her about it.

He liked making her lose her temper. It was exciting, in a primitive way, to watch those blue eyes narrow like a cat's. It was the final sign that he'd tormented her into attack. The day he'd thought she was an intruder and tracked her in the snow, then tackled her, her rage had startled him, caught him off balance, but it had excited him. Most people who knew Jay would never think she was capable of that kind of anger, or that she would physically fight anyone. It told him a lot about her, about the passionate, volatile side of her personality and about what it took to bring it out. Probably very few people could make her angry, but because she loved him, he could. And after he'd provoked her to anger, he liked to wrestle with her and love her out of her temper.

Physically she delighted him. She was still too thin, though she ate well, but he liked to watch her trim hips and rounded buttocks in her tight jeans too much to complain. Her skin was satiny, her breasts high and round, her exotic mouth full and pouty; no matter how she dressed, she turned him on because he knew what lay under those clothes. He also knew that all he had to do was reach for her and she'd turn into his arms, warm and willing. That kind of response enchanted him; there was something so new about it, as if he'd never known it before.

Then one morning they got up to find that it had snowed again during the night, and it continued snowing all during the day, not hard, just a continuous veil of flakes sifting down over the meadow. Except for trips outside to bring in more firewood, Jay and Steve spent the day in the cabin, watching old movies. That was an extra benefit of the satellite dish; they could always find something interesting to watch on television, if they were in the mood. It was perfectly suited to a lazy day when they had nothing better to do than to lie around and watch the fat snowflakes drifting down.

Just before dark, Steve left to check the area, something he always did. While he was gone Jay began cooking dinner, humming as she did so, because she was so contented. This was paradise. She knew it couldn't last; when his memory returned, even if he still wanted to marry her, their lives would change.

They would leave here, find another home. She would have to find another job. Other things would take up their time. This was time set aside, out of the real world, but she meant to enjoy every minute of it. Briefly a dark thought intruded: This could be all she had. Perhaps it was. If so, these days were all the more precious.

Steve entered through the back door, slapping snow off his shoulders and shaking it out of his hair before taking off his thick coat. "Nothing but rabbit tracks." He looked thoughtful. "Do you like rabbit?"

Jay turned from the cheese she was grating for the spaghetti. "If you shoot the Easter Bunny..." she began in a threatening tone.

"It was just a question," he said, and grabbed her for a kiss, then rubbed his cold, beard-roughened check against hers. "You smell good. Like onion and garlic and tomato sauce." Actually, she smelled like herself, that sweet, warm, womanly scent he associated with her and no one else. He buried his cold nose against her neck and inhaled it, feeling the familiar tension growing in his loins.

"You won't get any points for telling me I smell like onions and garlic," she said, returning to her chore even though he kept his arms looped around her waist.

"Even if I tell you how crazy I am about onions and garlic?"

"Humph. You're like all men. You'll say anything when you're hungry."

Chuckling, he released her to set the table and begin buttering the rolls. "How would you like to take a trip?"

"I'd love to see Hawaii."

"I was thinking more in terms of Colorado Springs. Or maybe Denver."

"I've *been* to Colorado Springs," she said, then looked at him curiously over her shoulder. "Why are we going to Colorado Springs?"

"I'm assuming Frank doesn't want us returning to Washington, even briefly, so he'll fly the doctor out to check my eyes. That means, logically, either Colorado Springs or Denver, and I'm betting Colorado Springs. I'm also betting he doesn't want the doctor to know the location of the cabin, so that means we go to him."

She had known he would have to have his eyes checked again, but just talking about it brought the real world intruding into their private paradise. It would feel strange even seeing other people, much less talking to them. But reading strained his eyes, and enough time had passed for them to realize his sight wasn't going to improve. She thought of how he would look in glasses, and a warm feeling began spreading in her stomach. Sexy. She gave him a smile. "Yeah, I think I'd like to make a trip. I've been eating my own cooking for a long time now."

"I'll get in touch with Frank after dinner." He could have done it then, but filling his stomach was more important. Jay made great spaghetti, and getting in touch with Frank could be time-consuming. First things first.

After the dinner dishes had been cleaned and Steve was in the shed contacting Frank, Jay stretched out on the rug in front of the fire, for the first time thinking about the chic little apartment in New York that Frank had been keeping for her. It contrasted sharply with the rustic comfort of the cabin, but she much preferred the cabin. She would hate to leave it; it would be beautiful here during the summer, but she wondered how much longer they would be here. Surely Steve's memory would return before then, and even if it didn't, how much longer would it be before Frank told him the truth? They couldn't let him live another man's life forever. Or could they? Had that been the plan? Did they somehow know he'd never get his memory back?

The mirrors kept reflecting back different answers, different facets to the puzzle, different solutions. And none of them fit.

"Are you asleep?" he asked softly.

She gasped and rolled over, her heart jumping. "I didn't hear you come in. You didn't make any noise." He always moved silently, like a cat, but she should have heard the back door. She'd been so deep in thought that the sounds hadn't registered.

"The better to sneak up on you, my dear," he growled in his best big-bad-wolf voice. He joined her on the rug, sinking his hands into her hair as he angled her mouth up toward his. He kissed her slowly, deeply, taking his time and using his tongue. Her breathing altered, and her eyes grew heavy lidded. Desire was a heavy warmth inside her, slowly expanding until it completely filled her.

They weren't in any hurry. It felt too good to lie there in the warmth of the crackling fire and savor their kisses. But eventually the heat was too much, and she moaned as he unbuttoned her flannel shirt, parting the edges to press his lips to the swollen curves of her breasts. He lay on top of her, his heavy legs controlling hers even though she twisted restlessly. She

wanted more. Moaning again, her voice sharp with
need, she turned until her nipple brushed against his
mouth. Lazily he extended his tongue and licked it,
then clamped his mouth over it and sucked strongly,
giving her what she needed.

The firelight burnished her hair with golden lights
and her skin with a rosy glow as he unfastened her
jeans and pulled them off. Her mouth was red and
moist, glistening with the sheen of his kisses. Abruptly
he couldn't wait any longer and jerked his own clothes
off. The flannel shirt still hung around her shoulders,
but even that was too much. He pulled it away from her
and knelt between her legs, draping her thighs over his
as he bent forward to enter her, fusing their bodies as
surely as their lives were fused.

They lay together for a long time afterward, too content to move. He put another log on the fire and pulled
on his jeans, then put his own shirt around her to stave
off any chill. She sat in the circle of his arms, her head
on his shoulder, wishing nothing would ever happen
to disturb this happiness.

He watched the waving yellow flames, his rough
chin rubbing back and forth against her hair. "Do you
want kids?" he asked absently.

The question startled her enough that she lifted her
head from his shoulder. "I…think I do." she replied.
"I've never really thought about it, because it just didn't
seem like an option, but now…" Her voice trailed off.

"Before, we didn't have much of a marriage. I don't
want it to be like that again. I want to come home every
night, live a normal life." He tightened his arms around

her. "I'd like to have a couple of kids, but that's a mutual decision. I didn't know how you felt about it."

"I like kids," she said softly, but guilt assailed her. They hadn't had *any* kind of a marriage before! He was feeling guilty for another man's acts.

"Yeah, I like them, too." He smiled, still watching the fire. "I get a kick out of watching Amy—"

Jay jerked away from him, her eyes wide with something like panic in them. "Who's Amy?"

Steve's face was hard, his mouth grim. "I don't know," he muttered. "I feel as if I just ran into a brick wall. The words just slipped out, then *bam*! I hit the wall and there's nothing."

Jay felt sick. Had she been so wrong in trusting that Frank wouldn't have set this up if Steve had been married? Was he a father as well as a husband?

Steve was watching her and sensed the direction of her thoughts, if not the content. "No, I'm not married and I don't have any kids," he said sharply, pulling her back to him. "It's probably just a friend's little girl. Do you know anyone with a little girl named Amy?"

She shook her head, not looking at him. The terror was back; she felt stiff with it. Was his memory returning? When it did, would he leave? Paradise could end at any time.

Steve lay awake long after they had gone to bed that night. Jay slept in his arms, as she had every night since the chinook blew, her hair streaming over his left shoulder and her warm breath sighing against his neck. Her bare, silky body was pressed all along his left side, and her slender arm was draped across his chest. She had looked so panicked for a second when he'd mentioned Amy's name, whoever Amy was. He held her closer, trying to erase that panic even from her sleep.

This would probably happen a lot, a casual remark triggering flashes of memory. He hoped they wouldn't all scare her so much. Was she truly afraid he wouldn't want her when his memory returned? God, couldn't she feel how much he loved her? It went beyond memory. It was in his bones, buried in the very depths of his existence.

Amy. *Amy.*

The name flashed through his mind like fire and suddenly he saw a little girl with glossy dark hair, giggling as she shoved a chubby, dimpled fist into her mouth. *Amy.*

His heart began pounding. His memory had actually supplied a face to go with the name. He didn't know who she was, but he knew her name, and now her face. The mental picture faded, but he concentrated and found he could recall it, just like a real memory. Just as he'd told Jay, she must be a friend's daughter, someone he'd met since their divorce.

He relaxed, pleased that the memory had solidified. His sexual satisfaction made his body feel heavy and boneless, and his chest began to rise and fall in the deeper rhythm of sleep.

"Unca Luke, Unca Luke!"

The childish voices echoed in his head and the movie began to unwind in his mind. Two kids. Two boys, tearing across a green lawn, jumping and shrieking "Unca Luke" at the tops of their lungs as they ran.

Another scene. Northern Ireland. Belfast. He recognized it even as a tingle of dread ran up his spine. Two little boys played in the street, then suddenly looked up, hesitated and ran.

Flash. One of the first two little boys looked up with a wobbly lower lip and tears in his eyes and said, "Please, Unca Dan."

Flash. Dan Rather stacked papers at his newsdesk while the credits rolled.

Flash. A bumper sticker on a station wagon said, I'd Rather Be at Disney World.

Mickey Mouse dancing... Flash...a mouse crawling through the garbage in an alley... Flash...a grenade sailing in slow motion through the air and hitting a garbage can with a loud thump; then a louder thump and the can goes sailing... Flash...a white sailboat with sassy red-and-white striped sails tacking closer to shore and a tanned young man waves... Flash flash flash...

The scenes ripped through his consciousness, and they were truly only flashes, following each other like pages of a book being flipped through in front of his eyes.

He was sweating again. Damn, these free-association memories were hell. What did they mean? Had they truly happened? He wouldn't mind them if he could tell which ones were real and which ones were just something he'd seen on television or in a movie, or maybe even imagined from a scene in a book. Okay, some of them were obvious, like the one of Dan Rather with the credits rolling across his face. But he'd watched network news many times since the bandages had come off his eyes, so that could even be a recent memory.

But... Uncle Luke. Uncle Dan. Something about

those kids, and those names, seemed very real, just as Amy was real.

He eased out of bed, being very careful not to wake Jay, and walked into the living room where he stood for a long time in front of the banked fire, watching the embers glow. Full memory was close, and he knew it. It was as if all he had to do was turn a corner and everything would be there; but turning that mental corner wasn't as easy as it sounded. He had become a different man in the months since the explosion; he was trying to connect two separate people and merge them into one.

He had been absently rubbing his fingertips with his thumb. When he noticed what he was doing, he lifted his hand to look at it. The calluses were back, courtesy of chopping wood, but his fingertips were still smooth. How much of him was left, or had his identity been erased as surely as his fingerprints had been? When he looked in the mirror, how much of it was Steve Crossfield and how much of it was courtesy of the reconstructive surgery? His face was changed, his voice was changed, his fingerprints gone.

He was new. He had been born out of the darkness, brought to life by Jay's voice calling him toward the light.

Regardless of what he did or didn't remember, he still had Jay. She was a part of him that surgery couldn't change.

The room had taken on a chill as the fire died, and finally he felt the coldness on his naked body. He returned to the bedroom and slipped under the quilt, feeling Jay's body warmth wrap around him. She murmured something, moving closer to him in her sleep, seeking her usual position.

Instantly desire fired through him, as urgent as if it hadn't been slaked only an hour or so before. "Jay," he said, his voice low and dark, and he pulled her beneath him. She woke and reached for him, her hands sliding around his neck, and in the darkness they loved each other until he had no room for memories other than those they made together.

CHAPTER ELEVEN

THEY LEFT THE cabin early the next morning so they could rendezvous with Frank at Colorado Springs that afternoon. Jay felt a wrench at leaving the cabin; it had been their private world for so long that, away from it, she felt exposed. Only the thought that they would be returning the next day gave her the courage to leave it at all. She knew that eventually she would have to leave it forever, but she wasn't ready to face that day right now. She wanted more time with the man she loved.

She intended to ask Frank the name of the American agent who had been "killed." He might not tell her, but she had to ask. Even if she couldn't say it aloud, she needed to know, she had to put a name to her love. She looked at him as he skillfully handled the Jeep, holding it steady even on the snow, and her heart swelled. He was big and rough-looking, not handsome at all with his rearranged features, but just one glance from those fierce yellowish eyes had the power to make her dizzy with delight. How could they ever have thought they could pass this man off as Steve Crossfield?

Their subterfuge was riddled with holes, but she hadn't seen them until she had been too deeply in love with him to care. They had relied on shock and urgency to keep her from asking the pointed questions to which they would have had no answers, such as why they didn't use blood type or their own agent's dental records to determine the identity of the patient. She had known at the time that Frank was hiding something from her, but she had been too concerned over "Steve" to think it was anything more than protecting the details of a classified mission. The truth was that she had been misled so easily because she had wanted to be; after the first time she had seen him lying in the hospital, so desperately wounded but still fighting with that grim determination of his that burned through unconsciousness, she had wanted nothing more than to be by his side and help him fight.

They were to stay at a different motel than the one they'd been in before, because Frank didn't want to take the chance the desk clerk might recognize them. They even used different names. When they got there, Frank had already arrived, and he'd made reservations for them under the names of Michael Carter and Faye Wheeler. Separate rooms. Steve looked distinctly displeased, but placed Jay's overnighter in her room without comment and went along to his own room. The eye specialist checked Steve's eyes immediately; then he was taken to an optometrist to be fitted for glasses, which would be ready for him the next morning. Jay remained behind, wondering what strings Frank had pulled and whose arms he had twisted to get everything done so fast.

They returned a little after dark, and Steve came immediately to Jay's room. "Hi, baby," he said, stepping inside and closing the door behind him. Before she could answer he was kissing her, his hands tight on her arms, his mouth hard and searching.

She shivered with excitement, crowding closer to his body as she dug her fingers into his cold hair. He smelled like wind and snow, and his skin was cold, but his tongue was warm and probing. Finally he lifted his head, a very male look of satisfaction stamped on his hard face. He rubbed his thumb across her lips, which were reddened from contact with his. "Sweetheart, I may freeze my naked butt off sneaking into your room tonight, but I'm *not* sleeping alone."

"I have a suggestion," she purred.

"Let's hear it."

"Leave your clothes on until you get here."

He laughed and kissed her again. Her mouth was driving him crazy; it had the most erotic effect on him. Kissing her was more arousing than actually making love had been with other women—and just for a moment, before they faded away, some of those other women were in his mind.

"The doctor is already on his way back to Washington. Frank is staying until the morning, so it's the three of us again. Are you hungry? Frank's stomach is still on Washington time."

"Actually, I am a little hungry. We don't keep late hours ourselves, you know."

He looked at the bed. "I know."

Jay hoped to have the chance to ask Frank about the agent's name; she couldn't take the risk of asking him in Steve's presence, because the sound of his own name might trigger his memory, and she couldn't face the possibility of that. She wanted him to remember, but she wanted it to be when they were alone in their high meadow. If the chance to talk to Frank didn't present itself, she could always call him after they'd retired to their individual rooms for the night, provided Steve didn't come straight to hers, but she didn't think he would. He'd probably take a shower first, and put on fresh clothes. She sighed, weary of having to second-guess and predict; she wasn't cut out for this business.

Steve noted the sigh, and the faint desperation in her eyes. She hadn't said anything, but that look had been there since he'd had that first flash of memory the day before. It puzzled him; he couldn't think of any reason why Jay should dread his returning memory. Because it puzzled him and because there was no logical reason, he couldn't let it go. It wasn't in his makeup. When something bothered him, he worried at it until it made sense. He never quit, never let go. His sister had often said he was at least half bulldog—

Sister?

He was quiet as the three of them ate dinner at an Italian restaurant. Part of him enjoyed the spicy food, and part of him was actively involved in the easy conversation around the table, but another part of him examined the sliver of memory from every angle. If he had a sister, why had he told Jay he was an orphan? Why hadn't Frank had a record of any relatives? That was the screwy part. He could accept that he might have told Jay a different version of his life, because he didn't know what the circumstances had been at the time, but it was impossible that Frank hadn't had a list of next of kin. That was assuming he was remembering "real" things.

A sister. His logic told him it was impossible. His guts told him his logic could take a flyer. A sister. Amy. *Unca Luke! Unca Luke!* The childish voices reverberated in his head even as he laughed at something Frank said. *Unca Dan.* Unca Luke. Unca Luke Unca Luke... Luke...Luke...

"Are you all right?" Jay asked, her eyes dark with concern as she put her hand lightly on his wrist. She could feel tension emanating from him and was vaguely startled that Frank hadn't seemed to notice anything unusual.

The pounding left his head as he looked at her and smiled. He'd gladly count his past well lost as long as he could have Jay. The sensory umbilical cord linking them was as acutely sensitive as the strings on a precisely tuned Stradivarius. "It's just a headache," he said. "The drive was a strain on my eyes." Both statements were true, though the second wasn't the cause of the first. Also, there hadn't been that much strain. His problem was the precise, close-up focusing needed for reading; his distance vision was as sharp as ever, which was better than twenty-twenty. He had the vision of a jet pilot.

Jay returned to her conversation with Frank, but she was as aware of Steve's fading tension as she had been of the fact that he'd been as taut as a guide wire. Had something happened that afternoon that he hadn't told her? A feeling of dread almost overwhelmed her, and she wanted badly to be back at the cabin.

When they returned to the motel, she noted with relief that Steve went to his own room rather than stopping to talk with Frank or immediately following her to

hers. She darted to the phone and dialed Frank's room.
He answered on the first ring.

"It's Jay." She identified herself.

"Is something wrong?" He was immediately alert.

"No, everything's okay. It's just that something's
been bothering me, but I didn't want to ask you in
front of Steve."

In his room, Frank tensed. Had they failed to cover
all bases? "Is it about Steve?"

"Well, no, not really. The agent who died...what was
his name? It's been on my mind a lot lately, that he died
and I never even heard his name."

"There's no reason you should have. You'd never
met him."

"I know," she said softly. "I just wanted to know
something about him. It could have been Steve. Now
that he's dead, there's no reason to keep his name secret, is there?"

Frank thought. He could give her a fictitious name,
but he decided to tell her at least that much of the truth.
She'd know his name eventually, and it might help if
she could simply think a mistake had been made. It
would give her a small fact she could focus on for reference. "His name was Lucas Stone."

"Lucas Stone." Her voice was very soft as she repeated the name. "Was he married? Did he have a family?"

"No, he wasn't married." He deliberately didn't answer her second question.

"Thanks for telling me. It's bothered me that I didn't
know." He'd never know how much, she thought as
she quietly replaced the receiver. Lucas Stone. She re-

peated the name over and over in her mind, applying it
to a battered face and feeling her heart begin to pound.
Lucas Stone. Yes.

Only then did she realize what a mistake she'd made.
If it had been difficult before to refer to him as Steve,
it would be almost impossible now. Steve had been a
stolen name, but one she'd used because there had been
no alternative. What if the name Lucas slipped out?

She sat on the bed for a long time while she mentally flailed against the hall of mirrors that trapped her
with its false reflections. The things she didn't know
bound her as securely as the things she knew, until she
was afraid to trust her own instincts. She wasn't made
for deception; she was straightforward, which was one
reason why she hadn't fitted into the world of investment banking, a world that required a certain measure
of "slickery," that balance of slickness and trickery.

Finally, too tired to open any more blank doors, she
took a shower and got ready for bed. When she came
out of the bathroom, Lucas—*Steve*! she reminded herself frantically—was stretched out on the bed, already
partially undressed.

She looked at the locked door. "Haven't we done
this before?"

He rolled to his feet and caught her arms, pulling
her to him. "With one difference. A big difference."

He smelled of soap and shaving cream, and the underlying muskiness of man. She clung to him, pressing
her face into his neck to inhale that special scent. What
would she do if he left her? It would be a life without
color, forever incomplete. Slowly she ran her hands
over his broad chest, rubbing her fingers through the

crisp, curly hair and feeling the warmth of his skin, then the iron layer of muscles beneath. He was so hard that her fingers barely made an impression. Bemused, she pressed experimentally on his upper arm, watching as her fingernails turned white from the pressure but had noticeably little effect on him.

"What are you doing?" he asked curiously.

"Seeing how hard you are."

"Honey, that's not the right place."

Her face was bright with laughter as she swiftly looked up at him. "I think I know all your other places."

"Is that so? There are places, and then there are places. Some places need a lot more attention than others." As he spoke he began moving her toward the bed. He was already aroused, his hardness pressing against her. Jay moved her hand down to cover the ridge beneath his jeans.

"Is this one of the places in need of attention?"

"A lot of attention," he assured her as he levered them both onto the bed. He felt her legs move, her hips lifting to cradle him, and all amusement faded out of his eyes, leaving them fierce and narrow. It was a look that made Jay shudder in exquisite anticipation.

She looked up at him, her face soft and shining as his hands began moving tenderly on her body. "I love you," she said, and her heart echoed, *Lucas*.

IT WAS DIFFERENT the next morning, as if the world had altered during the night, but he couldn't quite put his finger on the difference. It was an oddly familiar feeling, as if he were more at home with himself. Jay was in his arms, her sleek, golden-brown hair lying tangled on his shoulder. If they had been in the cabin he would have got up to rebuild the fire, then returned to bed for some early-morning loving. Instead he had to go to his own room to shave and dress. That damn Frank. He'd booked separate rooms knowing they needed only one. But Jay wasn't like all the other women; Jay was special, and maybe this was Frank's tribute to her specialness.

Other women. The thought nagged at him after he left Jay and returned to his own room in the biting cold of dawn. His memory was returning, not in one big, melodramatic rush, like a light switch being turned on, but in unconnected bits and pieces. Faces and names were surfacing. Instead of feeling elated, however, he was aware of a growing sense of caution. He hadn't told Frank his memory was coming back; he'd wait until it had truly returned and he'd had time to consider the situation. Wariness was second nature to him, just as he automatically checked his room to make certain no one had entered it in his absence.

He showered and shaved, but as he shaved he found himself staring at his face in the mirror, trying to find his past in the reflection. How could he recognize himself when his face had been changed? What had he looked like before? He wondered if Jay had a picture of him; it would be an old one, if she'd kept any at all. But women tended to keep mementos and their divorce hadn't been a bitter one, so maybe she hadn't destroyed whatever pictures she'd had. Maybe seeing one would give him a link to the past.

Hell, why should it? He stared at himself in disgust. He hadn't recognized Jay or Frank; why should he recognize his old face? The face he knew was the face he could see now, and it wouldn't win any prizes. He looked as if he'd played too many football games without a helmet.

Still, the sensation lingered that he was on the brink of…something. It was there, just beyond his reach.

It nagged at him in little ways, like the ease with which he slipped his shoulder holster on, and the familiarity of the gun in his hand as he checked it, then slid it into place. The ease and familiarity had been there before, but now they were somehow different, as if the link between past and present were returning. Soon. It would happen soon.

The day was uneventful, but the feeling of anticipation didn't leave him. They all met to eat breakfast; then he and Frank drove to the optical lab and picked up his glasses. On the way back he asked, "Have you found this Piggot guy yet?"

"Not yet. He surfaced a month ago, but he went underground again before we could get to him."

"Is he good?"

Frank hesitated. "Damn good. One of the best. His psychological profile says he's a psychopath, but very controlled, very professional. His jobs are a matter of pride to him. That's why he wants you. You screwed him up the way no one else ever had. You spoiled his job, killed his 'employees' and managed to hit him hard enough that he had to go underground for months to recover."

"I may have hit him hard, but it wasn't hard enough," Steve said remotely. "Do you have a picture of him?"

"Not with me. There's only one. We got him with a

telescopic lens, and it's grainy. He's about five-ten, a hundred and forty-five pounds, blond, forty-two years old. His left earlobe is missing, also courtesy of you. His reputation suffered."

"Yeah, well, some days I'm a little cranky."

That was vintage Lucas Stone. Frank felt the shock of it like a slap, but he kept his hands steady on the wheel. "Is your memory coming back?"

"Not yet," Steve lied. He could see Geoffrey Piggot, whiplash thin, malignant, cold. Another face to go with a name.

HE WAS VERY quiet on the drive back to the cabin. Jay glanced at him, but sunglasses hid his eyes, and she could read nothing in his expression. She still sensed the tension in him, just as she had the night before, during dinner. "Do you have another headache?" she finally asked.

"No." Then he softened the bluntness of his answer by reaching over to rub the backs of his fingers against her jaw. "I feel okay."

"Did Frank say anything that's bothering you?"

Briefly he considered the disadvantages of letting someone get so close to you that they could read your moods, but then he counted that battle well lost in Jay's case, because as far as he was concerned, she couldn't get close enough to suit him. And he hadn't *let* her get close; it had simply happened.

"No. He told me a few things about the guy who tried to make me into beef stew—"

"Oh, gross!" she said, slapping his hand away, and he laughed at her.

"I was just thinking about him, that's all."

After a moment she curled up in the seat and rested her head against the back. "I'll be glad to get home."

He was in total agreement with that. They had been alone together for so long that this trip had almost brought on culture shock. Neon lights and traffic were a definite jolt to a system that was used to fir trees, snow and a deep, deep silence. Right now he would welcome a trip to civilization only if he and Jay were getting blood tests and a marriage license.

Blood tests.

Suddenly he felt alert, just as he'd felt a thousand times before when his life hung in the balance. Adrenaline spurted into his veins, and his heart began racing, but not as fast as his brain. A blood test. Damn it, it didn't fit. Why had they needed Jay to identify him when they had all the means at hand? He was their agent. Granted, his fingerprints were gone, he'd been unconscious and his voice damaged, but they still had his blood type and dental records. It should have been easy enough to establish his identity. It followed, then, that they hadn't needed Jay at all, but had definitely wanted her for some reason.

He went over what Jay had told him. They had wanted her to identify him because they couldn't make a positive ID, and they'd needed to know if their agent had bought the farm, because Steve and this other guy had been caught in the explosion and one of them was dead. That meant there must have been two agents on location, but it wouldn't have changed the fact that Frank had the means at hand to identify both of them. Supposedly he and this other agent had physically resembled each other, about the same height and weight, and with the same coloring. There still wasn't any problem with identification, even if he stretched coincidence and allowed that they both might have had the same blood type. That still left dental records.

Damn, he felt like a fool. Why hadn't he seen this before? They had wanted Jay in this for some reason, but identification hadn't been it. What kind of scheme was Frank running?

Think. He had to think. He felt as if he were trying to put a puzzle together without all the pieces, so no matter how he moved things around they still didn't fit. If he could just remember, damn it!

Why would Frank lie to Jay? Why concoct the story that he and the other agent so closely resembled each other? Why insist that he needed her at all?

Why did they need Jay?

Voices tumbled in on him. *"Congratulations, Mr. Stone"*… *"I'm glad you're back, son"*… *"Unca Luke! Unca Luke!"* Stone…son…Unca Luke…son…Luke… Stone…

Luke Stone.

His hands jerked on the steering wheel. He felt as if he'd been hit in the chest. Luke Stone. Lucas Stone. *Damn Frank Payne to hell! His name was Lucas Stone!*

As soon as he'd turned that mental corner, all the memories came rushing at him in a confusing flood, filling his mind with so much clatter that he could barely drive. He didn't dare stop, didn't dare let Jay know what he was feeling. He felt… God, he didn't know how he felt. Battered. His head hurt, but at the same time he was aware of an enormous sense of relief. He had his identity back, his sense of self. Finally he knew himself.

He was Lucas Stone. He had a family and friends, a past.

But he wasn't Jay's ex-husband. He wasn't Steve Crossfield. He wasn't the man she thought she was in love with.

So that was why she'd been brought in. There had been only one agent at the explosion, and he was that man. Steve Crossfield must have been there for some reason, and he had died there. Lucas tried to form his memories of the meeting, but they were blurred, fragmented. They would probably never come back. But he did remember seeing a tall, lean man walking up the street, his outline reflected on the wet pavement under the streetlight. That could have been Steve Crossfield. He didn't remember anything after that, though now he was remembering making contact, setting up the meeting with Minyard, going to the meeting site. He'd looked up, seen the man…then nothing. Everything after that was a blank, until Jay's voice had pulled him out of the darkness.

His cover had been blown, obviously. Piggot was after him; that was the reason for the charade. Pulling Jay in, duping her into thinking he was her ex-husband, having him positively identified as Steve Crossfield, was the best cover the Man could concoct for him until they could neutralize Piggot. The Man never underestimated his enemies, and Piggot was, as Frank had said, very good. The extent of the Man's deception also told Lucas that the Man suspected there was a mole in his ranks and hadn't trusted regular channels.

So they'd "buried" him, and he'd awakened to another name, another face, another life, even another man's wife.

No, damn it! Savagery filled him, and his knuckles turned white as he automatically negotiated the icy patches on the road. Maybe he wasn't Steve Crossfield, but Jay was his. *His.* Lucas Stone's woman.

Silently and at length, he cursed the Man and Frank for everything he could think of, ranging back over several generations of their ancestors. Not Frank so much, because he could see the Man's fine hand in this. Nobody had a mind as intricate as Kell Sabin's; that was how he'd gotten to be the Man. They had probably—no, almost certainly—saved his life, assuming there was a mole passing information to Piggot, but they weren't the ones who had to tell Jay he wasn't her ex-husband. They didn't have to tell her that the man she loved was dead and she'd been sleeping with a stranger.

What would she say? More important, what would she do?

He couldn't lose her. He could stand anything except that. He expected, and could handle, shock, anger, even fear, but he couldn't stand it if she looked at him with hate in those deep blue eyes. He couldn't let her walk away from him.

Immediately he began examining the situation from all angles, looking for a solution, but even as he looked, he knew there wasn't one. He couldn't marry her using Crossfield's name, because such a marriage wouldn't be legal, and besides, he'd be damned if he'd let her carry another man's name. He would have to tell her.

His family probably thought he was dead, and there

was no way he could let them know he wasn't without jeopardizing them. If his cover was blown, his family would be at risk if Piggot ever found out he hadn't died as planned. The way things stood now, he'd have a hard time convincing his family of his identity anyway; he neither looked nor sounded the same. His hands were tied until Piggot was caught; then he supposed Sabin would arrange for his family to be notified that a "mistake" had been made in identification, and due to extenuating and unusual circumstances, et cetera, the error had only now been corrected. The Man probably already had the telegram composed in his mind, letter-perfect.

His family would be taken care of; they would be glad to get him back despite the way he looked, or the fact that his voice was ruined.

Jay was the victim. They'd used her as the ultimate cover. How in hell could she ever forgive that?

JAY DOZED, FINALLY awakening as they turned onto the track to the meadow. "We're home," she murmured, pushing her hair back. She turned her head to smile at him. "At last."

He was tense again, surveying every detail of the track. There was new snow on the ground, filling the tire tracks they had made the day before and also obliterating any other trail that could have been made after they'd left. All his training was coming into play, and Lucas Stone didn't take chances. Unnecessary chances, that was. There had been more times than one when he'd laid his life on the line, but only because he'd had no other choice. Taking chances with Jay's life, however, was something else.

As usual, Jay picked up on his tension and fell silent, a worried frown puckering her brow.

The snow surrounding the cabin was pristine, but when Lucas parked the Jeep he put a detaining hand on Jay's arm. "Stay here until I check the cabin," he said tersely, drawing a pistol from beneath his jacket and getting out without looking at her. His eyes were never still, darting from window to window, examining every inch of ground, looking for the betraying flutter of a curtain.

Jay was frozen in place. This man, moving like a cat toward the back door, was the man she loved, and he was a predator, a hunter. He was innately cautious, as graceful as the wind as he flattened his back against the wall and eased his left hand toward the doorknob, while the pistol was held ready in his right. Soundlessly he opened the door and disappeared within. Two minutes later he stood in the back door again, relaxed. "Come on in," he said, and walked back to the Jeep to get their bags.

It irritated her that he'd frightened her for nothing; it reminded her of the morning when he'd tracked her in the snow. "Don't do that to me," she snapped as she threw open the door and slid out. The snow crunched under her boots.

"Do what?"

"Scare me like that."

"Scaring you is a hell of a lot better than walking into an ambush," he replied evenly.

"How could anyone know we're up here, and why should anyone care?"

"Frank thinks someone would care, or they wouldn't have taken the trouble to hide us."

She climbed the steps and knocked the snow off her boots before entering the cabin. It was cold but not icy, because they had left the backup heat system on. She took the bags from him and carried them into the bedroom to begin unpacking while he built a fire.

Lucas watched the yellow flames lick at the logs he'd placed on the grate, slowly catching and engulfing the wood. He couldn't tell her, not yet. This might be the only time he'd ever have with her, an indefinite period of grace while Sabin's men hunted Piggot. He'd use that time to bind her to him so tightly that he could hold her even after she found out his real name, and that Steve Crossfield was dead. She had told him she loved him, but it was Steve Crossfield she'd been saying the words to, and, oddly, it had been Steve Crossfield hearing them. He was Lucas Stone, and he wanted her for himself.

His need was fast and urgent, like a fire low in his belly. He walked into the bedroom and watched her for a moment as she bent over to remove her boots and socks. She was as slim as a reed, her skin silky soft. He caught her around the waist and tumbled her on the bed, immediately following her down to pin her to the mattress with his weight.

She laughed, her blue eyes no longer filled with irritation. "The caveman approach must be fashionable this year," she teased.

He couldn't smile in return. He wanted her too

badly, needed to hear her say the words to *him*, not to a ghost. The yellow glitter was in his eyes as he stripped her and surveyed her nakedness. Her nipples were puckered from the chilly air, her breasts standing up round and firm. He circled them with his hands and lifted the tight nipples to his mouth, sucking at each of them in turn. She gasped, and her back arched. Her responsiveness did it to him every time, shattered his control and made him as hot and eager for her as a teenager. He could barely tolerate taking his hands off her long enough to hastily tear at his own clothing and throw it to the side.

"Tell me you love me," he said as he adjusted her slim legs around his hips and began entering her.

Jay squirmed voluptuously, rubbing her breasts against the hairy planes of his chest. "I love you." Her hands dug into his back as she felt the muscles ripple. "I love you." Slowly he pushed and slowly she accepted him, her pleasure already rising to an urgent pitch. Her body was so attuned to him that when he began the rhythmic thrust and withdrawal of lovemaking her sensual tension swiftly reached a crescendo. He held her until her shudders stilled, then found the rhythm anew.

"Again," he whispered.

She wanted to cry out his name, but couldn't. She couldn't call him Steve now, and she didn't dare call him Lucas. She had to bite her lips to keep his name unsaid, and a moan rose in her throat. He controlled her, his slow, deep thrusts taking her only so high and refusing to let her go any higher. She was on fire, her nerve endings exploding with pleasure.

"Tell me you love me." His voice was gravelly, the

strain apparent on his face as he kept his movements agonizingly slow.

"I love you."

"Again."

"I love you."

He wanted to hear his name, but that was denied him. Sometime in the future, when this was all over, he promised himself that he would have her as he was having her now, and she would scream his name. He had to be content with knowing it himself, and with the way her eyes locked with his as she whispered the words over and over again, until his control broke and sweet madness claimed them both.

He couldn't get enough of her, ever, and knowing that he might lose her was intolerable. Physical bonds were the most basic, and instinctively he used them to strengthen the link between them. He would make himself a part of her until his name no longer mattered.

TWO NIGHTS LATER, Frank had just gotten into bed when the telephone rang. With a sigh, he reached for it. "Payne."

"Piggot's in Mexico City," the Man said.

Forgetting about the good night's sleep he'd been anticipating, Frank sat up, instantly alert.

"Do you have a man on him?"

"Not at the moment. He's gone to ground again. It's about to unravel, and this move tells me who snipped the thread. I'll take care of that little detail, but you get Luke out of there. The cabin's location has been leaked."

"How much do you want me to tell him?"

"All of it. It doesn't matter now. It'll go down within the next twenty-four hours. Just see that they're safe." Then Kell Sabin hung up, wondering if he'd cut it too fine and endangered a friend, as well as an innocent woman.

CHAPTER TWELVE

AT THE FIRST beep from the palm-size pager lying on the bedside table, Lucas was on his feet and reaching for his pants. The tone told him it was the communications beeper, not the alarm caused by the laser beam being broken, but the very fact that Frank was contacting him in the middle of the night was alarm enough. Jay roused and reached for the lamp, but Lucas stopped her.

"No lights."

"What's going on?" She was very still now.

"I'm going out to the shed. That's the communications beeper. Frank's trying to get in touch with us."

"Then why not turn on a light?"

"He wouldn't contact us in the middle of the night unless it was an emergency. It might be too late. Piggot could already be close by, and a light would warn him."

"Piggot?"

"The guy who tried to make me into beef stew, remember?"

"I'll go with you." In a flash she was out of the bed and fumbling with her clothes in the dark. Lucas started to stop her, not wanting her to leave the safety of the cabin, but if Piggot had found them, the cabin wouldn't be safe. A hand-held rocket launcher in the hands of an expert, which Piggot was, could turn the cabin into a shattered inferno in seconds.

He stamped his feet into his boots and grabbed the pistol out of the holster, which he always kept at hand. As he left the room he lifted his jacket from the hook beside the door, then shrugged into it as he raced through the dark cabin to the back door. Jay was right behind him; she had on her jeans and his flannel shirt, her bare feet shoved into boots.

They slipped across the snow to the shed, staying in the shadows as much as possible. The ramshackle shed was a revelation; Jay had been stunned the first time Lucas had shown her what lay below its surface. He moved a bale of hay aside and revealed a small trapdoor, just wide enough to allow his shoulders through, then pressed a button on the pager that released the electronic lock. The trapdoor silently swung open. A narrow ladder extended downward, illuminated only by tiny red lights beside each step. Lucas urged her down, then he followed and closed the door, once more sealing the underground communications chamber. Only then did he switch on the lights.

The chamber was small, no more than six by eight, and crammed with equipment. There were a computer and display terminal, a modem hookup and a printer against the end wall, and an elaborate radio system on the right. That left about two and a half feet of room on the left for maneuvering, and part of that was taken up by a chair. Lucas took the chair and flipped switches on the radio. "On air."

"Get packed. Piggot has been spotted in Mexico City, and we have word the location of the cabin is no longer secure." Frank's voice filled the small chamber eerily, without the tinny sound radios normally produced, testifying to the quality of the set.

"How much time do we have?"

"The Man estimated four hours; less if Piggot has already put accomplices in the area."

"His usual method is to move people in, but keep them at a distance until he arrives. He likes to orchestrate things himself." Lucas's voice was remote, his mind racing.

Silence filled the chamber, then Frank asked quietly, "Luke?"

"Yeah," Lucas said, aware of Jay's sudden movement behind him, followed by absolute stillness. He hadn't wanted to tell her like this, but all hell would be coming down in a hurry. Four hours wasn't a lot of time, and no matter what happened, he wanted her to know his name. For four hours she would know whose woman she was.

"When?"

"A couple of days ago. Any chance of intercepting Piggot before he gets here?" That would be the best-case scenario.

"Slim. Nailing him there would be our best bet. We don't know where he is, but we know where he's going."

"He won't go through customs, so that means he's in a small plane and will land at a private airstrip, one close by. Do you have a record of them?"

"We're pulling them out of the computer now. We'll have men at all of them."

"Where's a safe place for me to stash Jay?"

Frank said urgently, "Luke, you're out of it. Don't

set yourself up as bait for the trap. Get in the Jeep and drive, and call me in five hours."

"Piggot's my mess, I'll clean it up," Lucas said, still in that cool, remote tone. "If I'd taken care of him last year, this wouldn't be happening now."

"What about Jay?"

"I'll get her out of it. But I'm coming back for Piggot."

Realizing the futility of arguing with him across two-thirds of the continent, Frank said, "Okay. Contact Veasey, at this frequency, and scramble." He recited the frequency numbers only once.

"Roger," Lucas said, and flipped the switch that cut them off. Then he shoved the chair back and stood, turning to face Jay.

Her entire body felt numb as she stared at him. He knew. His memory had returned. Her time of grace had ended, the mirrors had shattered, the charade was over. The violence that had brought him into her life was about to take him out of it again.

With the return of his memory, he was truly Lucas Stone again. It was there in his eyes, in the yellow gaze of the predator. His face was hard. "I'm not Steve Crossfield," he said bluntly. "My name is Lucas Stone. Your ex-husband is dead."

She was white, frozen. "I know," she whispered.

Of all the things he'd expected her to say, that wasn't one of them. It stunned him, confused him, and irrationally angered him. He'd agonized for days over how to tell her, and she already knew? "How long have you known?" he snapped.

Even her lips felt numb. "Quite a while."

He caught her arm, his long fingers digging into her flesh. "How long is 'quite a while'?"

She tried to think. She had been caught in a web of lies for so long that it was difficult to remember. "You… you were still in the hospital."

Scenarios flashed through his mind. He'd been trained to think deviously, to keep hammering at something until it made sense, and he didn't like any of the situations that came to mind. He'd assumed from the beginning that she was an innocent blind, used by Sabin and Frank Payne to shield him, but it was more likely that she'd been hired to do the job. White-hot fury began to build in him, and he clamped down on his temper with iron control. "Why didn't you tell me?" God, for a while he'd thought he was going crazy, with all those damn memories coming back and none of them connected with the things she had told him. He might have gotten his memory back sooner if he'd had one solid fact to build on instead of the fairy tales she'd woven.

He was hurting her; his grip would leave bruises on her arm. She pulled at it uselessly, gasping as he only tightened his fingers. "I was afraid to!"

"Afraid of what?"

"I thought Frank would send me away if he knew I'd discovered you weren't Steve! Lucas, please, you're hurting me!" At last she could say his name, even though it was in pain, and her heart savored the sound.

His grip eased, but he caught her other arm, too, and held her firmly. "So Frank didn't hire you to say I was Steve Crossfield?"

"N-no," she stuttered. "I believed you were, at first."

"What changed your mind?"

"Your eyes. When I saw your eyes, I knew."

The memory of that was crystal clear. When the doctor had cut the bandages away from his eyes and he'd looked at Jay for the first time, she had gone as white as she was now. That was odd, because he knew Sabin would never have overlooked a detail as basic as the color of his eyes.

"Your husband didn't have brown eyes?"

"Ex-husband," she whispered. "Yes, he had brown eyes, but his were dark brown. Yours are yellowish brown."

So his eyes were a different shade of brown than her husband's had been; it was almost laughable that Sabin's carefully constructed scam could have fallen apart over something as small as that. But she hadn't told them that they had the wrong man, which would have been the reasonable thing to do. She hadn't even told *him*, not then and not during the weeks when they'd been up here alone. Angry frustration made his voice as rough as gravel. "Why didn't you tell *me*? Didn't you think I'd be a little interested in who I really am?"

"I couldn't take the chance. I was afraid—" she began, pleading for understanding.

"Yeah, that's right, you were afraid the gravy train would end. Frank was paying you to stay with me, wasn't he? You were with me every day, so there was no way you could hold down a job."

"No! It isn't like that—"

"Then what is it like? Are you independently wealthy?"

"Lucas, please. No, I'm not wealthy—"

"Then how did you live during the months I was in the hospital?"

"Frank picked up the tab," she said in raw frustration. "Would you please listen to me?"

"I'm listening, honey. You just told me that Frank paid you to stay with me."

"He made it *possible* for me to stay with you! I'd lost my job—" Too late, she heard the words and knew how he would take them.

His eyes were yellow slits, his mouth a grim line of rage. "So you jumped at the chance for a cushy job. All you had to do was sit beside me every day and anything you wanted was given to you, while Frank paid your bills. This explains why you wouldn't marry me, doesn't it? You were happy to accept your 'salary,' but marrying a stranger was a little bit too much, wasn't it? Not to mention the fact that the marriage wouldn't have been legal. You saved yourself some sticky trouble by dragging up all those excuses."

"They weren't excuses. For all I knew you could have had someone who cared for you—"

"I do!" he yelled, his neck cording. "My family! They think I'm dead!"

Jay groped for control, managing to steady her voice. "I couldn't marry you until you'd gotten your memory back and knew for certain you wanted to marry me. I couldn't take advantage of you like that."

"That's a convenient scruple. It actually makes you look noble, doesn't it? Too bad. If you wanted the gravy train to keep running, you should have married me while you had the chance and just kept pretending I was Crossfield. Then, when I got my memory back, you could have been the poor victim and maybe I would have stayed with you out of guilt."

She shrank away from him, her eyes going blank. Somehow, during the long months she had spent with him, she had come to believe he loved her, though he had never said the words. He'd been so possessive, so tender and passionate. But now his memory had returned, and he couldn't have made it plainer that his absorption with her had ended. He didn't need her any longer, and he certainly wasn't going to renew his offer of marriage. It was over, and they weren't even going to part friends. The worst had happened; she had lied to him, kept his identity from him, and he would never forgive her for it. He thought she had done it just because the government had been willing to support her for as long as the charade had lasted.

He released her suddenly, as if he couldn't stand to touch her any longer, and she staggered back. Catching her balance, she turned toward the ladder. "Open the door," she said dully.

He clenched his fists, not ready to break off the argument. He didn't have all the answers he wanted, not by a long shot. But her movement recalled the need for urgency; he had to get her out of there before Piggot found them. The last thing he wanted was for Jay to be caught in the middle of a firefight.

"I'll go first," he said, and shouldered past her. He signaled the door open and climbed the ladder, the pistol ready in his hand. As soon as his head was above ground he looked cautiously in all directions, then climbed out and knelt on one knee by the hole to help Jay out. "All right, come on."

She didn't look at him as she crawled out, nor did she accept the hand he extended. He closed the trapdoor, then replaced the bale of hay over it. She started to just walk out of the shed, but he grabbed her and held her back. "Watch it!" he said in a furious whisper. "We go back the same way we came. Stay in the shadows." He led the way, and Jay followed him without a word.

He still wouldn't allow a light on in the cabin, so Jay stumbled to the bedroom and gathered a few clothes in the dark. He came into the bedroom as she took off his shirt to put on her own clothes, and after a moment of frozen embarrassment, she awkwardly turned her back while she struggled with her bra. Her hands were clumsy, and in the dark she couldn't manage to straighten the straps. Despairing of getting it on, she finally dropped it on the bed and simply pulled her sweater over her head.

Lucas watched her. Her pale breasts had gleamed in the faint light coming through the window, and in spite of his anger, his sense of betrayal and the need for haste, he wanted to go to her and pull her against him. Only a few hours before he had held her breasts in his hands and pushed them up to his avid mouth. He had made love to her until the building anticipation had bordered on agony, and they had writhed together on that bed. She had told him she loved him, over and over, and now she turned her back as if she had to hide her body from him.

It hit him hard, shook him. There was more to it than she'd told him, more than the mercenary motives he'd thrown at her. He needed to know what it was, but he didn't have time. Damn it. If only she didn't look so beaten and remote, as if she had withdrawn inside herself. He had to fight the urge to take her in his arms and kiss that look away. Hell, what did it matter why she had done it? Maybe money had been the reason at first, but he was damned certain it wasn't the reason now, or at least not all of it. Even if it had been, he thought ruthlessly, he wouldn't let her go. He'd get this settled between them as soon as he'd taken care of Piggot, but right now the most important thing was to make certain Jay was safe.

"Hurry," he urged roughly.

She sat down on the edge of the bed and jerked her boots off, quickly put on a pair of thick socks and put the boots on again. Then she got her purse and shearling jacket and said, "I'm ready."

He didn't see the need for her to get anything else, as they would come back to the cabin and pack after he'd taken care of Piggot, and he was pleased that she didn't insist on wasting time. Jay was a good partner, even though she was out of her depth.

He had to find a safe place to leave her. He doubted that Black Bull, the closest town, had a motel, but he didn't have the time to go any farther than that. He drove the Jeep at breakneck speed across the meadow, especially considering that he didn't dare risk turning on the headlights. But he had taken the possibility that he might have to do this into consideration and had walked the meadow over and over, mentally tracing the route he would take, estimating his fastest safe speed, noting all the rocks and ruts in his path. He edged so close to the tree line that branches scraped the side of the Jeep.

"I can't see," Jay said, her voice strained.

"I can." He couldn't see much, but it was enough. He had good night vision.

She held on to the door as they jolted across a hump, rattling her teeth. He'd have to turn on the headlights when they went down the mountainside, she thought; the track was only wide enough for the Jeep, with a steep drop on one side and vertical mountain on the other. Even in daylight she hardly dared to breathe until they had safely negotiated it. But when they made the turn that took them onto the track, he kept both hands on the wheel. The darkness in front of them was absolute.

Jay closed her eyes. Her own heartbeat was thundering in her ears so loudly that she couldn't hear anything else. There was nothing she could do. He had decided not to turn on the lights, to risk the drive in the dark, and nothing she could say would change his mind. His arrogant confidence in his own ability was both maddening and awesome; she would rather have walked down the mountain in ten feet of snow than risked this hair-raising drive, but he had simply decided to do it, and now he was.

She couldn't estimate how long the drive took. It seemed like hours, and finally her nerves couldn't bear the tension, and numbness settled in. She even opened her eyes. It didn't matter. If they went over the side, they would go whether her eyes were open or closed.

But then they were down and bumping across the second meadow. Suddenly he slammed on the brakes, swearing viciously. Jay saw what he saw: a set of headlights playing along the edge of the meadow in front of them. They were still safely out of range of the light, but she knew as well as he did what it meant. Piggot's men were drawing close, closing the net to wait for Piggot's arrival.

Lucas put the Jeep in reverse and backed the way he had come, keeping the Jeep at the tree line. When he reached the rear edge of the meadow he turned, taking the Jeep up the north edge. They were off the track now, and the snow tires dug in deep, spewing snow back behind them.

"Are we going around this way?"

"No. We won't be able to make it. The snow's too deep." He pulled the Jeep under some trees and got out. "Stay here," he ordered, and disappeared back toward the track.

Jay swiveled in her seat, straining her eyes to see what he was doing. She could barely make out his form, black against the snow; an instant later he was out of sight.

He was back in less than two minutes. He vaulted into the Jeep and slammed the door, then rolled the window down. "Listen," he hissed.

"What did you do?"

"I wiped out our tracks. There was only one vehicle. If it goes past us, we'll get back on the track and make it to the highway yet."

They listened. The sound of the other motor came plainly through the night air. The vehicle was moving slowly, the engine toiling in low gear as it cautiously made its way up the slick, snowy, unfamiliar track. The headlights stabbed the darkness, coming almost straight toward them.

"Don't worry," Lucas breathed. "They can't see us from the track. If they just don't notice where we turned and if they keep on going, we'll be okay."

Two ifs. Two big ifs. Jay's nails were digging into her palms. The headlights were close enough that their reflected light illuminated the interior of the Jeep, and for the first time she noticed that Lucas had on his thick shearling jacket, but no shirt. The odd detail struck her, and she wondered if she might be edging toward hysteria.

"Keep going," he said under his breath. "Keep going."

For a moment it seemed as if the other vehicle slowed, and the lights seemed to be coming over the slight rise straight toward them. Then they turned, and the noise of the engine slowly moved away.

She let out her breath. Lucas started the engine, knowing the sound wouldn't be heard over that of the other motor. He put the Jeep in gear and turned it around, praying they were hidden well enough that the red glow of the brake lights wouldn't reveal their position. But at least they were behind the other vehicle now. If he had to, he could make a run for the road. As rough as the track was, the chance that they would be hit by gunfire from a pursuing vehicle was small.

The Jeep lurched through the snow, and then they were on the track again. No other headlights disturbed the darkness, and they could just catch glimpses of light playing through the trees as the other vehicle moved slowly up the treacherous mountainside track.

Jay sat silently, even when they reached the road

and Lucas finally turned on the headlights. She was numb again.

They reached Black Bull at two in the morning. The local populace of one hundred and thirty-three souls were all in bed. There wasn't even an all-night convenience store, and the one gas station closed at ten at night, according to the sign in the window. A county sheriff's car was parked at the side of the gas station.

Lucas stopped the Jeep. "Can you drive this well enough to get out of here?" he asked brusquely.

She looked at the gearshift, but not at him. "Yes."

"Then drive until you hit the next town big enough to have a motel. Stop there and call Frank. He'll arrange for you to be picked up. Do you have his number?"

So this was it. It was over. "No."

"Give me a pen. I'll write it down for you."

Jay fumbled in her purse and found a pen, but she didn't have even a scrap of paper for him to write the number on. Finally he grasped her hand and turned it palm up, then wrote the number on her palm.

"Where are you going?" she asked, her voice strained but even.

"I'm taking that county car right there and radioing Veasey. Then we're going to catch Piggot and end this once and for all."

She stared out the windshield, her hand clenched tightly as if to keep the number from fading off her palm. "Be careful," she managed to say, the admonishment trite but heartfelt. She wondered if Frank would even tell her the outcome, if she would ever know what happened to Lucas.

"He ambushed me once. It won't happen again."

Lucas got out of the Jeep and strode over to the county car. It was locked, but that wasn't much of a deterrent. He had the door open in less than ten seconds. He looked at the Jeep, staring at Jay through the windshield. Her face was ghostly white. He wanted nothing more than to jerk her into his arms and kiss her so hard that they both forgot about this mess, but if he kissed her now, he might not be able to stop, and he had to take care of Piggot. It was just that he wanted her so badly, wanted to use the bond of the flesh to make certain she knew she was his. A sense of incompletion gnawed at him because they hadn't thrashed out the situation between them, but it would have to wait. Maybe it was better this way. In a few hours he wouldn't have to worry about Piggot any longer, and his temper would have cooled. He would be able to think clearly and not react as if she'd betrayed him. He didn't understand her reasons yet, but underneath everything, he knew she loved him.

Instead of climbing over into the driver's seat, Jay opened the door and got out to walk around. She paused in front of the Jeep, her slim body starkly outlined by the glare of the headlights. "It was the only way I could think of to protect you," she said, then got into the Jeep and put it in gear.

Lucas watched the taillights as she pulled out of the gas station and onto the highway. He felt stunned. Protect him? He was so used to being out in the cold, on his own by choice, that the idea of anyone protecting him was alien. What had she thought she could do?

She could keep the charade intact. She had been right; Frank would have quickly and quietly hustled her away if she'd told him there had been a mistake, that he, Lucas, wasn't her ex-husband. She didn't have his skill with weapons or in fighting, but that hadn't stopped her from literally setting herself up as his bodyguard. The charade had depended on her, so she had kept quiet, and shielded him with her presence.

Because she loved him. He swore aloud, his breath crystallizing in the frigid night air. His damned training had tripped him up, making him look for betrayal where there hadn't been any, making him question her motives and automatically assuming the worst. He had only to look to himself to understand why she hadn't said anything. Hadn't he kept quiet these past two days because he'd been afraid of losing her if she knew the truth? He loved her too much to accept even the possibility of losing her, until Piggot had forced his hand.

Swearing again, he folded his length into the county car and began the process of hot-wiring the starter.

DAWN THREW ROSY fingers of light across the snow, a sight Lucas has seen many times since coming to the mountains, but the scene wasn't peaceful this particular morning. The meadow was crowded with men and vehicles, the pristine snow trampled and criss-crossed by both feet and tires. Here and there the white was marred by reddish-brown stains. A helicopter sat off to the left, its blades slowly twirling in the breeze.

Ten guns snapped toward him as he stepped out from the trees, then were lifted as the men holding them recognized him. He walked steadily toward them, his own pistol held in his blood-stained hand down at his side. The stench of cordite burned his nostrils in the cold air, and a gray haze lay over the meadow, resisting the efforts of the breeze to disperse it.

There was a tall, black-haired man standing next to the helicopter, surveying the scene with grim, narrowed eyes. Lucas walked straight to him. "You took a chance, setting us up in your own cabin," he snapped.

Kell Sabin looked around the meadow. "It was a calculated risk. I had to do it to find the mole. Once the location of the cabin was leaked, I knew who it was, because access to that information is very controlled." He shrugged. "I can find another vacation spot."

"The mole blew my cover?"

"Yeah. Until then, I had no idea he was there." Sabin's voice was icy, his eyes like cold black fire.

"So why the masquerade? Why drag Jay into it?"

"To keep Piggot from finding out you were alive. Your cover was blown. He knew about your family, and he's been willing in the past to use someone's family to get to them. I was trying to buy time, to keep everyone safe until Piggot surfaced and we could get to him." Sabin looked up at the trees behind the cabin. "I assume he won't be bothering us again."

"Or anyone else."

"That was your last job. You're out of it."

"Damn straight," Lucas agreed. "I've got better things to do, like get married and start a family."

Suddenly Sabin grinned, and the coldness left his eyes. Few people saw Sabin like that, only the ones who could call themselves his friends. "The bigger they are," he jibed, and left the rest of the old saw unsaid. "Have you told her yet?"

"She already knew. She figured it out while I was still in the hospital."

Sabin frowned. "What? She didn't say anything. How did she know?"

"My eyes. They're a different shade of brown than Crossfield's."

"Hell. A little thing like that. And she still went along with it?"

"I think she figured out that the whole thing was to protect me."

"Women," Sabin said softly, thinking of his own wife, who had fought like a tigress to save his life when he'd been a stranger to her. It didn't surprise him that Jay Granger had put herself on the line to protect Lucas.

Lucas rubbed his jaw. "She doesn't even mind this ugly mug."

"The surgeons did what they could. Your face was smashed." Then Sabin grinned again. "You were too pretty anyway."

The two men stood and watched the mopping-up process, their faces becoming grim again at the loss of life. Three men were dead, counting Piggot, and four more were in custody. "I'll notify your family that you're alive," Sabin finally said. "I'm sorry they had to go through this, but with Piggot on the loose, it was safer for you, and all of them, as well, if the charade was played out. It's over now. Collect Jay from wherever you've stashed her, and we'll get the two of you out of here."

Lucas looked at him, and slowly the blood drained out of his face. "She hasn't called Frank?" he asked hoarsely.

Sabin went still. "No. Where is she?"

"She was supposed to drive to the next town, check into a motel and call Frank. Damn it to hell!" Lucas turned and ran for the shed, with Sabin right beside him. Suddenly he felt cold all over. There was a possibility Piggot could have gotten to Jay before coming here, as well as the slightly less terrifying possibility that she could have had an accident. God in heaven, where was she?

AFTER LEAVING LUCAS, Jay simply drove, automatically following the highway signs picked out by the headlight beams, and eventually wound up on U.S. 24, the highway that they had taken to Colorado Springs. She turned in the opposite direction. She didn't pay any attention to the time; she just kept driving. U.S. 24 took her through Leadville, and finally she connected with I-70. She took a right, toward Denver.

The sun came up, shining right into her eyes. She was nearly out of gas. She got off at the next exit and had the tank filled.

It would be over by now.

Exhaustion pulled at her, but she couldn't stop. If she ever stopped, she would have to think, and right now she couldn't bear it. She checked her money. She didn't have much—a little over sixty dollars—but she had her credit cards. That would get her back to New York, to the only home she had left, the only refuge.

I-70 went straight to Stapleton International Airport in Denver. Jay parked the Jeep and entered the terminal, carefully noting where she had parked so she could tell Frank where to retrieve his vehicle. She bought her ticket first, and was lucky enough to get on a flight leaving within the hour. Then she found a pay phone and called Frank.

He answered in the middle of the first ring. "Frank, it's Jay." She identified herself in a numb monotone. "Is it over?"

"Where the hell are you?" he screamed.

"Denver."

"Denver! What are you doing there? You were supposed to call me hours ago! Luke is tearing the damned place up, and we have every cop in Colorado prowling the highways looking for you."

Her heart lightened, the terrible dread lifting from it. "He's all right? He isn't hurt?"

"He's fine. He took a little nick on the arm, but nothing a Band-Aid won't cover. Look, exactly where are you? I'll have you picked up—"

"Is it over?" she asked insistently. "Is it really over?"

"Piggot? Yeah, it's over. Luke got him. Tell me where you are and—"

"I'm glad." Her legs wouldn't support her much longer; she sagged against the wall. "Take…take care of him."

"My God, don't hang up!" Frank yelled, the words shrieking in her ear. "Where are you?"

"Don't worry," she managed to say. "I can get home by myself." Totally forgetting the Jeep, she hung up the phone, then went into the ladies' rest room and splashed cold water on her face. As she pulled a brush through her hair she noticed the pallor of her cheeks and the dark circles under her eyes. "You guys sure know how to show a lady a good time," she murmured to her reflection, drawing several startled glances her way.

Yogi Berra had said, "It ain't over till it's over," but this was very definitely over. Jay couldn't sleep on the flight, despite the utter exhaustion weighing down her body. Nor could she eat, though her stomach was empty. She managed to drink a cola, but nothing more.

After the solitude of the meadow, New York's J.F.K. airport was bedlam. She wanted to shrink against a wall and scream at all the scurrying people to go away. Instead she got on a bus, and an hour and a half later she let herself into her apartment.

She hadn't seen it in months; it was no longer home. It had been well taken care of in her absence, as Frank had promised, but it was as empty as she was. She didn't even have any clothes with her. She laughed hollowly; clothes were the least of her worries. Frank would make certain they were shipped to her.

But there were sheets to go on the bed, and towels for the bathroom. She took a warm shower, then even summoned the strength to make up the bed. The afternoon sun was going down as she stretched out naked between the clean sheets. Automatically she turned, searching for Lucas's warmth, but he wasn't there. It was over, and he didn't want her. Acid tears stung her eyes as her heavy eyelids closed, and then she slept.

"JANET JEAN. Janet Jean, wake up."

The intruding voice pulled her toward consciousness. She didn't want to wake up. So long as she slept, she didn't have to face life without Lucas. But it sounded like his voice, and she frowned.

"Janet Jean. Jay. Wake up, baby." A hard, warm hand shook her bare shoulder.

Slowly she opened her eyes. It *was* Lucas, sitting on the edge of her bed, scowling at her. Those yellow eyes looked almost murderous, though his tone had been as gentle as his ruined voice would allow. He looked like hell; he badly needed a shave, his hair was uncombed, and a bloodstained bandage was wrapped around his left forearm. But at least he had on a shirt now, and his clothes were clean.

"I know I locked the door." Sleep still muddled her mind, but she knew she'd locked the door. In New York, one wasn't careless about locking the door.

He shrugged. "Big deal. Come on, sweetheart, go to the bathroom and splash some cold water on your face so you can focus your eyes. I'll make coffee."

What was he doing here? She couldn't think of any reason, and though part of her rejoiced at seeing him, no matter why, another part of her cringed at having to say goodbye to him again. She might not be able to stand it this time. At least before, she had been numb.

"What time is it?"

"Almost nine."

"It can't be. It's still daylight."

"Nine in the morning," he explained patiently. "Come on, get up." He lifted her to a sitting position, and the covers fell to her waist, exposing her bare body. Quickly Jay grabbed the sheet and pulled it over her breasts; she couldn't meet his eyes as a flush chased the pallor from her face.

His face was expressionless as he got to his feet and unbuttoned his shirt. "Here, put this on. I packed your clothes and brought them with me, but they're all tumbled together in the suitcases."

She took his shirt, still warm from his body, and pulled it around her. Without another word she got up and went into the bathroom, firmly closing the door behind her. She started to lock it, but decided not to waste her time. Locks weren't much good against him.

Five minutes later she felt much more alert, having followed his advice and splashed cold water on her face. She was very thirsty, after having gone so long without anything to drink, so she drank several cups of water. She would have felt more secure if she'd had on something more than just his shirt, but it almost swallowed her. His scent was on the fabric. She lifted it to her face and inhaled deeply, then let it drop and left the security of the bathroom.

He was lying on the bed. She stopped in her tracks. "I thought you were going to make coffee."

"You don't have any." He got to his feet, put his hands on her shoulders and shook her. "Damn you," he said in a shaking voice. "I went through hell when I found out you hadn't called Frank. Why did you run? Why did you come back here?"

Her hair had fallen over her face. "I didn't have any-place else to go," she said, and her voice cracked.

He yanked her into his arms, reaching up behind her back to lock his fist in her hair and hold her head back. "Did you really think I'd let you get away from me that easily?" he all but snarled.

"Was what I did so bad?" she pleaded. "I didn't know any other way to protect you! When I saw your eyes, I knew you had to be the agent Frank had told me had been killed, and I knew he'd gone to an awful lot of trouble to hide you, so you had to be in danger. You had amnesia. You didn't even know who was after you! Keeping the lie going was the only way I had of keeping you safe!"

The yellowish eyes glittered. "Why should you care?"

"Because I was in love with you! Or did you think that was a lie, too?"

His touch gentled. "No," he said quietly. "I think I've always known you loved me, right from the start."

Tears leaked from the corners of her eyes. "The first time I touched you," she whispered, "I felt how warm you were, and how hard you were fighting to stay alive. I started loving you then."

"Then why did you run?"

He was relentless, but then, she had always known that. "Because it was over. You didn't want me. I'd been terrified of what you would do when you found out. I was afraid you'd send me away, and you did. So I left."

"I only wanted you away from the danger, damn it! I didn't intend for you to go two thousand miles!" He picked her up and dropped her on the bed, then followed her down. "No excuses this time. We're going to get married as soon as we can legally do it."

She was as stunned as she had been the first time he'd mentioned marriage. "W-what?" she stammered.

"You told me to ask you again when I'd regained my memory. Well, I have. We're getting married."

All she could say was, "That's not asking, that's telling."

"It'll do." He began unbuttoning his shirt, uncovering her breasts.

"Is it because you think you owe me—"

His head jerked up, those eyes fierce and wild. "I love you so much I'm out of my head with it."

She was stunned again. "You never said. I thought—but then you made me leave..."

"I didn't think I could have made it any plainer how I felt," he growled.

Very simply she said, "Do you need the words?"

That stopped him. "I need the words very much."

"So do I."

He bent his head and kissed her, his hand stroking her bare body beneath the shirt. His muscled legs moved against hers, and she felt his hardness against her thigh. "I love you, Jay Granger."

The sun was exploding inside her, lighting her eyes. "I love you, Lucas Stone."

At last she could speak his name with love.

EPILOGUE

"Is Piggot really dead?"

"He's really dead." Lucas watched her face carefully across the breakfast table. He had gone out and bought the necessary groceries, and they had both eaten as if they were starved, which they had been. He hadn't been interested in food before, either. Finding Jay and getting her back where she belonged had been far more important. "I finished the job." The truth wasn't pretty, but she had a right to know that about the man she was going to marry.

She sipped at the hot coffee, then lifted those incredible dark blue eyes to his. "I'm glad he's dead," she said fiercely. "He tried to kill you."

"And came damn close to succeeding."

She shuddered, thinking of the days when his life had hung in the balance, and he reached for her hand. "Hey, sweetheart. It's over. That part is really over. This part—" he squeezed her hand "—is just getting started—if you're sure you can stand looking at this face over the breakfast table."

The smile broke over her face like sunshine. "Well, you're not good-looking, but you sure are sexy."

With a growl he grabbed for her, dragging her around the table and onto his lap. Her arms went around him even as he tilted her face up for his kiss. "By the way, I'm not an agent."

She jerked back, startled. "What?"

"Not any longer. I'm officially retired, as of yesterday. Sabin took me out of it. Once my cover was blown, there was no way I could go back without endangering my family. I've really been out of it since the explosion, but Sabin didn't make it official until Piggot was caught."

"Then I guess we'll both have to hunt for a job." He was retired! She felt like chanting hosannas. She wouldn't have to worry every time he walked out the door that she'd never see him again.

He rubbed his thumb over her bottom lip. "I already have a job, baby. I'm a businessman, in partnership with my brother in an engineering firm. I traveled all over the world. It was a good cover for the work I was doing for Sabin. Speaking of my brother, by now Sabin will have gotten the news to them that a mistake was made in identifying the victims of the explosion and I'm still alive. This is going to be a bad shock to them, especially my parents."

"You mean a good shock."

"It'll be a shock, of whatever nature. Given the changes in my face and voice, they may have trouble adjusting."

"And you're bringing a strange woman into the family," she said, concern darkening her eyes.

"Oh, that. Don't worry about that. Mom has been after me for years to settle down. It wasn't an option I had before, but that's changed." He gave her a raffish grin. "I'd already decided to retire, anyway, so I could spend my time keeping you satisfied."

He certainly did that. Jay put her head on his shoulder, absorbing his warmth and nearness. His arms tightened. "I love you," he said steadily.

"I love you, Lucas Stone." She would never tire of saying it, and he would never tire of hearing it.

He stood up with her in his arms. "Let's go make a phone call. I want to talk to my folks and let them know they're getting a daughter-in-law."

They did make the phone call, but not right away. First he kissed her, and when he lifted his head the expression in his eyes had intensified. He carried her into the bedroom, and then the mirror on the wall reflected the true image of two people entwined as they loved each other.

* * * * *

The "First Lady of the West," #1 *New York Times*
bestselling author

LINDA LAEL MILLER

brings you to Parable, Montana—where love awaits

Sheriff Boone Taylor has his job, friends, a run-down but decent ranch, two faithful dogs and a good horse. He doesn't want romance—the widowed Montanan has loved and lost enough for a lifetime. But when a city woman buys the spread next door, Boone's peace and quiet are in serious jeopardy.

www.LindaLaelMiller.com

Available in stores now.

The truth can't stay buried forever...

#1 *New York Times* bestselling author

LISA JACKSON

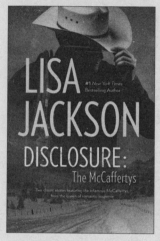

The McCaffertys: Slade

Slade McCafferty was a bachelor through and through—too busy raising hell to settle down. Case in point: fifteen years ago daredevil Slade had taken wild child Jamie Parsons's innocence, and then had broken her heart. But Jamie is back in town, a lawyer, all confidence and polished professionalism. And seeing her again is setting off a tidal wave of emotions Slade thought he'd dammed up ages ago. Back then, as now, there had been something about Jamie that made Slade ache for more. A hell of a lot more...

The McCaffertys: Randi

Is hiding the identity of her child's father worth risking her life? Randi McCafferty seems to think so, but investigator Kurt Striker is hell-bent on changing her mind. Hired by her well-meaning but overbearing brothers to keep Randi and her son safe, Kurt knows the only way to eliminate the danger is to reveal Randi's darkest secret...any way he can. Yet when protection leads to desire, will Randi and Kurt's explosive affair leave them vulnerable to the threats whispering in the shadows?

Available wherever books are sold!

The past can catch up to you....

MARTA PERRY

Rachel Weaver Mason is finally going home to Deer Run, the Amish community she left behind so many years ago. Recently widowed, she wants desperately to create a haven for herself and her young daughter.

But the community, including Rachel's family, is anything but welcoming. The only person happy to see her is her teenage brother, Benjamin, and he's protecting a dark secret that endangers them all.

Available in stores now.

REQUEST YOUR FREE BOOKS!

2 FREE NOVELS
FROM THE SUSPENSE COLLECTION
PLUS 2 FREE GIFTS!

YES! Please send me 2 FREE novels from the Suspense Collection and my 2 FREE gifts (gifts are worth about $10). After receiving them, if I don't wish to receive any more books, I can return the shipping statement marked "cancel." If I don't cancel, I will receive 4 brand-new novels every month and be billed just $5.99 per book in the U.S. or $6.49 per book in Canada. That's a savings of at least 25% off the cover price. It's quite a bargain! Shipping and handling is just 50¢ per book in the U.S. and 75¢ per book in Canada.* I understand that accepting the 2 free books and gifts places me under no obligation to buy anything. I can always return a shipment and cancel at any time. Even if I never buy another book, the two free books and gifts are mine to keep forever.

191/391 MDN FVVK

Name _____ (PLEASE PRINT)

Address _____ Apt. #

City _____ State/Prov. _____ Zip/Postal Code

Signature (if under 18, a parent or guardian must sign)

Mail to the **Harlequin® Reader Service:**
IN U.S.A.: P.O. Box 1867, Buffalo, NY 14240-1867
IN CANADA: P.O. Box 609, Fort Erie, Ontario L2A 5X3

Want to try two free books from another line?
Call 1-800-873-8635 or visit www.ReaderService.com.

* Terms and prices subject to change without notice. Prices do not include applicable taxes. Sales tax applicable in N.Y. Canadian residents will be charged applicable taxes. Offer not valid in Quebec. This offer is limited to one order per household. Not valid for current subscribers to the Suspense Collection or the Romance/Suspense Collection. All orders subject to credit approval. Credit or debit balances in a customer's account(s) may be offset by any other outstanding balance owed by or to the customer. Please allow 4 to 6 weeks for delivery. Offer available while quantities last.

Your Privacy—The Harlequin® Reader Service is committed to protecting your privacy. Our Privacy Policy is available online at www.ReaderService.com or upon request from the Harlequin Reader Service.

We make a portion of our mailing list available to reputable third parties that offer products we believe may interest you. If you prefer that we not exchange your name with third parties, or if you wish to clarify or modify your communication preferences, please visit us at www.ReaderService.com/consumerschoice or write to us at Harlequin Reader Service Preference Service, P.O. Box 9062, Buffalo, NY 14269. Include your complete name and address.

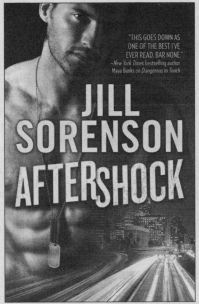

LINDA HOWARD

77569	TROUBLE	___ $7.99 U.S.	___ $9.99 CAN.
77430	MACKENZIE'S HEROES	___ $7.99 U.S.	___ $9.99 CAN.
77429	MACKENZIE'S LEGACY	___ $7.99 U.S.	___ $8.99 CAN.

(limited quantities available)

TOTAL AMOUNT	$ _____
POSTAGE & HANDLING	$ _____
($1.00 FOR 1 BOOK, 50¢ for each additional)	
APPLICABLE TAXES*	$ _____
TOTAL PAYABLE	$ _____

(check or money order—please do not send cash)

To order, complete this form and send it, along with a check or money order for the total above, payable to Harlequin HQN, to: **In the U.S.:** 3010 Walden Avenue, P.O. Box 9077, Buffalo, NY 14269-9077; **In Canada:** P.O. Box 636, Fort Erie, Ontario, L2A 5X3.

Name: _____
Address: _____ City: _____
State/Prov.: _____ Zip/Postal Code: _____
Account Number (if applicable): _____

075 CSAS

*New York residents remit applicable sales taxes.
*Canadian residents remit applicable GST and provincial taxes.

HARLEQUIN® HQN™
www.Harlequin.com

PHLH0113BL